HOPEBEARER

BOOK ONE OF THE HIGH REALM CHRONICLES

James Robert Wright

First published in August 2018

Copyright © 2018 James Robert Wright
Cover art created by Daniel E.J.
Based on original artwork by Alexander Smulskiy

ISBN 9781-1722417703

For Laura, my motivation
and inspiration.

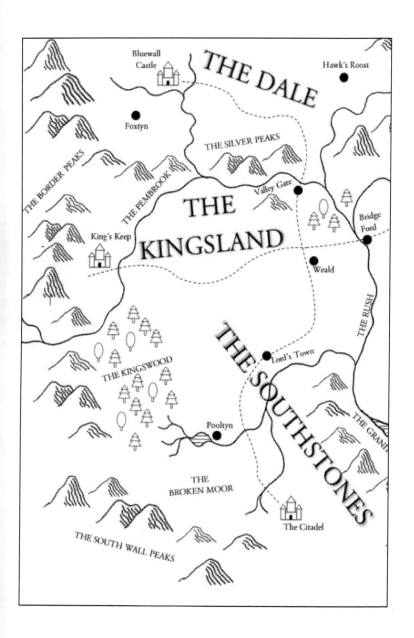

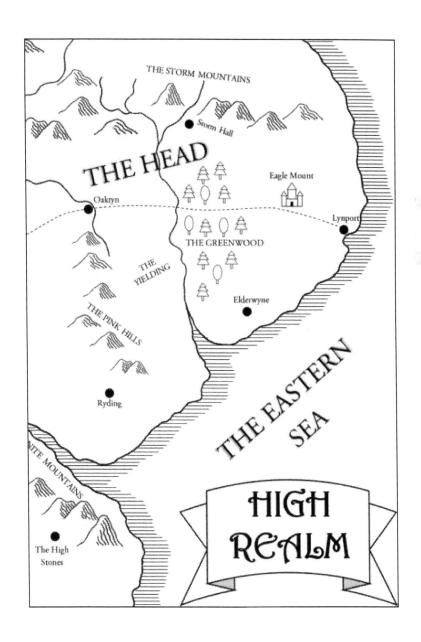

THE STORM MOUNTAINS

Storm Hall

THE HEAD

Eagle Mount

Oaktyn

Lynport

THE GREENWOOD

THE YIELDING

Elderwyne

THE PINK HILLS

THE EASTERN SEA

Ryding

ITE MOUNTAINS

HIGH REALM

The High Stones

Prologue

Night had fallen over the small village. The sun had set behind the tall mountains to the west, beyond the river, leaving the valley in darkness. Winter was on its way, and a flurry of snowflakes was blowing in from the south, threatening to cover the countryside with a thin blanket of white.

The snowflakes fluttered across trees and rocks and landed on the furrows of the fields, before being whisked off again by the cold wind. They danced through the air, glowing white in the darkness, before melting suddenly in the hot flames.

The village was ablaze.

Fire had already consumed the thatched roofs of the houses in the village, and flames roared angrily out of the windows. Black smoke billowed up into the air, hiding the stars from view.

The small boy sobbed as he searched for his parents. He could hardly see because of the darkness and the smoke, but he could make out the fire destroying his family's home. He had never seen anything so terrifying. Turning his back on it, he stumbled along the road that led between the buildings. The ground was cold and wet beneath his bare feet, but he did not notice. He was so frightened that all he could do was cry.

The shapes of people darted this way and that, screaming in panic, but none appeared to notice the small boy. Along with the sounds of the villagers' terrified cries came the loud jeers of the strange men carrying burning torches. They laughed as the fires spread. The roof of a nearby barn collapsed, sending a shower of burning embers into the night sky. Some figures beside the barn cheered and hooted, waving axes in the air. A woman's scream sounded a moment later, and the boy wondered if it was his mother.

He continued to shuffle along the road, getting nearer and nearer to the centre of the village. He could not see where he was going, and tripped on something that sent him tumbling into the mud. He struggled onto his hands and knees, his bottom lip trembling as he noticed the cut on his hand. He looked behind him and saw that he had tripped over the body of a man, but who it belonged to he did not know.

The boy coughed as the thick smoke found its way into his throat. He forced himself back to his feet, just as a group of the strange men ran past, roaring and waving their burning torches. The boy had never seen men like these before. They were nothing like the nice men who lived in his village; the fat baker who was telling him jokes, the blacksmith who would always smile at him with a toothy grin, and the fisherman who always smelt of fish no matter how many times he washed.

The village was getting quieter now, apart from the crackling of the fires that were burning the houses to cinders. A weak voice cried out but apart from that he heard no one. The boy suddenly felt very alone. He had stopped crying now, but felt even more afraid than before. It was at this moment that he saw the man.

As a cold gust of wind cleared some of the smoke from the road, the boy saw him standing silhouetted against the flames. He was a tall man and his armour made him even larger still, like something horrible out of the stories his maid used to tell to scare him.

The man noticed the small boy looking at him, and began walking towards him. He held his fearsome sword in a huge hand, and as he got closer and the light from the fires hit him, the boy could see the blade was wet with blood. The boy stood, transfixed in horror, and his eyes moved up to the man's face. His mouth was twisted into an evil smile. A great scar curved from his left eye to his mouth, which cast a gruesome shadow across his cheek. The boy wanted to run away, but found that his feet were frozen to the ground in fear.

At that moment the boy felt a hand suddenly grab him on the shoulder. He tried to cry out in terror, but no sound would come.

CHAPTER ONE

No place to call home

Merric Orrell woke with a start, alarmed by loud voices coming through his window from the courtyard far below. Panicking, he reached over to the table beside his bed and snatched up the dagger he kept there, clutching it in his shaking hand. As he lay there, breathing heavily, he felt the fear and alarm slowly leave him. The noises from outside were normal, and it was just the nightmare that had put him on edge. Despite the cool morning air Merric was coated with sweat, and he gave an involuntary shiver. Climbing out of his bed, trailing the sheets and furs messily over the floor behind him, he made his way over to the stone basin in the corner of his chamber. His forehead was clammy, so he dipped his hands into the water and splashed his face.

Merric looked up into the mirror that stood above the basin. Through the distorted effects of the glass he saw a small and skinny fourteen year old boy with slightly curly brown hair and piercing blue eyes staring back. People always said that Merric looked young for his age, and he hated that.

He breathed out slowly and thought about the nightmare he had been having. It was the same one he had dreamt many times, for as far back as he could remember. Like all dreams the details of it always faded when he woke, but there were some things he could always remember; the village, shrouded in fire and smoke, and the tall man, scarred, hideous and terrifying. Merric always woke when the hand grabbed his shoulder, filling him with horror. In the nightmare he never learned who the hand belonged to, nor what happened next.

Merric went to the large window and sat on the stone sill, eager to distract himself from the memory of the nightmare. Throwing the wooden shutters open, he allowed the sunlight to stream into the room. The fresh air rushed in too, and he felt the last remains of sleepiness leave him.

It was a fine spring morning. The cloudless skies promised a long and warm day; a day for farmers to bring in their harvests and for children to play in the streams. Merric was envious of them all. The birds that nested in the tall towers of the castle of Eagle Mount were in full song, and flew in circles across the sky high above.

The loud voices from below drew Merric's attention. Despite the early hour, the courtyard of the castle was already alive with activity. Servants scurried across the courtyard, carrying out their tasks, while others swept the stone ground itself with long brooms. Bright banners were

being hoisted up to hang from the wa
decorating the courtyard in bright colou
the horses in the stables to a glossy sheer
soldiers drilled under the watchful gaze of

Today was a big day for Lord R.....,
duke, but not for Merric. He had no desire to stay in the
castle today, and he felt the familiar urge to see the world
outside its thick walls. He looked enviously at the birds that
flew freely high above him, the whole world within their
reach.

Crossing to his wardrobe, Merric pulled the doors
open and tugged out a pair of simple woollen breeches and
a plain white shirt. He dressed quickly and made to close
the wardrobe again. Pausing for a moment, his eyes passed
over the richly engraved hilt of the sword that was poking
out from between the poorly folded clothes. The sword had
once belonged to his father; the only thing he had inherited
from a man he had no memory of.

Merric slammed the wardrobe shut, hiding the sword
once more. He pulled on his boots and slung his bag over
his shoulder, before exiting his bedchamber. He closed the
heavy oak door quietly behind him, keen for no one to hear
him leave.

He walked quickly along the hallway outside his
bedchamber, before descending the spiral staircase at the far
end. When he had first arrived at the castle many years ago,
Merric had regularly got lost in its many passages and
hallways, staircases and chambers. Now, he knew it as well

ho had lived there, and better than most. He
. preferred to be alone when in the castle, and his
wledge of the Eagle Mount's secrets came in useful at
times like these.

The stairs opened out into a much grander hallway than the one his bedchamber was on, and carved stone statues lined the walls. He made his way to a nearby door, but just as he was about to grab the heavy doorknob he heard voices at the far end of the hallway. He ducked into the shadow of one of the statues. He recognised the growl of the chief steward, Myk, who was issuing commands to one of the servants. Merric liked to call the stiff and strict steward "Old Myk", but never to the man's face; he was far too clever to do such a silly thing. Old Myk and the servant were walking towards Merric's hiding spot.

'The journey will have been long, so be sure that the chambers prepared for Lord Aric and his companions are ready: swept, clean sheets, and plenty of spare candles. It's warmer here than in The Southstones, or so I'm told, so the extra furs won't be needed.'

'At once, master,' the servant replied, hurriedly scribbling the instructions onto a piece of parchment with a scratchy quill.

'There will also need to be two extra seats placed at the head table for the welcoming banquet tonight. We had best make sure the Monforts are sat beside our duke, else they'll take offence. Have you ever seen what Lord Aric does to those who displease him?'

'No master.'

'Neither have I, and I wish not to see it now…'

The remainder of the conversation was lost to Merric as the two men passed his hiding place and disappeared out of earshot. With the coast clear, Merric pushed the door open and stepped outside into the bright sunshine.

Hurrying away from the huge castle keep, Merric disappeared into the shadow of the wall that ringed the courtyard. Rather than heading down towards the main gate of the castle, where Merric knew he would be challenged by the guards, he instead darted towards the stables that held the horses of the duke's family. The servants scurrying this way and that did not even glance in his direction, and Merric entered the stables without anyone calling out to him. He was happy to see that none of the stable boys were around, as they would have been sure to ask why he was there. Merric knew he would find a trapdoor hidden in the third stall from the left in the stables, concealed beneath the straw that was scattered across the floor, and he moved over to it. One of the horses watched Merric with interest as he located the trapdoor and pulled it open, before disappearing down the stone steps that lay beyond. Merric closed the door above him again, winking at the horse as he did so, and waited for his eyes to adjust to the darkness.

Merric had first discovered this hidden tunnel by chance when he was a young boy, playing hide and seek with Lord Roberd Jacelyn's son, Tristan. It had taken a few more years before Merric had plucked up the courage to venture down the long, dark passage to see where it went. But when he did, he found that it led out of the castle and into the bustling town of Eaglestone that lay outside its walls. Later, Merric had found a dusty old book in the castle library which looked as though it had not been read in years. Merric loved books, and poring eagerly through its pages he read that the tunnel had been built by one of Lord Roberd Jacelyn's ancestors long ago, who liked to visit the taverns and pubs of Eaglestone without anyone seeing him leave the castle. That was over two-hundred years ago, and it was possible that now only Merric knew of its existence.

Merric hurried down the tunnel, which headed gently downwards. It was pitch black, and was cut straight into the hill itself. It smelled damp and earthy, and water dripped onto Merric's head as he journeyed through the darkness. He kept one hand on the wall beside him, feeling the rough earth beneath his fingers. He had made this journey many times, and the darkness of the tunnel no longer scared him. It was his way out of the castle without anyone knowing, and he enjoyed the freedom it allowed him. Inside the castle walls he was nobody. Outside of them though he could be anyone he wanted to be.

After a couple of minutes the tunnel levelled out and Merric knew he had passed beyond the walls of the castle. Shortly after, he arrived at a door that was just about visible in the darkness. After putting his ear against it for a moment, to check the coast was clear, Merric pushed the door open. He emerged into a dimly lit wine cellar. Barrels filled the small underground room, and a ladder rose up through the ceiling. Merric closed the secret door behind him. It was cleverly made to blend in with a rack of wine bottles so that, once closed, it was invisible except to those who already knew it was there. Merric had never bumped into the owner of the tavern, and wondered what he would say if he knew there was the entrance to a secret passage on his property, which led into the castle.

Merric climbed the ladder and was soon in the sunshine again. A fence surrounded the tavern's yard, but it was old and in desperate need of repair. Merric hurried over to the usual section of fence where he knew there was a gap wide enough for a boy his size to wriggle through. Emerging on the other side, Merric brushed the dust and cobwebs from his clothes after his short journey underground.

Behind him, the walls of the castle towered over the town. The folk of Eaglestone were reassured by these impressive walls, but Merric could not help but think that they were there to keep him out, not stop enemies from getting in. However even these walls were in the shadow of the castle keep itself that lay beyond, stretching even higher into a blue spring sky. The castle had been named Eagle Mount many centuries ago, when the first stone had been laid, and it was well named. Many tall turrets and towers rose up from the keep, and like the rest of the castle they were built from a bright sand-coloured stone. Atop the tallest of these was the carved, stone likeness of a great eagle, perched watchfully as it looked proudly over the surrounding land.

It was still early, but the streets of Eaglestone were already crowded, packed with folk who were too busy about their day to give Merric a second glance, mistaking him for nothing more than a common boy. Today was a market day, and merchants, farmers, peddlers and street vendors were setting up their stalls, ready to sell their wares. As Merric set off down the cobbled street between tall timber-framed buildings he took in the sights and sounds that the bustling town offered, and which a boy raised in the great castle would not usually be able to experience. Merchants stood before stalls covered with bottles of wine and barrels of beer and mead, and many of the sellers appeared to have permanently red noses from too many years of tasting their own products. Other stalls were overflowing with vegetables fresh from the fields, as well as rare fruits from more distant lands. A strong smell of fish assaulted Merric's nostrils as he passed a vendor selling the morning's catch from the nearby Eastern Sea, though this was quickly replaced by the overpowering aroma of herbs and spices being sold by an exotic merchant from the lands beyond High Realm's northern borders. The busy harbour of Lynport lay not far from Eaglestone, and so traders from foreign lands would regularly visit to sell their strange products, such as silk, ivory and other luxuries.

A chorus of bleating sounded as Merric walked past a small square which had been fenced off. It was packed full of sheep being tended by a shepherd who was haggling loudly with some potential buyers. Further along, tailors sold bales of cloth of every colour, while an ironmonger proudly displayed his rack of finely forged swords, axes and armour. Laughter filled Merric's ears as he passed a juggler tossing daggers into the air, while a fool galloped past on a pretend horse made of wood. Children ran after him gleefully, while a pair of dogs fought over a scrap of meat which they had stolen from an unsuspecting butcher's stall.

There were stalls selling everything imaginable, from all four corners of the realm and beyond. The folk who wandered the streets were just as varied as the market itself. Merric had to dart to one side to avoid being trampled by a haughty knight on his towering warhorse, his bright yellow surcoat and shield bearing the symbol of a blue boar. His young squire hurried along behind him on a much smaller mount, clutching the knight's helmet under his arm. The knight was likely here for the jousting tournament that was due to take place in a few weeks, which would draw competitors from across the realm.

The knight had only just disappeared around the corner when Merric saw a group of brothers from the Grand Priory making their way up the street towards him, and he respectfully stepped aside with the rest of the crowd to make room for the religious men. Despite the pleasant warmth of the day they were dressed in their usual thick brown robes, with hoods pulled over their heads. Their feet were sandaled, and they slapped noisily on the cobbles as they passed.

As Merric walked deeper into the heart of the town, the crowds grew thicker. Soon he was having to push his way through the press of bodies. Still, none of the townsfolk paid Merric any attention. He was just another face among many. As he finally neared the edge of the town the crowds finally began to thin. Merric was now passing through the bakery district of Eaglestone. On both sides of the street were open-fronted bakeries that engulfed his senses with the delicious smell of freshly baked bread. He walked around a parked wagon, whose occupant was unloading a delivery of flour from a nearby mill, whilst a baker stood beside it counting out coins.

'Just three silvers for a sack of flour?' he said happily, 'things are looking up! Come along Bob, give me a hand.'

A small boy, his son or perhaps his apprentice, with a face smeared with flour ran to help carry the sacks.

Up ahead rose the wall that safely enclosed the town. The town wall was much lower than those that surrounded the great castle, but it still towered above the buildings nestled within it. Circular towers were spaced along its length every hundred paces, from where the guards could keep a watchful eye out for any danger approaching the town.

Cutting through an alley between two bakeries, Merric emerged at the base of one of these towers. He glanced to the left and right to make sure he was alone, and saw nothing apart from three pigs that were happily munching away in the small sty at the back of one of the bakeries. Satisfied that the coast was clear, Merric grasped hold of the rough stone of the tower and started the familiar climb. The tower was in need of repair but the missing stones provided Merric with plenty of handholds. His muscles protested, but he knew the climb; he had done it many times before. It was not long before he finally clambered onto the roof of the tower and slumped, short of breath, onto the distinctive blue tiles that made Eaglestone and the castle of Eagle Mount so unique.

Merric felt a drop of sweat bead its way down his forehead from the effort of the climb, and he welcomed the breeze which helped to cool him on his lofty perch. From this distance, Eagle Mount looked like a toy castle atop its hill behind him.. It would be a long time before Merric's absence in the castle was noted, and so he would not have to be back within its walls for hours yet. The light wind picked at his hair, and Merric closed his eyes for a moment, contented at last. He opened his bag and pulled out a book. It was centuries old, and the cover was tattered and worn. He opened it onto the first page where a scholar, hundreds of years ago, had hand-written the title of the book in ink that had started to fade into the yellowing pages. It was one of Merric's favourites. It was about the Fabled Isles, a small collection of islands rumoured to lay off the coast of High Realm somewhere. No one had ever seen them before because, according to legend, any ships that ventured too close sank in fierce storms. It was the kind of tale of adventure that Merric loved.

Merric flicked through the pages absent-mindedly for a few minutes, before closing the book again and looking out at the land that lay before him.

Eagle Mount, and the town of Eaglestone which surrounded it, sat idyllically among the beautiful gently rolling fields and woods of The Head. That was the name given to these eastern-most lands of High Realm, which were ruled by Lord Roberd Jacelyn on behalf of the king. His father had been Duke of The Head before him, and *his* father had been the duke before that. There had always been a Jacelyn at Eagle Mount, and under their guardianship the folk of The Head had lived in safety. Because of this, the folk loved their lord. On this morning the land itself seemed to mirror the happiness that the folk felt; the woods were green and the pleasant little streams that wound their way between the fields and flowery meadows were a deep blue in the spring sun. As beautiful as it was, Merric knew this was not his home. He was not a Jacelyn, after all.

Merric was the only son of a lesser lord who once held lands in The Head. Merric had never known his parents though, nor the small castle in which he had been born. When he was very young his home had been destroyed. Merric had only escaped with his life after he was rescued by Lord Roberd and his knights. They had been too late to save Merric's parents and the rest of the village, and the duke had taken pity on the small orphaned boy. He had brought Merric back to Eagle Mount and provided the small boy with a home, but as he had grown out of childhood Merric had felt more and more out of place in Lord Roberd's castle.

A voice suddenly called out, shaking Merric from his thoughts.

'I didn't think I'd see *you* here this morning, my lord.'

Merric turned and saw a girl emerge onto the roof of the tower behind him, her dirty blonde hair pulled back and tied loosely behind her head. Merric smiled for the first time that morning.

Since his arrival at Eagle Mount all those years ago, Merric had gradually felt more and more alone. He felt as though he was an outsider in a place that was not truly his home, and so found himself seeking his own solitary company. It was during one of these periods of loneliness that he had ventured down into the tunnel in the castle stables and discovered the way out of Eagle Mount without being seen. He had begun to explore the varied sights of the town of Eaglestone. Here he was able to forget who he was, and enjoy being simply another face in the crowd. The town was the centre of society and trade in The Head, so the streets were always busy with folk coming and going. There were plenty of things to see to occupy the curious mind of the boy, and he welcomed the distractions. At the end of the day though, Merric was a child of noble blood, brought up in the comforts and safety of the castle, and so the harsh world of the common folk came as a shock to him. Never more so than one such visit when he was nine.

It was at this time, during one of his first trips into Eaglestone, that Merric was set upon by a gang of scruffy street urchins, all of whom were bigger and stronger than he was. They had recognised the rich clothes that the young nobleman was wearing, and had picked him out as an easy target. Pulling him into an alley they attacked him with their small fists, and made to steal anything of value on him: his supple leather boots, his fine thick woollen cloak, including the silver brooch that held it in place around his neck, and the small coin purse that he wore on his belt. The coin purse was empty though, the young boy having no need for money.

He was rescued by the girl, Ana, who happened to be passing at the time. She had no idea who Merric was, but seeing him in trouble she quickly stepped in to stop the mugging. Being the daughter of a blacksmith, and dressed as if she was following her father into the trade, she could not have contrasted more with the richly dressed and well-groomed Merric. She was the same age as him, but working with her father had made her much stronger, and the street urchins fled away when they saw her coming. She had gathered up Merric's discarded boots, coin purse, cloak and even his brooch, and handed them back to him. Then, after finding out he was from the castle, she smacked Merric roughly across the back of his head. She scolded him for his stupidity in venturing into the streets alone while dressed like a prince, and had taken him back to the castle gates where he faced an even sterner telling off from a worried Lord Roberd. Merric had promised that he would never venture off out of the castle on his own again.

Merric broke that promise the very next day.

That following morning he once again snuck out of the castle and explored the streets of Eaglestone, though more plainly dressed this time, and with more respect for the danger. He spent a whole morning searching for his rescuer, having spent the past evening thinking constantly about the strange girl dressed in boyish clothes. In the castle, the only girl he saw was Sophya, Lord Roberd's daughter. She would never leave her chamber without having first bathed, put on one of her brightly coloured gowns and have one of her handmaidens style her hair. To see a girl with dirt on her hands was completely new to Merric, and Ana had fascinated him.

Merric had eventually found her down Forge End, the street dedicated to the town's blacksmiths. Amidst the din of the hammering and beating of metal and the whoosh of bellows pumping he had spotted Ana. She was outside her father's workshop, hammering at a piece of steel that glowed red hot on an anvil. In noble families, ladies would never even dream of working in the heat and noise of a blacksmith's, and Merric watched, mesmerised, as Ana worked. She was dressed practically, with leather breeches and jerkin over a grubby shirt, and her face and hair were caked in dirt and soot and sweat. Her hands were rough from handling the tools, and Sophya would have fainted at the sight of her fingernails.

As though sensing his gaze, Ana had looked up and recognised the noble boy standing across the street. Seeing him as a pest she had chased him off with her hammer. Merric had not given up though, and now, five years later, they were the best of friends.

Merric winced at her words as she sat down next to him on the tower.

'I told you, don't call me "my lord",' he said.

Merric was not a lord, but he was the only highborn person Ana had met, so she liked to tease him and call him it anyway. She just laughed and gave a mock curtsey.

'Sorry, my lord. But seriously, why are you up here? I saw you in the market heading this way. I thought you'd be in the castle today.'

'Why? Merric asked her.

'Oh I don't know,' Ana said sarcastically, rolling her eyes. 'I heard it was a pretty big day today at the castle. Something about some important guests? Maybe you didn't know.'

Merric had been moaning about little else over the past month, until Ana had finally told him to shut up as it was boring her silly.

'So? What does that have to do with me?'

'Surely all of his lordship's family should be there to greet them?'

'Exactly,' Merric said, picking at the corner of a chipped roof tile and not looking at Ana. 'His *family*. Lord Roberd won't want me there, and I don't want to be there either.' He was surprised to feel a lump in his throat.

Ana's voice softened. 'Of course he'll want you there.'

'I'm not a Jacelyn,' Merric said.

'That doesn't matter.'

Merric turned on her, his sadness fuelling an anger that had been building up in him for months. 'It does!'

'Where is this coming from?' Ana asked, shocked at her friend's tempter. 'You've constantly been feeling sorry for yourself over the past year; you never used to be like this.'

'I'm not feeling sorry for myself,' Merric said with a huff, turning back to the roof tile.

The tone of his voice was not fooling Ana. In truth, Merric was miserable, and it shamed him to think it. Lord Roberd had raised him as well as could have been asked, and Merric had everything that a young nobleman could need. He had been happy with his adoptive family for years, but nowadays he was always thinking about what he had lost. By rights he was Merric Orrell, son of Lord Willarm Orrell, the heroic baron and knight who had served Lord Roberd with loyalty and courage for many years. His mother, the Lady Chanelyse Orrell, had been renowned across the land for her unmatched beauty. Merric had been Lord Willarm's heir, due to inherit his castle and lands in the far corner of The Head. This was taken from him though, that night many years ago, and now he had nothing. He was a boy with no future, who relied on the charity of others.

'You need to stop distancing yourself from his lordship and his family,' Ana said.

'They're not *my* family,' Merric interrupted.

His friend's face flushed with frustration.

'Family is about more than just blood, Merric. His lordship has raised you as though you were his own son. You feeling like this is just part of growing up, you'll see.'

Merric breathed out slowly. He knew the truth in what she was saying, but he was not comforted by her words.

'You don't understand,' he said, causing Ana to raise her eyebrows.

'Then tell me,' she challenged.

Merric looked out across the fields and woods of the countryside that surrounded Eaglestone. His eyes finally settled on the distant white specks that were sheep grazing contently in a field under the spring morning sun.

'It's not just that I don't feel like I belong here…I don't belong anywhere! I had a home. I might not remember it, but it was there, and it was taken from me, along with my parents and any hope I had of a normal life. It's fine for you; you have a life here, and a purpose. You'll be a blacksmith like your father.'

'I've lost things too though, Merric, you know that.' Ana said to him. 'My mother died when I was very young. I never knew her, the same as you didn't know your parents. My father raised me as best he could but, well, he's a blacksmith. You know what he's like. He loves me more than the world, but he could never be a mother to me as well as a father. From as young as I can remember I've had to look after myself. I've had to cook, to clean, to wash my own things.'

She looked at her friend. He was of noble birth, with servants looking after his every need. It was doubtful that he had ever had to cook for himself, clean, or had to wash the dirt from his clothes in his whole life.

'I didn't grow up thinking I'd be a blacksmith like my father,' Ana continued, 'but I've had to get used to it. I always wanted to write songs, that minstrels across the realm might one day perform.'

Despite his bad mood Merric could not help sniggering at this.

'You're not serious?' he said to her.

'I'm not!' she said, embarrassed. 'Why's that so hard to imagine?'

This caused Merric to laugh even harder.

'Just promise me you'll never sing in front of me.'

'Well I'm glad I've managed to amuse you,' Ana said, slightly offended, but laughing alongside Merric all the same.

A loud fanfare suddenly sounded from the main gates into the town to their left, causing a flock of birds to take flight in shock from the neatly ploughed field just outside the walls. Merric and Ana snapped their heads around and peered into the distance.

'They're here,' Merric said.

Half a mile away, along the wide, rutted road, marched a brightly coloured column of horsemen. Though he could not make out any details, Merric could see that a single man rode proudly at the head of the column, wearing a white surcoat over his polished armour, while behind him rode a second man carrying a banner of the same colour. Around a hundred others followed them. This was the arrival of Lord Aric Monfort, Duke of The Southstones, which lay to the southwest of The Head. Lord Aric was to be Lord Roberd's guest for the coming weeks.

'They're an impressive bunch,' Ana observed.

'Not *that* impressive,' Merric said.

Ana smiled at him. 'I'd better be going, I've got to help father. I only came into town to get coal for the forge, he'll be wondering where I am.'

Merric nodded, but was sad to see his friend leave. Her father was contracted by Lord Roberd to supply the castle with horseshoes. With the visit of Lord Aric and his knights, and the jousting tournament that was due in a few weeks, Merric knew he must be busy.

'Okay,' he said. 'See you tomorrow though?'

'If you like,' Ana replied, standing. 'Are you certain you won't be missed at the castle today though? I think you should go back, just in case.'

'I'm certain.'

Ana did not push the subject, and Merric appreciated this. She put her hand on his back, and he found the touch strangely soothing.

'You give his lordship too much of a hard time. I've heard he's a good man; he wouldn't want you to feel this way. Talk to him, he might understand. He was a fourteen year old boy once too.'

'Maybe,' Merric said quietly, as he continued to watch the column of men riding towards them.

'Until tomorrow then. Keep out of trouble, *my lord.*'

Ana gave Merric a push, causing him to wobble dangerously atop the tower. He had to wave his arms around stupidly to stop himself from falling. With a laugh Ana disappeared before he could get her back. Merric smiled to himself, knowing that he could always depend on Ana to cheer him up.

He sat by himself for a few more minutes, before deciding that he would go into the streets to get a closer look at the southern knights. Clambering back to his feet he made his way back down the side of the tower.

Little did he know the trouble that waited for him there.

- CHAPTER TWO -

Monfort and Jacelyn

Merric dropped the last few feet, landing smartly at the base of the tower. However when he turned around and made to head back into the streets of Eaglestone, he found himself face to face with Tristan Jacelyn, Lord Roberd's son and heir. The older boy scowled down at him, his hands on his hips. Merric groaned, sensing the trouble he was about to be in. Tristan stood nearly a foot taller than him, and his disapproving eye looked Merric up and down.

'What in the Mother's name have you been doing?' Tristan asked, his voice deep.

'Nothing!' Merric replied, stupidly, unsure of what else to say.

Tristan raised an eyebrow. 'Nothing? Really? I thought your days of skulking around the back alleys of Eaglestone were behind you. Father's not going to be happy.'

Merric did not say anything, so Tristan continued.

'They say Lord Aric has the ear of the king. You know how important this day is for Father.'

Merric could hear Ana's words in his head, but Tristan's tone was making him annoyed.

'Then why are you down here looking for me? Get back up to the castle if it's so important.'

He did not want to speak like this to Tristan, who looked taken aback by Merric's words. It made Merric feel immediately guilty.

Tristan recovered from his shock, and raised a gloved finger at Merric, threateningly. 'Why are you making things so difficult? What has Father ever done to you?'

Merric did not reply, and looked at his feet.

Tristan let his hand drop, and his face relaxed. 'Come, Merric. Enough of this foolishness.'

Growing up Merric had always been in Tristan's shadow. Not only was Tristan the heir to Lord Roberd, and would therefore be Duke of The Head himself one day, but he was five years older, much taller, stronger and more handsome. Now he was a young man, and no longer a child. Tristan had already received his knighthood, and had ridden to war at his father's side. Merric had idolised the older boy as he was growing up, but as the years had passed and Merric had started to resent the fact that he was an outsider in Eagle Mount, Tristan had grown tired of Merric's lack of gratitude towards Lord Roberd. Now, the two barely spoke.

'How did you know where to find me?' Merric asked.

Tristan pointed a thumb back over his shoulder. Merric looked round him to see his own servant, Tomas. He was a small, round-faced boy, with a small mouth and a vacant expression. He always seemed to be nervous, and on this occasion he was stood shuffling his feet awkwardly, being careful to avoid Merric's gaze. Merric felt betrayed by his servant, but this feeling quickly turned to sympathy. Tomas was incredibly loyal to Merric, who he idolised. However he could never have refused to answer a direct question from Tristan Jacelyn.

With a last disapproving look at Merric, Tristan took the reins of his large black horse from Tomas, and swung himself smartly into the saddle.

'Come now. And try and make yourself a bit more presentable. You look like a vagabond, not a nobleman.'

He had brought a spare horse for Merric, and together they began threading their way through the alleys and narrow roads of the edge of the town and back towards the castle. As they rode, Merric hurriedly tried to scrape the dirt from his clothes that clung there from his journey in the tunnel and his climb, and used the horse's mane to clean his grubby hands. Tomas hurried alongside them on foot, his face red and sweaty from the effort. Tristan looked far more impressive than Merric, who was less comfortable on horseback than the older boy. Atop his strong warhorse he towered over Merric, and his long curly blond hair and handsome face caught the attention of the young women they passed.

In comparison to Merric, Tristan looked striking and lordly. He wore a sky blue jerkin bearing the golden eagle of the Jacelyn family on his chest, and over his broad shoulders hung a spotless white cloak. In honour of his status as a knight he carried a sword at his waist. The blade was heavy, impressively showing all those around that it was for battle, and not just for show. Tristan was the finest swordsman Merric had ever seen. While he had no talent for swordplay himself, Merric used to love to watch Tristan train when they were younger. On his other hip Tristan wore a highly decorated dagger, and its golden hilt was carved into the likeness of an eagle with its outstretched wings forming the cross guard. In High Realm, it was traditional for a father to gift his son with a dagger when he became a knight. The son would proudly keep it with him always, both as a reminder of his status as a knight and as a symbol of the love shared by father and son.

The back roads turned into larger streets, and their horses' hooves clip-clopped on well-worn cobbles. The townsfolk who crowded the streets, waiting eagerly for a glimpse of Lord Aric Monfort and his companions, had to part to give Tristan and Merric room to pass. The townsfolk bowed respectfully at Tristan and chattered excitedly once he had passed.

Tristan and Merric joined onto The Lord's Way, the main route from the town gate up to the castle, and here they found their going much easier. The buildings to either side were larger here, the homes and shops of Eaglestone's wealthier inhabitants. Up ahead the high walls of Eagle Mount soared dramatically into the air. Before the mighty gates of the castle stood The Square, a wide open space which served many roles. On some occasions it acted as a meeting place, at other times it was filled with fayres and other entertainments, but today it was the heart of the market. Here the hustle and bustle was at its busiest, and the voices of all the merchants calling out their prices merged into one chaotic noise. Merric watched a man haggle with a merchant over the price of a bolt of cloth. Another merchant had abandoned his stall and was pushing his way through the press of shoppers and was waving his selection of amulets in the air, claiming they could ward off old age.

On one side The Square was overlooked by the Grand Priory. It was an enormous stone building that soared over the heads of the folk of Eaglestone, second only in size to the great castle that it sat beside. At either end of the majestic building was a tall tower, each adorned with a huge bell that would toll out across the town, calling the folk to prayer.

All towns and villages across High Realm had a priory, but there were few as large as the Grand Priory of Eaglestone. Merric had visited the Grand Priory with the Jacelyns every week, along with most of the population of the town, to listen to the Arch Prior deliver his sermons. They bored Merric out of his wits, and when he was younger Tristan would keep Merric entertained by making faces and imitating the Arch Prior's wheezy voice. Those years had passed now, and Merric looked sadly at the back of Tristan who rode ahead of him. The playful boy who had enjoyed spending time with Merric had grown into a man, the memory of his younger self lost.

The crowds finally cleared as Tristan and Merric arrived before the huge gates of Eagle Mount. The tall oaken gates were flanked on either side by round towers, which when under attack would be filled with archers who could rain arrows down on anyone trying to force their way into the castle. Fortunately, on this day, Tristan and Merric suffered no such onslaught as they rode through the archway.

Beside the gates stood two Jacelyn soldiers, who saluted them respectfully as they passed. They were formidable and well-trained warriors, clad in knee-length padded leather coats which they wore over shirts of heavy ring mail. Their long, sky-blue shields were painted with the eagle symbol of the Jacelyn family, and in their other hand they carried long spears topped with wicked points. On their heads were simple dome shaped helmets, with a steel nose guard to protect their faces. All of their armour was well polished, and their shields did not show the scratches and dents that usually covered them from their hours of practice in the training yard. Clearly Lord Roberd was wanting everyone to look their best for their visitors.

As Merric rode through the gate and beneath the iron portcullis he could not help but notice that it was a far more dignified entrance than his usual return to the castle, scuttling through the filthy underground tunnel.

The courtyard of Eagle Mount opened up before them. The servants, who earlier this morning had been busily preparing the courtyard, were gone. Instead, directly ahead, with the vast castle keep behind them, stood the rest of the Jacelyn family. Merric was instantly taken aback by how striking they looked, and suddenly felt shamed by his still grubby clothes.

Lord Roberd looked proud in his finest armour with a sky-blue cloak draped over his shoulders. His brown beard, though now almost grey, was neatly trimmed. He was a tall man, though wider around the waist than he would have preferred. In his youth, Roberd had been a mighty warrior, but his responsibilities as Duke of The Head had kept him out of the saddle and behind his desk instead more often than he liked. To his right stood his lady wife, Cathreen of The Dale, and next in line was Sophya, Tristan's younger sister. Both wore their finest silk gowns, which were modest in decoration but were well fitted. They were belted elegantly around the waist and fell gracefully to the ground. In the fashions of High Realm their sleeves were extremely wide, and trailed almost to their feet.

Whilst Tristan had inherited his striking blond hair from his mother, Sophya shared her father's brown locks, which she wore plaited at the back of her head. For much of her life she had been the attention of many young suitors from noble families across High Realm, though Lord Roberd had still not agreed to promise her hand in marriage to any of these young men. Instead he wanted her to marry someone that she loved, but as yet she had not given her heart to anyone.

Behind the Jacelyn family stood Lord Roberd's household. Sir Gerard Velion, the captain of the Eagle Guard, stood as still as a stone, his face hidden as usual by his great steel helmet. The Lord's Counsel, Orderix, who was advisor to Lord Roberd in all matters, was there as well, looking thin and stiff in his tight-fitting black floor-length robes. Arch Prior Simeon stood beside him, slightly stooped, wheezing and coughing as always in his old age.

Assembled to each side of the gate were the twenty men of the Eagle Guard. They looked dazzling in their sky-blue surcoats, which they wore over their pristine armour. Each man was handpicked to serve on the Jacelyn family's personal bodyguard, and they were considered the finest warriors in all The Head.

High above all were the bright banners that hung from the castle walls. They flapped in the breeze, but everything else was silent. There seemed to be a nervous energy in the air.

Two stable boys darted forward and took the reins of Tristan and Merric's horses as the two dismounted, and quickly led the mounts away towards the stables. Tomas hurried after them, eager to keep out of the way. Tristan took his place between his mother and sister, and Merric joined the end of the row, feeling as shabby as ever in his scruffy clothes. He was keen to avoid Lord Roberd's eyes. He wondered if he should say something to the duke, but at that moment the sound of blaring trumpets announced the arrival of their guests.

The men rode through the gate beneath banners displaying the black marching knight symbol of the Monfort family, the rulers of The Southstones. The man who Merric assumed to be Lord Aric Monfort himself rode at the head of the column. Like Lord Roberd he had elected to wear his finest armour in honour of the occasion, and his shoulder length hair and neat beard were black and glossy, with only a few faint flecks of grey.

Behind him rode his companions for the journey, mostly made up of knights and servants and their guard of soldiers. From his viewpoint on the town walls the bright colours of the knights who accompanied their duke looked spectacular, but up close they were even more striking. Falcons, lions, towers, snakes, axes, fish and spiders looked down at Merric from the chests of the assorted visiting knights' surcoats. Each surcoat showed the noble family that the knight was a member of, and most were the sons of the barons who held land in The Southstones, and we proud to ride with their duke. Merric thought sadly that if his family still lived, then there may have been times in future years that he would have ridden with Lord Roberd, wearing the red surcoat with the golden deer symbol of the Orrell family.

Once the visitors were all assembled in the courtyard, Lord Aric dismounted, handing the reins of his black horse to his servant, and strode purposefully up to Lord Roberd. The two embraced as though they were old friends, though Merric could not help noticing that both men appeared to do so stiffly.

'Roberd, my friend, it has been too long.' Lord Aric had the drawling accent common among those from The Southstones.

'Aric,' Lord Roberd replied. 'The hospitality of The Head is yours.'

He then introduced Lady Cathreen. She offered Lord Aric hand to him, which he promptly kissed.

'My lady, I apologise that my own wife wasn't able to make the journey. She so wanted to meet you. Unfortunately her health prevented her. Her physician advised that the colder climates of the south would be better for her at this time.'

'I'm sorry to hear that my lord, I trust it's nothing serious?' Lady Cathreen replied, though in truth she did not sound sorry at all. Rumour had it that Lord Aric's wife was a vain, cold woman. Lady Lisbeth Monfort was the daughter of the King of High Realm though, and such pleasantries were expected.

'She'll be grateful for your concern,' Lord Aric said bowing slightly with a pleasant smile, 'but it's a minor ailment, the Mother be praised.'

Next, Lord Aric was introduced to Tristan, and he nodded approvingly at the young Jacelyn's broad chest and strong arms.

'Arms well used to the weight of a sword,' Lord Aric noted with a nod. 'How are you in the lists?' he asked.

'Well enough, my lord. I haven't been beaten yet.'

Lord Aric laughed boomingly. 'Very good, very good. I look forward to seeing you face off against my son. He has some skill with a lance as well.'

The approaching jousting tournament, being held to honour Lord Aric, was due to take place on the final day of his visit. Tristan had been looking forward to the opportunity to show off his talents atop his horse and skill with his sword and lance, and was the favourite amongst the common folk to win.

'And who have we here?' Lord Aric had turned his attention to Sophya.

'Sophya, my lord,' she said nervously, offering Lord Aric her hand as her mother had done. Like all daughters in noble families in High Realm, Sophya had been schooled in the behaviours expected of a lady.

Lord Aric obligingly kissed the offered hand.

'A beauty. You are truly your mother's daughter,' he said.

Sophya smiled modestly at the compliment. 'Thank you, my lord,' she said shyly.

Lord Aric continued smiling at her for a moment, before calling over his shoulder. 'Rayden, my boy, come here.'

A young knight, around Tristan's age, answered the summons. When he removed his helmet he revealed a head of long sleek, black hair, though unlike Lord Aric's his had not yet shown any signs of turning to grey. Merric heard Sophya take a sharp intake of breath, and he frowned at her. The knight's armour was the most elegant that Merric had ever seen, and was polished so much that it shined like a mirror. Merric could even see his own face reflected in the steel plates. Unlike the other knights, he did not wear a surcoat over the top of his armour. Instead the symbol of his family, the black marching knight of the Monforts, was picked out in rare black onyx stones that were attached to his shining breastplate. His face featured chiselled cheekbones that Merric assumed must be considered handsome. Sophya certainly seemed to think so, as she had quickly gone a deep shade of red. Lord Aric had noticed this, and a sly smile played across his lips. Rather than handsome, Merric thought the knight's heavily-lidded eyes made him look rather full of himself.

'Sophya,' Lord Aric said, 'allow me to introduce you to my son and heir, Sir Rayden Monfort. A knight, and the finest in all The Southstones. He's the pride of The Citadel, our castle home.'

'My lady,' said Rayden, shooting Sophya a charming smile and taking her hand, kissing it like his father had.

41

'Pleased to meet you,' Sophya said breathlessly, and she seemed hesitant to take her hand away from the young knight's lips. Rayden noticed, and winked at her.

At that moment, Lord Roberd stepped in, his voice slightly louder than normal.

'And here is my ward, Merric Orrell, once of Ryding.'

Lord Aric moved over to Merric, leaving his son with Sophya, and his face turned sombre.

'A pleasure to meet you Merric. I once knew your parents. Lord Willarm was a fine knight, and the Orrells a proud and honourable family. What happened to them and the village of Ryding was a true tragedy,' he said, putting a hand on Merric's shoulder. 'Seeing you well in Roberd's keeping brings a great happiness to me.'

Giving Merric's shoulder a strong pat that nearly forced him down onto his knees, Lord Aric turned his attention to the great keep in front of him, and craned his head back to look up at the tall towers.

'Ah, Eagle Mount, magnificent! It does me well to see it again. Thank you for your fine welcome, Roberd. I fear the road has made me weary. A chance to rest and soothe my sore limbs would be most welcome.'

'Of course, my friend.' Lord Roberd summoned his steward. 'Myk will show you and your knights to the chambers we have prepared for you. Your soldiers and servants will be welcome in my men's barracks for the duration of your visit.'

'That's most kind of you,' Lord Aric said with a smile.

The Monfort duke followed the steward towards the castle keep, his helmet tucked under his arm. Rayden walked beside him, and the two were deep in conversation. Lord Roberd watched them go, a dark expression on his face.

CHAPTER THREE

The lord and the lawbreaker

Lord Roberd waited until Lord Aric had disappeared through the main doors into the keep with his son and knights, and his soldiers had been shown the way to the barracks, before he walked over to where Merric stood.

'Come with me,' he said.

Merric swallowed nervously, and obediently fell in behind Lord Roberd. He followed him up the front steps of the keep in the wake of their guests. Once inside the cavernous entrance chamber, they climbed the grand staircase which led to where Lord Roberd's study could be found. The walls inside the keep were magnificently decorated with paintings and tapestries that depicted the rich and fascinating history of High Realm, but Lord Roberd did not stop to look at them. When they arrived at the door to his study, Lord Roberd held it open for Merric, and then gestured for him to sit in front of the duke's large oak desk. Lord Roberd himself sat behind it in his high-backed chair.

Merric was fascinated by this room, though he had only been in it a couple of times. On both occasions he had been in trouble. Just like the passage outside, three of the stone walls of Lord Roberd's study were covered in ornate tapestries, and soft furs covered the wooden floorboards beneath their feet. Merric's favourite feature of the room though was the vast map that covered the fourth wall, directly behind the desk. The map showed all four dukedoms of High Realm, from The Head on the eastern shore to The Kingsland beside the mountains to the west. The lands of The Dale laid to the north, and The Southstones, the dukedom of the Monfort family, was to the south. Every river, mountain and forest was lovingly hand-painted onto the map, along with countless castles, towns and villages. Merric's eyes rested on a small mark, nestled on the eastern bank of the Rush, the great river that ran down the middle of the realm. The writing next to the mark identified the village of Ryding, once home to Merric, but now nothing more than burnt stone walls overgrown with weeds.

Sensing what Merric was looking at over his shoulder, Lord Roberd's voice adopted a gentle tone. 'Do you ever think of it?'

'My lord?' Merric asked, drawing his attention away from the map.

'Do you ever think of Ryding? Of your parents?'

This was not how Merric thought the conversation would begin. 'Oh, no my lord. I mean, I try not to. I can't remember Ryding at all, or my mother and father.'

'You were very young when your parents were taken from you,' Lord Roberd said, understanding. He looked behind him at the map, and for a moment a look of sadness appeared on his face. 'I think about it every day, you know. I had received reports that a band of brigands had been seen in my dukedom, stealing and burning as they went. I summoned as many soldiers and knights as I could muster, but I was too late. By the time we arrived, Ryding was already ablaze. You were the only survivor.' Lord Roberd had kept his eyes on the map as he talked, but now turned back to Merric, a pained look on his face.

Merric stared at him. The man was strong, both of mind and of body. He was powerful and brave, as any good duke should be. But Merric had never seen him looking as vulnerable and old as he looked now. He was not sure that he liked it.

'I had a nightmare last night. I'm not sure, but I think it might have been about that night,' Merric confessed, 'I've dreamt the same thing before.'

'You have? Tell me about it,' Lord Roberd encouraged.

'It's always the same,' Merric said, feeling awkward discussing it. He had expected to be summoned to Lord Roberd's study to be told off for his trip into Eaglestone on this important day, and for no doubt causing extra stress on the duke. Instead, he found himself talking about the nightmare that had been worrying him for years. 'There's smoke everywhere, and folk screaming. The village is burning. Then I see a man. He has a scar on his face, and I think he's going to come for me, to kill me, but then I wake up.' He paused, waiting for Lord Roberd to speak, but the duke stayed silent. 'It's just a nightmare.' Merric said finally, with a shrug.

'Yes, it's just a nightmare,' Lord Roberd said, 'and whilst they may remind us of things we'd rather forget, they can't hurt us. That was a dark time for you Merric, and you suffered unimaginable loss. It is natural that your mind may wander there in the night. Live your dreams, Merric, but leave your nightmares in the dark where they belong.'

Merric smiled awkwardly. It felt good to have spoken to someone about the nightmare. He wished he had done so before.

'You've grown into a fine young man,' Lord Roberd continued, smiling at him, 'and I'm very proud of who you have grown to become.' His eyes still looked troubled though, and Merric sensed that the real purpose of this conversation had been reached. 'Why didn't you want to be here today, to welcome Lord Aric?' Lord Roberd asked. 'I had to send Tristan to find you, and you were hiding in the town? Why Merric? Have I done something to have upset you?'

'I'm sorry for any trouble I've caused,' Merric said, bowing his head in shame and fidgeting with the cuff of his grubby shirt.

Lord Roberd was well respected, and there wasn't a man in The Head with a kinder heart. The idea of disappointing him caused Merric's eyes to begin to sting with the threat of tears.

'You haven't caused any trouble at all,' Lord Roberd assured him kindly, raising his hands soothingly.

'I didn't think you'd want me to be here,' Merric admitted.

'Why in the Mother's name would you think that?' Lord Roberd looked surprised.

Merric took a deep breath, keeping his eyes on his feet, and his hands continued to fidget.

'I'm not a Jacelyn, I'm not a part of your family.'

Lord Roberd made a sympathetic sound, rose from his chair and sat on the edge of the table next to Merric.

'Do you like it here?'

'My lord?'

'Does Eagle Mount feel as though it's your home? Do you think of me like a father? Do you think I love you like a son?'

'I-I don't know,' Merric stammered. 'I've never known any other home, and you and Lady Cathreen have always been kind to me,' he admitted, feeling ashamed at his actions that morning.

The more he thought about it, he was feeling ashamed at how he had been acting for the whole past year. There had not been a week that had passed when he had not snuck out of the castle behind Lord Roberd's back. He did not think the duke would mind, but now Merric knew that was not the case at all.

Lord Roberd smiled warmly at him. 'My wife and I have raised you since you were very small. You weren't born from us, but you're as much our child as Tristan and Sophya are. You're not an outsider here. Merric, you may not be a Jacelyn, as far as the laws of our land are concerned, but you are an Orrell, and I can think of no greater honour than being a descendant of that noble and honourable family. One day you'll be a man grown, and a knight if you so wish it. Whatever path you choose to take, you'll serve your dukedom well.'

The twinkle had returned to Lord Roberd's eyes, and Merric forced himself to smile.

'I know that you have been struggling recently,' Lord Roberd continued. 'It is not easy being a young man, especially a young nobleman. For you it must be even harder, and I'm sorry that I have not spoken to you about this earlier. It may have caused us both to have worried less.'

'You've been worried?'

'Of course! I know you have been sneaking out of the castle. I did not try and stop you, as it was your decision to make. I do not wish to treat you like a child, Merric. I am

49

just glad that you no longer come back all covered in bruises,' Lord Roberd laughed. 'You need your space from time to time, I understand that. I only ask that, if you ever have any worries, you come and speak to me. Do not let your mind wander and come to the wrong conclusions. My lady wife and I would be very sad if you did not feel welcome here.'

Merric promised that he would. He knew that Lord Roberd was right. But there was something that bothered him still.

'Tristan really seems to hate me.'

Lord Roberd sighed, and rose once more from where he was sat on the desk. He moved over to the fire that crackled merrily in the grate, and looked deep into the flames. 'Tristan certainly doesn't hate you Merric, and it pains me to hear you think he does. He thinks of you as his brother.' He suddenly laughed. 'My brother and I were as different as two brothers could be. Some said he had the sharper sword, but I had the sharper mind. We would argue constantly as we grew up. Yet he was still my brother.'

Lord Roberd's brother had died before Merric had been brought to Eagle Mount, and the duke rarely talked about him. 'Then why does Tristan act so coldly towards me?'

'Have you ever seen two brothers around each other? They spend half their time fighting each other, but it is rare to see a bond stronger than the love they share. I've seen

50

you around Tristan, Merric, and you're not exactly warm towards him either. Do you hate *him*?'

'Of course not.'

'Then why do you think he hates you?'

Merric missed the fun that he and Tristan used to have, and hated that something as simple as age had come between them. He felt that he no longer even recognised the person that Tristan had become. He did not know how to put it into words though. When Merric did not answer, Lord Roberd sensed what he was thinking.

'Tristan has a lot on his mind. Being the son of a duke is not an easy role to play,' he said. 'I know, I was in that position once myself, remember. One day he will be a duke himself, and will have to rule The Head. Unfortunately, such an honour brings much pressure as well. Tristan has had to grow older much swifter than someone of the same age as him should normally have to.'

Merric knew that it was stupid of him to think that nothing would change as Tristan grew older. It was likely that, given a choice, the older boy would have preferred to live without the responsibility of one day having to lead the dukedom looming over him.

'I will admit,' Lord Roberd continued, 'that Tristan is not completely without blame. I've already spoken to him, this very morning in fact. He admitted, after some time, that he could show a greater kindness to you.'

'I don't suppose he liked that,' Merric smiled.

'No,' Lord Roberd said, his eyes twinkling in amusement. 'But he admitted that I was right. You are a part of this family Merric, even if you chose to exclude yourself from us.' Merric opened his mouth to protest, but Lord Roberd waved this aside. 'You are not a child anymore, and I'd be lying if I said I didn't go through my own rebellious streak when I was your age. We love you, Lady Cathreen and I, and Tristan does too, even if he's too proud to show it. Sophya even has her own affection towards you, and I've heard her call you her brother on more than one occasion.'

'Truly?'

'A duke isn't allowed the luxury of lying,' Lord Roberd laughed, before looking serious again. 'I see no reason why your friendship with Tristan cannot be as strong as it once was. All I ask of you is to remember that Tristan is not a boy anymore, so don't be frustrated when he doesn't act like one.'

'I promise I won't,' Merric said, meaning it.

'Good,' Lord Roberd smiled. 'Now, as you know, Lord Aric's visit will end with the jousting tournament.'

Merric nodded enthusiastically. He was as excited about this display of combat and skill as anyone. He had never spent much time practicing with a sword himself, despite the Swordmaster of the castle trying to insist that he train for five hours a day like all young noblemen. Merric had never imagined himself as a knight, preferring to spend his spare time buried in books rather than practicing in the courtyard. Lord Roberd, hearing about this, had allowed Merric to enjoy his reading instead. 'I will not tell you to move yourself from the library to the training yard,' Lord Roberd had once said to him. 'Your life is yours to live. There is as much power to be found in books as there is in a Reaver's war hammer; one only needs to know where to read it.'

However, Merric loved to watch Tristan fight, and over the years had seen the change in him from the boy who would practice his sword swings on a young Merric to the proud knight who rode his horse so gallantly.

'You will squire for Tristan during the tournament,' Lord Roberd said. 'You will clean his armour, carry his lance, and hold his banner when he competes. You two will be close again, I promise.'

'Yes, my lord, I'd like that.'

Merric was willing to try anything. He did not want to let Lord Roberd down again, and was desperate to make up for his attitude over the past year or so.

Lord Roberd's eyes shone as he looked at Merric, a smile on his lips.

'Not all of us can achieve greatness, my boy, or live through the ages immortalised in songs of bravery or valour. For those of us less remarkable than that, we can still measure the value of our lives through the effect we have on our loved ones around us. Myself, Lady Cathreen, Tristan and Sophya, and even a certain young daughter of a blacksmith who I've been told about; are our lives richer from having had you in it? The answer is "yes", Merric, we're rich indeed.'

There was a heavy knock at the study door, and Lord Roberd called for them to enter. The door opened to reveal Sir Gerard, captain of the Eagle Guard. He still wore his armour, but had removed his helmet to reveal his scarred and weathered face. He was not a young man and his beard and hair were grey. He was the brother to Lord Osworth Velion, Baron of Elderwyne. The Velion family had been loyal to the Jacelyns for many centuries, and in return they had been granted the warm, fertile lands south of Eaglestone. Here there were vast vineyards stretching for miles, providing all of High Realm with fine wines. Lord Osworth was the oldest brother, so inherited the barony when their father passed away. Gerard, once he had become a knight, dreamt of being the best swordsman in The Head. After years of riding and fighting for his brother he was invited to join the Eagle Guard of the Jacelyns. Being promoted to the captain of the Eagle Guard was the highest honour a man could receive. Even as an old man, his skill with a sword was famous across the realm and there was no knight more loyal to Lord Roberd.

Merric had always been nervous of Sir Gerard, with his grim face and swift anger. He did not say much, and instead preferred to let his sword do the talking. In this regard it was said that Sir Gerard gave the greatest speeches on either side of The Rush. Tristan had often told tales of

Sir Gerard to Merric when he was younger, often to scare him or to get him to behave when he was being bad.

'My apologies if I'm interrupting, my lord.' Sir Gerard's voice was gruff.

'Not at all, Sir. What is it?' Lord Roberd said.

'Orderix begs your presence in the Grand Hall. A poacher has been caught, and your justice is required.'

Lord Roberd sighed, and rose from his chair. 'I'm sorry, Merric, I must take my leave.' He made to follow Sir Gerard out of the door, but paused and turned back to Merric. 'Perhaps you would like to come with me?'

'Really?' Merric was taken aback.

Tristan was heir to Eagle Mount and so regularly took part in Lord Roberd's court, and accompanied him in matters of lordship. Merric had never before been invited, but was eager for the chance. He left the study with Lord Roberd, and the two of them followed Sir Gerard towards to the Grand Hall.

***

In honour of the visit of Lord Aric, the Grand Hall had been spared no expense in its decoration. At the top of the hall, behind the raised stage on which Lord Roberd's seat was placed, was a vast stained glass window, and for the occasion this was flanked by two great banners. To the left was a sky-blue banner, featuring the eagle of the Jacelyns delicately embroidered in rich golden thread, whilst to the right there was a white banner bearing the symbol of the black marching knight of the Monfort family. However, despite these towering banners, which hung all the way from the roof beams to the flag-stoned floor, it was the stained glass window itself that dominated the room.

This huge piece of art displayed the first Duke of The Head, Jace the Eagle Rider. He was one of the three companions of High Realm's first ever king, Eldred the Pure. They accompanied him when Eldred had fled for his life from his home of Ouestoria, and travelled east over the Border Peaks and first arrived in this land. The first settlement that was built was taken as the new king's home, and he named it King's Keep. To this day it was still where the King of High Realm ruled from. The realm was then split into four dukedoms, and he gave the other three to each of his companions, giving them the title of duke. They served their king, but were free to rule their lands as they chose. Jace, a master of all creatures, settled on the eastern shore of the new realm, and took his beloved giant eagle, Haerophon, as the symbol of his family. This was a thousand years ago, but every child knew the story of how High Realm was first created.

Along the side wall of the Grand Hall was a row of huge wooden shields. Each was decorated with the symbols of the six noble families that held baronies in The Head. The white ship of the Lyns sat beside the great oak tree of the Oakhearts. Next to them were the red fleur-de-lis of the Velions, the winged horse of the Blooms, and the blue bear of the Conways. At the far end was a shield bearing the golden stag of the Orrells, and it was this which always drew Merric's eyes. Despite Ryding being no more, Lord Roberd still chose to honour the Orrell family. Each of these great families ruled their lands in the name of the Duke of The Head, and the golden eagle of the Jacelyn's lay at the centre of the wall, on a shield even larger than the others.

The floor of the Grand Hall was usually covered with long tables, which could seat many hundred, but for the moment these had been pushed against the walls to clear a large space in the centre of the chamber. Lord Roberd took his place on his chair on the raised stage, whilst Merric and Sir Gerard stood behind him. Orderix, Lord Roberd's counsellor and advisor, stepped stiffly next to his duke.

Merric had never liked Orderix. His father had served as Lord's Counsel before him, and with his help Lord Roberd had many years of prosperity and peace in The Head. Orderix had been named the new Lord's Counsel when his father had become too old to continue the demanding role. But whereas Orderix's father had been wise and fair, Orderix himself was cold and ambitious.

The poacher who had been caught was brought in from a side door, his hands bound and two Jacelyn soldiers flanking him. The man held his back straight and his head high, but his clothing was scruffy and travel-worn, and of poor quality. He was of middle years, but looked strong for a man of his age. His thick arms and broad shoulders

57

showed that he was well trained in using a longbow. His jaw was unshaven, and he had to flick his dirty blond hair out of his eyes.

The man was brought forward to stand before the stage, where Lord Roberd addressed him.

'What is your name?'

'Kasper, of Little Harrow,' the man replied, his voice flat.

Orderix hissed with anger, and at his gesture one of the soldiers struck the poacher with the wooden shaft of his spear.

'You will address us "*my lords*",' Orderix snarled.

Merric noticed the emphasis the Lord's Counsel put on the word "us". Orderix was not a lord, but he felt that his high position in the dukedom allowed him to use this title if he chose to.

The poacher grunted and doubled over in pain, but immediately straightened up and looked brazenly up at Lord Roberd. The soldier went to hit Kasper again, but to Orderix's clear annoyance Lord Roberd raised a hand to stop the beating.

'That will do. Do you know why you have been brought before me, Kasper of Little Harrow?' Lord Roberd asked.

'Yes. I killed a deer.'

He still did not address the duke properly, and Merric could not help but me a little impressed by the nerve of the scruffy poacher. Or was it stupidity? The soldiers looked up at Lord Roberd for direction, but received no orders to strike the prisoner.

'And you confess to this crime?'

'I do,' the poacher said simply.

'You understand that the crime for killing one of the king's deer is death?'

Lord Roberd seemed dismayed by the poacher's lack of regret. The man seemed unafraid, and rather than grovelling and begging for forgiveness he just glared up at Lord Roberd, the look in his eyes turning into pure anger.

'My family is starving, clearly something you're not used to here.' He indicated around the luxurious room. 'I'll do what I must to provide for them, even if no one else will.'

'And yet you turned to poaching?' Lord Roberd asked sadly, shaking his head. 'If the folk of Little Harrow are starving then you should have appealed to your baron, Lord Tymon…'

'Tymon Conway is tucked up in his castle, the same as you are. He cares nothing for those outside his walls!'

The poacher's outburst was loud, and he took a step forward towards where Lord Roberd sat. The soldiers jumped forward and grabbed hold of his arms.

Lord Roberd kept silent for a moment. He had heard rumours that Lord Tymon, baron of the lands to the far west of The Head, had been neglecting the folk who lived under his rule. He knew that soon he would have to summon the baron to Eagle Mount, to ensure he was reminded of his responsibilities. The folk of The Head looked to their lords to offer them guidance and protection, and it was their responsibility to provide it.

In the silence that followed his outburst, the poacher spoke again.

'I have no fear for myself, only that my wife and child won't survive another winter. You have no idea what it feels like,' he said accusingly, 'to know your family is suffering and to not be able to help. To watch them, and be forced to tell them that everything will be okay. To lie!'

'I want to hear no more of your pathetic bleating,' Orderix said, his voice high, but he was silenced immediately by a stern look from Lord Roberd. Orderix bowed to his duke with gritted teeth, before taking a step backwards.

The poacher snarled at the Lord's Counsel, and strained against the men holding him.

'If I had my longbow in my hands you would not speak to me so, you snake,' he said to Orderix.

'You see, my lord,' Orderix said to Lord Roberd, accusingly. 'The folk of your dukedom need a heavy boot and a strong arm to keep them in line. This man is a prime example. I've spoken to you of this before. You are too soft, you need to be strong…'

'Enough!' Lord Roberd silenced Orderix once again, and looked down at the poacher.

Lord Roberd's face was set, knowing what he must do, but Merric could sense the hesitation in him. There was no doubt the man had committed the crime, he was willing to admit as much, but the poacher's words had made an impression on Lord Roberd. As Duke of The Head, it was he who had the responsibility to ensure that justice in his dukedom was upheld, and Merric could see that he was thinking hard. Eventually he rose from his seat. The two Jacelyn soldiers forced the prisoner to his knees.

'The laws of the Realm are clear,' Lord Roberd said. 'Poaching is a crime against our rightful ruler, King Cristoph of Eldred's line, and therefore a crime against the Mother herself. Kasper of Little Harrow, I hereby sentence you to death.'

Orderix cleared his throat, and all eyes looked at the Lord's Counsel. Not for the first time, he reminded Merric of a scheming spider, and an unpleasant one at that.

'My lord, if I may make a suggestion? I believe it wise for this criminal's execution to take place tonight, in front of our guests. It would certainly act as a message to any others who should choose to break the king's laws. The common folk need to remember who their betters are.' Orderix's voice was cold, as were his eyes.

Lord Roberd surveyed Orderix for a moment, with a look of intense dislike on his face. The poacher stared at him too, with loathing in his eyes. The silence was broken by Lord Roberd, and his words were directed at Orderix. Merric had the uncomfortable feeling that he was overhearing a private conversation between the two men.

'A man's execution is his punishment for his crimes, and this man will pay for his. An execution is *not* for the entertainment of others, and nor should a man be humiliated in his death,' Lord Roberd said quietly.

Orderix kept silent, but Merric could tell there were more than a few words that he wanted to say.

'What is more,' Lord Roberd continued, 'only the Mother can judge us; it is not for us to claim to be the betters of anyone. You would do well to remember that, if you care to continue serving as my counsel.'

Lord Roberd turned back to the condemned poacher. 'My men will take you to the dungeons where you will await your sentence being carried out.'

The two soldiers seized the poacher's arms, and began to lead him away.

'One moment,' Lord Roberd said, taking a step forward and raising a hand.

The soldiers stopped, but the poacher kept his eyes stubbornly on the door he was being led to.

'Kasper, look at me,' Lord Roberd insisted, his voice suddenly soft. The poacher reluctantly turned his head and looked back at him. 'Your family's suffering is my failing, not your responsibility to correct. I promise you, with the Mother as my witness, that I will do what I can to right this wrong. For your family, and for all the folk in my dukedom, highborn and low.'

'Were it not for you so-called "lords", who do us common folk more harm than good, my family would be just fine,' Kasper spat.

CHAPTER FOUR

The tournament

The larger part of the crowd cheered and whooped as Tristan's lance shattered against the shield of his opponent, sending the man tumbling from his horse. He was a knight from The Dale, the northern dukedom of High Realm, and bore the symbol of a leaping fox on his blue shield. Tristan wheeled his horse around and galloped alongside the stands, the splintered remains of his lance thrust into the air in victory. Merric, standing at the far end of the jousting field, waved Tristan's banner enthusiastically. He could see Lord Roberd and the rest of his family clapping from the centre of the stands, where seats had been set up to watch the jousting tournament. Lord Aric was there too, clapping slowly and studying Tristan with a professional eye.

It was the second day of the jousting tournament. The competition was taking place outside the walls of Eaglestone, and the towering castle of Eagle Mount atop its hill formed a striking backdrop. The stands had been temporarily erected on the meadows outside the town, and were filled with those who sat in the warm spring sun enjoying the jousting.

Tristan reined in his horse when he joined Merric at the edge of the field. The cheering of the crowd had filled the horse with a nervous excitement, so Merric reached up and took hold of the horse's bridle to help calm him. Tristan dismounted, and removed his helmet to reveal his blond hair plastered to his head with sweat. Like all competitors he wore his finest and most striking armour for the tournament, with every knight wanting to outdo the others. Merric had laboured for hours to polish the armour to a bright shine, and Tristan's brand new sky-blue surcoat was trimmed with gold embroidery.

'Well fought, Tris,' Merric smiled, as Tristan handed him his helmet. 'Just think, he rode all the way from Fox Hall for that. Bad luck to be drawn against Sir Tristan Jacelyn of Eagle Mount!'

'Many have ridden further to receive the honour of my lance,' Tristan grinned back.

Lord Roberd had been right, as usual, Merric thought cheerfully. Arranging for him to squire for Tristan had brought the two of them closer together again. Neither had apologised to the other for their behaviour over the past year, but it was not needed. Both had pushed it aside as though it had not happened, and once again they felt like friends, like brothers.

Tristan led the way back to his tent that had been set up beside the jousting field, and Merric secured his horse to a hitching post nearby. Tristan eased his weary body down onto a stool in the shaded doorway of his tent, and settled down to watch the next bout. Merric planted Tristan's banner into the earth beside the tent before going to his side. The eagle on the banner flapped proudly over their heads. Around them were over two dozen other tents and pavilions of different colours belonging to the other knights. Musicians moved around the tents, playing their lutes and singing. Jugglers tossed balls, flaming torches, and daggers into the air for the entertainment of the spectators, and caused bursts of laughter when they missed a catch. In the distance a blacksmith could be heard banging dented armour plates back into shape before the owner's next bout. It created a festival atmosphere, and Merric was enjoying every moment of it.

'Water,' Tristan asked.

It was the warmest day of the year so far, and Merric hurried into the cool shade of the tent and poured Tristan a goblet of water from a jug. Tristan took one sip of it before tipping the rest over his head. He sighed contentedly. A distant cheer came across from the next field, where the archery competition was taking place.

In the next bout of the jousting tournament, Rayden Monfort rode lance to lance against Sir Gerard Velion. Lord Aric's boasts of his son's skill were not lies, it seemed. So far in the competition Rayden had unhorsed all his opponents with an almost lazy ease. However, Sir Gerard had years of experience in the saddle, and so it promised to be a close fight. Leaving Tristan in the shade of the tent entrance to relax, Merric got closer to watch.

As Rayden spurred his horse onto the jousting field to take up his position, Merric could hear Sophya cheering loudly from the centre of the stands, and looking across he saw Lord Aric lean in close and laugh with her. Rayden was wearing the same armour he wore the day he arrived at Eagle Mount, and astride his great warhorse with lance in hand he looked even more gallant and heroic. He kept his head bare for as long as possible before putting on his helmet, letting the breeze flow through his long hair. Merric hated to admit it, but Rayden looked just like the knights in the stories and poems he had grown up listening to. In comparison to the flashy Rayden Monfort, the older and more restrained Sir Gerard was wearing the armour that was his uniform as captain of the Eagle Guard. The plates were thick and strong, but dull and plain in comparison to his opponent's. It was armour meant for battle, not for tournaments, and the steel plates were cut and scored from dozens of sword strikes over the years.

The bout began, and the two knights rode at each other on opposite sides of the central fence. There was a sharp crack as their lances struck each other's shields, but both men managed to stay in their saddles. Rayden and Sir Gerard turned their horses around so they faced each other again, and once more lowered the points of their lances and spurred forward. Sir Gerard aimed his lance for a second time at Rayden's white shield, hoping that strength alone could force the young knight out of his saddle. Rayden appeared to be doing the same, but at the last moment he adjusted his position and brought his lance tip past the older knight's shield. The lance struck Sir Gerard squarely in the chest. The older knight grunted and toppled backwards off his horse and fell heavily to the ground.

'The winner is Sir Rayden Monfort, of The Citadel,' cried the brightly dressed herald who stood at the edge of the jousting field. The two trumpeters standing beside him put their lips to their instruments and blared a few notes across the jousting field.

Lord Aric got to his feet and applauded his son loudly, each deafening clap as loud as thunder. Sophya's face flushed with pleasure.

Sir Gerard had remounted his horse, and made his way over to his tent. He handed his lance to his squire and bowed his head respectfully at Rayden. The younger knight did not bother to return the gesture, but thrust his armoured fist into the air in victory instead. As he rode off the field, Rayden passed close by Tristan's tent and saw Merric watching him.

'You're the Orrell boy aren't you, or are you pretending to be a Jacelyn these days?' Rayden said. 'Come and find me once you've grown up and can lift a sword, until then stop staring at me.'

He laughed at his own joke, and rode away.

'He's an ass,' Tristan said quietly, watching Rayden dismount beside his tent and throw his helmet at his small squire who fumbled the catch. Rayden then reached over and grabbed a horn of wine, which he gulped down.

Like Merric, Tristan had quickly grown sick of their visitors. The jousting marked the end of their month-long visit, and was to be followed by a huge banquet that evening. Merric did not know the purpose of the neighbouring duke's visit, and what had caused him to ride from his castle all the way to Eagle Mount, but he was looking forward to the next day when they would be leaving and the castle would be quiet once more. It had not taken Merric long to see that Rayden Monfort was arrogant and spoilt, and had an intense, and Merric was sure unhealthy, interest in Sophya.

Merric was less sure about Lord Aric. The Duke of The Southstones was quick to laugh and friendly enough at first appearance, but there was something Merric found unsettling about him. There were times when the two dukes had been enclosed in Lord Roberd's study all day, and none knew what they were discussing there. Neither seemed happy whenever they appeared again, hours later.

Spring had worn on towards summer and the rest of the Monforts's visit had been spent pursuing the popular pastimes of the nobility in High Realm. By night there were banquets and performances by actors and musicians from the surrounding land, while in the day the two dukes rode to the nearby Greenwood to hunt, with falcons perched on their arms and accompanied by knights. Merric had been invited of course, but his lack of skill in the saddle or ability with a bow or spear had stopped him from taking up the offer.

He had not been able to spend as much time with Ana over the past weeks as he would have liked. The visit of Lord Aric had been keeping Ana and her father busy, and so their recent meetings had been brief. Lord Roberd had promised Merric though that once the Monforts had left he could invite Ana to visit the castle. It was another reason why he could not wait for Lord Aric to leave.

Two more pairs of knights competed, and two more knights celebrated victory while their opponents stumbled, battered and bruised, off the field. It was then Tristan's turn again.

His next bout was against one of the knights who had accompanied Lord Aric and his son from The Southstones. As Tristan donned his eagle-crested helmet once more and climbed into his saddle, Merric watched his opponent make his way to his starting position. He recognised the knight as being one of Lord Aric's most valued companions, and he had rarely seemed to leave his duke's side throughout the visit. Merric had not seen him remove his helmet once though, and this had roused a mild curiosity in him. He was a tall man, and his shoulders were broad to match. He was clad in armour as black as the knight on the heraldry of the Monfort family. His chipped and splintered shield bore no symbol though, but was covered in a black and white chequered pattern.

'He's the biggest man I've ever seen,' Merric said to himself, and Tristan overheard him.

'Yes,' he said, turning his head to look down at Merric. 'Much too big for me. Would you like to fight him instead?' His voice was muffled by his steel helmet.

Merric grinned up at Tristan and handed him a new lance, made from a fragile wood that would shatter on impact to help reduce the chances of a fatal wound being caused.

The crowd cheered as Tristan walked his horse onto the jousting field. His opponent's huge warhorse was beating the grass with its hooves and gnashing its teeth in anticipation. The horse seemed as eager to fight as its rider, but the black knight had no trouble controlling the spirited animal. The herald dropped his arm, signalling the knights to fight, and they both immediately kicked their spurs back and charged at each other.

The black knight thrust his lance powerfully, with little regard for his own safety. When the tip of his lance connected with Tristan's shield it echoed like a drum, and Merric was sure his friend would be beaten. The shaft of the lance did not break, so the full force of the impact drove into Tristan. He barely managed to remain in his saddle, and in trying to keep his balance his own lance missed its target entirely. There was an audible groan from the amassed crowd, but Tristan was still in the fight.

The two knights reached the opposite ends of the jousting field, and turned their horses back to face each other along the length of the fence. Apparently eager to land a blow on his opponent, Tristan immediately launched his horse into a full charge. The black knight took his time, and allowed his horse to rear up terrifyingly before he too spurred forward. This second time Tristan fared better, but only just. His lance made contact with the black knight's chequered shield and shattered, but his opponent once more found his mark and struck Tristan on the arm, causing him to almost drop the splintered remains of his lance.

Merric hurried forward as Tristan reined in his horse at the edge of the field, and took the broken lance from him.

'He leads me three points to one,' Tristan said.

A knight scored two points for striking his opponent's body, and one point for hitting his shield. Whoever scored most points after three charges was the winner, though if a knight managed to knock his opponent off his horse then he won automatically, regardless of the score. Though Tristan's face was hidden by his helmet, his voice betrayed no concern that he was losing.

'Is your arm hurt?' Merric asked, as he passed a new lance up to him.

'A little,' Tristan admitted. 'But it was worth it.'

'Worth it?' Merric was confused, but he could see that the black knight was ready and the herald was signalling for the final charge to begin.

While Merric ran back off the field, Tristan turned and tucked his lance under his aching arm. The sound of thundering hooves filled the air once more, and Merric held his breath as the two knights came together for a final time. There was a loud crack, followed by the collective gasp from the crowd, before the black knight fell heavily with a roar.

The crowd cheered and Merric punched the air, more from relief than anything else. The black knight sprung back to his feet and stalked angrily from the field, with grass and earth stuck in the joints of his armour, leaving his squire to retrieve the loose horse and guide it back towards the tents. Tristan raised his gauntleted hand to the crowd.

'You see?' Tristan said over the cheering of the crowd once he had returned to where Merric stood.

'You let him strike you,' Merric said, understanding now.

'Of course,' Tristan said with a smirk. 'He as strong as an ox, but slow. I let him think he had me beaten, before using his own strength against him.'

A long gouge on Tristan's shield showed where he had allowed the black knight's lance to pass him on that last charge, throwing the larger man off balance.

'He's not going to like that,' Merric observed.

73

'What can he do?' Tristan said with a shrug showing that he was not concerned. 'The bout is over.'

With that victory, Tristan was through to the final, and by now the sun was sinking towards the horizon, marking the start of a pleasant evening. As expected by many, the two knights set to face off against each other in the final were the sons of the two great dukes.

As Tristan knelt in the grass briefly to offer a prayer to the Mother to give speed to his arm, Rayden Monfort trotted his horse smartly over to the stands. Since his last bout, his squire had brushed the horse until its coat was glossy and shone in the summer sun. Rayden stopped when he reached Sophya and, with a flourish, offered her a rose. This drew jealous glances from many other young ladies in the crowd. Sophya blushed heavily and took the offered flower with a nervous hand. In return she handed him her delicate silk handkerchief, which he stowed safely inside his metal gauntlet, before throwing Sophya a dazzling smile.

'I think I see love blooming,' Lord Aric observed with a smile as he watched his son ride off with his token from Sophya.

Lord Roberd gave a short laugh, which could easily have just been a cough, but said nothing.

At his end of the field, Tristan frowned at Rayden, disapproving of the other man's interest in his sister. He jammed his helmet back onto his head. There were many young ladies in the crowd who were eagerly clutching tokens ready to gift Tristan, and were trying to attract his attention. He did not approach them as Rayden had though, and kept his focus on the tournament.

A fanfare of trumpets sounded, and the excited chatter from the crowd died away. Lord Roberd rose from his place in the stands, and addressed the two knights.

'Your valour and skill have no bounds, and you've proved yourselves on this field today. You've both fought gallantly, and made the houses of Monfort,' he gestured at Rayden, 'and Jacelyn,' Tristan bowed his head, 'proud.'

'Well spoken,' Lord Aric boomed, clapping his hands together.

'May the Mother guide your arms, and help us to determine a final victor.'

The cheering of the crowd sounded again as Lord Roberd resumed his seat. In honour of her position as wife of the Duke of The Head, Lady Cathreen rose from her seat and took a silk pennant that was offered to her by a servant. She raised the pennant high above her head, where the light breeze caught the fabric. After a moment's pause she let it go, and the pennant fluttered gently down. The two knights kicked back with their spurs, and their horses darted forward.

Merric stood at the very edge of the field, as close to the jousting as he could get, along with the other squires and the knights who had not made it into the final bout. The two knights came together in a crash of steel and wood, and both rode away from the confrontation still in their saddles and both clutching broken lances. As most predicted, the two seemed to be equally matched.

Being at the wrong end of the jousting field to where Merric stood, Tristan retrieved a new lance from a nearby servant instead. When Tristan wheeled his horse around to face his opponent he saw Rayden, the visor of his helmet lifted, smiling at Sophya. A quick glance at the stands told Tristan his sister was returning the smile, and the sight seemed to boil his blood. Rayden turned his attention to his opponent and his smile turned into a mocking smirk.

The second charge started, with the knights on one point apiece. As the thundering horses neared, Tristan braced his shield, before relaxing his arm at the last moment to allow Rayden's lance to deflect past him. However the trick did not work on Rayden as it had on the black armoured knight. Rayden anticipated the move, and quickly brought his lance up to avoid the trick whilst at the same time parrying away Tristan's own strike. As they passed each other Rayden thrust out with his shield, smashing it into Tristan's own shield and almost dislodging him from his horse.

'No point!' the herald cried. 'Strikes may only be made with the lance tip.'

Most of the crowd were yelling in anger at this dishonest display, whilst the supporters of Rayden shouted their appeal. As the horses came to a standstill at the far ends of the tilt, Tristan looked furiously back at the Monfort knight, following his sneaky attack.

'Are you okay?' Merric asked, hurrying up to Tristan and reaching out to calm his horse.

'I'm fine,' he replied with gritted teeth. 'Does chivalry mean nothing to him?'

'Your shield,' Merric said.

Tristan looked down to see that Rayden's strike had shattered one edge of his shield which bore the ornately painted eagle of the Jacelyn family. Without a word Tristan took his arm out of the straps and handed the broken shield down to Merric.

'You can't,' Merric gasped, but Tristan had already turned his horse and was riding away from him, with no shield to protect him.

Seeing this, the crowd cheered for their hero. A smile played across Lord Aric's face, whilst Sophya bit her lip uncertainly, torn between her love for her brother and her infatuation for the handsome knight from The Southstones.

'You're either very brave, or very foolish, eagle knight. And I think I know which,' Rayden called from his end of the field.

Over the noise from the crowd only Tristan heard him. He ignored the taunt and readied his lance.

'You're beaten,' Rayden continued. 'Accept it, or watch me embarrass you in front of everyone.'

'Close your visor, Monfort,' Tristan snarled.

Rayden laughed harshly, but obligingly lowered the steel visor with a clang. The two knights darted forward one last time, and as he watched, Merric felt time slow. Each hoof beat on the compacted grass appeared to cause the ground to shudder, and his ears were filled with the heavy thudding and metallic jangling of armour. Tristan and Rayden had their lances pointed at each other's chests, though whereas the Monfort knight had his shield raised to protect him, Tristan was at the mercy of his opponent's lance.

The two came together heavily. Rayden struck first. At the last moment he changed the aim of his lance so that it connected heavily with Tristan's armoured head and it deflected upwards, tearing the carved eagle from the crest of his helmet. Tristan's lance impacted against his opponent a moment later, slipping past Rayden's raised shield and striking him square in the breast plate of his armour. The blunted wood carved a long gouge along the shining armour, sending some of the onyx stones that were embedded in the steel flying in every direction.

Merric held his breath along with everyone in the stands, and watched as both knights were flung violently backwards in their saddles as their horses continued to gallop past each other. Tristan appeared to slip, but reached out with his shieldless arm and grasped the reigns tightly, somehow managing to stay in his saddle. Rayden let out a shout of pain and toppled backwards, bouncing off his horse's bucking behind and landed unceremoniously on the hard ground.

The crowd were going wild, cheering for the young Jacelyn knight. Merric shouted as loudly as the rest, and began jogging onto the field to make sure Tristan was unhurt. The Jacelyn knight was struggling to pull the dented helmet from his head. The strike from Rayden had been underhand and sneaky once again, but he had still failed to win the tournament. Knowing this, Rayden scrambled to his feet and looked furiously from his opponent to the herald who announced Tristan Jacelyn as the victor.

Discarding his lance, Rayden wrenched his sword free of his scabbard and ran towards his victorious opponent.

Merric saw the threat a moment before the other onlookers, and shouted a warning to Tristan who had just dismounted from his horse. Tristan turned his helmeted head and saw Rayden charging furiously towards him. With a practiced speed he reached for his own sword. He met Rayden's attack head on, and their blades met in a shower of sparks. Lances were the only weapons allowed to be used in the fight. As such, the swords were not blunted, and the two young men faced each other with deadly steel.

'No!' Merric cried, and ran towards the fight.

The two knights exchanged heavy blows, and the air was filled with the sound of steel striking steel. The two were well matched, but one of Tristan's swings knocked Rayden's sword aside, leaving him vulnerable to a killing blow. He swung his blade back, furious at his dishonourable opponent, but at that moment Lord Roberd rose from his seat. His voice thundered across the field.

'PUT DOWN YOUR SWORDS!' he roared, and Tristan immediately obeyed his father, dropping to a knee. He bowed his head in shame.

Taking advantage of the pause, Rayden brought his sword up again, but seeing his opponent kneeling he too lowered his blade. Silence filled the crowd, broken only by the soft padding of Merric's feet as he reached the two knights.

'I'm sorry, father,' Tristan said, his breathing heavy. He knew he should have shown more control.

'Be at peace, Sir Tristan,' Lord Aric said, standing beside Lord Roberd. 'A knight must have nerves of steel to ride in the tournament, and sometimes we all allow ourselves to be overcome by the excitement.'

His words were kind, but the look he then gave his own son was cold. Rayden had removed his helmet, and after looking back at his father for a moment he reluctantly turned to Tristan and offered his hand.

'My apologies, too much wine perhaps,' he said.

Tristan stood and after a moment's hesitation he shook his hand, accepting his apology with a nod. Up in the stands, Lord Roberd still looked furious.

'Such passion is to be expected in young men,' Lord Aric said to him.

'That may be,' Lord Roberd said, his face flushed. 'Though I would expect more from the man who would one day rule The Head.'

Lord Aric smiled curiously. 'Let us not take anything from Sir Tristan's victory. A well fought tournament indeed. My congratulations to him.'

'Quite so,' Lord Roberd said, reluctantly pushing his anger aside.

He nodded to a squire who passed him an ornately decorated lance. Lord Roberd took it and Tristan, still slightly shamed, climbed the steps so that he stood before his father.

'Sir Tristan Jacelyn of Eagle Mount, in honour of your skill of arms as shown to us today, I present you with this. Treasure it always, as proof of your valiant victory'

Tristan took the lance and bowed his head. The crowd cheered, and even Lord Roberd himself clapped. With the attention no longer on him, Rayden's expression darkened and he watched Tristan sulkily.

Lord Aric then caught his son's eye, and two looked at each other for a long moment. Slowly, the corner of the young knight's mouth curled into a cold smile.

- CHAPTER FIVE -

Lord Roberd's tale

Merric had never seen the Grand Hall so full as it was for Lord Aric's farewell banquet. Hundreds of candles covered the long tables, each of which was packed with folk enjoying the many dishes of food laid out before them. Roasted boars sat beside chicken and venison, with mutton and duck also being plentiful and brought out by servants from the kitchens below. Tureens of stew, potatoes and other root vegetables were laid out, and platters of bread freshly baked. As Merric looked at all the food he spared a thought for the poacher, still locked in the dungeons, and his family who often struggled to find enough to eat.

Nearest to the raised stage at the head of the Grand Hall sat the knights, rich merchants, priors and other important guests, while at the far end were the Monfort and Jacelyn soldiers, sat side by side. Not used to the luxuries usually only enjoyed by noble folk and the rich, they ate and drank lavishly, as though afraid the fine food and drink would be taken away from them. Men wearing the white of Lord Aric and the sky blue of Lord Roberd sat together, banging their mugs of ale together and singing rowdy songs that were hardly appropriate for the Grand Hall. One of the Monfort men seized a serving girl around the waist and pulled her over to sit on his knee. She was only rescued when a senior servant saw her plight and clipped the man hard around the ear.

Over their heads, in the gallery that overlooked the Grand Hall, a troupe of musicians were playing. They scraped their bows across their instruments, straining to be heard over the din. Below them, jesters, acrobats and fools entertained the guests, whilst minstrels scrolled between the tables adding their own songs and poems to the noise.

Atop the stage stood the high table, facing out across the room, with the vast stained glass window depicting Jace the Eagle Rider at its back. Lord Roberd sat at the centre of the high table, on his carved stone chair that dominated the room. As befitting his status, Lord Aric sat in the place of honour on his right hand side, eating heartily and laughing often. Lady Cathreen sat on Lord Roberd's left, taking small delicate bites. Tristan's place was beside Lord Aric, with a cut on his brow the only reminder of the day's earlier jousting. Rayden was on Lady Cathreen's other side. Lord Roberd had seen it wise to keep the two young men separate, should their tempers flare up again.

Much to Merric and Tristan's annoyance, however, Sophya was seated next to Rayden, and she spent more time looking at him and laughing at his jests than she did concentrating on the food laid out before her. She looked less enthusiastic about having Orderix sat on her other side. The Lord's Counsel sat as stiff as ever, taking disinterested bites of the chicken on his plate. Before long he grew bored of the food and took to studying the occupants of the tables nearest him with his unfriendly grey eyes.

Merric was seated at the far end of the table with Simeon, the wizened old Arch Prior, beside him. Merric liked the kind, elderly man, but his good heart and gentle nature did not disguise the fact that he was possibly the most boring man Merric had ever met. The Arch Prior could drone on for hours, sending anyone within earshot into an easy sleep. As expected, he was wheezing on to Merric, though Merric could not have said what Simeon was talking about.

A few seats along the table, Lord Roberd and Lord Aric were deep in conversation, their plates being ignored for the moment. The Duke of The Southstones appeared enthusiastic and passionate, but Lord Roberd seemed less so, and kept trying to change the subject. Merric watched them curiously, trying to hear what they were saying over the noise of the banquet. A minstrel had moved over to the head table. He was singing a ballad well known to Merric, and all young folk across High Realm.

Brave Sir Keldin, the Knight of the Moon,
His shield a shining disk.

His lance aglow with a silver light,
And blessed with the moon's own kiss.

The song was the *Ode to the Knight of the Moon*, the tale of Sir Keldin, one of the most famous knights in High Realm history, though perhaps for the wrong reasons. Merric was not interested in the long-dead knight at this moment though, and tried to blank out the singing, along with the Arch Prior's droning. He kept his attention on the two dukes, trying to hear their words, however something Simeon then said to him suddenly brought Merric's attention snapping back to the old Arch Prior.

'What did you just say?' Merric asked.

Simeon blinked, looking confused, and hesitated. 'I said too much, clearly. Ignore me, my child.'

'Tell me,' Merric urged. 'You mentioned my father.'

'Yes, well I think I did.'

The Arch Prior suddenly seemed very interested in a loaf of bread in front of him, and began tearing bits off and dipping it into a stew with frustrating slowness.

Merric was not put off. 'What were you saying about my father?'

Simeon glanced up at Merric cautiously, and seeing the young nobleman staring at him he quickly looked back down at the stew.

'I thought you already knew,' he said, 'it's not my place to say. Forget I spoke.'

'I don't know anything about my father, not really. I didn't even hear what you said, I just heard you mention his name. No one talks to me about him.' Merric could see the discomfort on the old man's face, and felt sorry for him.

The minstrel's song continued to invade their ears.

His banner bore a shimmering crescent,
Of the house into which he was born.
His armour forged not of this world,
Such was its godly form.

'Very well.' Simeon took a breath and nervously dabbed at his mouth with a cloth. He looked at Lord Roberd, but could see he was still deep in conversation. 'As I was saying, your father and his lordship, I'm sorry to tell you, didn't get on. Quite the opposite in fact.'

'My father and Lord Roberd were enemies?' Merric asked in shock, certain the Arch Prior must be wrong.

'No, no,' Simeon chuckled nervously, raising a wrinkled hand, not wanting Merric to jump to the wrong idea. 'No, my poor child. As I said, they merely did not see eye to eye.'

'But my father was Baron of Ryding. Lord Roberd was his duke.'

The Arch Prior nodded. 'Indeed, and his lordship couldn't have asked for a more loyal and capable baron, I assure you! In his time, the lands Lord Willarm Orrell ruled were never more prosperous.'

86

'Then I don't understand.'

Simeon thought for a moment, as though he did not know how to continue. He kept quiet for several moments, and Merric did not try and hurry him. Finally, the old man spoke again.

'Your father and Lord Roberd were once good friends, closer than most friends would ever be. But they had grown apart. In the years before your father passed away...'

'Was murdered,' Merric corrected.

The Arch Prior flinched.

'Quite so, quite so. In the years before he was murdered he was an obedient baron to Lord Roberd, but no more than that.'

'If he and Lord Roberd did not get on, why did my father continue to serve him?'

Simeon chuckled again.

'Honour, my dear child. Your father was a knight. He had sworn his sword to his duke when he was made Baron of Ryding. No knight could ever go against an oath, and nor would Lord Willarm have wanted to. Chivalry, the code of honour all knights live by, far outweighs any petty grievances two men may have with each other.'

'What grievance stopped them from liking each other?'

The smile faded from the Arch Prior's aged face.

'Please don't make me say any more, I fear I have said too much already. I thought you already knew this, which is why I mentioned it. I would never have spoken had I known.'

E'where he went maidens flocked to him,
And gazed on his silver hair.
None could explain how a mortal man,
Could ever be so fair!

A sudden thought occurred to Merric.

'Is this why Lord Roberd feels so guilty that he didn't arrive in time to save my parents, and the village?'

Simeon looked as though he was about to nod, but shook his head instead.

'Forgive me, but I would truly prefer it if you spoke to his lordship about this. I do hope I haven't upset you.'

It had not upset Merric in the slightest, which surprised him. He was curious though. His father, who had ridden to war with Lord Roberd countless times, had not been on speaking terms with his own duke. Why? He decided that he would indeed ask Lord Roberd about it when he next had the chance. With Lord Aric and his companions leaving the next day, Merric knew that Lord Roberd would be less busy, and was sure that an opportunity to discuss the subject with him would arise.

He looked again to where Lord Roberd was still in deep discussion with Lord Aric, whose voice had gotten louder. Merric, his conversation with Simeon finished, leant in closer to listen. He could now make out their words.

'A joining of our great two families, Roberd! Why not?' Lord Aric said.

Lord Roberd smiled patiently across at the other duke.

'I'm afraid Sophya is already promised, as I've told you before,' he shrugged apologetically.

Merric knew this was not true, Sophya was not arranged to marry anyone. He wondered why Lord Roberd was lying to Lord Aric.

'To the son of that fat baron of yours?' Lord Aric asked, angrily, his friendly tone fading.

Roberd ignored the insult to Lord Arran Lyn, Baron of Lynport, the harbour town to the east of Eaglestone.

'The match to Lord Arran's son is a good one. Sophya is a daughter of The Head, and she belongs here.'

Lord Aric's voice was sour, almost threatening.

'I'm offering your daughter the hand of my son, the *heir* to The Citadel. This is a great honour for her, and for you. You think the son of a mere baron compares to that?'

'And yet I must decline, Aric. Sophya will one day marry the Lyn boy.'

Somehow Lord Roberd had allowed himself to remain calm, despite Lord Aric's angry tone.

Yet Sir Keldin, the Knight of the Moon,
At first sign of trouble turned and fled.

Sword unused and unbloodied in battle,
Judge a knight by his deeds not his armour,
wise men have always said.

'Will you please give us silence?' Lord Aric shouted at the minstrel, causing the man to take a step backwards in shock.

Those sat nearby looked up at the southern duke, stunned. Lord Aric breathed deeply, before waving apologetically at the minstrel. His face softened as he looked back at Lord Roberd.

'You'll forgive my persistence, of course. You're entitled to choose a worthy husband for your daughter without being harassed by the likes of me. Perhaps my son isn't the only one who allows his judgement to be clouded by wine.'

'There's nothing to forgive,' Lord Roberd said, and the other duke nodded his head in thanks.

The rest of the banquet passed without incident, but Merric sensed a prickly mood around the room. When the final dishes had been cleared away, Lord Aric got to his feet and spoke to the room.

'Allow me to offer a toast.'

It took several minutes for the last of the laughter and singing to die down at the far end of the hall.

'My lords and ladies,' Lord Aric said, addressing all. 'I thank you for your hospitality. My son and I,' he gestured to Rayden and one of the Monfort soldiers whistled loudly, to the amusement of his fellows, 'have been overwhelmed by the warmth offered to us. We go back to The Southstones tomorrow, but do so with our special relationship with the honourable Jacelyn family even stronger. For a thousand years the Jacelyns and the Monforts have stood side by side, and helped safeguard the realm.' He gestured with his arm, as though speaking about all of The Head. 'I love these lands as though they were my own, and will stop at nothing to help protect them if I can.'

Lord Aric raised his goblet of wine. Lord Roberd mirrored him, as did all others present in the Grand Hall.

'The Jacelyns, and the king!' Lord Aric said.

'The Jacelyns and the king,' Merric echoed, along with three hundred other voices. Lord Roberd and his family, in High Realm tradition, respectfully returned the toast to Lord Aric.

It was close to midnight when Merric left the Grand Hall, and by that point most of the others from the top table had already left the banquet and gone to bed. The soldiers at the far end of the hall seemed far from ready to sleep though. They had entered into a ridiculously complicated drinking game against each other, which the Jacelyn men appeared to be very poor at. As such many were dozing happily with their heads slumped over the table. Merric rarely got to try wine, but Lord Roberd had allowed him to on this night. He was unused to the drink though, and his head felt slightly dizzy as he stumbled towards his bedchamber. He was not sure he liked the feeling.

As he passed the door to Lord Roberd's study he could hear a raised voice, along with the loud crying of Sophya. This made Merric pause, one hand resting on the wall beside him for support.

'But I *love* him,' she wept.

'Sophya-,' her father tried to calm her, but she was despairing and pounded her feet on the floor.

'Please father, I beg you. Please let us marry.'

'My daughter, you don't love him, you only think you do. I'll help find you a good man, I promise. A better man.'

'I don't *want* anyone else! I want *him*! I hate you!'

The door suddenly flew open and Sophya stormed out, her eyes awash with tears. She did not even notice Merric, who had to dive clumsily out of the way to avoid her barrelling into him. A moment later Merric heard the sound of her bedchamber door slamming a floor above.

Footsteps sounded in Lord Roberd's study, and the door was pushed shut. Despite him hating seeing Sophya upset, Merric could not stop a smile from forming on his face. Within a month she will have forgotten all about the handsome knight from The Southstones, and all would be back to normal. Merric wondered if Tristan knew, and he considered going to his chamber to tell him. He was stopped, though, by further voices coming from Lord Roberd's study.

'She'll come around, she doesn't hate you,' came Lady Cathreen's voice.

'I know,' Lord Roberd replied wearily.

'I was once very much like her, don't you remember?' Lady Cathreen chuckled but Lord Roberd merely grunted, and Merric heard the creak of his chair as he sat down. 'Tell me, dearest,' Lady Cathreen continued, 'why is it you so object to Aric's offer? Why did you lie about Sophya already being promised to Lord Arran's son?'

'I will do what I can to protect my daughter,' Lord Roberd replied with a sigh.

Lady Cathreen was taken aback by these words.

'Protect her? Surely a marriage to the Monforts would be a good match, and a strong one. Your son will one day be Duke of The Head, and your daughter could be lady of The Southstones.'

'I do not trust Lord Aric Monfort,' Lord Roberd said, his tone harsh, 'nor do I trust any man who bears that name.'

There was a moment of silence, and Merric moved closer to the door to make sure he did not miss anything.

'You don't trust him?' Lady Cathreen said at last, 'he serves the king, does he not?'

Her husband gave a hollow laugh. 'He serves himself, and the king only when it suits him.'

'What are you saying?'

'There is more to Lord Aric than you know.'

Lady Cathreen was shocked.

'I don't believe it, this is Aric Monfort we're talking about, Duke of The Southstones. He's the hero of the Battle of King's Keep; he saved the realm!'

'Ah yes,' Lord Roberd said, his voice darkening, 'and the world will always remember it. However I was there, Cathreen, twelve years ago. I recall it as if it was yesterday.'

Merric heard the sounds of Lady Cathreen sitting down beside her husband. She knew the histories of High Realm, as Merric did. The story of the Battle of King's Keep told of a great victory by Lord Aric, and was sung by minstrels across the realm.

'The Ouestorians took the realm completely by surprise,' Lord Roberd began. 'The Ouestorian army had crossed the Border Peaks in their latest attempt to seize High Realm for themselves. They reached as far as King's Keep before we even knew what was happening. The king was forced to flee with the remains of his army before their might, leaving the folk of the capital to the mercy of the Ouestorians. They continued their advance, reaching as far as the Rush before we were able to strike back. The king called all of his dukes to come to his aid, and we in turn summoned our barons. I assembled The Head for war, and your father gathered the forces of The Dale. Only the Monforts did not answer the king's request. I led the army of The Head across the Rush and met the army from The Dale, and together we joined with the king's forces and marched on the invaders.'

'I remember the day you left,' Lady Cathreen said. 'I wondered if I would ever see you again.'

'The war was hard fought,' Lord Roberd admitted, 'but eventually we began to push the Ouestorians back with the combined might of the dukedoms of The Kingsland, The Head and The Dale. Finally, on the slopes outside King's Keep, the final battle took place. The capital was back within our grasp, and we could sense victory was close. But I've never known a bloodier battle. We lost many men that day.'

'Including my father,' Lady Cathreen said sadly. 'He was an old man, and close to a natural death as it was. He should have allowed my brother to lead the army of The Dale, or one of his barons.'

'I saw your father lead his knights against the flank of the Ouestorian army, like a true duke. He may have died but it was not in vain. His bravery caused the Ouestorians to break. Victory was ours, and our enemies began fleeing back towards the Border Peaks. It was at that moment that another army appeared, trapping the defeated Ouestorian army and stopping them from reaching their homeland in the west. Above the newly arrived army the banner of the black marching knight of the Monforts flew. Aric had finally arrived, and we managed to capture the fleeing Ouestorian army. They swore they would return to their homeland and never draw swords against our land again. They knew the power of a united High Realm, and knew it was no longer a land they could hope to conquer.'

'The stories are true then,' Lady Cathreen said, as Lord Roberd paused. 'The arrival of the Monfort army secured the victory.'

'The battle was already over, and the war won,' Lord Roberd corrected. 'The king, overwhelmed by his gratitude towards Aric, named him the hero of the battle. The countless men who had died in the war, who had answered the king's call from the start, were discarded from his memory as though they had not existed. Your father, one of realm's dukes, was among them. But Aric and the Monforts were rewarded with gold and honour.'

Lord Roberd paused in his story, and Merric held his breath. Was Lord Roberd's distrust in Lord Aric purely down to jealousy, and anger that his own part in the defeat of the Ouestorian army was not recognised? Merric could not believe that would be the case.

'I know the truth though, even if the king was blind to see it,' Lord Roberd said. 'Aric is ambitious. Ambitious and greedy, and will do whatever he can to further his own gains. When the Ouestorians invaded they looked to have the upper hand, and until the dukedoms of The Kingsland, The Dale and The Head united, the victory of the invaders was certain. Aric did not answer the king's call because he wanted to side with the winner, it is as simple as that. The king thought that the arrival of the Monfort army won the battle, but the battle was already won. Aric didn't join the fight until he knew which the winning side was. Had the battle turned ill for us then I know for certain that Aric would have turned the swords of his army on us and sided with the Ouestorians instead. The man has no honour, and I want my children to have nothing to do with him or his family. I show him courtesy as befitting his position as Duke of The Southstones, but I will never trust any man who bears the black marching knight on his coat.'

'I can't believe it,' Lady Cathreen said, when Lord Roberd had finished. 'Lord Aric is a duke of High Realm, descended from one of the three companions who followed the first king to this land. He swore loyalty to the king, as all dukes have. He is even married to the king's own daughter! He wouldn't allow the realm to fall.'

'There is nothing he would not do for power,' Lord Roberd replied grimly.

Lady Cathreen was silent, as was Merric. No matter how unbelievable the story may be, Lord Roberd would not make it up, and would only share it with his lady wife if he knew it to be true.

Merric was deep in thought about this when he was brought back to earth by Lord Roberd's voice.

'Come, let us retire. It is late, and Aric and his party will be leaving early. The sooner they are gone from my lands, the happier I will be.'

Merric heard their chairs scrape, and he hurried away from the study door. He did not want Lord Roberd to know that he had been listening. He knew the conversation was not for Merric's hearing.

As he headed up to his chamber his head was filled with the conversation he had heard. It explained a lot. He knew that Lord Roberd and Lord Aric had known each other for years, and had fought together for the king many times, yet their friendship always seemed forced. In the past, hundreds of years ago, it was not unknown for the Jacelyns and the Monforts to be on the verge of war against each other over some disagreement, but that was history. At least Merric hoped it was. He had experienced enough death in his life without wanting to see any more.

The fuzziness in his head from the wine had disappeared, but Merric felt suddenly exhausted as he arrived at his chamber. Without stopping to take off his clothes or boots, he collapsed onto his bed and fell straight to sleep.

- CHAPTER SIX -

Swords in the night

He dreamt again that night, but the nightmare that invaded Merric's sleep was new. Perhaps the things he had overheard that evening had unsettled his thoughts. He dreamt he was on a ship, like those he had seen at anchor in the harbour of Lynport. He had often marvelled at the huge wooden ships that travelled there from far and wide, their holds filled with exotic items from lands beyond High Realm. In his dream, Merric was aboard one of these vessels, but far from being thrilled by the experience, he was filled with fear.

The steely grey ocean spread out in all directions. There was no land in sight, apart from a fog bank on the horizon which hid a cluster of mountainous islands. The feeling of isolation terrified Merric, and he turned and tried to leave the deck of the ship. The captain blocked his path to the safety of his cabin though, and looked, arms crossed, down at Merric.

'You can't go down there, boy,' he said, his voice gruff.

'I don't belong here!' Merric cried at him.

'Too right,' the captain said, and pointed at his crewmen who were climbing the mast to bring in the sail. 'They're sailors; born and bred to be here on the open sea. Who are you?'

'I'm not a sailor,' Merric confessed.

'You're not a sailor,' agreed the captain. 'You're of no help to anyone. This ship is for sailors, not lost boys. Now get out of our way, there's a storm coming.'

Merric looked in horror at the ocean that surrounded him. Only a moment before it had been calm, but now it had suddenly turned into crashing waves that rose and fell around the ship. The vessel was buffeted from all sides, and Merric was knocked from his feet as a wave smashed into the side of the ship. Rain began to fall in heavy sheets, drenching them all within seconds. The first roar of thunder sounded overhead, but still none of the sailors looked scared. The captain was laughing at Merric.

'You truly are no sailor; you should have stayed at home.'

'I have no home!' Merric moaned.

Wind howled across the deck, adding to the heavy storm. Lightning cracked in the night sky, and the ship crashed through the breaking waves that towered over them. The ship was solidly built though, and no matter how hard the churning ocean struck them, the wooden planks of the ship's sides held firm.

Suddenly Merric understood why none of the sailors were scared. The ship was invincible. *Walls of Oak* it was named, written across its stern in proud golden letters. No matter what the sea threw at them, the ship would not be beaten. The waves were crashing against the vessel, but it ploughed through them and kept on towards the journey's end. Light showed on the horizon, the first sign of the coming day. Merric thanked the Mother, and the captain grinned at him.

All of a sudden the captain's smile faded. From deep below the deck there came a deep gurgling sound, and with that all the colour drained from the captain's face.

'What is it?' Merric asked, the fear with him once more.

His answer was the screams from below decks, followed by the rush of water streaming up between the planks under his feet. The hatch behind Merric, which led below, burst upwards, and with it came torrents of icy sea water. The flood engulfed the ship, which quickly began to sink. The mast snapped in two and fell into the raging ocean, and the sailors were now screaming with terror as they plunged into the sea.

'How is this possible?' the captain cried aloud, 'this ship is impregnable!'

Even as he said it, he was dragged beneath the waves. The ship continued to sink until only the figurehead at the prow remained above the cold water. Merric clung onto the carved figurehead and saw that only one sailor was there with him, all others having been lost to the sea.

'Help me!' Merric begged.

The sailor turned his head, shaking his black hair from his face. Merric cried out as he recognised him, and Lord Aric smiled wickedly back. In his hand was a great axe, which he had used to sink the ship.

Lord Aric laughed as the ship sank below the waves, taking himself and the terrified boy with it. The carved figurehead was the last to go, its outstretched wings and beaked head straining against the grey water, before finally succumbing and disappearing into its watery grave.

* * *

At first, Merric thought it had been the nightmare that had woken him from his sleep, but then he felt the pair of panicked hands shaking him. His eyes opened a fraction to show him that his chamber was still dark. He doubted he had been asleep for more than an hour. The hands continued to shake him with urgency, so Merric opened his groggy eyes further to reveal the terrified face of his servant, Tomas.

'What's wrong?' Merric slurred, sitting up, ignoring the banging in his head from the wine he had drunk earlier that evening.

Tomas looked as though he had lost the ability to speak, such was his fear.

'Tomas,' Merric repeated suddenly wide awake, feeling his own heart racing, 'what's wrong?'

'The Monfort men,' his servant stammered, but the next words were jumbled and Merric could make no sense of them.

'Slow down,' Merric urged. 'What about the Monfort men?'

'They're here to kill you!'

Merric ogled at his servant.

'*What?*'

'And your family,' Tomas said, his eyes filled with panic and tears.

'My family?' Merric said, unable to think.

It took a moment for him to realise that Tomas meant the Jacelyns. This was not the time to correct him though. He felt fear creep into him. His heart turned as cold as ice, and his arms and legs felt weak

'What are you talking about? How do you know this?'

'I heard them, milord, I did. I passed the Grand Hall on the way back from the privy and I heard some of the Monfort soldiers talking.'

Merric was about to tell Tomas that he must be wrong, but stopped himself when he saw the look of sheer horror on the boy's face. Merric knew Tomas was not mistaken.

At that moment, a woman's scream echoed from somewhere above him. Merric almost fell from his bed in shock. He could not tell who it was, but he felt the colour leave his face. The sound of swords crashing together echoed through the walls. What was happening?

Like a flame flickering into existence, the realisation sunk in.

Was this was why Lord Aric had travelled for over two weeks from his own castle to get to Eagle Mount? Had he plotted this all along? The memory of the previous evening came back to him, and he heard Lord Roberd's words about Lord Aric.

'There's nothing he wouldn't do for power.'

It was all beginning to fall together. The Monforts had not visited The Head in over ten years, yet all of a sudden Lord Aric had felt a desire to visit the eastern dukedom of High Realm? Lord Aric had pretended that he was there to try and arrange a marriage between his son and Sophya, but it was truly The Head that he wanted. Merric thought of the Jacelyn soldiers lying asleep on the tables down in the Grand Hall, filled with the wine and ale forced upon them by the Monfort men. If there was a time to seize Eagle Mount when their defences were weakest, it was now.

'No!' Merric said, to no one in particular.

He had already lost one family, he would not allow the same thing to happen to the Jacelyns. They had taken him in when he had nowhere else to go. They were not his blood relations, yet they had cared for him, and treated him as though he were one of them.

At that moment, Merric's bedchamber door rattled as someone tried to open it. Tomas had bolted the heavy door behind him when he had entered. The rattling turning into a heavy bang, as someone threw their shoulder against the door. The wooden door held though, and whomever was outside started kicking at it, to try and open it by force.

Merric thought quickly. He knew that if the Monforts were trying to force their way into his chamber then it could only be for one reason: they wanted to kill him too. Perhaps killing the Jacelyn family was not enough, they wanted there to be no witnesses. Tomas had most likely saved their lives for a few more moments when he bolted the door, but they were far from safe. Merric knew he only had one option. He had to find Lord Roberd, and pray he was not too late.

Terrified of the heavy booms coming from the door, Tomas collapsed onto Merric's empty bed. He clutched his face, rocking back and forth.

'They're going to get us,' he cried over the banging.

'No they're not!' Merric said, his eyes on the window opposite the door. He darted over, ignoring the noises from the door behind him, and wrenched the window's shutters open. The scene below him was revealed.

In the open space of the courtyard, beneath the stars, the Monfort and Jacelyn soldiers fought, and Merric's ears were filled with the ringing and crashing of swords against shields. The Jacelyn men were outnumbered and caught unawares, and were being pushed back by the men from The Southstones. Some Monfort archers had taken the walls, and were shooting their bows and crossbows down into the courtyard. Cries from those struck down rose up to Merric, and he was filled with horror at what he saw.

The beating on Merric's door continued with a new intensity. The door was built of strong wood, but Merric knew it would not hold forever. He could not be there when the door gave way at last, and knew there was only one other way for them to get out of his chamber.

Merric climbed through the window and crept out onto the narrow stone ledge beyond. The night air whipped across his face. There was dampness in the air, and a promise of rain. He had never noticed before just how high his bed chamber was, and the drop to the ground below was a long one. He waved at Tomas to follow him, but his servant just shook his head frantically in terror. A metallic hammering now sounded on the door behind him. Perhaps someone was hacking at the wood with an axe, and this caused Tomas to reluctantly approach the window, wringing his hands nervously. He looked fearfully at the drop beyond the window.

'Come, Tomas,' Merric urged with desperation, trying to force a calming smile. 'I'll help you.'

Faced with the threat of the men outside the door, Tomas screwed his eyes shut and climbed clumsily through the window. He almost lost his balance and fell, but Merric seized the boy's shoulders and held him tightly

'I've got you, now go that way!' Merric said, having to raise his voice to be heard over the noise from the courtyard below.

He pointed along the ledge to where it led into the darkness. Tomas gulped as he looked again at the drop below, but obediently made his way gingerly along the ledge, keeping both hands firmly fixed on the rough stone of the castle keep beside him.

'Don't look down,' Merric advised him, struggling to keep his voice calm.

He had awoken from one nightmare just to be thrown into a real one. He feared the men pounding on his door, yet felt even more terror when he thought about the Jacelyn family in danger.

Just as Merric was about to follow Tomas along the ledge and away from his chamber window, the door finally gave way to the triumphant cries of those on the other side. The door crashed to the floor, its hinges broken, revealing three brutish men wearing padded leather coats that bore the symbol of the black knight of the Monforts on their left breast. The leader of the three soldiers, a heavily scarred serjeant, had his sword in his hand, and the faces of the other two twisted into wicked smiles beneath their helmets. Together they hefted their axes as they spotted their quarry in the window.

'Don't let 'im get away!' the serjeant said, and the men ran eagerly forward towards Merric.

The fastest one dove through the window at him, but Merric stepped quickly to one side, causing his attacker to miss and go tumbling with a scream to the courtyard far below. Merric's dodge caused him to lose his footing on the ledge, and he slipped. His heart leapt into his mouth, but somehow Merric's flailing hands managed to grip onto the ledge and stop his fall.

'He got Hwell!' one of his attackers roared with anger, and his ugly face appeared in the window.

Merric hauled himself up onto the ledge again, and shouted at Tomas to hurry. His servant had frozen in fear when he had seen the Monfort man fall through the night sky, but at Merric's shout he continued his way along the ledge.

'There's two of 'em!' the soldier at the window said, looking, 'there's a fat boy too.'

'Kill 'em both,' came the serjeant's impatient reply from Merric's chamber.

Merric and Tomas edged along the narrow ledge, away from Merric's chamber window. Up ahead there was another window, which Merric knew led into a passageway. He hoped that they would reach the window and be able to scramble back through before their pursuers knew where they were heading. Frustrated shouts came from behind him, as the Monfort men realised they were too large to fit out onto the ledge themselves.

As he followed Tomas slowly along the ledge, Merric allowed his mind to dart to Lord Roberd. *'The Monfort soldiers, they're here to kill you. And your family.'* Tomas's words swam around in his head. Despite the battle going on in the courtyard of Eagle Mount below, and the men who had tried to kill Merric a moment ago in his chamber, he could not bring himself to believe it. Were Lord Roberd and his family really in danger?

Tomas's frightened mumbling brought Merric's mind back to the moment. They had reached the next window, and Merric looked through at the wide, torch-lit passage that lay beyond. It was deserted. At the end of the passage was a spiral staircase which Merric knew travelled all the way to the top of the north-eastern tower. They could take that staircase to get to Lord Roberd's chamber, where he was sure to be.

If he was still alive of course.

There were no shutters on this window, and the night air blew freely into the draughty passageway, causing the torches to stutter. Merric was about to step through when he heard a shout of glee. His heart sank as he saw the two remaining Monfort men from his bedchamber come rushing around the corner of the passage, and they skidded to a stop when they saw the two boys cowering in the window.

Merric suddenly thought of his father's sword that he had left in the wardrobe in his chamber. He cursed himself for not thinking of it before, and looked frantically around the passageway in search of something he could use as a weapon. There was nothing. He positioned himself to put Tomas behind him. His young servant was shaking, and Merric felt a surge of guilt. He had come to warn Merric, and that choice had probably cost him his life. If he had stayed with the other servants it was likely he would have escaped the bloodshed.

'Leave Tomas,' Merric said, his voice shaking. 'Don't harm him.'

He reached backwards and put his arms protectively around his servant. The two Monfort men just laughed and advanced slowly towards them.

'Kill me, just let him be,' Merric said.

The men were nothing but ruffians, each as ugly and stupid as the other, but with weapons in their meaty hands they would have no trouble taking down Merric. Even if he had taken his father's sword he was not sure he would have stood a chance. He had never been any good with a blade.

'They won't kill either of you.'

The voice which spoke was familiar to Merric.

Tristan appeared around the corner of the passageway. He was still dressed in his night clothes, but his expression was determined. The grins faltered on the faces of the two attackers, and they instinctively took a step away from Tristan. His sword was in his hand, and the blade was already red with blood. No doubt some other Monfort men had been sent to his chamber to kill him, but they had not been successful.

Merric's heart soared when he saw Tristan, and hope filled him.

'You're alive!' he gasped.

'It takes more than these rats to kill me.' Tristan snarled at the Monfort soldiers. 'Get back, Merric.'

Merric and Tomas edged back onto the ledge and into the rain that had started to fall. Tristan moved to put himself between them and the Monfort men. The two soldiers looked at each other hesitantly, all confidence gone. To kill an unarmed boy was easy, but a knight was something else entirely. As Tristan had shown in the tournament, he was one of the best warriors in the entire realm and could easily outfight them, even when outnumbered two to one. After a moment of indecision the serjeant made up his mind, and pushed his friend towards Tristan. The man stumbled for a moment and swung his sword wildly at the Jacelyn knight. Tristan stepped aside to avoid the clumsy attack, and struck forward with his own blade, his golden hair shining in the flames of the torches. The Monfort man cried out in panic, and managed to escape with no more than a scratch on his cheek.

'Run, Merric, now!' Tristan said over his shoulder.

The castle would be swarming with Monfort men, and in a moment more enemies were sure to arrive in the passage. But Merric could not leave Tristan on his own. He opened his mouth to speak, but Tristan stopped him.

'You need to get as far from here as you can. Away from the castle. Go for help. Go to Elderwyne, to Lynport.

Anywhere!' He looked back at the two soldiers, and went on the attack. He struck once, twice, and a third time. The Monfort serjeant fell beneath his blows and did not stand up again. The other man looked anxiously around him, clutching at the cut on his cheek, and wondered if the knight would catch him if he tried to run. He could not outfight Tristan. His expression of panic was replaced with one of victory though when the sound of approaching feet came from behind Tristan.

Two more figures emerged in the passage, the torch light glimmering off their full plate armour. Rayden Monfort smiled with satisfaction when he saw Tristan.

'I looked for you in your bedchamber. I saw you made a mess of the men I sent to detain you.'

'Don't send others to do your dirty work if you want it doing properly,' Tristan retorted, raising his sword.

Rayden took a moment to reach up and tie his long black hair behind his head. He then turned and took his sword from the second new arrival. Merric recognised him as being the tall, black armoured knight from the tournament, and his black and white chequered shield was slung across his back. Though Merric could not see his face from this angle, the knight had finally removed his helmet for the first time since he arrived at Eagle Mount, revealing a shaved head.

'I'm not going to pretend this won't give me pleasure,' Rayden said. He swung his sword in a couple of practice strokes, and the razor sharp blade hissed through the air. 'You can have your little victory in the tournament, but the real victory is mine and my father's.'

'Where is your honour? Murdering innocent folk in their sleep?' Tristan said with hatred in his voice.

'No one is innocent,' Rayden said, running his fingers along his sword blade and studying it closely, testing its sharpness. 'We have unfinished business, you and I, and your father isn't here to stop us this time.'

'Unfortunately for you,' Tristan snarled.

Rayden chuckled. Apparently satisfied with his sword's edge, he lifted his eyes to meet Tristan's. All of a sudden and so quick that Merric almost missed it, Rayden darted forward, aiming his blade at Tristan's head. His opponent knocked the attack away with his sword, and the two young men began to slowly circle each other. Tristan lunged at his opponent and the two exchanged quick blows, the ringing of steel on steel echoing through the passage. The two knights were equally matched, and each strike was met by the other's sword. Their blades attacked and parried, countered and blocked quicker than Merric had ever seen swords move. Neither was able to get past their opponent's defences.

The fighters stopped for a moment, weighing each other up. Tristan changing his grip so that he was wielding his sword with both hands. He looked vulnerable in his shirt and breeches, and appeared smaller than Rayden who was clad in his full armour.

Having caught a few breaths, Rayden let out a roar and unleashed his full fury on his opponent. But Tristan was ready for the attack. He parried the slashing sword, and with both hands swung his own blade back at Rayden. His strike was so heavy that had it hit an unarmoured man it would have killed him with ease. The sword blade instead hit against the armoured plates on Rayden's side, sending sparks showering into the air. Tristan quickly brought his sword up for another strike, but he was instead met with Rayden's armoured fist which flew out of nowhere. It connected hard with the side of Tristan's head, and blood began to run down into his eye. The bald knight laughed as he watched.

Tristan went on the attack again next, shaking the blood from his eye to clear his vision. He seemed dazed from the blow, but gritted his teeth. His sword was a blur as he struck again and again, but Rayden sneered as he stopped the blade each time. Merric was filled with hope every time Tristan swung his mighty sword, but felt his heart drop each time the ring of steel on steel told him that Rayden had blocked the attack.

Tristan's blows were strong and Rayden was forced to give ground and back away from the ferocious attack. Suddenly, the cold stone of the wall at Rayden's back. He could retreat no further. The sneer on his face turned to a grimace as he realised he was being outfought by the Jacelyn knight. With one final two-handed sweep, Tristan knocked Rayden's sword from his hand, and the blade clattered onto the stone floor.

'You came into our home,' Tristan said, panting slightly from the effort of the fight and weakened by the wound on the side of his head. 'You accepted our hospitality. How many good men have died this night because of you and your father? Where is he anyway, skulking in the shadows while you do the dirty work? Tell your men to put down their weapons. This betrayal is over, and you and your father will be taken to the king to explain this cowardly act.'

Rayden just laughed, ignoring Tristan's sword that was pointing directly at his face.

'You're so weak, Jacelyn,' he said. 'You are too merciful. You should have killed me while you had the chance.'

The bald knight in black armour stepped up behind Tristan, and without a word thrust his own sword forwards into Tristan's back. Merric gasped in horror. Tristan's face turned into an expression of surprise. He did not cry out, but looked in confusion at the sword blade protruding from his chest. He sunk slowly to his knees, and all strength seemed to seep out of him.

With his opponent beaten, Rayden picked up his own sword again and leered down at Tristan. He pressed his blade against Tristan's neck. The rain began to fall harder outside where Merric stood, and far off he heard a rumble of distant thunder.

'Do you hear that?' Rayden said to his defeated opponent, nodding towards the sound. 'A storm rises, and there's nothing you can do to stop it. I wish you could have seen the look in your father's eyes when I took him from this world. Your mother screamed as if that would bring him back to her, before I killed her too. You lose. Your family is gone. A thousand years of legacy, all gone. The Head is ours now.'

A single tear rolled down Tristan's cheek. He reached to his hip to where he wore his dagger, given to him by his father. He gripped the hilt and closed his eyes. Rayden swung his sword back, ready to strike. Merric watched in horror, unable to do anything to stop what was about to happen. With a grunt of effort, Rayden brought the blade hissing back through the air. As he did so, Tristan slowly turned his head and looked at Merric who was still stood frozen beyond the window. Their eyes locked for a moment.

'Go,' Tristan mouthed weakly, a moment before the sword struck.

Tomas clapped his hand over his mouth in shock. Merric could only let out a strained cry. The bald man in black armour whipped around at the sound, having not previously noticed Merric.

Then Merric saw his face; hideously scarred, with an old wound running from his eye down the side of his face to his mouth; a face which had haunted his nightmares for over ten years.

The next thing Merric knew, he was falling. The night air and rain drops whipped past his face, and the shape of the window and Tomas huddled on the ledge grew smaller as he fell. Merric span around as he fell, and watched as the ground below rushed up to meet him.

- CHAPTER SEVEN -

Fight or flight

The fall lasted no more than a few heartbeats, but to Merric it felt like a lifetime. He spam around once more as he fell, the stormy night sky now stretched out above him. He knew that he was about to die. Surely that would be better than the pain he was feeling now though.

The idea of dying did not frighten him. Tristan was gone, along with Lord Roberd. Lady Cathreen, and Sophya as well most likely. He had lost his parents all those years ago, at the hands of the bald knight who he now knew served the Monforts, and now the other family he had loved had been taken away from him as well. He kept his eyes closed, and waited for the worries to slip away.

The air was knocked from his lungs as Merric's fall was stopped suddenly, but other than that he was unhurt. Somehow, he was still alive.

He forced himself to open his eyes, and looked at the castle keep that rose up far above him.

Through the rain that pattered on his face he could see Tomas, nothing more than a speck, on the ledge outside the high window. Seeing that Merric had not been killed by the fall, and after a terrified glance over his shoulder Tomas let himself drop. He squealed all the way down, before landing next to Merric.

Directly below the window from which Merric had fallen was a shelter used to store the horses' hay. Landing flat on his back on its thatched roof had winded Merric and sent a shooting pain through his body, but the soft straw stopped him from coming to any further harm.

High above Merric, a face appeared at the window. The head of Rayden Monfort looked down directly at Merric, and he let out a shout of frustration. He screamed orders down to those in the courtyard, pointing at Merric.

'Seize him!'

Merric's instinct took over, and he lurched to his feet. He stumbled across the thatched roof, grabbing Tomas as he went. Together they jumped off the roof and felt firm ground beneath their feet, just as a group of Monfort soldiers came charging towards them. Merric and Tomas were trapped with nowhere to go. At that moment, a shout drew the Monfort soldiers' attention, and they turned to see Sir Gerard appear from the main doors of the keep, leading a dozen of his Eagle Guard. The Monfort men turned their backs on Merric and Tomas, ready to meet the new threat.

'No!' Rayden shouted. 'The boy, get the boy!'

The weapons of Sir Gerard and his men already showed signs of use in the battle, and all appeared to have suffered wounds at the hands of Lord Aric's men. They charged at the Monfort soldiers, disregarding their own safety, without even noticing Merric or Tomas. Their swords and spears hacked and slashed and thrust at the Monfort men, and slowly they pushed their enemies back. Lord Aric's soldiers struck back though, and men on both sides cried out as they fell. More Monfort soldiers hurried towards the Jacelyn warriors, but Sir Gerard fought on firmly, felling three of his enemy with a single swipe of his sword.

Merric and Tomas darted through the fight, dodging soldiers and ducking beneath swords. A man fell dead in front of them and they jumped over the body, not stopping. Arrows fell around them from the Monfort archers on the walls, striking friend and foe alike. Merric and Tomas kept running across the courtyard, and the men they passed did not pay them any attention. Merric did not look back, but kept his eyes forward. If he stopped, even for a moment, he knew they would never escape.

He led Tomas into the stables and out of the rain, leaving the battle behind them. It was likely that the Monforts had already seized control of the gatehouse, and were guarding it against any attempt for anyone in the castle to try and escape. They would also be stopping anyone else for trying to come into the castle to help the

Jacelyns. Merric knew their only way to escape was through the hidden tunnel.

He guided Tomas through the stables, where the horses looked nervously at them, their ears pricked at the sounds of battle outside. Merric raced to the usual spot and wrenched the trapdoor open. He pushed Tomas through the hole in the floor first, before going down himself and shutting the door quickly behind him.

Almost instantly the sounds of the battle disappeared, and everything was oddly silent. All Merric could hear was his own heavy breathing, and Tomas' quiet sobs. The tunnel appeared safe, but they could not stay there. If anyone had seen them disappear into the stables then it might not take them long to find the hidden entrance to the tunnel and discover them there.

Merric led the way down the dark passage, and he could hear Tomas following. Merric kept one hand on the earth wall beside him, but reached out behind him and clutched Tomas's hand with his other. Tomas had never been down here before, and the pitch dark was not going to be any sort of comfort after the night's events so far.

The journey seemed to take only moments, and they soon emerged into the wine cellar of the tavern. They climbed up the ladder to the yard above, with Tomas needing a push to help him up. Even once they could feel the night air and rain on their faces once more they did not stop. Merric edged through the gap in the fence and hurried down the road beyond. They kept on running, turning left and right and left again, putting as much distance between themselves and the castle as they could. Merric did not know where he was going, but Tristan had told him to flee, and he knew the castle was a dangerous place for him to be near. Folk were emerging into the street, looking in confusion and fear towards the castle where the sounds of the fighting could be heard.

Merric led the way down an alley, ignoring the stares of the folk they passed. All of a sudden Tomas tripped with a yelp, and went sprawling onto the cobblestones. He sat up and rubbed his grazed knee, fighting back fresh tears. Merric took the moment's pause to lean back against the cold stones of a building they had stopped next to and breathed out slowly.

They were all dead. Lord Roberd, who had taken him in and treated him like a son, and Lady Cathreen, who had always made Merric feel welcome in their home; Sophya, who had never hurt anyone in her life, and who only yesterday was dreaming of marrying the very man who had gone on to murder her family; and Tristan, the brother that Merric had never had.

They had been murdered. Murdered by those who had been welcomed into the Jacelyn's home as guests. They were murdered on the orders of Lord Aric. And for what? Rayden's last words to Tristan haunted him. '*The Head is ours now.*'

Earlier that very night, Merric had overheard Lord Roberd tell his wife that Lord Aric would do anything for power. It appears that he had not been wrong. Is that why they had killed the Jacelyn family as they slept, to take the dukedom of The Head for themselves? But if that was the case then why did they also try to kill Merric? If it was Eagle Mount and The Head that they wanted, then Merric would never be able to oppose them. In the laws of the realm he could have no claim over The Head. He was the orphaned son of a mere baron, and could never rival the power of Lord Aric Monfort, the Duke of The Southstones.

All that left Merric's mind, as he once again realised what it truly meant. The Jacelyns were dead, they were gone. He did not care why, only that he was lost and alone for the second time in his young life. Everyone he loved had been taken away from him again. He would never see Lord Roberd again, or Lady Cathreen, or Sophya. And he had watched Tristan die, he had seen Rayden's sword strike him down, and he knew he would never forget that image. Tristan had been Merric's best friend when they were children, and had grown into a strong young man and a perfect knight. He would never become duke like his father; never marry and have children of his own.

'Milord?'

The sound of Tomas's scared voice, barely more than a whisper, drew Merric's attention. It was only at this point that he noticed that there were floods of tears mixing with the rain on his cheeks. He hurriedly dried his eyes.

'Yes?' Merric said, trying to keep his voice steady.

'What do we do?'

I have no idea, Merric thought, but he did not say it. 'Follow me, quickly. We're not safe here.' He tried to sound confident.

They set off again at a run. Would Lord Aric send men to look for Merric, or would they just be happy to know they had forced the boy out of the castle? He was a young nobleman, used to the luxuries that came with living in a castle. They would know he would not last a day on his own in the outside world.

Merric and Tomas continued down the alley, which emerged beside the Grand Priory and looked out over The Square. Crowds had gathered there, drawn by the sounds coming from the castle.

'Look!' Tomas said.

Reluctantly Merric glanced back towards Eagle Mount and, in the moonlight, saw the gates swing open and three men ride out on horseback. They walked their horses through the rain away from the castle, and stopped when they reached the centre of The Square. The townsfolk drew in close to them, eager to hear any news of what was happening.

'What's going on?' a voice called.

'I can hear fighting!' came a second.

'Is it the duke? Is he safe?' another asked.

The horsemen were hooded and cloaked, to protect them from the rain, but Merric recognised their leader instantly, when he looked out over the crowd and spoke.

'Folk of The Head,' Orderix, the Lord's Counsel, called out. 'Grave tidings! Our beloved duke is dead.'

His words were met with horrified murmuring, and many of the townsfolk dropped to their knees and prayed. An elderly woman began wailing.

'Lord Roberd has been murdered, along with his family. None were spared.' Orderix's voice echoed around The Square. 'His ward, Merric Orrell, once of Ryding, is missing. If anyone here knows his whereabouts then please let him or herself known.'

'It's safe milord,' Tomas said to Merric with relief, 'they must have beaten the Monfort men.' He took a step forward, and raised his arm so that Orderix could see him.

But something did not seem right to Merric.

'No, stop!' he said, too late.

Orderix saw the gesture and turned his horse to look over the crowd at the two boys stood by the entrance to the alley. He squinted at them with a hand to protect his eyes from the rain, trying to see who it was through the darkness. Suddenly Orderix shouted to the two spear-armed horsemen with him.

'That's him! Get him!'

The crowd scattered with alarm as the two horsemen kicked back with their spurs and charged their horses across The Square towards where the two boys stood. Tomas's hand was still raised, but his mouth dropped open in shock. As their horses galloped, the wind caught at the cloaks of the riders, revealing what they were wearing underneath.

On the breast of their padded coats was not the eagle of the Jacelyns, but the black knight of the Monforts.

'Run!' Merric shouted, grabbing the back of Tomas's jerkin and pushing him back into the alley from where they had come.

Merric ran like he had never ran before, with his servant just in front of him. He could hear the heavy clattering of hooves close behind, loud on the cobblestones. Merric gave Tomas another push to urge him on. The Monfort horsemen were forced to ride one behind the other as the alley narrowed, with buildings crowding in on both sides. The first horsemen could see that the two boys could not possibly escape, and in a matter of seconds would be ridden down beneath his horse. He shouted in eagerness as he levelled his spear and aimed it at Merric's fleeing back.

'Faster!' Merric urged Tomas, but his shout was echoed by the horseman behind him, and the pursuers spurred their horses on.

Merric was running so fast that he felt as though he was going to trip, but he kept his legs pumping. The hoof beats were right behind him, and he knew that it was hopeless, and they would never make it. He tensed his back and waited for the pain of a spear thrust. The leading Monfort horseman was just a few feet behind Merric, and he lunged forward with his spear.

It never reached its target.

A crossbow bolt punched into the horseman, right in the centre of his chest. He cried out more in surprise than pain, and fell from his saddle. His horse, confused without its rider, skidded to a halt on the cobbles, and the second horseman following along behind was forced to rein in his mount with a shout of alarm. In an attempt to avoid the spear thrust, Merric had dived forward and clattered onto the cobbled road. Lifting his head he saw the most unlikely thing he could have imagined.

Ana, her blonde hair plastered to her head by the rain, had emerged from a side alley ahead, a look of grim determination on her face. She quickly notched another bolt in her crossbow, and sent it sailing towards the second horseman. The shot missed, but it was enough to cause him to turn his horse in panic, and ride back the way he had come, leaving his companion lying motionless on the cobbles.

'Merric!' Ana breathed, hurrying over to him. The heavy crossbow looked massive in her arms, and she slung it over her shoulder. 'What's happening?' she asked, looking shaken at what she had just done. She reached down and helped Merric back to his feet.

Whilst Tomas slumped on the ground, exhausted from his frantic run, Merric and Ana hugged tightly.

'They're dead!' Merric said, letting the grief overcome him again. He felt his eyes welling up once more.

Ana broke away from Merric's embrace. Holding tightly onto his arms she looked at him for a moment in stunned silence.

'Who?' she asked.

'Lord Roberd,' Merric said, his eyes filled with tears. 'Tristan, Sophya, Lady Cathreen. Everybody. The Monforts murdered them. They tried to murder me too.'

Ana hugged him again, her eyes filled with horror. She looked at Tomas over Merric's shoulder, and he simply nodded to confirm it was true.

'Orderix is one of them, he must have betrayed them,' Merric continued, suddenly feeling angry.

'We need to get you out of here,' Ana said, looking up and down the alley. 'You've got to get far from here.'

'No!' Merric pulled away from Ana, surprised by his own words.

'What?' Ana looked at him in confusion. 'Those men just tried to kill you.'

'I can't go,' Merric said overcome with his anger. 'They murdered them!'

He did not know what he meant to do, but he knew all he wanted to do was cause Lord Aric and Rayden as much pain as possible. He wanted them to feel the loss that he now felt. He wanted them to hurt like he did.

'But you've got to go! Sir Tristan told you to,' Tomas pleaded.

'And he was right,' Ana said. 'If they wanted to kill you then they won't stop. More men will be heading this way. The only way to keep you safe is to put as much distance between us and them as we can.' She grabbed hold of Merric's arm.

Merric shook Ana's hand off him, and took a step back towards the castle.

'What are you *doing*?' Ana said to him, disbelieving.

'I have to go back,' Merric insisted.

'No!' Tomas moaned.

Merric looked hard at them both, his eyes determined. 'I have to go back,' he repeated. 'The Jacelyns were my family, I won't let Aric and Rayden get away with this.'

'But there's nothing you can do milord,' said Tomas. 'It's…it's too late.'

'He's right,' Ana said bluntly. 'They're dead, and getting yourself killed isn't going to bring them back. We need to go, now!'

The sounds of new hoof beats sounded, growing steadily nearer. It sounded like at least half a dozen more horsemen were heading their way.

'The whole town is going to be swarming with Monfort men, all looking for you. I'm not going to let you die here, Merric,' Ana continued.

'I'm not just going to leave, to let them get away with what they've done' Merric said angrily making his hands into fists. 'Ana, I'm sorry.'

He turned to leave and head back towards the castle. In the Grand Priory the bells began to toll, announcing the death of the duke. The sound was sombre, and it made Merric all the more determined. He did not know what he intended to do, but he could not bring himself to abandon

Eagle Mount, to abandon the memory of the Jacelyns. The rain continued to fall in sheets, and he had to brush his sodden hair out of his eyes. But he was filled with a desire, and nothing would stop him.

Ana stepped up behind him. 'No,' she said, hitting him hard on the back of his head with the heavy wooden stock of her crossbow. '*I'm* sorry.'

- CHAPTER EIGHT -

Fugitives

When he opened his eyes, all Merric could see was green. He was sure he was outside though; a gentle breeze was touching his face and fresh air filled his nostrils. He blinked, and the green turned into leaves. He was lying on his back, with trees full of leaf towering overhead. The ground was soft and mossy beneath him. His head throbbed painfully, but he felt oddly peaceful, with the sound of the birds and the calm wind rustling the branches above him.

Something was itching him, and he gingerly moved his hand up to his forehead to find a bandage wrapped tightly around his head. It was then that he noticed the throbbing pain at the back of his skull. Slowly turning his head to the left he could see that he was lying in a forest, with trees spreading into the distance as far as his eyes could see. Judging by the light that filtered down through the leaves to speckle on the forest floor he guessed it was around midday. The last thing he could remember was standing in the rain, looking back up towards Eagle Mount. The rain had since cleared, and the spring sun was warming the air again.

Merric rubbed both hands gently over his face, but even that made his head ache. He groaned and turned his head the other way. He could see Tomas hunched over a pile of sticks, trying to light a fire. The sight of his servant was comforting; a feeling of familiarity in an unexpected and unfamiliar place. Tomas was striking two flints together to try and make a spark, though his attempts did not seem to be going very well.

Merric tried to sit up, grunting from the effort. Looking up from his work at the sound of the groan, Tomas saw that Merric's eyes were open.

'You're awake, milord!'

Tomas's face flushed with relief. He boy jumped to his feet, leaving the fire unlit, and hurried over with a broad smile stretched across his face.

Again, Merric tried to sit upright, but cried out when a lance of pain shot through his head. Tomas rushed to his aid, and helped him lay back down again.

'You lie there a moment longer, milord. I'm sorry about your head. Does it hurt much? Ana had no choice. She had to stop you from going back.'

Merric recalled the pain of something hitting the back of his head, and realised that this had been Ana. The emotions of the recent events came rushing back to him; the loss of the Jacelyns, and his hatred towards the

Monforts. He felt anger towards Ana, for stopping him from going back and getting his revenge on them.

'Where is she?' Merric asked slowly, his eyes looking around the small clearing where she and Tomas appeared to have made a small camp. She was nowhere to be seen, which was perhaps wise given Merric's sudden mood.

'She's hunting. We haven't eaten in three days, and we saw some wild boar hereabouts yesterday.'

'Three days?' Merric stared at his servant. 'I've been unconscious for *three days?*'

Tomas looked apologetic, his face going red.

'Yes milord, I think Ana hit you harder than she meant to.'

'Where are we?' Merric asked, fingering the lump on the back of his head. 'The Greenwood?' It was the largest forest close to Eagle Mount, so assumed that was where they were.

Tomas nodded. 'A day's walk from Eaglestone. We haven't been able to move quickly, what with you being unconscious. We had to hide from some Monfort soldiers who have been searching for you as well,' he added.

Merric did not reply. Was it really three days ago that it had all happened?

'I know you wanted to go back, milord. You would be dead if we had let you though,' Tomas said nervously, as though reading Merric's thoughts.

'I have nothing left,' Merric suddenly snapped, 'maybe I wouldn't mind getting killed.'

'Maybe we should have let you then,' Ana said as she walked into the clearing, her crossbow in hand and a small boar draped over her shoulder. She set both down beside Tomas's attempt at a fire and stood over Merric. 'Maybe we should have let you go back,' she repeated. 'But they're all gone, I'm sorry if that sounds blunt, Merric, but it's the truth. There's nothing you could do to bring them back.'

'It was my choice!'

'Not when you make foolish decisions like that!'

'Don't call me a fool!'

'Merric,' Ana said, trying to calm things. 'All I was doing was trying to help you. I know the pain you're feeling, but you're not thinking straight.'

'But what's the point in me just running away, I've lost everything…again.'

'You're not the only one that's lost everything,' Ana said. 'Folk saw Tomas and me leave with you, and it won't have taken the Monforts long to learn who helped you to escape. I can never go back to Eaglestone, they'd snatch me as soon as I stepped through the gate. I doubt I'll ever see my father again. And Tomas can't go back to his family, otherwise they'd be put in danger too.'

Merric reflected on this, ashamed. Tomas had four younger sisters who looked up to him. Merric had never asked either of them to help him though. They could have left him if they had wanted to.

But the point was that they had not wanted to, and Merric began to feel guilty for his outburst.

'We've sacrificed everything to help you,' Ana continued, prodding Merric in the chest with her finger. 'A little more gratitude would be welcome, *my lord*.'

She turned to walk away, but then spun around again.

'Don't wish your life away so easily,' she went on. 'There are still people in the world who care about you.'

Without another word she stormed over to Tomas's half-finished fire. With a deft strike of the flints she lit it, and within a few minutes the fire was crackling merrily. Merric looked at Tomas, who smiled encouragingly at him.

Ana seemed content to ignore Merric entirely as she busied herself with preparing the boar, her mood grumpy. She seemed irritated for allowing Merric to make her angry. Tomas checked the bandage on Merric's head, and was satisfied that the wound was healing nicely.

An hour later they were tucking into the roasted boar, but still no one had said anything since Ana's outburst. When they were finished, Tomas packed up the leftover meat while Ana stamped out the fire. She then shouldered her crossbow and started walking away from the clearing.

'Where are you going?' Merric called after her, the temporary silence broken.

'The same place you are,' she said coolly over her shoulder. 'As far away from Eaglestone as we can get.'

Merric still felt reluctant to leave Eagle Mount. It had been his home for over ten years, and he could not bear the thought of Lord Aric sitting in Lord Roberd's seat. He tried one last attempt to convince Ana.

'But I don't want to leave, this is our –'

'Merric, that place *isn't* our home, not anymore. Didn't you hear what I said earlier? I don't know what we're going to do, but now that you're awake we only have one option; getting away from here. Now *come on*!'

She set off, and did not look back.

Tomas helped Merric to his feet, and put his arm round him to take some of his weight. Merric felt too weak to object any further, and allowed Tomas to lead him through the trees in Ana's wake.

The day wore on and they kept walking. The trees seemed never ending, and in an attempt to distract himself from his sorrow, Merric wondered what the names of the different trees were. He had come across writings about trees in his books, and their names were varied and many; willows and oaks, redbeams and warriorpines, silverbeech and oldalders. The ground was littered with mushrooms and small flowers, white and yellow and purple, and at one point Merric saw a rabbit hop up to them. It waggled its nose at them for a moment, before deciding they were of no interest and scurrying away again.

And still the trees continued, stopping briefly for the occasional stream or animal trail that cut its way through the forest, before continuing on again as thickly as before. Merric, Ana and Tomas followed no road or route, but kept walking in the same direction, weaving between trees and thick bushes. Merric and Tomas made slow progress, and Ana had to keep stopping and wait for them to catch up, her foot tapping the ground impatiently. Merric decided it would not be a good idea to remind her that it was she that had hit him, and therefore her fault that he could only move slowly.

The high sun started to set as the afternoon moved towards evening, and it blinded them as it glared through the gaps in the trees ahead.

'We're heading west,' Merric said, realising.

'There's nowt east of Eagle Mount but the sea. Not much use going that way,' Ana said.

Shortly after that Ana stopped, at last, at the foot of a gentle rise. Merric fell gratefully to the ground. They had hardly paused all day, and he was exhausted. The pain and throbbing in his head had lessened over the course of the day, but he was still feeling weak after being unconscious for so long. While Merric and Tomas made themselves comfortable in the lengthening shadows of the trees, Ana disappeared for a few moments. She returned a short while later and told them to get back on their feet. Merric groaned unhappily as he stood, but Ana explained that she had spotted some shelter at the top of the hill. The prospect of being able to stop for the night gave Merric a final burst of energy.

The climb only took a couple of minutes, but sweat had beaded on Merric's brow by the time they crested the rise. Tomas clutched a stitch on his side, but as always he kept his complaints to himself. Merric had expected the crest of the hill to offer a spectacular view of the forest around them, and part of him had even hoped to be able to glimpse the distant shape of Eagle Mount from this vantage point, but to his dismay the trees continued to tower over them even here. As promised by Ana though, the hilltop made a good spot to set up camp for the night.

At first glance Merric assumed the top of the hill was just covered in a jumble of rocks, but as he took in his surroundings he realised it was in fact the ruins of an old priory. It had fallen into disrepair many years ago, and the ages had eaten away at the stone, leaving merely the skeleton of the building that had once existed. The roof had long since disappeared, but they soon found a comfortable spot beneath the remains of a wide arch. The Greenwood was once a much smaller forest, so Merric guessed that this spot had once been a thriving village. The forest must have spread outwards and swallowed up the village over the years, leaving only the stone of the priory as evidence of its existence.

Ana busied herself with lighting a fire for them. In an attempt to make amends for their earlier argument, Merric helped her roast some of the boar for their evening meal. The last thing he needed was for her to stay angry with him. He was not much help as it turned out, having never cooked anything in his life, but Ana appreciated the effort and even gave him a smile.

Tomas quickly fell to sleep once they had eaten. The boy was even less at home in the wilds than Merric, and was finding the great outdoors exhausting. Merric lay awake, listening to Tomas's steady snoring, and was glad that the nights were not chilly. In their hurry to leave Eaglestone, Ana and Tomas had been unable to gather any supplies or grab any blankets or cloaks. Merric could not complain though, as the amount of care and loyalty they were already showing him was overwhelming. Every time his mind was warmed by this though, it was quickly turned to ice as the reason for their journey into the Greenwood and away from Eagle Mount came back to the front of his mind. He was struggling to come to terms with the idea of the Jacelyns being gone.

There was a soft murmuring coming from the other side of the fire, and Merric glanced across at Ana. Her eyes were closed and she was fingering the amulet she wore around her neck. It had been a gift from her father when she was very young. It was a simple leather cord with a pendant shaped like a leaf hanging from it, made from pure silver. It was the symbol of the Mother, the god of High Realm. It was the most valuable thing Ana or her father had ever owned.

'Does She hear you when you pray?' Merric asked.

Ana kept her eyes closed. 'She always hears me, though She doesn't always reply.'

While Merric had attended priory masses regularly, as all in High Realm did, he had never put much faith in what

Grand Prior Simeon had preached. Merric loved to read the thousands of dusty books that filled the shelves in the Eagle Mount library, and his mind was absorbed with the histories that filled those yellowing pages. This left little space for any god. Ana was a devout follower of the Mother, but she never judged Merric for his lack of belief.

'What are in your prayers tonight?' Merric said.

He immediately wished he had not asked, as he realised it was a very personal question. However Ana did not seem to mind, though Merric saw her blush slightly.

'I'm praying for you.'

This answer took Merric aback, and he went quiet. Sensing his discomfort, Ana continued.

'I'm praying for the Mother's guidance, and for her to protect you over the coming days. And…'

'What?'

'And I'm praying that she takes his lordship and the others into her warm embrace when they reach her.'

Merric felt his eyes begin to sting, so he got up and busied himself with throwing a few more sticks onto the fire. He did not want Ana to see his tears.

The priors and prioresses taught that The Mother was the creator of the world, and that every plant, animal, bird and person are her children. She was the creator of everything, and so many turn to her for protection, for guidance and for strength. A knight may pray to The Mother to guide his sword in battle, a farmer may pray to

Her to grant a bountiful harvest, and a parent may pray for the health of their child.

'I know you don't believe in Her,' Ana said, 'but I find it helps in times of sadness to believe there's someone watching over us.'

Merric forced a smile onto his face, and tried to distance himself from the thoughts of Lord Roberd and the others which were trying to invade his mind. He looked up into the darkening sky. The remains of a tower rose from the eastern end of the ancient priory, and though its bronze bell had fallen to the ground many years ago to become green with age and almost hidden by weeds, he knew that centuries ago it would have rung across the land each week, calling folk to prayer.

'Did you know,' Ana said, sensing Merric's sadness and wanting to distract him, 'that hundreds of years ago King Odo the Pious once saw the Mother?'

'He *saw* her?'

This is where Merric's patience with the preaching of the priors ran out. He could understand folk finding comfort in believing there was someone looking out for them, and wanting to become a better person through the priory's teachings, but could did not believe that the Mother was real, and certainly did not think that anyone could have seen Her.

'It's true,' Ana said, seeing the mocking smirk on Merric's face. 'He said that she took the form of a beautiful woman, rising out of a lake.'

'Wait a moment,' Merric said, 'that's just the story of the Lady of the Lake. Lady Cathreen used to tell me that bedtime story when I was young.'

'King Odo's vision of the Mother is what inspired that legend,' Ana explained patiently. 'The tale of the Lady of the Lake has become better known across the realm than the original account of King Odo being visited by the Mother, but there are many who believe both are telling the same story.'

Merric knew the story of the Lady of the Lake well. Surrounded by a host of sprites and nymphs and ethereal folk who answered her every beck and call, the Lady of the Lake was the very definition of beauty. Young knights would ride far and wide to search her out, desiring nothing more than the honour of having her kiss their swords, blessing them for the rest of their lives. In the story though, only one knight ever actually found her, and he immediately fell deeply in love. He has since served as her guardian, known as the Paladin of the Lady. It was just a story though, meant to help young boys to grow up loving and respecting the ladies in their life and understanding the virtue of loyalty and commitment.

'Do you believe it?' Merric asked Ana. 'Do you really believe that there's a God living somewhere in High Realm? Someone can't live in a lake! I mean, how could that even be possible?' he laughed.

Ana smiled at him. 'Believing in something means not having to ask how.'

* * *

Merric rose early the next day, to the rays of the first summer sun of the year. He could not guess the hour, but the sun was still low. He unwound the bandage from his head. The pain was almost gone, and even the bump could hardly be felt beneath his hair. Leaving Tomas and Ana to rest a while longer, Merric strolled sleepily to the edge of the clearing and gathered some wood. He tossed it onto the smouldering fire, looking forward to some of the leftover boar for breakfast. Stifling a yawn he looked up at the ruined priory bell tower which rose above their campsite. He wondered how far you could see from its top, and if you could tell how much further the forest stretched. Ana rolled over but slept on, and Merric made his way over to the old tower.

It was surprisingly easy to climb. The ancient stone was pockmarked and cracked, providing plenty of hand and foot holds. On some parts the ivy was so thick and strong that he was able to use it to grip onto and pull himself up. He soon reached the top, and sat himself on the broken stones. Up here the tower cleared the surrounding trees, and Merric was surrounded on all sides by an ocean of green leaves. To the west the forest seemed to stretch on endlessly. That was the direction they were heading, and Merric knew they would have to walk for several more days at least until they reached the far side. He took a breath before turning and looking to the east, nervous of catching a glimpse of the towering castle of Eagle Mount atop its hill. The castle was nowhere to be seen though, the glare of the rising sun hiding much from view in that direction.

'Merric?' called a panicked voice, and he looked down to see that Ana was awake. She was on her feet, looking frantically around.

'I'm up here,' Merric called back.

Ana raised a hand to shield her eyes and looked up at him. Her look of worry turned to amusement as she spotted her friend perched at the top of the tower like a bird.

A sudden rustling came from some bushes at the edge of the clearing, and Merric felt a surge of fear. Had the Monforts found them? Tomas awoke with a start, and Ana swept up her crossbow, aiming at the spot where the noise had come from. With trembling hands Merric made to climb down, but Ana signalled for him to stay where he was.

'Maybe it's some sort of animal?' Tomas said, afraid.

Ana shook her head. She could hear footsteps.

'Who's there?' she said loudly, trying to sound confident.

As if appearing from nowhere, two cloaked and hooded men suddenly emerged from the shadows and walked into the ruins of the priory. One of them carrying a longbow. Ana's finger tightened on the trigger of her crossbow.

'Stay where you are!' she cried, and took a step forward.

The men obediently stopped, appearing to eye her crossbow warily.

'Who are you, and what do you want?' Ana demanded.

The men stayed silent. Deciding that Ana did not pose a serious threat, the man with the longbow stepped towards their fire. Merric was frozen in panic. The second man seemed to be limping, but even so they could easily overpower Ana and Tomas. Ana seemed to be thinking the same, and she aimed her crossbow directly at the first man's head. He just chuckled and squatted down by the fire, rearranging the burning wood with a well-practiced hand, but his injured companion lowered his hood to look better at Ana.

Merric gasped when he saw who the wounded man was.

'Sir Gerard!'

The elderly knight and the other man looked up at him.

'The boy sits in his nest,' the man with the longbow laughed, but Sir Gerard ignored the jest.

'It is indeed me,' Sir Gerard said to Merric, bowing his head. 'I'm glad to have found you at last.'

His face was pale, and he seemed to be in a fair amount of discomfort. This was the first time Merric had seen the old knight not wearing his armour. He looked far smaller and less fearsome in the grubby shirt and breeches he now wore beneath his cloak instead of his heavy steel plate. Merric looked at the other man, who helped Sir Gerard sit down on the mossy ground. He had now lowered his own hood now, and his long, dirty blond hair was curiously familiar.

Ana slowly lowered her crossbow, but Merric suddenly recalled who the other man was and told her to keep it up.

'He's a criminal!' Merric explained, hurrying down from the tower. Once he was standing beside Ana, he pointed at the blond man. 'He's a poacher. Lord Roberd sentenced him to death. He shouldn't be here.'

'Be at peace, Merric,' Sir Gerard said weakly, raising a hand. 'Kasper helped me escape the dungeons of Eagle Mount.'

'Besides, if anyone is a criminal, it's you,' Kasper the poacher said.

Merric looked at him in confusion.

'What are you talking about?' he said.

Kasper scowled. 'Word on the streets of Eaglestone is that a boy named Merric Orrell murdered the Jacelyns, and Lord Aric Monfort wants to bring him back to Eagle Mount in chains to deal out justice to him.'

Silence filled the clearing following Kasper's words, eventually broken by Sir Gerard who had found the leftover boar and began roasting it over the fire.

'What?' Merric managed to choke out at last.

146

'That's a lie!' Tomas piped up.

Sir Gerard shrugged, looking up from the fire. 'That's what Aric has announced,' he said, before wincing and clutching his side. 'According to him, you were hungry for power. You slew Lord Roberd and his family to take Eagle Mount for yourself.'

Merric balled his fists and felt rage surge through him. 'That's not true!'

The unfairness of the accusation stung like a pain he had never felt before. Ana raised her crossbow again and pointed it at the two men.

'So that's why you're here,' she said, 'to take Merric back? I expect you've been offered a reward or something have you?'

'He hardly seems worth all of this,' Kasper said to Sir Gerard, hefting his longbow and making to walk away. 'Let's leave these children to their tempers. I've done what I promised.'

Sir Gerard laid a hand on Kasper's arm to stop him, before turning back to Merric.

'If we believed the story to be true, do you really think we'd be stood here talking to you? As a member of the Eagle Guard my duty is to the Jacelyns, in life or death, and always will be. If you were Lord Roberd's killer, I'd have slain you already. We're not here to harm you,' Sir Gerard said.

Ana sighed in relief, and trusting that the two men meant no harm, she put down her crossbow. Sir Gerard turned back to the boar which he stuffed hungrily into his mouth.

'Why were you in the dungeons?' Tomas asked the old knight timidly. 'What happened that night?'

Finishing his boar and licking the grease off his fingers, Sir Gerard told his story.

'Rayden led some of the Monfort soldiers into the keep in the dead of the night, killing any of our guards that they came across. They murdered the Jacelyns family. It was a cowardly act, from men with not a shred of honour. I was later told that Tristan had been found with a sword in his hand, so at least he went down fighting. Once we were aware of their attack we tried to fight back, but they had taken Eagle Mount by surprise and we were outnumbered. In the end we were forced to yield, and the Monforts took the castle for themselves. I felt so ashamed, I wish I'd fallen beside my men and my duke. Aric then made us an offer; if we chose to serve the new masters of The Head then we would be unharmed, but if we refused then he said he we would be imprisoned. Not a single Jacelyn man took him up on his offer,' Sir Gerard added with pride.

'The next morning, Aric and that serpent, Orderix, spoke to the folk of Eaglestone. He announced that Lord Roberd and his family had been betrayed by Merric and the Jacelyn soldiers who were already languishing in the dungeons. According to him, many Monfort men died fighting against these traitors, trying to *save* Lord Roberd and the others. Of course, the opposite is true. For not taking Aric up on his offer to join him, I myself was labelled as one of these traitors. According to Aric, you escaped, and are now being hunted to answer for the crime of murdering the Jacelyns and trying to seize power yourself. Aric has named Rayden as the new Duke of The Head for the time being, to keep order in dukedom.'

'Surely no-one believes it,' Ana exclaimed. 'No-one can believe that Merric is capable of doing something like this, nor that the Jacelyn soldiers would ever turn on their duke. And they especially can't believe that the Monforts are there to *help* the folk of The Head.'

'What makes you think that Aric cares what people believe?' Kasper said, impatiently. 'Since when has the opinion of common folk mattered to lords?'

'Of course no-one believes it,' Sir Gerard said, ignoring Kasper's jibe. 'Everyone knows the truth. Aric is ruthless and power hungry, and has wanted The Head for his own for years. But who would dare stand up to him? Who would dare tell him that he's lying, and that Merric is innocent? It would gain nothing, except punishment and death.'

Merric knew this made sense, and wondered what choice the folk really had. He thought about Ana's father and Tomas's family. Not only were their children missing, but they were now facing uncertain futures under the rule of an evil family.

Sir Gerard had not finished. 'Aric had brought far more men with him from The Southstones than he had led us to believe. The rest were left a few miles back along the Great East Road, hidden from Eagle Mount. With these men they were easily able to overwhelm us defenders. There are now nearly a thousand Monfort soldiers and knights at Aric's command here in The Head.'

'Why though?' Ana asked. 'Why would Aric take the risk? What's in The Head that he wants?'

'Power?' Sir Gerard shrugged. 'Land? Income? With The Head in the hands of his son, the Monforts now rule half of High Realm. The Head has always been the most important dukedom, with it bordering the sea.'

'He had tried to do it all without bloodshed,' Merric said, thinking. 'Aric wanted to arrange a marriage between Rayden and Sophya. That way I suppose he could have had his son become duke of The Head the legal way, without having to resort to murder.'

'No, that makes no sense,' Sir Gerard said, shaking his head. 'It would have been many years before Lord Roberd would die of natural causes. And anyway, Sir Tristan would have been the heir to the dukedom, not a husband of Sophya's.'

That was true, Merric realised. The attempt to arrange the marriage must just have simply been a ruse to give Lord Aric a reason to travel to Eagle Mount to carry out his plan, without arousing suspicion.

'So how did you come to be here?' Merric asked, 'How did you escape the Monforts?'

'I have Kasper to thank for that,' Sir Gerard said, looking across at the poacher. 'I was locked in the same cell as where he was sent to when he was sentenced to death for killing that deer. Fortunately for both of us, the sentence had not yet been carried out. I was weak. Aric had tortured me, determined to find out where you had gone. I did not know, in truth, but I wouldn't have told him even if I did. I serve the Jacelyns, and always will. Lord Roberd always thought of you as a son, and so I will defend you with my life. Two nights ago, when they opened the cell door to bring us food, Kasper subdued the guard and led me out. We managed to secure weapons, and once we were out of the castle Kasper was able to track you into the Greenwood.'

'How?' Ana asked suspiciously.

Kasper laughed. 'Two sets of footprints, dragging an unconscious body? It doesn't need a skilled hunter like me to follow those tracks.'

'So what do we do now?' Tomas piped up.

'We need to get Merric as far away from Eagle Mount and the Monforts as we can,' Sir Gerard said looking across at Merric, and Ana nodded. 'It's not safe, and Aric won't stop hunting you, I'm certain of that. You were supposed to die that night. With you alive, Aric and Rayden will be in constant fear that the truth would get out. It'll be a hard road, but with Kasper and me by your side your chances of survival have greatly improved.'

'I never agreed to protect the boy,' Kasper said to Sir Gerard, his voice gruff. 'I only promised to bring you to him, and I've done that. It's time for me to go back to my family.'

'And I thank you for that, my friend,' Sir Gerard replied. 'But the only hope for Merric is to get him far from here. I need your help. You saw the posters up in Eaglestone. A handsome reward has been offered by the Monforts for Merric's capture. There's a chance that the loyalty of not all folk can be trusted.'

'No one from The Head would betray Merric,' Ana said.

'Money can be a strong lure,' said Sir Gerard regretfully. 'Do not forget that Orderix turned on his own duke. I can't imagine what the Monforts promised him. The further we get from Eagle Mount, the safer Merric will be.'

'Excuse me,' Merric interrupted, a little irritated, 'but I still think I should have a voice in the matter.'

Ana looked at him, and raised a threatening finger.

'We're not discussing this anymore, you're not going back.'

'She's right, Merric. There's nothing left for you there,' Sir Gerard said to Merric. 'The Head is lost, the Jacelyns are gone. I, we, must focus on you now.'

'But we've got to do *something* about what has happened.' Merric urged.

'What can we do?' Sir Gerard shrugged. 'The Monforts are the most powerful family in High Realm. The remaining Jacelyn soldiers are imprisoned in the castle dungeons. I can try and protect you, but I certainly can't fight a war for you.'

'What about the king?' Tomas suggested.

'What about him?' Sir Gerard asked.

'We could go to him,' Tomas said. 'If we tell him what has happened, he might help us.'

Sir Gerard just laughed sourly.

'You're only young, my lad, and naïve. It's a good plan, but it would be Merric's word against Aric and Rayden's. Aric's wife is the king's own daughter, so who do you think the king would believe murdered Lord Roberd? The noble Duke of The Southstones, his own son-in-law and the hero of the Battle of King's Keep? Or the orphaned son of a baron, with nothing to lose but a whole lot to gain?'

'Your home is gone, Merric,' Ana said to him, taking his hand. 'I'm sorry. Everything you held dear there is gone, you need to move on. Start a new life, somewhere Aric won't find you.'

'And we'll come too,' Tomas said.

Merric felt a surge of affection towards his friends, grateful for the sacrifices they had made, and were willing to continue making for him. With them by his side, life had a glimmer of hope of not being all bad.

'But where would we go?' Merric asked. 'To one of the barons? Or will they believe the lie that I murdered Lord Roberd, and so now serve the Monforts?'

Sir Gerard shook his head.

'The barons of The Head will be loyal to the Jacelyns until the end of all days. They will never believe that you murdered Lord Roberd, and they will know the truth. But they're too weak to oppose the Monforts on their own. They'll be forced to bend the knee and swear loyalty to their new duke, Rayden Monfort. My own brother, the Bron of Elderwyne, included. They wouldn't dare stand against the Monforts, for fear of what would happen to the folk they had a duty to protect. In times of trouble each baron can muster maybe a handful of knights and perhaps two hundred soldiers. What good could that do against the might of all The Southstones?'

'So what do we do then?' Merric asked, frustrated. He was being told that his own plan of returning to Eagle Mount was stupid, but they were not offering anything better.

Sir Gerard spoke to Kasper. 'There's a way, perhaps, that both of our desires can be satisfied. You wish to return to your family, and I want to get Merric far away from here.'

Kasper had been leaning against the ruined priory wall, waxing the string on his longbow, as though trying to keep himself separate from the conversation. He seemed to have been deep in thought.

'I'm an archer, not a wet-nurse. I'm not here to babysit the boy.'

'I heard what you spoke of during your trial,' Sir Gerard said. 'You said that times are hard in your village at the moment. I know your baron, Lord Tymon Conway of Bridge Ford. I can speak to him, to try and get him to help your village.'

Kasper frowned. He looked from Ana to Tomas, before his eyes finally settled on Merric. After a pause, he spoke.

'Alright, I'll take you to my village. But,' he put up one finger, 'if any of you slow me down then I'll leave you behind.' He put up a second finger, 'if you turn into a burden, then you're on your own.' Finally he made a fist, 'and if you put my family in any danger by being in my village then I'll kill you myself,' he said.

'We agree,' Sir Gerard said, while Tomas looked alarmed.

'I'm only doing this for you,' Kasper warned Sir Gerard. 'I care little for the boy, or the business of lords, but you're a decent man.'

'Lord Tymon's lands,' Merric said, thinking, 'they're on the western border of The Head aren't they?'

'They're far from here, aye,' Kasper agreed, already thinking that Merric was more of a bother than he was worth.

Sir Gerard put a strong hand on Merric's shoulder, sensing the boy's hesitation.

'It's time to put Eagle Mount behind us. Everything you held of value there no longer exists,' he looked up at Ana and Tomas, 'or else is here with you.'

There was sadness in Ana and Tomas's eyes, as they thought of the loved ones they were leaving behind, never to see again, but Ana smiled encouragingly at Merric.

'If his village is many miles from here then we can hope that Aric won't stretch his arm that far in his search for you,' she said.

'Precisely,' said Sir Gerard. 'The village of Little Harrow is many days' march away if we're staying off the roads, and the journey may not be safe. Let's be on our guard, and on our way.'

They set off beneath the green leaves of the forest. Their group had swelled to five, and Merric felt reassured by the presence of Sir Gerard. He was less certain about Kasper, but the poacher's longbow would no doubt be useful. Every step felt heavier as they walked further and further away from Eagle Mount. Merric found himself turning his head and looking back the way they had come. If he tried hard enough he felt like he could almost see the gleaming, bright towers of Eagle Mount looking back at him; the castle which had been his home, and which he knew he could never see again.

- CHAPTER NINE -

The wandering minstrel

The Great East Road snaked through the Greenwood, its rutted surface dusty and bright against the endless green of the forest. It had once been a simple track that headed across The Head, from Lynport in the east all the way to the crossroads at the centre of High Realm where it joined with the Great West, North and South Roads. Now, after centuries of use, it was wide enough for two carts to pass each other, and was the main route to the Eastern Sea. Many inns and villages had sprung up along it, but in the Greenwood, where the trees pressed in on all sides, they were few and far between.

Sir Gerard insisted that they stay away from the Great East Road, wary of the Monfort men who were scouring the land looking for Merric. On the first day since Sir Gerard and Kasper had joined them they walked until sundown, before making camp for the night. As they had travelled, Kasper had walked a little further ahead than the rest, keeping an eye out for danger and using his longbow to hunt anything that might go towards their meal that evening. Ana was relieved to be able to give up this job to the skilled hunter, as her love towards the animals of the forest caused her to be filled with sorrow when she had to aim her crossbow at them. She would follow close behind Kasper though, and would pick any wild mushrooms and roots that she saw growing in the patches of sunlight beneath the trees. Merric was feeling back to his old strength, and could travel without help from Tomas. This allowed his servant to aid Sir Gerard along whenever the old knight appeared to struggle. He was stone-faced and proud, and would not let on how much pain he was in after his torture at the hands of Lord Aric.

Once they had made camp for the night, Ana and Tomas busied themselves with preparing the food for their dinner. Kasper disappeared into the forest, scouting the way ahead. Merric tried to help his friends with the pheasant and wild onions, but could quickly see that he was more of a hindrance than a help. He instead settled down with his back against a tree, and watched as the darkness descended. Just as he was getting comfortable, Sir Gerard approached him and retrieved a spare sword from the bundle he had been carrying across his back.

'Here, take this,' he said, tossing the sword to Merric.

The blade landed with a metallic ring in the soft grass by Merric's feet, and he reached forward to pick it up. He stood and gave the sword a couple of practice swings, but Sir Gerard tutted.

'That'll never do,' he grumbled.

Despite the pain he was in, Sir Gerard drew his own sword. Both swords were plain, taken from the Eagle Mount armoury when Sir Gerard and Kasper had escaped. Merric guessed the knight's personal blade, which he had carried for years, had been taken from him when he was thrown into the dungeons.

'Stand ready,' Sir Gerard ordered.

Merric planted his feet and held the sword out in front of him.

'Don't point it at me,' Sir Gerard said. 'Hold it straight up. Merric obeyed, and lifted the sword so the point was looking straight at the sky above. 'It's easier to bring a sword down, than it is to raise it up,' Sir Gerard explained. 'If you hold it high, then no matter where your opponent attacks from, you're in the best position to defend it.'

Sir Gerard swung his sword low, and Merric brought his own blade down sharply to block the strike. He immediately lifted his sword again, ready to defend the next strike.

'Good,' Sir Gerard said, before quickly bringing his sword up towards Merric's shoulder. Again, the attack was parried away to the sound of ringing metal. The third attack was aimed at Merric's sword itself, and he cried out in surprise as the heavy blow knocked the blade from his hands. As Merric stooped to pick up the dropped sword, Sir Gerard pressed the tip of his blade against his chest.

'Never lose your weapon,' the elderly knight said. 'Your enemy will take full advantage of it. Now let's go again, and quicker this time.'

They continued to fight, with Merric getting better with every swing. He had never shown much interest in using a sword when Eagle Mount's swordmaster had been training him and Tristan, but Merric now knew that the skills could save his life one day. If the events from the other night had shown Merric anything, it was how defenceless he was. By the time Kasper had returned to the camp and the roasted pheasant that had been caught that day was ready, Merric's arms ached, but he felt good. He was looking forward to further tutoring from Sir Gerard, wondering what Tristan would have said if he could see him now. He buckled the sword's scabbard to his belt, and slid the blade into the leather sheath. It felt strange carrying a sword at his waist, and the weight of it was unfamiliar. But he liked how it felt.

Kasper kept to himself all that first night, and Merric found the man unsettling. He trusted Sir Gerard with his life, but the poacher he was less sure about. Kasper certainly had no love for Merric or the Jacelyns, and Merric hoped that Kasper found no reason to turn on them. With his knowledge of the wild and skill with his longbow they could not afford to lose him, and he would be a dangerous enemy should his loyalties prove to lie elsewhere.

The next day passed, and still the forest showed no signs of ending. By staying in the depths of the forest they were safer, but the going was far slower. On the third morning after Sir Gerard and Kasper had joined them, the poacher told them that the Crags were ahead; tall, impassable rocks that rose like shards of huge grey glass. They had no choice but to turn north and travel closer to the Great East Road in order to pass this natural obstacle.

As Sir Gerard had feared, danger was close.

Voices and laughter drifted across to where they walked. The Great East Road was visible through the trees to their right, and Kasper muttered that it may just be travellers. He edged towards the road to look, and Merric followed, curious. As they reached the treeline, they ducked behind some thick bushes that grew beside the road, and peered out. Kasper took one look before grabbing Merric and pulling him back into the shadow of the trees.

Fifty paces down the road was a small inn, with a stable where travellers could rest their weary horses. Three men were seated on benches outside the tavern, mugs of ale in their hands. They appeared relaxed and off guard, and another burst of laughter drifted over to where Kasper and Merric hid. The men were clad in plain leather and ring mail, but their shields that were leant against the wall beside them bore the symbol of the black marching knight.

'Monfort soldiers?' Merric asked, his heartbeat quickening.

Kasper nodded.

'They're yeomen. They're the eyes and ears of Aric's army, mounted on the swiftest horses.'

161

'Are they looking for us?'

'Looking for you, you mean?' Kasper corrected, looking across at him. 'Yes, it's likely.'

Merric felt his anger rise as he looked at the symbol on their shields. It was not any of these men who had held the blade that had killed Lord Roberd or the others, but they served Lord Aric and Rayden, and that was enough. Merric balled his hands into fists, and then remembered the sword he was wearing at his waist. He felt himself reach for the blade, but another hand was suddenly on his and he stopped himself. He looked round to see that Ana and the others had joined them at the treeline, and it was her comforting hand that had reached out to him.

Two more of the yeomen walked around the corner of the inn from the stables, leading six horses by the reins. One of them looked young, with a faint wisp of moustache on his upper lip, and he seemed nervous around the older and more experienced men. Another of the yeomen, their leader, exited the inn through the door, and shouted for them all to mount up. There was a small amount of grumbling, but the serjeant grabbed them one at a time by the scruffs of their necks and pulled them away from their drinks. They were soon in their saddles, riding away from the inn, westwards along the Great East Road in the same direction Merric and his company were heading. The clip-clopping had faded into the distance before Kasper and Sir Gerard were satisfied that it was safe for them to continue.

Their close call with the Monfort yeomen made Merric appreciate how much danger they were in. Lord Aric and Rayden were likely to be determined to find him. And if they did, Merric would be dragged back to them, and no doubt be killed. They caught glimpses of the same Monfort men several more times that day as they galloped up and down the road, on the lookout for Merric. On one occasion Merric and his companions even saw a group of Monfort soldiers on foot, heavily armed, and led by one of Lord Aric's knights. They had intercepted a poor farmer and his mule-drawn cart, and had loudly demanded to know if he was concealing Merric. The farmer had pleaded that he was not, but the soldiers had emptied his cargo of carrots from the cart anyway to see if their quarry was hiding there, ruining the vegetables while they were at it. They had marched on, leaving the farmer weeping for his lost produce. Each time Merric and his company had one of these encounters with their hunters they had no choice but to hide, laying low in the forest until the Monfort men had passed by. On more than one occasion the enemy had been no more than a handful of paces away from where Merric lay hidden, but the dense undergrowth of the forest floor had meant he was able to go undetected

The sense of danger was never far from Merric's mind, and he was sure the others felt the same. As they continued south-west through the forest, the Crags and the Great East Road now behind them, he jumped every time he heard a twig snap, or the leaves of a bush rustle. More often than not it was the wind, or one of his travelling companions, and Merric kept telling himself to stop letting his nerves get the better of him.

For some unknown reason there were fewer animals in this part of the forest. What few small birds and rabbits they did see proved too hard a target even for Kasper's longbow. Their dinner each evening became a simple affair, limited to the roots and mushrooms that they chanced upon, but even these started to get rarer. They were all beginning to suffer from the lack of food, but none would say so; they just tightened their belts and continued on their journey.

Kasper continued to walk a little further ahead, his eyes scanning the oak trees around them, wary that there were always more Monfort men close by. Ana was more concerned about keeping her eyes on the forest floor, picking anything she decided was edible. She kept on throwing concerned glances at Merric and Tomas, both of whom seemed to be suffering worst from the lack of food. Merric had never gone hungry in his life before this, and Tomas and the other servants had grown up with the luxury of the leftovers from the banquets the Jacelyns enjoyed. Sir Gerard had often ridden to war, and so had gone for long stretches without enough to eat, but his injuries were still bothering him. Still, he did not say a word and managed to keep up with the others. Eventually the hunger took over the fear that Merric was feeling, and he decided he would happily trade a run-in with the

Monfort yeomen's long spears if it meant a good meal afterwards.

The following day they saw a smudge of black smoke rising above the trees half a mile ahead of them. Kasper told them it looked like the smoke from a campfire, and Sir Gerard suggested they take the longer way round to avoid whoever was there. It could be the Monfort yeomen, or it could be other travellers like themselves, choosing to keep off the main road for some reason. Either way, it would be better to avoid contact with whoever it was. He did not want word of their movements to reach the ear of Lord Aric or Rayden.

A camp was sure to have food though. The day was nearing its end, and they would soon need to stop anyway. A campfire, if friendly, would be a welcome place to rest. Merric mentioned this, but still Sir Gerard felt uneasy, saying it was still too dangerous. The others looked at Kasper, who had temporarily taken charge of the group because of his knowledge of the land as they journeyed through the Greenwood. Kasper ran his fingers through his dirty hair and looked at Sir Gerard. They exchanged a few words, and eventually the poacher said he would go and have a look to see who the campfire belonged to. Sir Gerard reluctantly agreed to this, knowing that he was outnumbered.

'I'm going too,' Ana said.

Merric watched as she and Kasper disappeared into the trees ahead of them. Merric did not like Ana being alone with Kasper, but she and the poacher returned after a short while to report that a single man sat by the camp fire, with his small horse tethered nearby.

'A Monfort soldier?' Tomas asked, often fearing the worst.

'Far from it, boy,' Kasper said, 'unless Aric is hiring singers as soldiers now. Perhaps he means to sing his enemies to death.'

'A minstrel? All the way out here? That seems unlikely' Sir Gerard said, suspicious.

Minstrels were singers and musicians who filled the halls of lords great and small with music and merriment. They went wherever folk would pay them to sing, and that was rarely the depths of the Greenwood.

'Exactly, you see?' Ana said, turning to Kasper.

'What's going on,' Merric asked, looking from his friend to the poacher.

'The girl seems to think that our minstrel friend is a Monfort spy,' Kasper said.

'Sir Gerard just said it himself,' Ana said. 'Why would a singer be all the way out here in the wilderness all on his own, with Monfort men everywhere? He must have a reason, maybe he's a lookout for them!'

'Or perhaps,' Kasper retorted, 'he's just a brainless fool, like all minstrels. Let's send him on his way, use his campfire and help ourselves to the contents of his saddlebags.'

'And then if he is a spy,' Ana said hotly, 'he'd go to the first Monfort patrol he sees and point them in our direction. We should keep away from him.'

'He's not a spy,' Kasper said impatiently.

Sir Gerard seemed reassured by Kasper's confidence that the minstrel was no one to be suspicious of. The two had been through a lot together, so if Kasper was satisfied then so was he.

'We'll let Merric decide,' the old knight said, turning to him.

Merric was surprised to be given the decision, and they all stared at him. He respected Ana's instincts, but the prospect of good food was overwhelming.

'Let's go to his camp. If he turns out to mean us harm, then we're five against one.'

Ana seemed uncertain, but accepted his decision. They set off through the trees towards the plume of smoke. Tomas was almost tripping over himself in his excitement at the prospect of food.

It did not take them long to arrive at the small clearing where the minstrel had made his camp. A welcoming fire sat in the centre of the clearing, beside a fallen tree. A small pony grazed nearby, and baggage surrounded the camp. Clearly the minstrel did not like to travel light and enjoyed home comforts. A couple of small iron pots were hanging above the fire, and the delicious smell of cooking stew wafted across to them.

The minstrel jumped up in alarm from his perch on the fallen tree when he saw the group of armed travellers appear suddenly in his clearing. Having no weapon of his own he scooped up a small fallen branch that he saw by his feet, and waved it threateningly at them. A few leaves fell off in protest as he shook it.

'Get back! Back I say!' the minstrel cried, his face filled with panic. 'I'm armed! Don't come any closer, or I'll…oh.'

The branch had snapped, leaving just a small twig left in his hand.

Kasper merely laughed and raised his hands to show that he meant no harm.

'Be at peace, friend.' Sir Gerard said, 'we only seek the warmth of your fire and a bite of your food, if you offer it to share.'

'Who are you all?' the singer asked, lowering the twig slightly. His voice was high pitched.

'My name is Kasper of Little Harrow,' Kasper said, in his best attempt at a pleasant voice. This is Grodon,' he continued, plucking a name from his head and indicating the grizzled Sir Gerard. 'These other three are my servants. I'm afraid we were set upon by bandits. We escaped with our lives, but our horses and baggage were lost.'

There was a pause, whilst the minstrel weighed this up in his head, deciding whether they were safe or not. He was biting his lip, and looking at each of them in turn. Eventually his face relaxed.

'My friends, my poor friends!' he exclaimed.

Apparently deciding that the travellers posed no threat, he threw down the twig and spread his arms out in welcome. The hair on his head was glossy and shoulder length. and was topped by a flashy red hat with colourful feathers. The sleeves of his matching red jacket were baggy and puffy, and made him look an odd shape when combined with his extremely tight green breeches. His shoes were curled up outrageously at the toes, and small bells jingled as he moved.

'Come, join me by my fire, we'll sing and feast the night away,' the minstrel said.

Merric could not help but smile at the strange man; he understood now why Kasper found it amusing that Ana thought the minstrel could possibly be an enemy. The minstrel sat on the fallen tree he had taken as a seat, and took up his lute. He plucked the strings of the musical instrument absent-mindedly as the others joined him around the fire.

'Grodon?' Sir Gerard muttered to Kasper, with a raised eyebrow.

'Aye,' Kasper replied, 'I once knew a Grodon when I was a boy. An uglier man I've never seen.'

Sir Gerard just smirked at him.

'My name is Mortin,' the minstrel introduced himself, and took one of his hands off of his lute for a moment to give them a deep bow. 'I hail from Rosewood, a small village far to the north of here. I'm sure you've never heard of it though.'

Merric had, in fact, heard of Rosewood. It was a beautiful town in the foothills of the Storm Mountains, with summer fayres that Lord Roberd would visit each year.

'What brings you so far from the Storm Mountains?' Ana asked, still suspicious of the minstrel. She alone remained standing as the others sat. 'This seems a strange place for you to be.'

Mortin seemed unaware of the rudeness in her voice. Like many who lived to entertain, the singer appeared to enjoy talking about himself.

'I, Mortin of Rosewood, am a wandering minstrel, my fair maiden,' he said, causing Merric to snigger. Ana scowled across at him. 'I travel the lands, from King's Keep in the west to Lynport in the east, The Shining Castle in the north to The Citadel in the south. Common folk and lord alike shower me with coin to hear me sing and tell tales. I'm on my way to Elderwyne as we speak. The noble Velions are true enthusiasts of my songs.'

'Don't count on it,' Sir Gerard muttered. Merric, who overheard him, grinned.

Mortin did not notice. He continued to speak about his life to them all. His voice was accompanied by the gentle strumming of his lute, making everything he said seem like a song. It quickly became annoying, but this at least seemed to distract Ana from her suspicions. She too, was soon sat by the fire and beginning to relax.

They gradually drifted into silence, feeling the aches leaving their legs from their long march. The smell of the stew made Merric's mouth water. Several times Mortin opened his mouth as though to speak, but could see his companions were weary of conversation so closed his mouth again, disappointed. As the sky turned dark, Tomas piped up and asked for a song whilst they waited for their dinner to cook. Mortin seemed delighted by the idea, and flexed his fingers dramatically.

'Unfortunately,' Sir Gerard said, not sounding sorry at all, 'we have no coin to pay for a song.'

'On an evening as perfect as this, how could I possibly ask for payment?' Mortin said with a smile. Sir Gerard looked disappointed. 'Have you fine folk heard *The Ballad of The Lady and the Dragon*?' They all shook their heads, so the minstrel began strumming a mournful tune on his lute.

> *Save me, my lord, the maiden said,*
> *the beast has come for me.*
> *With lance and sword, he did fight,*
> *for he was in love with she.*
>
> *The beast was a dragon, fierce and great,*
> *a giant wreathed in flame.*
> *But brave he was, a brave lord knight,*
> *eager for love and fame.*

'Slay it' she cried 'my brave strong lord,
you are my true hero.'
So charged he did, armed with her love,
to fight the dragon foe.

With a roar, with a spit of flame,
the brave knight was no more.
And the beast did seize the fair maiden,
with his enormous claw.

No tears, she shed, for her brave knight,
that they were now apart.
For the dragon she loved, all along,
the knight never had her heart.

'What a ridiculous song,' Sir Gerard grumbled, 'now I'm truly miserable.'

Kasper and Merric laughed.

'What happened to her?' Tomas asked, his eyes wide. He had hung onto every word the minstrel had sung. 'What happened to the lady? Did the dragon love her back?'

'Aha! That is the wonder of song, young sire,' Mortin said enthusiastically, 'none know. Some say she and the dragon flew far to the cold south to live out their lives together, others say the dragon ate her there and then. After all, a dragon's only love is his next meal, so they say.'

'And I say it's utter rubbish,' Sir Gerard said grumpily. 'It's just a song, and a poor one at that. Give me a good foot-stomper any day. Something you can dance to.'

Merric could not imagine the elderly knight dancing, but then remembered that Sir Gerard must have been a young man once, without the worries and concerns that now filled him.

The minstrel opened his mouth to argue, but Kasper interrupted.

'That's enough, let's eat.'

They ate heartily, and not a drop of stew was left in the pot when they were finished. Afterwards none, save perhaps Mortin, wanted to do anything other than sleep, and Kasper offered to take the first watch. Tomas, Ana and Sir Gerard laid down beneath blankets lent to them by Mortin, and fell quickly to sleep. As had been the case every night since he had watched Tristan be killed, Merric found that sleep did not come easily. He laid awake, watching the bright ashes from the campfire drift upwards towards the stars. It was then that he realised he was not the only one who was still awake.

'I knew your father,' Mortin said softly beside him.

Alarmed, Merric looked across to where the singer still sat beside the fire. He could see the rosy-cheeked face looking at him in the firelight.

'I-I'm sorry?' Merric asked, certain he had misheard.

'Your father,' the minstrel repeated, 'I, Mortin of Rosewood, knew him.'

'You're mistaken, I'm sure.'

Nervousness struck Merric, and he felt his shaking hands edge towards his sword. He swallowed. Was Ana right after all? Merric wondered if there was more to the harmless-looking man than met the eye.

Mortin smiled kindly, trying to sooth Merric's sudden fear, and kept his voice low so as not to wake the others.

'As I said, I've travelled far and wide throughout my years. Your father was always very welcoming to me, inviting me into his hall. It was a tragedy what befell him, and his charming village of Ryding.'

Merric felt his heart stop, but before he could reply, the singer continued.

'I recognised you the moment you appeared with you friends. The archer said you were his servant, but I wonder if it's perhaps the other way around.'

Merric considered telling the minstrel that he was wrong, but knew there was no point.

'How did you know?' Merric asked.

'I've frequented Eagle Mount on many an occasion, and saw you seated at the top table often, though I confess your dress and general cleanliness were much improved back then.' He eyed Merric's grubby hands, tangled hair and dirty clothes. 'I have something of a talent of remembering faces. I'm sure you wouldn't remember me; to most, one minstrel is as alike as the next. We're as different to each other as cows are in each other's eyes, but I forgive the ignorance of common folk.' Mortin realised he was getting side-tracked, and gave Merric an apologetic smile. 'It was a wonder that you survived when Ryding was destroyed all those years ago, but surely it's a miracle that you've escaped danger once again. Yes, word of the awful events at Eagle Mount have reached my ears. Terrible, terrible! However I, Mortin of Rosewood, heard a story, not two days past, from a merchant out of Eaglestone, which may be of some interest to you –,'

'We've got a long day ahead of us tomorrow, you should get some rest.' Kasper said to them.

He had heard them speaking, and he too was showing alarm at realising that Mortin had known who Merric was. Kasper had risen from his position at the edge of the circle of light cast by the fire, and stood between Merric and Mortin, halting their conversation. Merric was curious about what the minstrel had been about to say, but Kasper had beckoned to the minstrel and the two were walking away to the other side of the fire deep in conversation. Merric knew there was no point in trying to find out what it was now. Reluctantly he rolled over and wrapped his blanket tightly round his body.

As he slowly drifted off to sleep he could hear Kasper and Mortin talking in hushed voices. Kasper sounded angry. It was too quiet for Merric to hear, so he forgot about them and closed his eyes.

***

175

Merric felt more relaxed than he could remember feeling in days when he awoke the next morning. He was greeted by the delicious smell of frying bacon and tomatoes, and had never smelt anything so good in his life. Despite the previous night's stew, the hunger from the past few days still gnawed at his stomach. He jumped up eagerly, letting his blanket fall to the grass, and moved over to where Tomas prodded the bacon around a pan with a fork. Ana watched him absent-mindedly, toying with a loose thread on her jerkin. Mortin was in his usual place on the fallen tree with his lute, and wished Merric a casual good morning. The minstrel acted as though their secret conversation the previous night had never taken place. This was not the time to ask him about it though. Sir Gerard was sitting with his back propped against some of the minstrel's packs. He grimaced at the injury that was still troubling him, and sharpened his sword with a whet stone, using long, slow strokes.

'Has Kasper been gone long?' Merric asked. He assumed that, as usual, the poacher was scouting the way ahead.

Ana started, noticing Merric awake for the first time. She gave her head a shake. 'An hour or so. I'm sure he'll be back soon.'

'Aye, and then we can be off,' Sir Gerard growled.

'Can't we stay with Mortin a little longer?' Tomas said, looking up from the pan. He was clearly enjoying the benefits that the singer's camp offered, with its food and comforts.

'No, we can't stay in one place for too long. These woods are crawling with Monfort men, remember?' Ana explained patiently to him, after making sure that the minstrel would not overhear her. She had grown fond of the servant boy over the past few days.

Mortin played the first few notes of a song, which echoed pleasantly around the clearing. With the sound of the tune mixing with the early morning calls of the birds and the smell of breakfast, Merric closed his eyes and smiled contentedly.

A loud musical twang sounded suddenly, and Merric glanced across at Mortin. The minstrel was sat with his eyes wide with shock as he looked down at the snapped strings of his lute. It was not until Ana leapt to her feet that Merric realised what he was seeing. A crossbow bolt had struck Mortin's beloved lute and shattered it. The feathered bolt was impaled on what remained of the wooden instrument.

At that moment the Monfort yeomen charged into the clearing on their horses, one carrying a crossbow that he hurried to reload. They were whooping and shouting with glee as they rode towards the travellers, eager for the rewards they were sure to receive from their duke for being the ones to find and capture Merric.

Tomas screamed, diving behind the fallen tree, while Sir Gerard struggled to his feet, casting the whet stone aside.

'To arms!' the old knight bellowed, as though he were commanding his Eagle Guard. 'Defend yourselves!'

Ana darted across to her things, gathering up her own crossbow. She aimed it at their attackers and the string twanged. One of the Monfort men fell from his saddle. Mortin remained where he was sat, and looked in horror at his destroyed musical instrument. A few inches higher and the shot would have struck him in the heart. Having quickly reloaded, Ana shot a second time. This time she missed her target, and suddenly the charging yeomen were upon them.

There was nowhere to run. Merric clumsily tugged his sword from its scabbard and raised it as Sir Gerard had taught him. He met the charge of the first horseman, who steered directly for him. The man aimed his spear at Merric, who ducked to avoid it, falling to the ground. The spear whistled harmlessly over his head. The momentum of the yeoman's charge took him several yards away from his target, and he shouted in annoyance. Merric took a few heartbeats to glance around and see how his friends were faring against the sudden attack in the clearing.

Gritting his teeth, Sir Gerard was fighting off two of the mounted Monfort men at once, hacking and parrying with his sword with well-practiced skill. As Merric watched, one of the attackers managed to wheel his horse around behind the knight, and the swipe of his sword caused Sir Gerard to shout out in pain. The shout turned into a snarl though, and he turned and cut the man down from his horse with a single blow. Ana had abandoned her crossbow, it being of no use when their enemies were so close. She pulled a slender dagger from inside her jerkin and duelled with a young Monfort yeoman who had jumped down from his horse. They lunged and blocked each other, neither able to gain an advantage over their opponent. The young yeoman seemed almost hesitant as he fought, and his face showed fear. The final Monfort man had grabbed Tomas by his ankle and was dragging him, kicking and screaming, from his hiding place.

'Is this him? I've got him!' the yeoman was shouting.

None of the attackers seemed concerned by the minstrel, who had finally noticed what was going on around him. With a terrified yelp he jumped up and ran from the clearing, the jingling of the bells in his shoes fading away. His pony broke free of where it had been tethered, and ran after him.

Kasper was nowhere to be seen.

The yeoman who had charged at Merric climbed down from his horse, and advanced towards him with his long spear grasped in two hands. A bushy beard and wild hair sprouted out from beneath his helmet, and both looked greasy and unwashed. With a shout he jabbed his spear at Merric, who had to step back from the deadly spear tip. The Monfort man roared and lunged at Merric's chest, and only a desperate sweep of his sword saved Merric's life. He tried to remember what Sir Gerard had taught him, but the lessons were slipping from his mind and in the moment he was acting on instinct. He just kept blocking every attack from the yeoman's spear with his sword, each strike jarring his arms and the blade threatened to drop from his sweaty hands.

Tomas kicked at the man who had grabbed him, and his heel struck him in the face. The yeoman cried out in pain and dropped the boy, clutching at his broken nose. Ana and the young yeoman were still circling each other. She was not as skilled with a blade as she was with her crossbow, and her attacker still seemed reluctant to fight.

The remaining man fighting Sir Gerard shouted in triumph as he managed to disarm the knight with a vicious chop to the older man's arm. The grizzled Captain of the Eagle Guard did not give up though, and despite his many wounds he reached forward and grabbed the yeoman's wrist, pulling him from the horse with a crash.

The two wrestled for a moment, each trying to gain possession of the yeoman's blade, before Sir Gerard was triumphant. With a snarl he managed to loosen the Monfort man's grip on the sword, and in an instant the blade was in the knight's hand. He raised it high above his prone opponent, his eyes searching for a weak spot through in the yeoman's ring mail armour.

All of a sudden the Monfort man reached down to his boot and drew out a long dagger.

Before Merric could cry out a warning, the man had thrust the blade towards Sir Gerard's chest. The yeoman hooted with victory as his attack struck home. Climbing back to his feet he took his sword back from Sir Gerard's weakening fingers, as the old knight fell slowly to his knees.

CHAPTER TEN

The fallen knight

The Monfort yeoman shouted again in triumph. It was a rare thing to defeat a knight in combat, even an older knight who was without horse and armour and who was already wounded before the fight began. Ignoring the battle still going on around him, the man squatted down beside Sir Gerard's body, eager to see if he had anything valuable on him that he could steal. Before he could find anything though there was a sharp whooshing sound, and an arrow caught the yeoman in his side, sending him sprawling on the ground.

Kasper appeared from the treeline, loosing a second arrow from his longbow which struck the yeoman who had been dragging Tomas from his hiding place. Merric's bearded opponent was momentarily distracted, looking in surprise at Kasper's sudden appearance, and Merric took advantage and charged past his spear, driving his sword forward. He heard the yeoman grunt in pain, and look back in shock at the boy who had struck him, before falling to the ground.

Kasper charged into the remains of the campsite, his longbow aimed at the last yeoman, the young man who had been duelling with Ana. When he saw Kasper's fingers about to release the arrow at him, the yeoman let go of his sword and dropped to his knees.

'Mercy! I yield!' he pleaded, filled with terror.

Merric took a step back from the man he had just killed, shocked. His hands began to shake at the realisation of what he had done. To keep them occupied he snatched up a handful of grass and used it to wipe the blood from his sword, before sliding the blade back into its scabbard. He suddenly remembered Sir Gerard.

While Kasper picked up a discarded sword and kept it pointed at the captive yeoman, Merric, Ana and Tomas hurried over to where Sir Gerard was lying in the grass. The grizzled old knight was still alive, but his strength was leaving him fast. Sir Gerard's face was white, and Merric knew that the elderly knight was close to death.

'I'm done, lad,' Sir Gerard said through clenched teeth when he saw Merric.

'No, Sir! No, you can't die.' Merric tried to keep his voice level.

'Save me your tears,' Sir Gerard said, seeing the grief on Merric's face. 'I'm a knight, sworn to serve and protect, fated to die in battle.'

Merric could not answer, so Ana spoke for him.

'You fought well, Sir,' she said.

'Aye, though not as well as I used to.' Sir Gerard looked directly at Merric. 'Continue onwards. Don't stop, don't turn back. I joined the Eagle Guard to protect the Duke of The Head, and his family. I failed to save Lord Roberd. No, don't interrupt,' he said when Merric opened his mouth to protest. 'Lord Roberd always treated you as his own, and that is why I followed you here. I am sworn to serve you, and I have done that. You must survive, you must. Otherwise, Lord Roberd's legacy is gone.' His body tensed with pain. 'It's time.'

Merric retrieved Sir Gerard's sword from where he had dropped it when he had been disarmed, and put it in the old man's hand. It was not his own blade, forged at his home of Elderwyne and carried by him for fifty years, but it was still a sword, the most treasured possession of a knight. Sir Gerard gripped it with all the strength he had left. His eyes slowly closed and his laboured breathing ceased. All the pain appeared to leave him. Merric bowed his head. Tomas's crying had stopped now, but his eyes were wet with tears. Ana put an arm around Merric, who felt warmed by the touch. The three of them knelt in silence for a moment, looking at the fallen knight.

At last, Tomas looked away from Sir Gerard's still body.

'What about him?' he said, gesturing at the captured yeoman.

The young man was hardly older than Merric, and kept glancing nervously at Kasper and the sword in his hand. Merric recognised the wisp of moustache on his upper lip, and realised that the yeomen who had attacked them were the same group that they had seen outside the inn several days past.

The yeoman had heard Tomas's question.

'Please, don't harm me none!'

'Do you know who we are?' Kasper snarled.

The captured yeoman looked up at him, terrified by the poacher's fierce eyes.

'They don't tell me nothing, honest. I just follow my orders, I do what I'm told,' he stammered.

Merric strode over to him and looked him in the eyes. 'I don't believe you. Do you know who I am?'

'N-no,'

Kasper tickled the yeoman's cheek threateningly with the point of his sword.

'I'd love to play dice with you, boy. You couldn't lie if you tried.'

'Okay, okay! My serjeant said that the Orrell boy is wanted for the murder of Lord Roberd, and that him, and any that help him, are outlaws. We was ordered to bring him back to Eagle Mount. Are you him?'

Merric felt his anger swell up once more.

'And do you believe these lies?' he said.

'I don't! I promise!'

'Do you really believe I could kill Lord Roberd and Lady Cathreen? They treated me like a son. Do you really think I could murder Tristan, or Sophya?'

The yeoman's sniffling stopped all of a sudden, and he looked at Merric in surprise.

'What is it?' Merric asked, confused. His anger disappeared slightly.

'You've got it wrong. See, I'm not like the rest of them, I want to help you.' The young yeoman spoke quickly, bringing his hands up and reaching up for Merric's. 'I promise, if you swear you won't harm me. There's something you don't know, but I can tell you. Just promise-'

Kasper's sword arm lashed out, and the young man fell to the ground, dead. Merric stepped back in shock, and he looked at Kasper in anger.

'Why did you do that?'

'He was a Monfort man,' Kasper replied with a shrug. He tucked the sword into his belt, and retrieved his longbow.

'He was a boy, barely older than I,' Merric countered, 'and he was about to tell me something.'

'He had nothing to tell. He was just trying to save his skin.'

Merric was unconvinced.

'But it's not right, he was unarmed! He'd surrendered to us.'

Kasper lost his temper.

'And you think they would have treated us any differently if they'd captured us? We'd be dead now if they had their way. Don't ever underestimate what the Monforts would be willing to do.'

Several birds flew up in alarm from the nearby trees at the sound of his raised voice. Kasper pointed at Sir Gerard's body.

'There's your evidence. That old knight was a good man, I hope your life is worth him losing his.'

'That's not fair,' Ana said hotly. 'Don't speak to Merric like that.'

'Not here,' Tomas pleaded, looking at Sir Gerard's body.

Kasper shrugged and kicked a discarded Monfort helmet that laid at his feet.

Merric did not need Kasper to say those words for him to feel responsible about the death of Sir Gerard. Death seemed to follow Merric wherever he went. He still felt a pang of guilt at the young yeoman's death. He was just a simple boy serving his lord, the same as any who carried a shield bearing the eagle of the Jacelyns. He was not responsible for what Lord Aric and Rayden had done. Merric glanced across at Sir Gerard's peaceful body, and then at the young Monfort man lying face down in the grass, and took a deep breath. This was Aric and Rayden, all of it. It was they who caused all of this death.

'What should we do with them?' Tomas asked quietly, his eyes still red.

'We'll bury Gerard, but the others we'll leave for the crows,' Kasper said.

Merric looked up.

'We can't leave them like this,' he said, 'that's not right.'

'You're much mistaken if you think they'd treat your body any better,' Kasper replied. 'We don't have time to bury them all, we need to be away from here. Where's Mortin?' he added when he had noticed that the minstrel was neither stood with them nor lying with the other fallen.

'He was one of them,' Ana said, 'I'm certain of it. He played a song, just before they appeared. Like it was a signal or something.'

'Another reason for us to be gone, if that's the case,' Kasper said.

'Or it could have just been a coincidence,' Tomas said, shaken after the fight. 'He might not have anything to do with it.'

'It matters not,' Kasper said. 'Let us be finished here and leave this place behind us.'

Tomas used whatever he could find from the camp to start digging a hole for Sir Gerard's grave, and Ana moved across to help him. Kasper rounded up some of the horses left by the Monfort yeomen and tied them to a nearby tree. With horses, they would be able to make much faster progress. To keep himself busy, Merric looked through the packs left by the minstrel. He had been carrying plenty of spare food, along with some fodder for the horses. He stowed as much as he could on one of their horses, throwing moody glances at Kasper. Despite the poacher having come to their aid, Merric was liking him less and less. The sooner they got to his village the better. He did not enjoy Kasper's company one bit.

Within an hour they were ready to leave. They had spent a few quiet moments by the fresh mound of earth that marked Sir Gerard's resting place. Then they swung themselves up into the saddles of the horses, and Kasper led them out of the clearing and into the trees, holding onto the reins of the packhorse.

Merric's own horse was a spritely and friendly beast, brown in colour but for white socks and a small white diamond on his forehead. The horse quickly grew comfortable with his new owner, accepting him without question, and trotted along happily. Merric wished he shared the horse's mood.

As they rode they were silent, each thinking about the morning's events. So many had died, though death no longer seemed such a stranger to Merric. First his parents had died, and then the Jacelyns. Now Sir Gerard was gone too. A man had even died at Merric's own hand, but this had left a smaller impression than he thought it would. He did not regret it. It was either going to be the Monfort man or him, and Merric had no intention of it being him. Sir Gerard had told Merric that he had to survive, and he was now even starting to believe it himself.

And then there was Mortin the minstrel. Ana believed that he was in league with the Monforts, but Merric did not know what to think. He kicked his heels into his horse's flank, and sped up until he was level with Kasper, who led the procession through the trees.

'Do you think that Mortin could have been working with the Monforts?' he asked. 'He seemed so pleasant.'

'It's the pleasant ones you need to be wary of; the unpleasant folk are the only ones you can really trust. It's possible that the minstrel was a spy, and welcomed us to his camp in order to keep us occupied whilst he waited for the Monfort yeomen to arrive. Or maybe he was a simple traveller who was in the wrong place at the wrong time. It's done though, there's no point dwelling on it.'

One thing was disturbing Merric though.

'But if they were working together then why would they try and kill him?'

He was thinking of the crossbow bolt that had shattered the singer's lute. It would have been an impossible shot if the yeoman had been trying to aim for the instrument, so he must have been try to kill Mortin, just as they were trying to kill the rest of them.

'The Monforts aren't known for their honour. Maybe they simply didn't want to share the reward with him,' Kasper offered.

Merric thought for a while in silence about Mortin.

'I don't think he betrayed us.'

'Good for you, it doesn't matter,' Kasper said without interest.

'It matters to me,' Merric countered hotly. 'He may have been nothing more than a kindly man who took us in and provided for us, even though he knew it would put him in danger.'

'You have a softer heart than I, boy,' Kasper finished, before calling over his shoulder to the others. 'Let's pick up the pace. One more day of hard marching and I want to be out of this forest.'

***

They were nearing the western border of the Greenwood at last, and the trees were finally beginning to thin. More and more daylight filtered down through the leaves and onto their heads as they continued west. It was the start of the summer and the still air of the forest was stuffy, so when the trees ended at last early the following day they enjoyed the feeling of the fresh breeze on their faces.

'Do you think we can trust him?' Ana said quietly to Merric, glancing at the back of Kasper who rode a little ahead of the others.

'He promised to help us,' Merric said, wishing he could convince himself.

'He promised to help Sir Gerard,' Ana corrected, 'and Sir Gerard is gone, so can no longer uphold his end of the bargain. What reason would Kasper have for helping us now?'

Merric looked at Kasper, trying and failing to judge the poacher's body language. *Could* they trust him? There was a suspicion at the back of Merric's mind about Kasper that he just could not shake.

'Do we have a choice?' he said,

'We always have a choice, Merric,' Ana said, surprised. 'We could turn our horses around now, and get far away from him.'

'He would track us, we'd never get away. There are Monforts behind us, and I would rather not take our chances against them on our own. We'll stay with Kasper, but keep on our guard. We're out of the forest now and he's brought us this far.'

The western edge of the forest had ended at the top of a rise that overlooked The Yielding, an expanse of rich, fertile lands. From their vantage point they could see for leagues. Before them stretched mile after mile of brightly coloured fields filled with barley, wheat, and countless types of vegetables, besides orchards and meadows of grazing animals. A line of trees several miles to the north showed where The Great East Road cut through the land after emerging from the Greenwood. Any Monfort patrols were sure to be focused around there. But Merric wondered if the bodies of the yeomen had been found yet in the clearing. If they had then the Monforts would know that

Merric and his companions were travelling across country, so would broaden their search.

They walked their horses downhill, away from the Greenwood and towards the patchwork of fields and meadows of The Yielding. A small river meandered in front of them, blocking their path.

'Is that The Rush?' Tomas asked as he spied it, his voice filled with awe.

'Hardly,' Kasper laughed. 'Believe me; you'll know The Rush when you see it.'

'The Rush is many miles from here,' Merric told Tomas patiently, 'on the border between The Head and the dukedoms of The Dale and The Southstones.'

The great river was said to be half a mile wide, and only one bridge crossed the fast flowing water along its entire length.

'You may even see it one day,' Kasper said. 'Though not on this journey, it's still miles beyond my village, and that's as far as we're going.'

They spurred their horses down to the bank of the river. Recalling the map in Lord Roberd's study, Merric knew that this was the Bluebottle, named for the bluebottle birds that were often seen landing on its surface and plucking fish from the water with their long beaks. Morning mists clung to the surface of the river, and it looked beautiful in the early sun.

'I once heard a prior say that mists are the spirits of good, honest folk going up to the eternal halls of their ancestors,' Ana said wistfully, looking at it. 'Maybe it's Sir Gerard.

Tomas looked in wonder at the gently moving mist as it floated over the slow flowing water of the Bluebottle. Kasper just scoffed.

'A man from my village once insisted that mists are nothing but wisps of water floating on the air, no different from the clouds in the sky. Folk say all sorts of rubbish. It doesn't mean they're true.'

A few hundred paces downstream there was an old stone bridge that crossed the river. It had been built many years ago, before the Great East Road had existed. In those days another road had crossed the river here. While the road was long gone, the bridge still stood firm. As they crossed, Merric's horse began nuzzling at the packs on Tomas' horse with his nose and whinnied cheerfully. Tomas laughed and looked back at him.

'What are you looking for in there?' he asked. 'You're a nosy one aren't you?'

Tomas pulled an apple from his pack, and Merric's horse ate it happily from his hand.

'Nosy,' Merric smiled, patting his horse's neck, 'that'll be your name.'

Fields of crops surrounded them as they continued west. In the northern-most lands of The Yielding there were even olive groves and trees on which exotic fruits grew, such as oranges that were grown from seeds once brought to High Realm from the Northern Kingdoms far beyond the realm's borders. The farmers of The Yielding provided not only for the inhabitants of The Head, but for much of the rest of High Realm as well. The Head was vital to High Realm because of its fertile lands, and Merric wondered if this was maybe why the Monforts wanted it for themselves.

Many little blue streams trickled across the land, supplying the fields with fresh water, and in the summer sun Merric would have loved to splash in the cool water. It was much nicer to be surrounded by the picturesque fields with the blue sky over their heads, rather than being surrounded by nothing but trees.

Ana seemed to be the only one not happy to be out of the Greenwood.

'We're very exposed, crossing this land,' she pointed out.

'True, girl,' Kasper answered, 'but so will our pursuers. I have keen eyes; we'll spot them long before they see us.'

Despite his confidence, Ana was not convinced.

As they rode along a simple, rutted track used mainly by farmers and their wagons, Merric once again brought his horse alongside Kasper's.

'How is it you came to be so skilled with a bow?' he asked him. He wanted to learn as much as he could about the man.

'The Conways bid that all boys from the age of seven practice with a bow at least two hours every week,' Kasper replied. 'Just in case he ever needed us to march to war for him.'

Lord Tymon Conway ruled his barony from the castle of Bridge Ford, which sat on the eastern bank of The Rush. It stood on the Great East Road, by the many-arched bridge which crossed the great river that gave the castle its name. Most barons in The Head, and in the rest of High Realm too, had a similar practice of training men to wield weapons, ready for when they needed them to fight. Few could afford to keep a large army all the time, so most would ensure that all able-bodied men in their lands were trained and able to join his army should he ever need to march to war. In times like this, common folk may be called upon by his baron to fight, either for the baron himself or for their duke. In return the barons protected the folk in their lands and looked out for their interests. Merric could understand Kasper's bitterness about Lord Tymon Conway not fulfilling his duty as a baron.

Merric wondered what his own father had been like as a baron. He hoped that Lord Willarm Orrell had been generous and kind, as Lord Roberd had been. Before Ryding had been destroyed, had the folk in Lord Willarm's lands been well looked after? Did the folk look up to him, or was he disrespected and disliked as Lord Tymon was?

There were five barons in total in The Head, each ruling their lands in the name of Lord Roberd, though Merric supposed that they now served the new duke, Rayden Monfort. As well as Lord Tymon Conway of

Bridge Ford and Lord Osworth Velion of Elderwyne, Sir Gerard's brother, there was elderly Lord Horin Oakheart of Oaktyn, who lands included The Yielding where they were now. Lord Arran Lyn of Lynport was baron of the lands on the shores of the Eastern Sea, while Lord Temothy Bloom, known as the Hornsword, ruled the mountainous lands on the northern border of The Head. Of course once there had been a sixth baron, Lord Willarm Orrell of Ryding. Now, the lands that had once been the Orrell's lay empty.

The farm track that Merric and his companions were now travelling along wove between fields thick with wheat that grew taller than Merric had ever seen before, towering over their heads even whilst on horseback. Merric began to feel nervous and blinded by the tall crops, and out of the corner of his eye he could see that Ana's hands were never far from her crossbow. Kasper seemed unconcerned though, and continued to walk his horse down the track.

A few hours later Kasper held up a hand when they reached a small crossroads, where a wider farm road crossed the track along which they were travelling. Merric strained his ears, trying to hear what had alerted Kasper, and could hear the faint sound of men singing. It was coming from south of them, along the larger road. From where he stood on the crossroads, the tall wheat stopped Merric from being able to see far down the road to the south, so could not tell who the singing voices belonged to. He looked nervously at Kasper, wondering what they should do. The poacher did nothing, except cock his head and listen. Merric glanced back at Ana.

'Should we get out of sight?' Ana asked Kasper.

He did not move, and the voices were getting closer.

'Come on,' Ana muttered to the others, dismounting and leading her horse off the track and into the wheat. Merric and Tomas followed her. 'Kasper, quickly' she said, 'in here!'

Still the poacher did not move, and stayed atop his horse in the middle of the crossroads.

'He's going to betray us,' Ana said, watching through the stalks of wheat and raising her crossbow. But she did not pull the trigger.

All of a sudden a group of men appeared around a corner of the road fifty paces away. Merric watched them, trying to make out who they were. A man in full plate armour and riding a large horse led twenty soldiers, who sang together as they marched along behind him with their spears over their shoulders.

Kasper raised his hand in greeting, and by now Merric could see that they weren't Monfort men.

Their shields and the knight's surcoat were yellow, and displayed the symbol of the bumble bee. It was the symbol of the Ashbee family, a minor noble family who had a small castle in Lord Horin Oakheart's lands. Merric let out a sigh of relief, and realised that he should have known that the Ashbee family's castle stood near here. He had looked at the map in Lord Roberd's study enough times.

As the Ashbee men neared the crossroads, the knight looked across at Kasper.

'Hello there! To where do you travel, may I ask?' he called.

'To Little Harrow,' Kasper replied.

At that moment, Merric, Ana and Tomas emerged from the wheat and joined Kasper. The knight's face showed amusement.

'And what were you up to in there?'

His eyes passed over Merric and Tomas, but did a double take when he saw Ana. He reined in his horse when he reached them, and his soldiers came to a halt.

'You're Danell the blacksmith's daughter,' he said with surprise. 'Your father was of service to me the day before Lord Roberd's tournament at Eagle Mount not long ago; my horse had thrown a shoe. My name is Sir Amalric Ashbee. I'll be honest, I had not imagined seeing you here in the South Yielding.'

Ana remembered the knight. It had been she herself who had re-shoed his horse. She looked apologetically at him.

'Yes I remember, Sir. But it's probably best that you pretended you hadn't seen me, or any of us,' she said.

Sir Amalric looked at her companions, and his eyes settled on Merric.

'I understand,' he said, realising who Merric was. 'You had best be on your way, and quickly. We've had reports that Monfort men are heading in this direction. I'm

199

taking my men to block the road. No Monfort man will come to my castle uninvited and force me to bend the knee to the so-called new Duke of The Head.'

He spat onto the dusty road and cursed Rayden Monfort's name.

Ana and Tomas looked anxiously at Merric. They had just about convinced Merric to give up his idea of fighting back against the Monforts. Finding this knight who wanted to fight them might be enough to make Merric go back to his old way of thinking. Sir Amalric had little power though, being from a minor noble family. He would only have a handful of men at his command, and his small castle was little more than a thick-walled house, and so would not be able to defend itself against the strength of the Monforts.

'Don't,' Merric said after a moment's pause, to everyone's surprise. 'You can't win, Sir.'

'When honour calls, winning doesn't matter,' Sir Amalric replied proudly. 'I won't shame my baron or the memory of my duke by allowing these invaders to walk all over me.'

'By now your baron, Lord Horin Oakheart, will probably have already sworn not to take up arms against the Monforts. Doing the same would not cost you your honour, Sir,' Ana said.

'And Lord Roberd is dead,' Merric continued, swallowing the pain that the words caused. 'Getting yourself and your men killed as well won't help that.'

Ana looked proudly at her friend, for having the strength to say that. What Sir Amalric was planning to do was no different to what Merric had wanted to do himself that night in Eaglestone.

Sir Amalric frowned at them all, while his soldiers looked nervously at each other. Merric's words had made sense to them. They were loyal to their knight, but had no desire to throw their lives away for no reason. Eventually, Sir Amalric's face broke into a soft smile.

'I see your lips move,' he said to Merric, 'but it's Lord Roberd's words that come out. You're as wise as he was.'

As Sir Amalric turned his horse and gestured for his men to begin marching back the way they had come, Ana called to him.

'Forget you saw us,' she reminded, 'it's better that way.'

'Saw who?' Sir Amalric replied, peering from side to side in mock confusion, before grinning. 'May the Mother watch over you all. And Merric, I hope we meet again one day.'

With Sir Amalric on his way back to Ashbee Castle, Merric and the others crossed over the farm road and continued west. It had been good to meet Sir Amalric, to know that they were not alone. It pained Merric to admit that fighting back would be fruitless, but he knew it would be the right choice. He did not want more death on his hands, and Sir Amalric and his men opposing the Monforts could only have one result.

After several hours more hours of riding, as the sun was sinking in the sky, the wheat ended to be replaced with fields of potatoes, cabbages and carrots that stretched as far as the eye could see. The Greenwood was a long way behind them now, nothing more than a green smudge on the distant horizon.

'There's a farm, not too far away from here,' Kasper said to them. 'We'll be safe there for this night. The farmer is honest, and hates anyone not from The Head. He'll be having no love for the Monfort's rule, so we can trust he won't be in league with them.'

'How do you know about this farmer?' Merric asked.

'He was a friend of my father's. He'll be old now, but I've heard he's still living, and his ways won't have changed at all. I haven't seen him in years, and it's likely he won't recognise me. I don't plan on letting him know who I am though, nor who you are. It's safer for us all that way.'

'Maybe we should keep going, and make camp somewhere,' Ana suggested, wanting to avoid any unnecessary contact with folk.

'They'll have shelter,' Kasper said, insisting. 'We'll stay there for the night.'

Following Kasper's guidance, they soon came across a modest cottage. Beside it were a small barn and a yard containing a stone well and some chickens which allowed to wander freely. A dog, which had been dozing in the early evening sun, was alerted to their approach and began barking, prompting an aged farmer to emerge from the cottage to investigate.

'Quiet, boy,' the farmer said when he saw the strangers approaching on their horses. He took a scythe from where it leant against the cottage wall.

The dog fell silent, but watched the newcomers with wary eyes. The farmer strode forwards to meet the travellers, stopping a few yards away from them, and leant on the scythe. The tool was used to cut down wheat, but made for a threatening weapon.

'Who might you be?' he asked them.

Kasper reined in his horse, and looked over his shoulder to indicate that the others should do the same. He turned back and replied to the farmer, keeping his arms away from his body to show that he meant no harm.

'We're simple travellers, journeying across your land. With your permission, of course. We mean you no trouble.'

The farmer nodded. 'Land is land. Who am I to say you can't travel across it? And what could I do to stop you? I'm an old man' He laughed.

Looking at the wicked long blade on the scythe, Merric was sure the old man could do quite a lot to stop them if he wanted to.

'Are you easterners?' the farmer asked, suddenly serious.

'We're from The Head, yes,' Kasper said.

'Good, good,' the farmer replied with a toothless smile. He seemed to be a kindly man. 'Do you seek shelter for the night?'

'And something hot to eat,' Tomas piped up.

Kasper gave Tomas a stern look, but the farmer just laughed.

'The boy is honest,' the farmer said, 'can't say fairer than that. You can sleep in my barn, but I want no trouble and you're to be gone at first light.'

'Who is it, Hary?' a woman's voice called from the cottage.

'Simple travellers, apparently,' Hary the farmer called back, 'put some extra vegetables in the soup, Grid.'

Tomas's eyes lit up and he licked his lips.

'We can provide some food for the cooking pot,' Merric said, 'we have plenty.'

'That would be most welcome,' Hary said. 'Come, inside. You can tie your horses outside the barn, and leave your weapons there as well. I won't have weapons in my house.'

They stowed their horses and left their weapons as requested, and followed Hary into his cottage. It was small, but warm and friendly. The main room contained a large fire, over which hung a large iron pot. A portly woman was tipping vegetables into the pot as they entered. Smoke coiled around the ceiling, before disappearing up through the chimney.

'This is Ingrid, my wife, and that outside was Chicken. A strange name for a dog I know, but instead of chasing chickens around like a normal pooch he just follows them around. I reckon he thinks he's one of them,' Hary said. 'I won't ask you for your names, as I wouldn't expect you to tell me them anyway. There's been lots of strange folk around the past few days, and some stranger tales coming from the east; Lord Roberd dead, and Southerners ruling in their place. I've lived on this good land for seventy-four years, the Mother be praised, and I never thought I'd see such a thing. Of course, you must know this already. If you don't then you must have been living under a stump somewhere. Mind you, you look strange enough…'

'We've heard the rumours, yes,' Kasper said, not wanting to say more.

'I've been around long enough to have outlived Aric Monfort's father, and his grandfather too. They're tyrants and rogues, the lot of them. If I was five years younger I'd have a mind to dig out my sword and give the Monforts my mind.'

Ingrid scoffed.

'Alright then,' Hary said, 'if I was twenty-five years younger.'

Ana gave the farmer's wife some of the meat from their packs to add to the soup, and soon after Ingrid spooned the broth into their bowls. After they had eaten,

Hary took them back to his barn, where he showed them the stack of hay which he said they could sleep on.

'It's no feather mattress,' the old farmer admitted, 'but it's better than the hard ground.'

They thanked him for his kindness, but he waved it off, saying it was no hardship on him. He told them to take the saddles off their horses and store them along with their weapons in the barn with them. There was no room in the small barn for the horses too, so they would need to stay outside. As they settled down for the night, Merric and the others listened to the sounds of the chickens in the yard outside. The noises were oddly comforting to Merric, and he felt his heavy eyelids begin to droop. Just as he was falling asleep though, he heard a new noise, one that caused his heart to quicken.

Quiet at first, but getting louder and louder, he heard a soft drumming sound. He laid there in silence, his ears pricked, listening to hear if the hoof beats would pass the farm. But, as he had half expected, the horses slowed and then stopped at the farm.

'Wake up,' Merric whispered to his companions.

Kasper had not been asleep, but Ana and Tomas required a shake to rouse them.

'What's wrong?' Tomas asked, too loudly, and then clapped his hand over his mouth when Merric put his finger to his lips. 'Who is it?' the boy whispered when he heard the neighing of the newly arrived horses.

Merric was sure that he knew who the visitors were. He only needed one guess. The barn had no door, so Kasper crept around the old broken down wagon that was parked in the centre of the barn so that he could peer out into the yard.

'Monfort yeomen,' he mouthed back at Merric, confirming their fears.

Chicken began barking, and shortly after came the sound of Hary's voice.

'Hey, this is my farm! What business have you got here in the dead of night?'

'We're looking for a boy,' came the gruff voice of the serjeant who led the yeomen. 'We've had reports of him heading this way.'

Orange light flickered through the gaps in the wooden walls of the barn, from the burning torches held by the Monfort men.

Merric's eyes snapped to Kasper, as did Ana's. Kasper had certainly been keen for them to stay the night in this farm. Had he known the Monforts would come this way?

'That sounds fun for you. Why are you bothering me with this?' Hary said in reply. 'There's no boys here, just me and my wife.'

Chicken barked.

'Yes, and my dog too, as you can see.'

The serjeant was not satisfied. 'He may not be travelling alone. We found some of our own men dead in the Greenwood. They're dangerous criminals. Have you seen them?'

'No, I'm afraid not.'

'Whose horses are those?' a new voice exclaimed.

'Mine,' Hary said, 'I use them to pull my wagon to Oaktyn. That's where I sell my crops.'

Merric looked at the wagon in the barn. It was old and the wood was rotten. If one of the Monfort men got a good look at it, he would see that it had not been used in years.

'Now, do you mind if you leave me to return to my bed?' Hary said.

'What's your hurry, old man?' the serjeant asked.

'I am indeed an old man, like you say, and I feel the cold in my bones,' Hary admitted. 'This chilly night air does nothing to help with my knee. I was on the wrong end of a Ouestorian axe at the Battle of King's Keep, and it's not been the same ever since. Now, good night to you, sirs.'

'Now wait a moment, come back here! If you have nothing to hide then you won't mind if we search your house and barn.'

Merric looked hard at Kasper, and slowly drew his sword. If the poacher had been planning to betray them then the moment had come. Ana likewise quietly pulled her knife from its sheath, ready to stop him if he tried to call out to the Monfort yeomen. Kasper looked back at them both, confusion in his eyes as he saw them pointing their weapons at him.

'I would mind very much,' the old farmer countered. 'I live in The Head, under the protection of Lord Horin Oakheart. You're a long way from The Citadel, and you can't order me to do anything.'

'Careful,' the serjeant warned, 'my men would kill you in an instant if I ordered it, and there's no one who could stop us.'

Merric continued to glare at Kasper, who continued to look back at him with curious eyes. The poacher made no move to call out to the Monfort men.

Hary did not seem concerned by the Monfort serjeant's threats.

'I hear your duke's whelp rules Eagle Mount now. Jacelyn or Monfort, whoever rules needs my crops to help feed The Head. If you kill me then thousands will go hungry, and you'll have an uprising on your hands. If a revolt sounds like fun to you, then go ahead.'

There were a few moments of silence as the yeoman serjeant weighed this up.

'Have it your way,' he said, knowing that he was defeated. The sound of hooves told Merric that the yeomen were leaving, but the serjeant stopped and turned his horse back to the farmer.

'The boy we're searching for is Merric Orrell. He's an outlaw, wanted for the murder of the Jacelyns. If you see him, or hear of his whereabouts, then you find us and let us know.'

'Right you are,' Hary said.

Merric and his companions sighed a breath of relief when they heard the hoof beats of the yeomen disappear into the night. The light from their torches faded, before disappearing completely.

Hary appeared at the entrance to the barn, his face lit up by the burning torch that he held out in front of him. He knew that his visitors had overheard his conversation with the yeomen.

'If what they say is true,' he said, 'then I should hand you over to them.'

Merric felt Ana stiffen beside him, her knife still in her hand.

'But I've never trusted the word of a man not of The Head before, and I don't plan on starting now. However, I don't want no trouble on my farm, so I want you gone before I get up in the morning.'

The old farmer and his torch disappeared, plunging the barn once more into darkness.

* * *

Rayden Monfort looked up at the colossal stained-glass window, depicting Jace on his giant eagle. Behind him, the Grand Hall of Eagle Mount was still and silent and filled with shadows. Ever since he had killed Roberd Jacelyn and his family the castle had seemed cold and empty, as though all life had been taken from it. This suited

Rayden though, who was more happy with his own thoughts than with the company of others.

He could not help but admire the huge window, cut from thousands of pieces of glass of many colours. Even in The Southstones, Jace was admired as a hero, and Rayden felt a small surge of honour to be standing in the place where Jace himself had stood a thousand years ago. It was said that on his giant eagle, Jace was able to inspire the whole realm, unifying them all with his mere presence. It was said that in the years following the arrival of the first king, it had been Jace that had held the fledging realm together, not King Eldred.

Rayden brushed the thoughts aside quickly, and reminded himself that Jace was ancient history. He was glad to have rid the realm of the Jacelyns, Jace's weak descendants.

His hand stroked the hilt of the sword that Rayden carried at his waist, remembering fondly the memory of the lives he had taken with it in this very castle. Already the folk right across High Realm admired him as a fine swordsman, and soon they would learn to fear and respect him too.

'You disappoint me, my son.'

Rayden turned, and was annoyed to see that he was no longer alone. Lord Aric was striding up the length of the Grand Hall, followed by his bald-headed and scarred henchman. Rayden let Aric walk all the way up the length of the hall to him before answering.

'I disappoint you, father?'

Aric looked at his son. For the benefit of their former hosts he had put on the guise of proud and loving father, but with Roberd gone he had no reason to pretend any longer.

'I would have hoped to have seen some results from you by now, but I see this was too much to expect from you.'

Rayden looked moodily away from his father's disapproving eyes.

'The library is vast, and the Arch Prior here is being...uncooperative,' he replied.

'My heir, foiled by some books and a dusty old man,' Aric mocked. 'Perhaps it would be better if I carried out this task myself.'

'No father,' Rayden said, stepping closer. His pride was hurt. 'I can do it. You won't regret giving me this task.'

Aric raised a fist, and Rayden flinched as he had done as a child whenever his father had beaten him. While Aric's fist did not touch him, Rayden could see the menace and the threat in the gesture.

'Make sure I don't,' Aric said, and he lowered his fist again.

'Have you had any word on the Orrell boy?' Rayden asked, taking the opportunity to change the subject.

'He heads west. Once I return to The Citadel he will be yours to deal with, if you can manage it. You must be sure that he is silenced, permanently. By sword would be preferable, but him fleeing will be proof enough to the simple folk of The Head that he's guilty, and then his voice will lose all worth anyway.'

'Yes,' Rayden agreed. 'If he thinks he can stop us then he is sorely mistaken. He will soon learn than none can resist the power of the Monforts. He saw me strike down his beloved Tristan, and would wet his breeches if he dared to oppose me.'

Aric ignored his son's bravado, and spotted the decorative shields of the barons of The Head that hung along the wall.

'Why have they not yet been removed?' he asked.

'My apologies,' Rayden said, 'I'll see it done at once.'

Aric smirked. 'With your hold over The Head not yet assured, why bother?'

'With Roberd and his heir gone, if the barons chose to resist us they would be nothing more than irritating wasps on a summer day. They cannot do anything to oppose us. Nothing will stand in the way of your plans. Still, the barons will all be under our control soon.'

'That's something I'd rather not leave to chance,' Aric said. 'I'll send my own man to sway them, and bring them under Monfort rule.'

The scarred knight stepped forward at his duke's mention. Aric looked hard into his son's eyes.

'He will stay with you to make sure you don't suffer any further setbacks. It's a sad day when a father cannot trust his son to do his bidding. Don't continue to disappoint me.'

'I won't, father,' Rayden said.

With one last disgusted look at his son, Aric turned and walked away. Rayden swallowed away his hurt pride. He looked at the scarred knight.

'See to the Velions first, and then the Oakhearts,' Rayden said to him, 'they're the strongest of the barons. The others will swear their loyalty easily enough once they've seen them bend the knee.'

The knight looked coldly at Rayden.

'You don't order me,' he growled. 'I'm your father's man, not your lap dog. I do as Lord Aric asks, not you.'

The knight left the Grand Hall in Aric's wake.

Rayden turned back to the image of Jace and his giant eagle. He clasped his hands behind his back, trying to control his rage. His father spoke to him like he was still a child, and even that jumped-up barbarian who his father had knighted all those years ago looked down on him too. Rayden had done much to make his father proud, but Aric never thought him worthy as an heir. To Aric, Rayden was just a tool to be used to achieve his aims; a face to win favour, and a sword to strike death, always to remain in his father's shadow.

Rayden would not fail in the task given to him though, and he would make the Monfort family more powerful than any of his ancestors ever had.

And then his father would see his quality.

- CHAPTER ELEVEN -

The grip tightens

The sunrise filled the eastern sky with a brilliant orange, which slowly turned the blackness of night into the light of dawn, but Merric and his companions had their backs to this sight as they headed ever further west. As requested by Hary, they had left the farm a couple of hours before dawn, and had not seen the old farmer or his wife. Tomas had given Chicken a pat on the head, and the dog had growled happily at his touch.

'Why didn't you tell Hary the truth?' Tomas asked as they rode.

'That I'm innocent, and that Lord Roberd was murdered by the Monforts, not me?' Merric replied. 'What would that have gained us?'

'He might have helped us, if he knew.'

'If he had helped us, and the Monfort men found out, then they would have killed him for sure. Ingrid too,' Merric explained. 'I'm not putting more in danger; enough have died for me already. No more will.'

The land they passed through was still filled with fields and farms, but the ground was growing hillier. The track they were following twisted and turned, seeking the best route through the hills and valleys that dominated this side of The Yielding. The fields of crops, orchards and vineyards clung to the sides of the hills, with the farmers eager to make use of every space of this fertile land. Ahead of them, dominating the skyline, rose a range of low but rocky and impassable mountains that lay across their path.

'Those are the Pink Hills,' Kasper said, pointing. He had not mentioned what had happened the night before, and Merric had not brought up the subject either. The fact that Kasper had not made their presence known to the Monforts did not prove that he was not in league with them. If he did intend to bring harm to Merric, then at least he now knew that Merric and Ana were on to him.

'That is where the realm was saved, during the Dark Days,' Merric marvelled, forgetting his concerns and looking in wonder at the Pink Hills.

He knew of the mountains, but had never been this close to them before. Six hundred years ago war had broken out within High Realm. The cause of this war had long been forgotten, along with who had started it. Baron had fought against baron, and duke against duke. The conflict was on the verge of tearing the realm to pieces, and through this chaos the savage Reavers sailed their longships up The Rush. They were a barbaric folk, from the cold, harsh icy wastes beyond High Realm's southern border. They put the countryside to the torch, and castles and towns alike fell to their cruelty. With High Realm facing its destruction, the lords put aside their differences to unite against this common enemy. It was here, on the lower slopes of the Pink Hills, where the lords of The Head, united once more under the leadership of the twelfth Duke of Eagle Mount, Lord Lowan Jacelyn, fought off the Reavers and managed to push them back. With their success, the other dukedoms were inspired and united their own warring barons, and the Reavers were forced all the way back to their cold homeland. For his part in saving the realm, Lord Lowan had been given the title *The Sword of the East*. It was something his ancestors had been proud of ever since.

'You know your history,' Kasper observed. 'My village lies just beyond those mountains.'

'Then we're nearly there,' Merric said with relief.

Kasper shook his head. 'The Pink Hills are steep and impassable, thick with rocks and covered in rough gorse and heather. It's that what gives the hills their name. We can't cross them, so we'll have to go around. They stretch for fifty leagues to the south,' he said, 'but to the north it's less; a few days ride at most.'

'Then we'll head north?' Merric said.

'We will, but that will take us close to Oaktyn, which is likely to have a Monfort presence now. We'll have to be on our guard.'

'Are you certain that we can't turn to Lord Horin Oakheart? He was one of Lord Roberd's most trusted barons and friends. He will help me, I'm sure of it.'

'Horin Oakheart is an ancient man, and as near blind as makes no difference,' Kasper answered. 'In any case, I expect he's now a baron in title only. Like as not the Monforts rule his lands now, or soon will, along with the rest of The Head. Our best choice is to stay with the plan that we came up with, the plan that Sir Gerard agreed to. We'll go to my village. The Monforts won't concern themselves with such an unimportant place, so you'll be safe there.'

'And then what?'

'You'll start a new life,' Kasper said simply. 'It might be a far cry from the life you had at the castle, but you'll be alive.'

'Why are you helping us?' Ana blurted out, surprising Kasper.

'I'm a man of my word,' Kasper said, looking irritated that it was being questioned.

'But you only swore to help us in return for Sir Gerard helping your village, and Sir Gerard is gone now.'

'I'm a man of my word,' Kasper repeated. 'Believe me, it would be easier if you weren't with me. After your little game last night it's clear you don't trust me, so feel free to leave me in peace if that's what you desire. I would make far quicker progress on my own, and getting back to my family is all I want.'

Merric, Ana and Tomas did not leave, and stayed with Kasper, following him as they guided him along the track.

They turned north as they reached the foothills of the Pink Hills, following the mountain range as it snaked north. The mountains, while small compared to the Storm Mountains on the northern border of The Head, still dominated the skyline. As the afternoon wore on the shadows of the mountains stretched over them. With the darkness quickly surrounding them they had no choice but to stop for the night. It would not do for one of their horses to stumble on the rocky ground.

They set off again the next morning once it was light enough, but the going was still difficult and at times they were forced to dismount from their horses and guide them on foot across some of the more treacherous areas of rocky ground.

Merric had grown fond of his horse. Nosy seemed as attached to his new master as Merric was to it. He had an innocence that Merric envied, oblivious to the terrible events that had rocked The Head. He wondered what life Nosy had led before he had come into Merric's possession. He had likely come from The Southstones, and Merric reflected that at least not everything from the Monfort family's dukedom was all bad.

In the afternoon the land began to grow less rocky and wild. The steeply angled vineyards that had clung to the uneven ground were replaced by more gentle meadows of flowers of many colours. The Grand Hall of Eagle Mount had often been filled with bunches of brightly coloured flowers, usually at Lady Cathreen's request, and Merric had never before spared a moment to think of where these flowers came from. Most of The Yielding was dedicated to the growing of food for folk to eat, but some parts had to make sure that the luxuries enjoyed by the noble folk were provided for.

The mountainous high ground to the west of them continued, and their heights remained rocky and barren, except for the thick patches of heather that covered the high hills. Merric knew Kasper was right when he said it would be impossible to pass through these mountains, even though it would make the journey far shorter. He wondered what it would have been like for Lord Lowan, all those hundreds of years ago, when he was leading all the men he could find towards those hills, ready to fight one last, desperate battle against the terrifying bloodthirsty Reavers. Those southern men wore their beards long and thick and wild, and would drink a potion before a fight to make themselves mad with bloodlust. Merric shuddered, and was thankful that he lived in a more civilised place than they did.

There was no track which led the way they now journeyed, so they cut across the rolling grassy fields. Rather than the neat rows of crops seen in the fields up until now, there was less order here. The crops seemed to spring up in the grassy meadows at random, as though the farmers had not wanted to disturb anything that was already growing. Tall bushes covered in flowers rose up around them, and birds sung from the many trees that dotted the landscape. Ana told them that it is said that the few folk who live around here are firm believers of The Lady of the Lake. Every tree, bush and flower were her children, so no tree would ever be cut down nor bush removed to make room for their fields. It was not a crime, in their eyes, to grow their crops and harvest it, as The Lady understood that this was the way of things. There was a need for crops to be eaten, but to cut down the trees that were already there was a selfish act.

This was an area largely untouched by man, with few roads, settlements or farms in sight, only the pleasant grassy meadows that stretched on for miles and shone in the summer sun. A bright orange butterfly fluttered from a bush next to them, disturbed by the passing horses. It flew over and landed on Ana's outstretch hand, where it perched happily enough. She looked at the butterfly with affection, and kept her hand still so as not to disturb it whilst she rode. Eventually her arm began to ache, forcing her to regretfully put her hand back on the reins. The butterfly danced back into the air, and circled her for a few minutes before spying some more bushes and flying over to them instead.

As the sun soared above them in the sky they heard the soft rushing of water. The day was the hottest of the year so far, and their mouths were dry, so they followed the sound of the stream, eager for a drink. The sound drew them into a large copse of trees, which contained a clearing featuring a spectacular waterfall. The stream was narrow, a man could step over it with ease, but over thousands of years it had carved the tall waterfall which fell thirty feet into a clear, blue pool below.

Merric and the others dismounted from their horses and carefully picked a route down through the trees to the pool. There they gladly removed their boots and rolled up the legs of their breeches, before wading knee-deep into the cool water.

Ana scooped up some water with both hands and threw it over Merric, who responded by splashing her back. Tomas laughed until he lost his footing, disappearing beneath the water. A second later he emerged, spluttering, much to his friends' amusement. He laughed with them, and soon all three were splashing around in the pool, forgetting their troubles and acting, for the first time in days, like the children that they were. Kasper leant against a nearby tree, shaking his head with a smile. Sometimes he forgot how young his travelling companions truly were.

They decided to camp in the clearing that night, and one by one they fell asleep with the soothing sound of the waterfall in their ears. As ever, Kasper remained awake, sat alone at the top of the waterfall. The poacher only seemed to need a few hours of sleep each night, and was always at full alert, listening and looking for any signs of danger.

As with any pleasant sleep, morning seemed to come too soon. It was dawn when Merric felt himself being shaken awake again by Kasper. The poacher's face looked tired and drawn, but his eyes were wide awake as always. They had a quick breakfast, packed up their things, and were soon on their way again. Oaktyn was ahead of them, and once past it they were onto the final step of their journey.

Oaktyn was a very old town, first settled soon after Jace had built Eagle Mount. The Oakhearts of Oaktyn had always been loyal subjects of the Jacelyns, but Lord Horin, who currently ruled the Oakheart lands, was now old and frail. He had two grown up sons, strong knights both, but Merric knew that Kasper was right; like the rest of the barons, Lord Horin lacked the strength and power to oppose Aric and the Monfort armies. To protect their folk, his only option would therefore be to bow down to their new masters. Honour and pride did not compare to ensuring the safety of the folk who depended on their baron. Merric and his companions therefore had no choice but to continue past Oaktyn, and accept that they would not be able to receive any assistance from the Oakhearts.

They reached the edge Oaktyn in the afternoon, but being summer there were many hours of daylight left. The Pink Hills came to an end at last, and a wide, low valley opened up in front of the travellers. The Great East Road stretched east and west down the length of the valley, disappearing off towards the distant Greenwood in one direction and The Rush and the border of The Head in the other. At the centre of the valley, built inside the curve of a small but fast flowing river, was the town. Oaktyn sat directly on the Great East Road, and so over the centuries had benefitted from the wealth of passing travellers. The town had prospered. The homes and inns were built from stone rather than wood, as was seen in most towns and villages in this part of High Realm, and at the very centre of town stood an ancient oak tree. In times of winter the tree looked cruel and harsh, its bare branches gnarled and unfriendly, but in the height of summer it was clothed in green leaves and made a pleasant centrepiece to the town.

It was not known which came first, the tree or the town, but it was widely believed by most townsfolk that if the tree was ever to fall then a great misfortune would descend upon them all. It was beneath the branches of this great tree that it was said that Jace had first kissed his beloved Lyn, who he went on to make his wife.

The oak tree was positioned on a wide green, beside which the castle and home of the Oakheart family had been built. Its ancient stone walls rose in a high circle, around a stout but strong keep. The castle was small compared to Eagle Mount, but still the fortress dominated the town. It was built from the same strong grey stone as the rest of Oaktyn, and no enemy had ever taken the castle. As was customary in High Realm, to the left of the gates of the castle hung the long green banner bearing the symbol of an oak tree of the Oakheart family, while to the right of the gate hung the banner of the duke the baron served. This banner was still sky blue and bore the golden eagle.

Merric and his companions stood at the top of a rise and looked at the town in the low valley before them.

'They're still flying the Jacelyn banner,' Merric said, squinting. 'What does that mean?'

'It doesn't mean anything. Proud old Horin may still be loyal to the Jacelyns, but it just simply means that the Monforts haven't yet forced him to bring the banner down,' Kasper replied.

'I want to go down there,' Merric said

Kasper looked across at him.

'No chance. We head west from here, now that we've reached the northern end of the Pink Hills. My village is just a day's ride. We can follow the Great East Road west for a couple of hours, before turning south.'

'But these are Lord Roberd's folk, look at his banner. I want to know they're safe,' Merric said.

'They'll be safe if they don't do anything stupid. There's nothing we can do. It's too dangerous.'

'It's looking quiet down there,' Tomas observed, peering at the town.

'It doesn't look like Aric's men have taken control of Oaktyn yet,' Merric agreed, 'they must still be looking for me back in The Yielding and the Greenwood. I just want to have a look. I won't make myself known, I swear.'

Kasper leaned forward on his saddle and frowned at Merric for a moment.

'Fine,' he said eventually, suggesting that Merric's fate was of no concern of his. 'Ana, you seem to have some sense in that head of yours. Go with him, and make sure he stays out of trouble.'

'I want to go with you too,' Tomas said to Merric.

'No you stay here with Kasper,' Merric said. 'We won't be long.

'Just get in, have a look, and then get out again,' Kasper said. 'We'll wait for you at the western edge of the town. If you're not there in an hour then I'm continuing on my way. I'm not waiting around for you.'

Merric and Ana left their horses with the poacher and made their way down towards Oaktyn. They soon came across a farm track which led into the town, and they followed it. Oaktyn was not surrounded by walls, so they had no trouble entering the town without drawing attention to themselves.

The townsfolk they passed did not give them a second glance. They were used to seeing strangers pass through Oaktyn, and Merric and Ana looked like any other travellers in their worn clothes and the travel cloaks they had taken from Mortin's baggage. The townsfolk went about their day as normal, and Merric was reminded of the folk of Eaglestone on market day. They passed two Oakheart soldiers, with an oak tree symbol stitched onto the breast of their padded coats and green shields slung over their backs. They chatted casually as they walked, and the sight of them reassured Merric that this town was yet to be brought under the Monfort's tightening grip. A baker was selling freshly baked bread, and the smell made their mouths water. Ana had brought a few coins with her when they had fled Eaglestone, and she used some coppers to purchase a small loaf. They ate the warm bread as they walked towards the centre of the town. Some townsfolk began hurrying past them, heading in the direction of the green. Curious, Merric and Ana followed them.

All of a sudden the pleasant atmosphere of the town faded, and the folk seemed to be gripped by nervousness. Going with the flow of people, Merric and Ana turned a corner and saw the ancient oak tree ahead of them. A crowd was forming on the green beneath the branches of the oak, and Merric forced his way to the front, wondering what was happening.

Before him stood the squat castle home of the Oakhearts. A group of Oakheart soldiers stood around outside the gates, peering worriedly up the Great East Road that ran past the castle. At a word from the serjeant leading them, one of the men hurried back through the castle gate and disappeared. Merric frowned, wondering what was going on. All of a sudden Ana grabbed hold of his arm, pulling him back into the safety of the crowd.

'What-,' Merric began, but he choked on his next words.

A column of horsemen galloped into the green from the east. They were Monfort soldiers, fully armed and mounted on powerful warhorses. A man at the front of the column carried a large white banner bearing the black marching knight. Beside him rode the tall bald-headed knight with the scarred face from Merric's nightmares, and who had been there that night when Tristan had been murdered. Merric felt his blood freeze at the sight of him. He and Ana tugged up the hoods of their cloaks.

The townsfolk all took a step back away from these new arrivals, and looked with fear at the gruesomely scarred knight who led them. Aric and his men would have passed through Oaktyn on their journey to Eaglestone all that time ago, but their passing would have been peaceful. These men, though, looked fierce and threatening, and rode with their weapons drawn.

The scarred knight reined in his horse in front of the gates of the Oakheart castle, and his men gathered around behind him on the green, the hooves of their horses churning the grass into dust. The nervous Oakheart soldiers guarding the gate took a few steps backward, unsure of what to do. They half-heartedly levelled their spears at the new arrivals, but it was a futile gesture; if the Monfort men charged they'd ride straight over the handful of Oakheart soldiers without even breaking their stride.

'Come out, old man!' the scarred knight called, his voice loud and harsh.

It was the first time Merric had heard him speak. His accent was strange, not from anywhere in High Realm.

The gathered townsfolk murmured, shocked at hearing their baron addressed in such a way. Lord Horin was well respected, and had ruled these lands for longer than most of them had been alive. The faces of the Oakheart soldiers went from nervous to downright scared, and Merric could see their spears shaking in their hands.

For several minutes there was no reply from the castle, except for the appearance of several crossbow-armed soldiers on the battlements above the gate, who took one look at the Monfort soldiers below and disappeared again. At last, just as the scarred knight appeared to grow bored, the gate of the castle swung open with a creak. Lord Horin Oakheart walked slowly from the castle towards where the Monfort men waited. He struggled in his old age, and his arm was supported by a tall, strong man, clad in full plate armour with a green surcoat beating the oak tree of the Oakhearts. A second man, identically dressed and just as huge, accompanied the baron on his other side. Behind them strode ten soldiers, one carrying the green Oakheart banner.

Lord Horin stopped in front of the scarred knight, his back bent and his breathing heavy. The knight remained sitting atop his horse, and did not dismount to greet the older man as was High Realm custom. Lord Horin glanced at the Monfort soldiers who sat idly behind the knight with their weapons drawn.

'May I ask your name, Sir, who means to threaten me outside my own keep?' Lord Horin asked, his voice weak but proud.

'Mind your own business,' the knight growled. 'I'm here on the orders of Lord Rayden Monfort, Duke of The Head.'

'Since courtesy is unknown to you,' Lord Horin said, 'allow me to make our introductions; Sir Oskar Oakheart and Sir Orsten Oakheart; my sons. I am Lord Horin Oakheart, Baron of Oaktyn and servant of Lord Roberd Jacelyn, Duke of The Head.'

Merric was impressed by the elderly baron's courage. He was a man well past his prime, and the men before him without a doubt intended him harm.

'I ask you again,' Lord Horin repeated, while the scarred knight just smirked at him, 'what is your name? And what brings you here, with so armed a company? As you can see, I do not even wear my sword.' He spread his arms to show that he carried no blade.

'You think speaking well will make a difference with me? You old fool,' the knight said, spitting at their feet. 'Go and fetch your blade, let's see if your ancient arms could hold the weight.'

Whilst his brother pulled their elderly father back a step to avoid the glob of phlegm, Sir Orsten Oakheart wrenched his sword from its scabbard and held it out before him. It was a vast blade, two-handed and taller than Merric. Sir Orsten wore his hair short, and the beginning of a beard covered his jaw, whereas Sir Oskar was clean shaven and had hair down to his shoulders. But that was where the differences in their appearances ended. Both brothers were near to seven feet tall, with muscles to match their height. They were twins, equally skilled with swords in their hands, however while Sir Orsten chose to strike first and ask questions later, his brother preferred to use his mind if it could avoid bloodshed.

'How dare you!' Sir Orsten roared, pointing his sword at the scarred knight. 'You dare to insult my father. You watch your words, Sir. You speak to Lord Horin of Oaktyn, a baron of The Head.'

The scarred knight just laughed.

'And I speak for Lord Rayden Monfort,' he leant forward in his saddle, '*Duke of The Head.*'

Sir Orsten tightened his grip on his sword, and glared at the knight. The scarred man smiled at the effect his words were having, knowing that if Sir Orsten tried to strike him then the Monfort soldiers would kill him before his sword reached its target. The scarred knight eventually looked away from Sir Orsten and addressed the crowd that was assembled.

'I'm here to receive your baron's oath of fealty, and to hear him announce his loyalty to Lord Rayden, your new duke.'

Lord Horin shrugged off Sir Oskar's hand, and took a step forward. His eyes were failing him, his sight almost gone, but he looked directly into the scarred knight's cold, grey eyes.

'You want me to swear allegiance to the family who murdered my duke?'

'You've got it wrong,' the scarred knight said, still smiling, 'he were murdered by the boy in his keeping. The whelp was hungry for power and blamed Lord Roberd for failing to save his parents' lives, all those years ago. If it hadn't been for Lord Rayden stopping him, the boy would have succeeded in taking Eagle Mount and The Head for himself.'

Merric felt his blood boil, and his hands clenched at his sides. He could not bear to hear the scarred knight speak of his parents, seeing as, if his nightmare was true, it had been he who had murdered them.

At that moment Sir Orsten took one of his hands off his great sword, and grabbed hold of the bridle of the scarred knight's horse.

'Dismount and face me like a man!' he roared, 'I'll cut you down, you liar! You have no honour, you are no true knight!'

Three Monfort soldiers appeared from nowhere and grabbed Sir Orsten, wrestling the sword from his other hand and throwing him down to the dirt. The Oakheart soldiers who stood behind their baron thrust their spears forward towards the Monfort men, but then half a dozen crossbows were suddenly aimed back at them.

'Stop!' cried Lord Horin, wanting to avoid any blood being spilled.

'You threaten the messenger of Lord Rayden?' the scarred knight asked Sir Orsten mildly, as the Oakheart knight was kicked in the side, sending him sprawling.

'When you speak to me, you speak to the duke. To threaten him is treason, punishable by death.'

'No,' Lord Horin said, his voice strained. 'Please, Sir. Don't harm my son. I'll swear my loyalty to your lord. I'll do whatever you want.'

'I know you will,' the scarred knight said confidently. 'But to make sure you keep your word I'll be taking your son with me back to Eagle Mount. A spell in the dungeons ought to calm his temper, and should Lord Rayden decide your loyalty is in question then he will have an appointment with the executioner's axe. Bring the other one as well,' he said, pointing at Sir Oskar, 'two are better than one after all.'

Monfort soldiers seized Sir Orsten's brother, and the two were forced onto horses. 'Twenty of my men will join your garrison, Oakheart, to make sure you keep yourself in line. Tear that banner down!'

One of the Monfort men jumped from his horse and hurried over to the side of the gate where the Jacelyn banner hung. None of the Oakheart soldiers moved to stop him, they did not know what to do. The sky blue banner of the Jacelyns was ripped down, and the white banner of the Monforts was hung in its place. The black marching knight flapped gently against the grey stone of the castle, looking mockingly at the gathered folk.

With that, the scarred knight turned his horse and spurred away down the road in the direction of Eagle Mount. Except for the twenty that would stay in Oaktyn,

233

his men followed him along with Sir Orsten and Sir Oskar who were forced to ride alongside.

The townsfolk who had gathered were silent after what had just occurred. Most had not been born when the last baron of Oaktyn had been alive, so Lord Horin had always been their ruler. He had been a strong baron, and fair and honourable. To see him so helpless was a shock to them. As if to confirm their worries, Lord Horin collapsed into the rutted road as he watched the distant specks that were his two sons being herded away. Seeing this, Merric darted forward, pushing his way clear of the crowd.

'No!' Ana cried, reaching to grab the hem of his cloak, but missing.

Merric ran to Lord Horin's side, and knelt down beside him on the dusty road.

'Are you alright, my lord?' he asked, concerned.

The elderly baron had visited Eagle Mount on many occasions, and he often took time to speak to Merric. His kindness was always genuine, and he always had an interesting tale to tell. Lord Horin looked at the arm that was offered him, and after a moment he took it and allowed himself to be lifted up from the dusty road.

'Yes,' Lord Horin wheezed, his voice weak, 'thank you, my boy.'

Merric smiled comfortingly at him, and the elderly baron seemed to notice him properly for the first time. He squinted at Merric's face for a moment, before his eyebrows shot up towards his thinning hair.

234

'*Merric Orrell?*' he breathed, hardly believing his failing eyes.

'Step away there, you!'

One of the Oakheart soldiers stepped forwards, looking shaken after the recent events, and eager to help his baron now that the Monforts were gone. He gestured at Merric to move himself out of the presence of Lord Horin. He assumed Merric was a common street urchin, but the elderly baron waved the soldier away.

'Thank you, Aarod. This young man is just helping an old man back to his feet.'

The Oakheart soldier bowed and stepped back respectfully, turning his attention instead to the Monfort men who were already pushing the Oakheart soldiers around. One of the Monfort men was munching noisily on a raw onion. Lord Horin glanced at them before whispering to Merric.

'It's not safe here, you must go!'

'Yes, we must,' Ana said.

She had followed Merric out of the crowd, and now tugged at his arm subtly, trying not to catch the attention of the Monfort men. But Merric did not budge.

'I'm sorry they're treating you this way,' he said.

'It is me who is sorry,' Lord Horin replied. 'I will always be loyal to Lord Roberd, you must believe me. But I must ensure the safety of my folk. It is my duty and honour as baron.'

'I understand,' Merric said, smiling at him comfortingly, 'and Lord Roberd would agree with you.'

Lord Horin's wrinkled face seemed to ease at Merric's words, as though his actions had truly been causing him a great shame.

'Thank you,' he smiled. 'Now go. Please! I could not live with myself if something happened to you too.'

'YOU!'

The booming voice caused everyone in earshot to pause and look at the serjeant who had been left in command of the group of Monfort soldiers. He was a bull of a man, with a nose covered in broken veins and teeth stained black. His eyes were as ugly as the rest of him, and they were both fixed on Merric. Nobody else may have noticed that the seemingly simple boy was in truth Merric Orrell, but the rich, though dirty, clothing he wore had not escaped the keen eyes of the serjeant. Whether he knew Merric's true identity, or simply saw him as a source of wealth that he could steal, the serjeant was not going to let him get away.

'You! Stay where you are. Grab 'em, boys!'

A handful of the Monfort soldiers closed in around Merric and Ana, blocking off any route of escape back into the town.

Merric felt Ana tense up next to him, and she pulled him close.

'By the Mother! Merric, we're trapped!'

- CHAPTER TWELVE -

A helping hand

Merric thought quickly. Grabbing Ana's hand he launched himself to his feet and ran as fast as he could in the one direction that was clear to them; into Oaktyn Castle. Together they sprinted through the open gates, passing the Oakheart soldiers who stood to either side of it. The men were too surprised to make a move to stop them, and they ignored the shouts from the Monfort soldiers who yelled at them to give chase. The Oakheart men did not know who the two young intruders were, but they had no intention of helping the Monfort men with their struggle.

Merric and Ana emerged into the courtyard of the castle, and they knew from the pounding of feet behind them that the Monfort soldiers were close on their heels. Merric and Ana were faster than their pursuers, who were carrying their spears and shields, and wore heavy ring mail beneath their padded coats. The courtyard of Oaktyn

Castle was filled with farriers and stable boys, blacksmiths and Oakheart soldiers. They all scattered as the chase passed them.

As he ran, Merric knocked over a barrel of apples, and the contents spilt over the ground behind him. The Monfort pursuers had to check their run to avoid slipping on the sudden obstacle. The Monfort men soon fell behind. Their serjeant yelled for the Oakheart soldiers on the castle walls to shoot them, but they deliberately raised their crossbows too slowly, and their targets were soon out of sight.

The stout keep stood before Merric and Ana, and the grey stone was thick with patches of moss and ivy. This gave the castle an earthy green colour, and the folk who lived in sight of its walls fondly called Oaktyn Castle the Green Keep. Merric led Ana through the tall carved wooden doors and into the keep, yelling at the stunned guards to get out of the way.

In the entrance hall, he and Ana darted through a side door, and came face to face with a spiral staircase that led both up and down. Here Merric faced a choice; upstairs to the upper floors of the keep, or down to the store rooms and dungeons below? Either way would eventually lead to a dead end. After only a moment's pause, encouraged by a yell from their pursuers behind them as they entered the entrance hall, he and Ana ran upstairs.

They climbed. And then went through the first door they reached, emerging into a passage that appeared to contain the Oakheart family's bedchambers. The walls were decorated with tapestries showing the history of the family, though Merric did not spare them a glance as they hurried past. They ran past a couple of the doors that lined the passage before entering the third at random, shutting it again behind them once they were safely through.

A gasp came from behind them, and they span round to see two ladies in the chamber. One was elderly and the other younger, though both were richly dressed in velvet gowns. They looked alarmed at Merric and Ana's sudden appearance. They had been seated with embroidery in their hands, but had jumped up in surprise at the Merric and Ana's entrance. Now they stood in the corner of the chamber, looking at the intruders with wide eyes.

Ana put a finger to her lips to hush who she assumed to be Lord Horin's lady wife and daughter, whilst Merric put his ear to the door and listened. There were distant shouts, but it seemed that their pursuers had taken a wrong turning somewhere and were searching for them in another part of the castle. Oaktyn Castle was small though, and so it would not be long before the Monfort men found them.

Despite the danger, Ana was furious at Merric.

'What were you *thinking*?' she hissed angrily at him, turning her back on the confused ladies. 'You should never have let them see you!'

'Shh!' Merric silenced her with a raised hand, his ear still pressed to the door.

Ana waited until they were certain their pursuers were still elsewhere in the castle before asking him again why he had been so foolish.

'Lord Horin was one of Lord Roberd's barons,' Merric explained. 'I couldn't just stand there and watch him be treated like that.'

Ana just rubbed her eyes, frustrated with Merric. No matter how many times he promised that he understood he needed to leave his old life behind, Merric would go and do something like this. But she knew that this was not the time to discuss it.

'We've got to get out of here. If they catch us…' she gave a shudder.

Merric gave a nod, and he did not need Ana to tell him that this was entirely his fault. He knew it was.

They were trapped here. The only way in and out of the castle was by the main gate, and that was sure to be guarded by the Monfort soldiers now. Kasper and Tomas will have seen the arrival of the scarred knight and the Monfort soldiers, and would now be wondering what had happened to Merric and Ana. Merric wondered if Kasper really would leave without them if he and Ana missed the hour deadline.

Merric glanced over at where Lord Horin's lady wife was cowering by the far wall of the chamber. Her fear and surprise was turning into curiosity though, as she realised the intruders meant she and her daughter no harm. Her eyes were peering at Merric, trying to work out where she recognised him from. Before she could remember his face, Merric turned back to Ana.

'Let's go. We'll find a way out of here.'

He gently eased open the door and peered out. Seeing the passage was clear, he slipped through the opening, closely followed by Ana. They had entered the passage from the spiral staircase to their right, so they headed left this time to where an identical staircase led to the floors above and below. Merric had just placed his foot on the first step that led back downstairs when he came face to face with one of the Monfort soldiers. The man had been coming up the stairs, and looked up with surprise as he saw them just a few steps above him.

Before he could react, Merric thrust both of his arms hard into the chest of the soldier. The man had his sword drawn, but Merric's attack had been too quick. All he could do was flap his arms wildly and grab onto the wall beside him to stop himself from falling backwards down the spiral staircase. He shouted out, alerting his fellows downstairs, and Merric was attacked by the smell of the soldier's oniony breath. Without waiting, Merric and Ana fled away from him up the stairs, and away from the triumphant shouts of their pursuers.

'Upstairs!'

'They're up there!'

Merric knew that heading further upwards was the last direction they wanted to go, as eventually they would run out of stairs to climb. He cursed his bad luck that the

Monfort man had happened to be on the stairs at that exact moment. The only way out of the castle was on the ground floor, and that was getting further and further away from them with each step they climbed.

They rose up two more floors, but on each they were faced with a door that was locked when Merric tried to open it. After a quick shove with his shoulder to try and break them down, they had no choice but to follow the spiral staircase as it wound its way up the castle keep. Their legs were burning from the climb, but they dared not slow down. They finally reached the top of the staircase, and once more their path was blocked by a door. Such was his desperation Merric muttered a prayer to the Mother, forgetting that he did not believe in Her, before pushing the door. To their relief the door was unlocked and opened at his touch with a loud creak. As they stepped through the doorway, though, their hearts dropped.   Instead   of opening out into a passage, the door led to fresh air. They were stood on the very roof of the castle, with the sun on their faces and a breeze in their hair. The spiral staircase had been in one of the four towers at the corners of the square keep, but the other three towers had no such door. Clearly this one was the only way to get onto the roof.

And the only way to get down from it again.

'We're trapped,' Merric said simply, looking around the empty square space hopelessly.

Battlements ringed the roof of the keep, but beyond them Merric could only see the forests and hills that surrounded Oaktyn. Ana closed the door behind them, but finding nothing to wedge it shut with she just took Merric's hand and led him away from the door to the very centre of the roof, her eyes scanning her surroundings, trying to come up with a plan.

After a couple of moments they heard the pounding of feet on the stairs, and a second later the door crashed open to reveal five of the Monfort soldiers, their serjeant at the front. They looked out of breath after the chase, and irritable that the Oakheart men had not helped them, but they now grinned horribly as they saw they had their quarry trapped.

Merric stepped in front of Ana. They had left their weapons with Kasper and Tomas, not wanting to draw attention to themselves in the town, so Merric could do nothing more than raise his fists in defence.

'Don't be a fool, Merric,' Ana said. 'I have an idea, do you trust me?'

'What?' Merric replied.

The Monfort men who were slowly making their way towards them. They were in no rush; they knew Merric was trapped. Merric looked over his shoulder at his Ana.

'Follow me!' she insisted.

Ana grabbed Merric by the arm and began sprinting away from their pursuers, whose looks of delight turned quickly to confusion. Merric went with her, equally confused. They were heading towards a spot directly between two of the towers. The battlements which marked the edge of the roof got closer and closer.

'Ana?' Merric said uncertainly as they ran.

In one fluid motion she leapt into the air, and Merric was forced to do the same. The battlements passed beneath them, and then there was nothing below them except for a long drop. Merric opened his mouth to cry out, but his breath was caught in his throat, and then they were falling.

They hit the water of the Willowbank River with a huge splash. The coldness of the water after the heat of the day hit Merric like a punch to the stomach as his body plunged deep into the river. He gasped at the shock of it, but succeeded only in swallowing a large amount of water. He kicked hard, and his head broke through the surface. He coughed and spluttered to clear the water from his lungs, before breathing the air in deeply. Ana surfaced a few feet away from him, and she coolly brushed her soaking hair from her face.

'Are you okay?' Merric called across to her, but she just grinned in response.

Merric laughed, the thrill of the jump coursing through him. At that moment a crossbow bolt pierced the water next to them, followed by another that missed Ana by inches. Her grin turned to a grimace as she turned and looked up at the battlements of the keep. Three Monfort soldiers on the roof had crossbows, and now lined the battlements far above. They aimed their weapons down at Merric and Ana as they sat there treading water in the river.

The fall had been over in seconds, but the height they had jumped was at least fifty feet. Fortunately, the keep of Oaktyn Castle backed directly onto the Willowbank River, which curled around the town. Ana must have spied this from the ridge above the town, and so up there on the roof she had realised their one and only escape route. The river was fast flowing, and it was already carrying Merric and Ana out of range of the deadly crossbows.

A third crossbow bolt was aimed desperately at Merric, but it fell short. He could hear the frustrated shouts of the Monfort men who realised that they had been beaten. Merric had been within their grasp yet he and Ana had slipped through their fingers. Merric dreaded to think what Lord Aric and Rayden would do to the soldiers when they found out.

'We're safe now,' Merric said to Ana as they were taken steadily downstream by the current.

The town of Oaktyn passed by on the southern bank, while the northern bank was dotted with trees. As they passed the last houses of Oaktyn, and were swept beyond the town's boundaries, the river grew more violent. The current of the river picked up its pace, and the rocky riverbed turned the calmly flowing water into tumbling rapids.

'Erm, Ana?' Merric glugged, and he accidentally swallowed a mouthful of water.

The blue surface of the river turned white as the water swept over and past boulders, and Merric cried out in pain as he was struck against a large rock. For the second time that afternoon he felt a stab of fear.

'Merric!' Ana shouted, and she tried to swim towards him.

Merric was smaller than she was, and was fast being swept out of her reach. The rapids forced them further apart, and Merric panicked as he felt frothy waves crash over him and throw him about. The willow trees which now lined the river closed in around them, blocking out the sun and casting the river into shadow. In this half-light Merric found it harder and harder to keep his bearings, and lost all idea of which way he was facing. He was being tossed around like a cork, and was constantly dragged beneath the surface of the water where he fought to breathe. He occasionally caught a glimpse of his friend's terrified face as she fought to reach him, but every time she got close they would be forced apart again.

He was pushed against another huge boulder, its surface smooth after centuries of erosion by the river. He felt his head crack against the hard stone, and stars swam before his eyes. He frantically tried to keep his head above water, but dizziness overcame him and he felt himself slip beneath the surface of the raging river.

'The Mother protect me,' he thought, praying again, as he sank slowly downwards. Everything started to turn black.

All of a sudden, just as he felt certain he was going to drown, Merric felt a hand grab his own and heave him upwards. The hand felt small but strong, and he clutched onto it for dear life, knowing that it was his only way to avoid death.

His head broke through the surface of the river.

If he had any breath left in him he would have cried out in relief, but instead he just coughed up the water that had filled his lungs. His saviour dragged him clear of the river, until he smelt the fresh grass of the riverbank beneath him.

'Thank you, Ana,' Merric said when he had finished coughing.

She did not reply, so he rolled onto his back and looked up at the willow trees above him. He was on the south bank of the Willowbank River, and he could see the tops of the towers of Oaktyn Castle beyond the trees in the distance. The river had carried them around a mile downstream, though for Merric it had almost swept him all the way to his death. He felt his breathing begin to slow as he tried to relax.

There was a splash upstream, and Merric saw Ana drag herself clear of the water and collapse onto the riverbank. She looked exhausted, but otherwise fine. She looked over and saw Merric.

'Thank the Mother you're alright,' she cried.

'How did you do that?' Merric said, confused.

Ana looked back at him, not understanding.

'Do what? Look, Merric, if I'd have known the river was so powerful I'd never have… If we'd got this far only for my mistake to get you killed…'

Merric waved this away, and looked at his friend closely as she came over to where he sat on the grassy bank.

'You pulled me out of the river,' he said. 'So how come you were all the way over there?'

'I thought I'd lost you,' Ana mumbled, not hearing him. She was shaking slightly. 'I saw you hit that rock and disappear underwater and I feared the worst. But then I saw you climb out of the river, the Mother be praised, and I knew you were safe.'

'Climb out? It was you, wasn't it?'

Ana studied him for a second, confused.

'It was me *what*?'

Merric finally drew his eyes away from his friend and looked at the trees around them. They were alone.

'It wasn't you. It can't have been. You were still in the river. So who pulled me out?'

'Nobody pulled you from the river, you climbed out by yourself,' Ana said, concern in her eyes.

She wondered if the knock to Merric's head was messing with his mind.

'I didn't climb out! I thought I was going to drown. I was about to give up, but then someone grabbed hold of me and pulled me up and out of the river.'

'Merric,' Ana said slowly, 'I saw you. You climbed out by yourself. There was no one else there.

'But…I felt them. I felt a hand,' Merric said quietly, looking once more around them for whoever it had been who had saved him.

Ana hesitated, looking worriedly at her friend.

'Some folk say that when we're in real danger we find strength in us that we didn't know we had.'

'I didn't imagine it,' Merric said hotly, but already he felt less sure. He had almost died, and had struck his head hard against the rocks. Could he have imagined it? He rubbed his hand as he thought. The hand that had grabbed him had felt so real.

'Merric! Ana!'

The joyful shout came from their right, where Tomas came scurrying out of the trees. He was followed by a less than happy-looking Kasper. Tomas was breathless as he stopped in front of his friends.

'We saw the Monfort men arrive soon after you went into the town. We thought they had got you,' Thomas said, looking shaken but relieved.

Ana gave him a hug, but kept a concerned eye on Merric.

'I hope you're happy with yourself,' said Kasper

Merric turned nervously to look at him. The poacher was glaring at him, an angry look on his face.

'So, what happened?'

Ana told them everything, from the moment they entered Oaktyn, to them emerging from the river. She told it true, but kept out Merric believing someone had pulled him to safety from the river. He was grateful for this, as he had no desire for Kasper to think he was imagining things. The poacher was angry nonetheless, and for the first time they heard him raise his voice.

'You both could have been killed! I haven't brought you all this way just for you to do something so foolish, Merric. It was pure luck that saved you.'

'Actually, it was Ana that saved me from those men,' Merric said defensively.

Kasper glared at him.

'It must be nice to have such a reliable friend, but getting her killed wouldn't have been a good way to repay her,' Kasper said coldly.

'I'm sorry,' Merric said, meaning it. 'I should never have insisted I go into Oaktyn. I should have listened to you.'

He was burning with disappointment in himself, knowing that he had almost ruined everything they had risked for him.

Kasper appeared to have used up all his anger, and let out a deep breath.

'So, did you learn anything useful?'

'Lord Horin said he would always be loyal to Lord Roberd,' Merric said.

'Aye, but loyalty to a dead man will only get you so far. Sooner or later, even if it takes years, he and the other barons will all become loyal to the Monforts, you'll see.'

Kasper knew that they had outstayed their welcome in Oaktyn, so demanded that they press on. They therefore set off through the willow trees to where Kasper and Tomas had tethered their horses. Merric and Ana's clothes quickly dried in the sun as they rode back towards the Great East Road, and as the day wore on their moods rose again. Merric put the mystery of the hand that had pulled him from the river behind him. Perhaps Ana was right, and that he had imagined the whole thing. Kasper seemed almost guilty for losing his temper. He apologised to Merric, saying he had just been worried.

'You're not getting attached to us after all, are you?' asked Ana, causing Merric and Tomas to laugh.

Kasper forced his face into his usual scowl, before giving in and letting a smile appear on his lips.

'Yes, I suppose I am.'

Kasper cheered them up further by letting them know that they should arrive at his village that night. Their journey was almost over, and they all shared the same relief. They followed the Willowbank River for a few more miles, where it slowed to a pleasant gentle flow, the raging rapids now behind them. They then turned south and suddenly the Great East Road lay before them. They paused when they reached the wide road, watchful for any unfriendly eyes. After a few minutes of waiting, and seeing only a farmer leading a tired-looking donkey, they decided that the coast was clear. Fearing the sudden appearance of Monfort men who seemed to always be just one step behind them, they quickly darted across the road and disappeared into the trees on the far side.

They were on the final stretch, and they felt invigorated at the thought of finishing their journey. None more so than Kasper, who was itching to see his family again. After a few hours they came in the lands that surrounded the village, and the fields either side of the narrow road along which they now travelled were thick with wheat which grew tall in the warm sun. Merric frowned in confusion.

'I thought you said your family were starving?' he asked Kasper. 'There looks to be enough wheat here to make bread for half of Eaglestone!'

Kasper indicated the fields around them.

'These fields all fall within the lands of Sir Hestor Peggleswade, the last and least gallant of an old family who live under Lord Tymon. They're farmed by the folk of my village. We have plenty of wheat, but no way to turn it into bread.'

'Why not?'

'The only way wheat can be turned into bread is if it first can be ground into flour.'

'And you have no mill?' Merric asked.

Back at Eagle Mount he took it for granted that bread appeared on their table, and had previously not thought about how much effort the common folk went to in order to put it there.

Kasper shook his head.

'No, we do have a mill in Little Harrow. It's our miller that's the problem though. Oh, Ketch is perfectly skilled,' he added, as Merric opened his mouth to ask the question. 'He's greedy though. He knows that he's the only one that can grind the wheat, and the power of that has gone to his head. He refuses to accept the wheat of most, and the crops are wasted. When he does agree to take in someone's harvest he takes so much of the flour as his payment that it hardly makes it worth it anyway.'

'Why doesn't someone do something about it?' Merric asked, shocked that such a thing could be allowed to happen.

'What can we do?' Kasper replied, opening his arms as though open to suggestions. 'A miller's trade takes years to master. If we displease him then he'll stop grinding the wheat all together, and then where would we be? We have no choice but to pay him the outrageous rates he demands.'

'What about Sir Hestor?' Ana said from behind them. 'If he owns this land then surely he owns the mill as well? Why not order the miller to do his job?'

Kasper gave a hollow laugh.

'The Pig Knight might be in charge according to the laws of the land, but in reality he's a man who only cares about where his next cup of wine is coming from. He sold his sword years ago to help him afford his next few barrels. He spends most of his days in the inn, and the rest of them trying to scrub the muck out of his beard. The miller,

253

Ketch, runs things in the village really. We've appealed to Lord Tymon, but he isn't interested in the petty issues of our small village. All we can do is struggle through. This last winter was a bad one though, and I nearly lost my child to the cold and hunger. Our crops of vegetables failed, and with no bread I had to rely on my longbow to hunt and provide meat for my family. Soon the wild boars disappeared from the woods and for weeks I couldn't find anything, until one day a deer came across my path.'

Merric guessed what came next. 'You were caught?'

Kasper nodded with a scowl.

'Some Conway soldiers found me with the deer, when I was only a few miles from home. They arrested me immediately, and dragged me to the Lord Tymon. He wouldn't accept that I was desperate, and so ordered them to take me to Lord Roberd for sentencing.'

Merric had seen Lord Tymon Conway a few times when he had visited Lord Roberd. He had no wife and no children, and seemed to have little interest in fulfilling his duties as one of Lord Roberd's barons. He was an unpleasant man too, and Merric always thought that if Lord Tymon had been kinder then he would not struggle to find a wife, and would then have sons and daughters to carry on his family name.

They rode on in silence for another hour, and as the sun was setting beyond the horizon Kasper turned to Merric.

'It's unlikely that the Monforts will have any presence in my village, but in any case the name "Merric Orrell" is not be safe to use. You'll need to think of another name for us to call you.'

The thatched roofs of the cottages of Little Harrow could be seen up ahead, with smoke gently rising from their chimneys. A stream lay across the path to the village, which could be crossed by a simple wooden bridge.

'I have a cousin named Podmore,' Tomas suggested from behind them. 'I've never met him, but I think he lives in Lynport.'

'That'll do,' Kasper said with half a smile. 'You'll be Tomas's cousin, and if you're to remain safe you'll need to stick to that story.'

And so Kasper, Ana, Tomas and Podmore rode their horses over the small wooden bridge and towards their new home.

CHAPTER THIRTEEN

Little Harrow

Little Harrow was a smaller village than Merric had been expecting, but was pleasant and welcoming. A few thatched cottages sat on either side of the small road that passed through the village, while up ahead a cluster of slightly larger buildings gathered around a central village green. Merric could spy a blacksmiths, a carpenters and a friendly-looking inn. No village folk were in sight, and the smells from the cottages they passed told them that most were sitting down to their meagre suppers. The evening light gave everything a pleasing soft, orange glow.

Just beyond the borders of the village, sat beside the stream, Merric could see a tall stone building. He assumed this to be the mill that was causing all the trouble in the village. Its water wheel sat lazily in the gentle stream, unmoving. Clearly the miller was not in the mood to grind any wheat into flour this evening.

The green opened up before them as they walked their horses further into the village, and light spilled out of the open door of the inn. Their ears were met with the sound of laughter and the musical scraping of a fiddle. Unlike the wood and thatch that the cottages of the village were made from, the ground floor of the two-storey inn was built from sturdy stone that looked like it had been there for hundreds of years. A sign hung over the door, squeaking slightly as it swung back and forth.

'The Golden Wheel,' Merric read off the sign. 'That's a strange name for an inn.'

'The story of The Golden Wheel is well known around here,' Kasper said. 'Long ago, King Lycal the Lavish was travelling along the Great East Road, not far from here. He was travelling in his luxurious carriage, which was clad in pure gold. It was a ridiculous, heavy thing though, and the axle broke. Rather than repair the carriage he simply chose to abandon it and have a new one built when he returned to King's Keep. Naturally, it didn't take long for folk to learn this, and soon folk from far and wide came to find the carriage and take what gold from it they could. One man from Little Harrow managed to secure himself one of the carriage's wheels, and even that on its own was worth a fortune. He used the gold to build the inn, and named it for the wheel that had made it possible.'

Curious about his new home, Merric turned away from the inn and looked over to his left. Beyond the smithy and cottages on that side of the green he could spy the two bell towers of a small priory, poking up out of a cluster of trees. The two towers were tiny, no larger than chimneys, and like as not held bells no bigger than a man's hand. This was a far smaller building than the Grand Priory in Eaglestone, which could seat the entire population of the town and still have room to spare, and the bells in its two towers were each taller than Merric. He had once been allowed to climb the hundreds of stairs inside the tower to see one of them.

'Up ahead,' said Kasper, shaking Merric from his thoughts, 'is Harrow Manor.'

Beyond the last cottages of the village stood a stone building, modest in size and not in its prime. It was surrounded by a wall, built more for privacy than protection, and its gate was guarded by a bored looking soldier, who leant on a pink shield.

'That's the home of the ancient and proud Peggleswade family,' Kasper said, with a slight curl of his mouth. 'There you'll find our brave Sir Hestor; most likely fast asleep, surrounded by empty wine cups.'

They turned off the road as they neared the last cottages, and this narrower track led towards fields and a distant wood. Merric could see Kasper pick up the pace on his horse as they neared the edge of the village, and he had a look of both excitement and nervousness on his face. Up ahead, a door was thrown open from a cottage, and a woman stepped out into the darkening road. An apron was tied round her waist, and she was drying her hands hurriedly on it as she looked curiously up the rutted track towards them.

She gave a cry as she saw the four travellers on their horses, and began running towards them. She had to lift her skirts to stop herself from tripping on them, and was met by Kasper who leapt from his horse. After an outburst of angry words from the woman, she suddenly burst into tears and the two embraced tightly. It was a few minutes before they broke apart. Merric and the others kept their distance, looking awkwardly around.

'I thought I'd never see you again!' the woman cried.

'I'm home now. I'm so sorry,' Kasper soothed, his voice low, as though he was trying to keep their conversation private.

Merric had never heard Kasper's voice sounding so gentle, and to distract himself he looked out over the nearby fields. While the crop of wheat was thick and tall, there were black patches where it had gone rotten. Although he was certainly no expert on farming, Merric assumed that whoever this field belonged to was not bothering to harvest the crop, seeing as it would likely go to waste anyway. For what felt like the hundredth time since Kasper had told him the story of the village, Merric wondered why Ketch the miller was being how he was. Kasper had said that various members of the village had gone to the miller, himself included, to try and convince him to change his ways, but he would not listen to anyone.

'Papa!' cried a squeaky voice, and Merric turned to see a small girl run out of the cottage after her mother, and with a squeal of glee she charged up to her father. Kasper gave her a long hug, and then hoisted her up onto his shoulders. She had inherited her father's dirty blonde hair. Kasper then looked round at his companions.

'This is my wife, Maryl,' he said to them, gesturing at his wife, 'and this little one is Daysee. Maryl, let me introduce Ana, Tomas and Podmore.'

'Pleased to meet you all,' she beamed, her eyes still wet from her tears of joy. 'Come in, come in, all of you!'

When they had all dismounted from their horses, Kasper asked Merric to help him tether the mounts to the hitching post around the back of the cottage. Nosy looked around his new surroundings with interest and whinnied happily.

'Do you like it here, boy?' Merric asked him, patting the horse's neck with affection.

With their mounts secure, Merric made to follow Ana and Tomas into the cottage, but Kasper threw out an arm to stop him in his tracks.

'Remember,' he said, 'the name Merric is behind you. You're Podmore now. Don't forget.'

'I won't,' Merric assured him, trying to imagine not using his own name.

The inside of the cottage was simple, and a far cry from the halls and chambers of the castle Merric had grown up in. The main room housed a hearth, where a fire crackled pleasantly, and a simple wooden table that was covered in many years' worth of scratches and burn marks. The floor beneath their feet was no more than dirt covered with straw, with no floorboards or stone in sight. An open doorway led to a second, smaller room where Kasper and his family slept, while overhead was a loft where they stored their belongings away from the damp.

Maryl had been cooking a soup in a large black pot over the fire in the hearth, and she quickly found four extra bowls into which she ladled the soup. Merric and his companions gratefully sat at the table and ate greedily and noisily. The soup was little more than water with a few small vegetables floating in, but they did not complain. The moment Kasper finished, Daysee jumped up onto his lap and let him stroke her hair.

'We've got some food still,' Kasper said to his wife, 'left over from our journey. Tomas, could you go and fetch it?'

Maryl smiled her thanks at Tomas when he brought the small bundle of food in from outside, and she climbed a ladder up to the loft and stowed the food safely away. 'I'll cook something special with it, for the summer feast,' she said, as she came back down.

Merric had forgotten that this celebration was coming. It was a special day each year when all folk across High Realm would feast and be merry, letting all worries leave them. It was a day dedicated to the Mother, to give thanks for the bountiful summer. It would be the first time, which he could remember, that he would spend the summer feast without the Jacelyns.

'How did you come to be with my Kasper?' Maryl asked them warmly once she had returned to the table and seen their bowls were empty.

'Once the Monforts had taken control of Eagle Mount we knew it was no longer safe, even for common folk like us,' Merric explained, with some truth. 'We fled the town and met Kasper in the Greenwood. With us having no place to go, he offered to guide us here.'

Maryl shook her head sadly.

'We heard rumours, but I still can't believe it. Our great duke...dead! They say Lord Roberd's own ward, a boy only a few years older than our Daysee, murdered him and his family. Do you think he could really have done that?'

'No!' said Merric, with a little too much anger.

'No, me neither,' said Maryl. 'I mean, a mere boy? To kill a family while they slept is beyond what most folk could be capable of, let alone someone so young.'

'Let us speak of something more pleasant,' Kasper said, with a look at Merric. 'Has your friend's daughter had her baby yet?'

Merric sat in silence while the others talked. Soon though, Tomas slumped over the table, exhausted. The sound of his gentle snores filled the room. The rest saw this as an indication that it was time for bed. It had been a long time since any of them had enjoyed a proper night's sleep.

'I'll clear some space in the loft,' Kasper said to Merric and Ana, rising from the table. 'You can all sleep there.'

* * *

Merric must have been more exhausted than he thought, as the sun was well risen by the time he, Ana and Tomas awoke from their peaceful sleep in the loft of Kasper's cottage. He initially wondered where he was, not recognising the sloping thatch above his head. He quickly remembered, and felt strangely comfortable and safe for the first time since the night Lord Roberd and his family had died.

He rolled over and poked his head over the edge of the loft to see Maryl busy sweeping the floor of the main room, preparing to scatter it with some fresh straw. Daysee sat playing by the open door with a kitten.

'Good morning,' Maryl called up at him kindly when she saw him.

Merric smiled back, and carefully climbed down the wooden ladder that was propped against the loft. As he sat himself down at the table, Kasper appeared in the open doorway, bathed in sunlight. He had already been up and about, and looked as well rested as Merric had ever seen him. Being back in his village seemed to have taken ten years off Kasper; his face looked less troubled, and a smile was quicker to appear on his lips.

'Finally awake,' he said, seeing Merric sat at the table and the faces of Ana and Tomas peeping over the edge of the loft above. He sat himself down opposite Merric.

'If you're going to stay in our village you're going to need to work. Everyone needs to do their bit to keep a village like this in working order. I've asked around and, Ana, the blacksmith has agreed to take you on as his assistant.'

She looked relieved and keen to get a hammer in her hands once more. This was the longest she had gone without beating a piece of red-hot metal, and she would always be more comfortable forging a sword than wielding one.

'Tomas,' Kasper said next. 'To no one's surprise, Sir Hestor Peggleswade's latest servant has had enough and left, so you'll be taking his place. I warn you, expect a lot of cleaning and putting up with his wine-soaked state. He usually sleeps in late though, I'm told, so you don't need to get to Harrow Manor until the sun has well risen each day.'

Tomas looked nervous, but nodded. He looked over at Merric, feeling guilty. He was technically still the young nobleman's servant, but Merric had no need for a servant anymore.

Kasper lastly looked at Merric. 'Podmore, you'll be helping old Hamm in his fields. His back isn't what it used to be, so he has need for a young, able-bodied man.'

Merric opened his mouth to protest, but glanced at Maryl. Unaware of his displeasure, she kept on sweeping, and eventually took her broomstick into the other room.

'I can't work in a field!' Merric hissed once she had gone.

Kasper raised his eyebrows.

'And why not? Is such a thing beneath you?'

'I've never tended to a field in my life!'

'After this afternoon you will have,' Kasper replied as though that settled things, but after seeing Merric's face he explained further. 'Unfortunately, your lack of skills makes your benefit to a village community small. Can you forge a horseshoe? No. Can you tan leather? You cannot. Therefore you'll be helping Hamm in his field.'

Merric knew Kasper was right, but the thought of working in a field made him miserable. He had been born in a castle, and raised as a nobleman, first by his baron father, and then by Lord Roberd. The thought of that life being behind him made him feel sad, but he knew he needed to welcome this opportunity for a new life. If Kasper had not brought them to Little Harrow then they would likely have been caught by the Monforts, and would probably be dead by now. Merric also remembered his promise to Kasper.

He therefore swallowed his pride and nodded.

Within a couple of hours of working in the fields, however, Merric knew that he would never be much of a farmer. He did not have the strength or skill required to guide the plough as it carved deep furrows into the soil as they prepared the winter crop of wheat, and his attempts at wielding a scythe to cut down the fully grown summer wheat caused Hamm to yelp in fright and leap back to avoid the wickedly sharp blade. He was therefore given the boring and unskilled job of walking alone in front of the plough, picking up and discarding any stones that could damage the blade. In that first afternoon he was also tasked with scaring birds away from the newly planted fields, to stop the winged thieves from taking the seeds. It was tedious and tiring work, and Merric found a new respect for the hardworking folk of The Head who he had previously never really spared a thought for.

At least the days were warm. Summer was at its height, but before long they would be faced by autumn and then the cold snows of winter. Spending the days in the fields then would be horrible, and Merric would no doubt bitterly remember the warm fires and thick furs that he would have had in Eagle Mount to help ward off the cold.

Ana returned from the blacksmith's on her first day dirty and sweaty, but with a huge smile on her grubby face. Working by a red-hot forge and beating glowing metal was her skill and passion, and she appeared to have settled in to her new role in the village quickly. Tomas, likewise, felt at home tending to the needs of his new master. Sir Hestor spent most of his days asleep, and so Tomas's duties were few.

Each evening most of the village folk could be found in The Golden Wheel. There they would relax and laugh after a hard day's work. The landlady of the inn was a young woman named Lora, whose quick smile and easy laugh made her popular with her customers. Understanding that most of the villagers were poor due to their harvests of wheat going to waste, she charged the lowest prices in The Head for her ale and mead. The farmers of the village repaid her kindness by providing her with any spare vegetables from their fields and a loaf or two on the rare occasions that Ketch the miller ground their wheat into flour. Lora's father had left Little Harrow to seek his fortune in the capital city of High Realm far to the west, and had opened a new inn in the shadow of the King's towering castle. The Golden Wheel had therefore passed to his daughter. Lora would laugh and joke with her customers at the bar whilst her fluffy cat wandered the crowded tables, happily accepting strokes from the friendly hands of the villagers.

With them being nervous of entering the crowded inn on their own that first evening, Kasper and Maryl took Merric, Ana and Tomas and introduced them to the villagers. Despite them being complete strangers to most, the villagers were welcoming and kind towards them. All except Ketch the miller, who Kasper pointed out to Merric. Ketch alone did not raise a hand in greeting to Merric and the others when Kasper announced them. He peered at the new arrivals with narrowed eyes, before turning his focus

267

back to the game of Kings and Castles, the popular High Realm board game, that he was engaged in with one of his cronies. He frowned in concentration at the chequered board laid out on the table in front of him.

The miller could nearly always be found in the inn, as could his cronies. They were a group of big-fisted but thick-headed ruffians, who answered Ketch's every beck and call. They shadowed him day and night. It was rumoured that the miller was a coward, but none had ever been able to get Ketch on his own to see if that was true or not. They would occupy the same table close to the fire every evening, and demand ale from Lora in loud voices. Everyone else gave them a wide berth, and tried to avoid his attention. The landlady seemed to be the only person who did not give in to the miller's bullying. Whenever Ketch and his cronies tried to leave at the end of the night she would block the way out with her palm outstretched. She would not let them leave until, with scowls on their ugly faces, they had paid the few coppers they owed for their drinks.

Merric, Ana and Tomas quickly fell into a routine as their first week in Little Harrow wore on. Merric and Ana would rise at first light each morning. They would leave Tomas to lie in for a few hours more, until the time when Sir Hestor Peggleswade would be in need of his services. After a simple breakfast Merric would wander to the fields west of the village, and Ana would make her way to the smithy in the centre of the village. There she would spend her days repairing tools and forging shoes for the horses.

Kasper would take his longbow into the nearby woods in the hope of bringing some meat back for their supper.

They would return to Kasper's cottage in the late afternoon, where Maryl had their supper prepared. The food was far from the luxurious fare that Merric was used to at Eagle Mount, but after a hard day toiling in the fields he would wolf it down all the same. They would end the day at The Golden Wheel, where they would relax and laugh together with everyone else. On their third visit to the inn, Ana had spied Tomas watching Lora secretively out of the corner of his eye when he thought the others were not looking. He went a deep shade of red when Ana pointed it out.

On their fifth morning it was the God's Day, and as such there was no work for anyone. Merric, Ana and Tomas made their way to the small priory with Kasper and his family, along with most of the village folk. Even Sir Hestor was there, wearing his finest and least stained clothes, with Tomas providing a supportive arm. The priory was a simple building, hardly bigger than Kasper's cottage. The prior was a well-liked man though, portly with a jolly face, who spoke of the strength they all possessed by remaining true and honest with each other. His words seemed to be directed at Ketch, but to no one's surprise the miller had not bothered to turn up that morning. Apart from Sir Hestor, who dozed peacefully in the front row, all the villagers seemed to hang on to the prior's every word as he spoke.

After the service, the men headed over to a tree-lined meadow that bordered Harrow Manor. There they spent a couple of hours at practice with longbows, aiming the arrows at straw targets thirty paces away. By Lord Tymon's law, they were required to do this every week. Kasper shot shaft after shaft into the very centre of one of the circular targets, before turning and helping some of the less abled men of the village. Merric and Tomas were also required to put in this practice each week. Despite the agony in his shoulder from the effort, Merric pulled the string back all the way to his ear. His first shot missed the target completely, but he continued to practice with a grim determination.

Life in the village was simple, and Merric was slowly getting used to this new way of living. However, the ever present issue with the miller was never far from his mind. With Ketch usually refusing to grind wheat to produce flour, there was rarely any bread to eat. As Kasper had said, meat was hard to come by, and when summer ended they would soon not be able to rely on their small crop of vegetables either. Winter would be difficult, Merric knew. Ketch was the cause of all this, and it would only be a matter of time before Merric experienced the miller's cruel side first hand. Little did Merric realise how soon it would be.

After a week of working in the fields, Hamm asked Merric to load his rickety old wagon with freshly harvested wheat, while the elderly farmer harnessed a frail looking ox to it. He explained that the harvest would rot if it did not get ground into flour now, so they were going to take it to the mill to see if Ketch would grind it for them. The farmer did not sound hopeful, but Merric was eager to come face to face with the cruel man who was causing all the trouble. The journey through Little Harrow to the mill was slow; the ox seemed as elderly as Hamm, and the wheels on the wagon were coming loose and closer to square in shape than round. Eventually, though, they turned off the main road when they reached the bridge out of the village, and headed up the track that led to the mill.

It was a strong-looking building, but it had been allowed to go to ruin. Moss was growing between the stones, and parts of the wooden waterwheel were rotted away completely. It appeared that Ketch did not take a great deal of care of his mill, and it was falling further and further into disrepair.

Ketch's cronies were sat relaxing on the steps which led up to the mill's door, but rose to their feet when they saw Hamm and Merric approaching. The biggest and stupidest one of them banged a meaty fist on the door, while keeping a watchful eye on the new arrivals. Merric heard a girl squeal and laugh from inside. A moment later the door opened with a rusty squeak, and the miller appeared. Up close, Merric could see that Ketch was younger than he had previously thought, perhaps around the same age that Tristan had been. He had a square jaw with a few missing teeth, and a thick mop of hair that he flicked out of his eyes as he looked down the stairs at Hamm.

'What do you want, old man?' Ketch asked, his voice sounding bored.

The question was rudely asked, but Hamm forced himself to smile.

'It's a fine morning isn't it?' he said to Ketch.

The miller rolled his eyes, and seeing this, one of his cronies took a step towards Hamm.

'We don't care none how nice a day it is,' the man growled threateningly, his simple mind straining to string the words together. The knuckles on his huge hands were like conkers, and he massaged them menacingly.

Merric instinctively took a step forwards to protect the older man, but this just made Ketch grin crookedly at him.

'And who is this? You're new around here aren't you, whelp?' he said, flicking his hair out of his eyes again. When Ketch did this it made him look like he was twitching. He had a wisp of a moustache growing on his top lip, and his fingers played with it as he looked at Merric. Far from making him look older, which Ketch clearly thought it did, Merric thought the moustache made him look even more childish.

Hamm put an arm out to stop Merric.

'This is Podmore. He's a friend of Kasper's.'

'I wouldn't brag too much about being a friend of that waster,' Ketch replied. 'It's a shame he came back. I've seen his pretty little wife making eyes at me.'

His cronies laughed, and Ketch watched Merric closely, as though daring him to try and start a fight. Merric forced himself to keep his face blank, and Ketch quickly grew bored. He therefore turned his attention back to Hamm.

'You still haven't answered my question. What are you doing here? You're interrupting my morning.'

The farmer took a step up towards the miller, taking his hat off as he did so and holding it tightly in both hands.

'My harvest is going to go to waste,' he said, nodding his head at the wagon over his shoulder. 'I would be much obliged if you could take it from me and use your mill to turn it into flour.'

Ketch laughed coldly.

'You were here two weeks ago, old man, asking me the same thing. I said "no" then, so what makes you think I'd say "yes" today?'

'Please sir,' said Hamm, his heart dropping as he realised that it had been a wasted journey and another wasted crop, 'just a bit of flour could go so far. Young Lidia in the village has just had a baby, I heard, and she needs to keep up her strength. You can keep some of the flour for yourself of course.'

Ketch laughed again at this.

'You'll let me keep some of the flour for myself? Hopper, show him.'

One of the cronies, a particularly fearsome looking thug with few teeth and small eyes, disappeared inside the mill. He emerged moments later clutching two large sacks of flour. He deposited them in front of Ketch with a heavy thud, before going back inside and returning with a third bulging bag. Hamm looked sadly at the sacks, and Ketch smirked at him.

'As you can see, I have plenty of flour for myself. I have enough to last me for weeks, so until that's used up I have no need to grind more.'

'Do you not realise that everyone else is going hungry?' Merric said, pushing past Hamm and looking angrily up at Ketch. 'How can you be so selfish?'

Hamm urged Merric to hush, but Ketch descended the mill steps and walked up close to them. His face was right up to Merric's, and his breath smelt terrible.

'Where are you from?' he asked, menacingly. He flicked his hair once again.

Merric drew himself up as tall as he could, looking into the sneering face of the miller.

'Lynport,' he lied. He would have loved to tell Ketch who he was really, but knew that would do little to discourage him.

'A town boy,' Ketch said, causing his cronies to guffaw. 'Well you're not in Lynport anymore. Here,' he waved his arm around to indicate the whole village, '*I'm* in charge of Little Harrow. This is my mill, and I can do what I please with it. Why should I be of service to every beggar who comes to my door? Who says I have to grind every bit of wheat that these cretins bring me? I deserve a little more thanks from you lot for everything I do for you. Don't think I don't know what you all say about me, behind my back. Now, get off my land, and take your wagon with you before it falls to pieces where it stands.'

'We're sorry to trouble you,' Hamm said, backing away and pulling Merric with him.

Merric reluctantly allowed himself to be steered away, but kept eye contact with Ketch. The miller smirked at him, before spitting on the dusty ground and returning to the mill and shutting the door behind him.

On the way back to Hamm's fields, the farmer walked ahead of Merric and did not speak to him. Merric knew that Hamm was unhappy with him, but this did not come close to matching the anger Merric felt towards Ketch. After all the things he had faced, and the terrible situation The Head was in, he could not believe there were people as selfish as Ketch. Folk in The Head needed to help each other if they are to survive the tyranny of Monforts, and another tyrant in the shape of Ketch would not help anyone.

As Merric walked, his fists clenched and unclenched. When he arrived back at Kasper's cottage later that day, he found Ana and Maryl sat at the table. Maryl could sense the fury in Merric and asked him what was wrong. He explained what had happened at the mill.

'It's been like this for a couple of years, Pod,' Maryl said, wearily. 'We get by; it's not that bad really.'

'But what about Kasper being forced to break the king's laws to provide for you? He was almost killed for it,' Ana asked.

She was trying to scrub the dirt from her hands after a day at the forge, and Maryl turned to her.

'This last winter was bad,' she admitted. 'While we struggle to have enough wheat to make bread, we can usually rely on our other crops; potatoes, turnips, carrots. But recently the crops have just been failing to produce as much as we really need.'

'I'll pray to the Mother for you, for a bountiful harvest' Ana said.

'For *us*,' Maryl smiled, grateful. 'You all live here now, too.'

'If Ketch started doing his job, everything would be okay?' Merric asked.

'Yes,' Maryl reluctantly agreed. 'With bread and what vegetables we have, and with Kasper back to hunt for anything he can find, we could get through this coming winter. It wouldn't be comfortable, but we'd survive. But Pod, what you did today, it can't happen again.' Merric opened his mouth to protest, but Maryl politely raised her hand to stop him. 'It *can't* happen again. Ketch provides enough flour for us to get by, just. He could easily stop grinding the wheat altogether, and then where would we be? We can't risk upsetting him. Kasper once tried speaking to him, as have most folk here, but he just does not listen. With his thugs behind him he's the law around here. There's nothing more we can do.' She could see that Merric was not happy, so she added 'I appreciate you wanting to help, I really do.'

Merric knew she was right, but he could not sit by and let the whole village be bullied by this man. Maryl excused herself, and took a basket outside to collect the clean washing from the line. Once she was gone, Merric directed his frustration at Ana.

'They can't just put up with him,' he said moodily. 'After villains like Lord Aric, and Rayden, and that knight with the scars on his face, I can't believe there's someone like Ketch that we're having to deal with!'

Ana just put her hands up in defence, suggesting that she agreed with him.

***

They went to the inn again that evening, though as they walked across the village Merric dragged his feet and hung back from the rest. He was not in the mood, and did not want to come face to face with Ketch again.

One of the villagers had brought his fiddle, and he struck up a tune on the musical instrument. The gathered folk cheered and before long the inn was filled with the sound of their singing. Merric gradually felt his frustrations slip away, and smiled as he saw the village folk looking so merry. Despite the hardships they suffered, they were able to always see the best in their lives, even if that was just a pleasant evening together in the inn to take their minds off things. Unaware of Merric's earlier actions, Kasper and Tomas joined in with the other villagers' singing, though Ana looked worriedly across at Merric.

'I'm fine,' he said to her, with a smile, 'truly.'

She smiled back, but this vanished quickly when Ketch and his cronies strode into the inn.

'Ale. Now,' Ketch said loudly, to no one in particular.

Two of his cronies shoved a couple of villagers off the best chairs by the fire, and Ketch sat down, putting his feet up. The fiddler had stopped playing when Ketch had entered, but now struck up a new tune. The singing resumed, and everyone did their best to ignore the new arrivals.

'Where's my ale?' Ketch asked the room.

'That'll be five coppers, if you and your friends want a drink,' Lora said from behind the bar. She was the only one that Ketch obeyed, and rumour had it that it was his desire to one day marry the barmaid. She had tried to take advantage of this, and appealed to Ketch herself to get him to carry out his duty as miller. Even she, though, could not change Ketch's stubbornness.

'It seems I left my coin purse at home,' Ketch said with a fake sigh. 'Someone give Lora some coppers, so me and my boys can have our drinks.'

No one moved, and all avoided eye contact with him. The fiddler continued to play determinedly, but fewer were joining in with the singing.

'I asked a question.' Ketch rose from his seat angrily, unhappy about being ignored. 'And stop that racket!' One of his cronies walked over to the fiddler and yanked the instrument from his hands. With one swift motion he snapped it in half, dumping the two pieces on the floor.

'That's better,' Ketch said. 'Now, how about you?'

He was pointing at Ana, as though noticing her for the first time.

'You're a pretty one. Give the woman some coins. Now.'

The inn had gone completely quiet now, but Lora caught Ana's eye and shook her head. Ana looked silently at Ketch, unsure of what to do. The miller looked around the room, not used to not getting his way. Eventually his eyes rested on Merric.

'Well, if it isn't the town boy. We're going to have a serious disagreement soon,' he snarled.

Merric tried to rise to his feet, but Ana reached out and stopped him. Kasper was looking from Merric to Ketch in confusion.

A moment later, seeing that he was not going to get his way, Ketch and his cronies got to their feet and headed for the door. The villagers were giving them a wide berth as they passed.

'I don't think I want a drink anyway,' Ketch said to Lora. 'Not from here, not with the kind of customers you let in.'

They disappeared out into the night, and Lora strode out from behind the bar and closed the door behind them.

'What was all that about?' Kasper asked, looking from Merric to Ana, and then to his wife.

Maryl was sat beside her husband, with Daysee sleeping on her lap, but she just shrugged and looked away.

'Something *needs* to be done about him,' Merric said, his voice shaking with silent fury.

'Merric, nothing *can* be done,' Ana said soothingly, though her own anger was clear.

'He's just a bully,' Merric snarled. Most of the villagers were listening now, the room still silent. 'Bullies only answer to strength.'

'We've tried,' a thickset farmer said, from behind a thick beard. 'I've tried speaking to him, so has Patt at other times, and Howel, and even Aulden.' The men around him murmured their agreement. 'Even Kasper has tried, but Ketch won't listen to anyone.'

'Then perhaps we need to try a new way,' Merric said.

'What are you suggesting, Pod?' Maryl asked, her eyes narrowed at him.

To everyone's surprise, the anger suddenly disappeared from Merric's face, and was replaced by a grin.

'I've got an idea.'

- CHAPTER FOURTEEN -

A time of change

Ketch always snored loudly as he slept. It did not bother him though; he never heard it after all. It was the dead of night, and a few stalks of wheat fell gracefully onto his face, tickling his nose. He grumbled sleepily and brushed them away. Another couple of stalks followed them soon after, falling from the rafters of the mill far above him. These, too, were brushed onto the floor.

He was a deep sleeper, but even Ketch could not notice when a whole pile of wheat was then dumped onto him in one go as he lay on his bed.

'What in the name of…!'

Ketch jumped up, crying out, and shaking the pile of stalks off him. He looked round the room angrily, expecting to see some of the children from the village playing a trick on him.

Where were his cronies when he needed them?

Another big bundle of wheat fell into the centre of the room with a muffled crash. Jumping out of the way, Ketch looked up into the shadows above him. He balled his hands into fists.

'If I find out who did this, they'll pay!'

The only reply to this was a constant, heavy stream of wheat stalks that fell from the ceiling. They landed on the floor, on Ketch's bed, and even on Ketch himself. He shouted in alarm, and darted for the door that led outside. He tugged at the handle but the door did not budge. He spun back around, looking for another way out, and saw to his horror that the floor of his home had already disappeared, covered by a thick layer of wheat. The bed was almost lost from sight too, but still the wheat kept falling.

'Stop it!' he cried, 'leave me alone!'

***

'Another sack, quickly!' Merric called from the rooftop, to those gathered below.

He held a sack upside down and was shaking it, letting the contents fall through the hole they had made in the roof of the mill. All the wasted wheat in the village had been cut into shorter lengths after Ketch had refused to grind it, and packed into sacks ready for threshing and for easier storage. A pile of these sacks, now empty, lay on the roof tiles of the mill next to Merric.

'Here,' a man said, climbing the ladder they had placed up against the mill and dumping a couple more sacks at Merric's feet.

Merric grabbed one, whilst Kasper picked up the other. These, too, were upended, and the contents fell down into the mill with the others. They could hear the miller's cries all the way up on the roof, and they laughed. Two of the villagers were holding the door of the mill shut, grinning as they heard Ketch try and wrench it open again. Another group of villagers, armed with their farm tools, had the miller's cronies backed into a corner of the yard, where they could do nothing to help their master. All the folk of Little Harrow were gathered outside the mill, including a jolly Sir Hestor Peggleswade and the portly prior who grinned along with the rest as they watched Ketch's plight.

Several dozen sacks of wheat later, Ketch had gone quiet inside the mill, except for the occasional sob. Merric climbed back down the ladder to ground level, and ordered the door be opened. As it swung open, the villagers roared with laughter.

The ground floor of the mill had been almost entirely filled with wheat, and a flood of stalks came pouring out, carrying Ketch along with it. He was dumped unceremoniously at Merric's feet, where he panted with fury and fear.

'Why didn't you do something?' Ketch cried angrily at his cronies, his eyes red. Whether this was from tears or from the wheat, none could know for sure, but all had their suspicions.

'There were too many of 'em,' Hopper, the chief crony, replied simply. 'You don't pay us enough to get hurt.'

He was looking at the large crowd of villagers that were gathered.

'You don't pay us at all,' another grumbled.

Ketch looked up at Merric, as though seeing him and the folk of Little Harrow for the first time. His voice suddenly sounded scared.

'What do you think you're doing?'

He seemed to twitch his hair out of his eyes more when he was nervous.

'Laying down the new law,' Merric answered.

'You can't do this,' Ketch said, his voice shaking.

'Kasper, Aulden,' Merric called, and the archer and the village blacksmith walked over. 'Get him back into the mill, and lock the door behind him. The rest of you, get some more sacks of wheat onto the roof.'

It felt strange to be ordering the villagers, but they all made to follow his orders without question.

'No!' Ketch cried, as they grabbed his arms. 'Please, don't!'

'Why should I listen to you?' Merric asked. 'You never listen to anyone else.'

'I'll do anything!' Ketch screamed as he was dragged back up the steps.

'Wait,' Merric said, holding his hand up to stop Kasper and Aulden. He looked at Ketch. 'I think you've got a job you're meant to be doing. You live in a mill; that should give you some clue as to what it is. Any ideas?'

'Yes,' Ketch said miserably.

He felt his power over the village folk leaving him. He had found it easy to bully the villagers when they kept out of his way, or when they came to him one by one. With the protection of his cronies he felt as powerful as any king. But seeing all the villagers here in front of him, with his thugs unable to help, Ketch realised that it had all been a trick. He was not a king, and he had no power over these folk really. It had just taken one boy from a distant town to realise that all it took was for the villagers to show strength and unity.

'I'll make you flour. All of you,' Ketch said, defeated.

He looked at the faces of the villagers that were now gathering round. They carried torches as though for a witch hunt, and for the first time in his life Ketch was afraid of them. They no longer looked intimidated by him, and in fact they seemed to almost pity him. Kasper and the blacksmith let go of Ketch, and he slumped feebly in the pile of wheat which was still spilling out of his door.

'I know you will,' Merric said, with a smile.

He crouched down to where Ketch now laid, sobbing. Merric pointed up at the door to the mill.

'There's plenty in there to get started with. And I'm sure if you ask them nicely, all these farmers will let you come to their fields and collect their harvests. You'd better get started; you're going to be busy.'

* * *

The very next morning there was a definite change in the mood of Little Harrow. The villagers awoke to find a small sack of flour outside each of their front doors, and when Merric and Hamm arrived in their field they saw Ketch and a pair of his cronies, pitchforks in hand, loading a wagon with wheat. Their faces were tired, after working through the night. Merric and Hamm watched from a distance with small smiles on their faces, as Ketch and his men finished the work and silently took the wagon back towards the distant mill.

That day, the work in the fields felt easier than normal, as though an invisible weight had been lifted. It was not just Merric who was feeling this. As he passed through the village that evening he was greeted by the smell of freshly baked bread from every home. The air was filled with the sound of laughter and high spirits, as the families sat down for their supper. Even the rain that had started to fall could not dampen their moods.

For the first time in months the folk of Little Harrow had enough to eat. Merric had half a loaf of bread to himself as he sat down with Kasper's family for their supper, and he used it to soak up the soup that tasted even more delicious than it had before. Later that night, Merric, along with nearly everyone else in the village, fell asleep with a smile on his face.

The change in fortunes for the folk of Little Harrow could not have come at a better time. A few days later was the summer celebrations, and the folk of the village, along with the rest of High Realm, would be spending the day giving thanks to The Mother for watching over them for another year. The day would include a feast on the village green, shared by all the villagers. In Eagle Mount, Merric used to celebrate the day along with the Jacelyns, and the banquet that was laid out for them and their guests was a wonder to behold. Eye-watering foods from across the realm and beyond were served, and everyone would forget any troubles they had and enjoy the day. The banquet here in Little Harrow would be simple in comparison to the vast array of foods and entertainment offered in the Grand Hall of the Jacelyns, but in a strange way Merric found himself looking forward to this year's celebrations even more. Though, whenever he found himself alone, his mind wandered to the memories of himself with Lord Roberd, or Lady Cathreen, or Tristan and Sophya. He pushed these sad thoughts from his mind, knowing they would not want him to be unhappy. He instead he tried to remember the happy times he had spent with them, and he let it bring a smile to his face.

The day of the summer celebrations dawned like any other, but all work finished at midday. Merric returned eagerly from the fields, and hurriedly bathed his hands in the barrel of rainwater beside Kasper's front door. Maryl seemed to be enjoying herself, straightening Merric's shirt and brushing his hair. Kasper rummaged around in a chest and dug out an old scarlet and blue cloak that he had long grown out of, and he draped it around Merric's shoulders. Maryl gave Ana a dress that she had not worn since her wedding day, but it fitted the blacksmith's daughter perfectly.

'It doesn't fit me any longer, so it's yours now,' Maryl said. 'The green will bring out your eyes wonderfully.'

Ana tugged awkwardly at the dress's skirts, unused to wearing anything like it, but smiled shyly when Merric saw her in it.

Tomas alone was not with them as they prepared, as he had to help Sir Hestor make himself as presentable as he could. As the lord of the village, he was expected to be in charge of the day's proceedings, but truthfully most villagers would be surprised if he could even last until the end of the banquet.

By the time the celebrations were due to begin, the rain had cleared up and it promised to be a pleasant evening. The village green was full of folk when Merric, Ana and Kasper's family arrived, and all seemed joyful and happy. This was the first time Daysee had been to the summer celebration feast and been old enough to understand what was going on. She skipped along excitedly, causing the others to have to hurry to keep up with her.

Merric felt warmth fill his heart as he watched the villagers looking so happy. Along with everyone wearing their finest clothes it made him feel like he was in another village entirely, compared to how it had been a couple of days ago. Many of the folk greeted Merric with genuine affection. All knew it had been him who had had the courage and determination to unite the villagers and stand up to Ketch, and without him it was likely they would have continued to live under the miller's bullying for many years to come. Merric blushed at the attention, but enjoyed it all the same. He was proud of the difference he had been able to make, even if he was too humble to admit it. He was glad that he had been able to repay the folk who had welcomed him and his friends into their village.

When the banquet started, Merric tucked in to the modest selection of food with everyone else. Vegetables, soups, piles of freshly baked bread, and a few roasted hare that Kasper had managed to hunt were piled onto a long table that stretched across the green. Everyone sat at the same table, equals for the day, and ate beneath the evening sky. Merric and the others were seated halfway down the long table, a few places away from where Tomas sat beside Sir Hestor. The knight was dressed in his best pink doublet, but he had already dripped gravy down his front. Tomas tried to wipe it away, but threw down the cloth and gave up when a second dollop of gravy dripped down from the joint of meat in Sir Hestor's hands. The servant caught Merric's eye and laughed. All around them, folk talked happily and ate and drank their fill.

Eventually, Sir Hestor rose unsteadily from the bench he was seated on, and addressed his fellow diners.

'Good folk of Little Harrow,' he said, slurring his words, 'we give thanks to our blessed Mother for watching over us, and for providing us with her care and love over this past year.'

At Sir Hestor's signal, the villagers all stood, and raised their cups to the Mother.

'To the Mother,' they all chorused.

'And here's to Pod!' a voice cried out, and it was echoed all along the table.

Merric blushed.

As the sun began to sink in the sky a couple of men lit a great fire at the other end of the green, and another retrieved his fiddle, recently repaired following his run-in with one of Ketch's cronies. As he started to play, the villagers began to rise from the table and make their way over to fire.

Logs had been arranged around the fire, and Merric sat himself on one close to the flames. The evening was a little chilly, and the fire gave off a pleasant warmth. The flames rose high into the sky, where they turned into spots of light that disappeared amongst the thousands of stars that filled the night. A merry tune had been taken up by the man playing the fiddle, and several of the villagers began to dance. As Merric watched, Kasper offered Maryl his hand

and the two of them held each other close as they danced around the green, their faces glowing in the light of the fire. Kasper was unrecognisable from the dour poacher who had helped guide them across The Head. Here he was a loving husband and kind father, with happiness written across his face.

Merric smiled as he watched at Kasper and Maryl dance, before gazing into the fire. He often found that watching flames played with his mind, which would wander to strange places. As his eyes followed the dancing flames, Merric thought of the stories he had read growing up. *The Lady of the Lake and the Green Knight, Sir Balleus the Barmy and his Willow Sword, The Witch of the Haunted Wood* and *The Tale of Eloria and Holion* were some of his favourites, and he had many fond memories of Lady Cathreen reading them to him when he was younger. He had lost hours of his life charging around the castle of Eagle Mount, slaying griffins and dragons and chimeras with imaginary swords, and rescuing damsels from the clutches of evil kings. He had always dreamt that one day he would take part in a story of his own. But now that it had happened he found that his own adventure had turned out to be quite different to anything he could have imagined.

Ana walked across to where Merric sat. Out of the corner of his eye Merric could see some of the boys of the village watching her from across the fire. Noticing this, he felt a strange aching in his stomach. Ana sat down next to him on the bench.

'They all look so happy don't they,' she said.

Merric nodded and looked around at the smiling faces.

'It's you that has brought them this happiness,' Ana said, looking at him. 'Lord Roberd would be so proud if he could see this.'

The flames were illuminating one side of her face, and for the first time Merric noticed the shape of her cheekbones.

'You really think so?' he said, distracted, watching her tuck her hair behind her ear.

'Of course,' she said, beaming at him. When she saw the look of doubt on Merric's face, she added, 'it's those of us who consider ourselves unremarkable that do the truly remarkable things.'

She put a hand on his knee, and Merric instinctively pulled his leg away.

'Sorry,' he said clumsily, when Ana's hand flinched.

She looked embarrassed and gazed into the fire, toying absent-mindedly with the cuff of the dress's sleeve. At that moment, one of the boys who had been watching her from across the fire walked up to where they sat.

'May I?' he asked, holding his hand out to Ana.

With a glance at Merric, Ana took the offered hand and allowed herself to be steered to where the other villagers were dancing to the music. Merric watched them go, feeling the unpleasant sensation in his stomach again, only this time it was twice as painful. Looking for something to distract himself he scanned the faces around him and saw Ketch seated alone at the very edge of the firelight. The miller looked smaller without his cronies around him, and he looked shyly around. As Merric watched, Daysee wandered over to where Ketch sat and tugged at his arm, trying to get him to stand up and join in with the dancing.

A sudden laugh brought Merric's attention back to Ana, and he saw her dancing with the boy. The fiddler was playing a foot-stomping tune, and the dancing was getting faster and faster. Ana looked so different in Maryl's dress, rather than her more practical blacksmith's clothes, and she had a broad smile on her face as she danced.

The aching in Merric's stomach got too much for him. He was confused, and frowned as he rubbed his brow. He did not know why he was suddenly feeling like this, but knew he could not bear to keep watching Ana and the boy. He looked around to try and find Tomas, but he must have been taking Sir Hestor back up to Harrow Manor, as he was nowhere in sight. With no one to distract him, Merric instead stood and walked quickly and silently away from the green. He left the crowds and the fire and the music behind him, and eventually reached the edge of the village. It was dark and cold after the warmth of the fire. He could still hear the music and laughter of the villagers behind him, but all the enjoyment of the night had left him.

He stopped and leant heavily on a rough wooden fence. He sensed footsteps behind him, and was surprised when he heard Ana's voice.

'Merric?'

He did not turn to face her.

'What?' he answered.

'What's wrong?'

'Nothing's wrong.' He did not know what else to say.

Ana leant on the fence next to him, but still Merric did not look at her.

'I know you're lying,' Ana said.

'Who was that you were dancing with?' Merric asked, trying to sound casual.

'Jule,' she said, 'he's the son of Aulden.'

Aulden was the village blacksmith, and no doubt Ana had got to know his son during her days working there. They probably worked together. Merric felt a surge of jealousy towards him.

'Do you not like me dancing with him?' Ana said to Merric, annoyed at his silence.

'I don't like him.'

'And why in the name of the Mother is that?' Ana asked, her patience gone.

Merric just shrugged. He did not know what he disliked about the boy, nor where this anger towards his best friend was coming from suddenly.

'Okay, let me get this straight,' Ana said, 'you won't dance with me, but you don't want anyone else to either?'

'What?' Merric said, spluttering.

'Just because you don't want to ask me to dance, it doesn't mean that someone else won't want to.'

'I...'

'I'm not going to wait around for you forever, Merric!' Ana said, her eyes beginning to well up.

Merric had never seen her cry, and it made him feel uncomfortable. He made to put his arm round her, but she shook it off.

'I didn't think you'd want me to ask you to dance,' he said, confused.

Merric's anger quickly returned, as he realised that Ana was being very unfair. His face flushed.

'I never knew you even *liked* to dance. If I'd known, I'd have asked you to.'

Ana threw her arms up in frustration.

'This has nothing to do with dancing, Merric. Don't be so thick.'

'What do you mean...?'

'Oh never mind,' she said, her eyes streaming with tears. 'Forget it! You clearly don't get it, do you?'

Ana turned from him, and ran away into the darkness. Merric took a step after her, but stopped. He waited for a moment, biting his lip, before taking another step. He paused again, and with a final shake of his head he changed his mind and went in the opposite direction.

His head was a mess. What had all that been about? Had Ana meant what he thought she did? They had been close friends for years, but perhaps she thought of Merric as more than that. That was the only explanation for how she had acted just now. And how did he feel about her? The jealously he felt when Ana was around the blacksmith's son, and the hollow feeling inside him, certainly pointed to him thinking of her as more than a friend too. He did not know how long he had felt about her in this way, nor what it meant now for their friendship, if they even had a friendship left.

Ana was the daughter of a blacksmith, so surely Jule was a better match for her than he was. Merric was the son of a baron, and a nobleman. They were as unsuited to each other as a prior and wine. But then again, he was a nobleman no more. In Little Harrow he was nothing more than a farm helper, with his past life in Eagle Mount now far behind him. Maybe he and Ana as a pair *could* work. But if he was a true friend to her then surely he should be happy for her, whether she chose to include Merric in her life or not. All he knew was that he could not bear the thought of him and Ana not being friends. He would need to find her, to talk to her, but perhaps that should wait until morning.

Merric had been walking without realising. The fire-lit village green lay in front of him again, and the folk were still enjoying their evening. Not wanting to speak to anyone, Merric made his way instead to the table that had been set up outside The Golden Wheel, and which was straining under the weight of the casks of ale and mead.

Merric grabbed a mug and quickly filled it, leaning back against the wall of the inn.

He raised the mug to his mouth, but then, through the night, he spotted a horse-drawn wagon entering the village. For a moment Merric feared it was the arrival of the Monfort men hunting him. It had been days since he last worried about those who were sure to be searching for them still, and he had dared to hope that they would be able to continue to live in Little Harrow in peace. Merric thought of his sword, safely stowed away in Kasper's cottage, and felt defenceless without the blade by his side. If the visitor turned out to be a Monfort man then he would be unable to protect himself. Merric considered ducking back into the shadows, to hide himself.

However, as the wagon neared, Merric could see that the driver was no Monfort soldier, but rather a richly dressed merchant. He stopped the wagon outside the inn, and jumped down from the driving bench. He was followed by a stocky and grim-faced man clad in leather and ring mail, who Merric assumed to be the merchant's personal bodyguard. It was not safe to travel alone on the roads in some parts of High Realm, let alone during the night and when you are carrying a bulging coin purse.

The merchant walked up to Lora, who was stood in the doorway of the inn cleaning a mug with a cloth, while enjoying watching the folk celebrating. The merchant bowed gracefully to her, twirling a finger around his oiled moustache. Lora's cat rubbed up against the merchant's leg, purring happily.

'Forgive me for my untimely arrival,' the merchant said silkily, 'I appear to be interrupting your charming village's summer celebrations. I hope The Mother takes no offence; being on the road I've unfortunately lost track of the day.'

The merchant spoke pleasantly, as did most who made a living selling their wares to others.

'I'm wondering if I could trouble you for a room for the night, and a stable for my horse? My man requires no room; he's more than comfortable in the open air

'I'm sure I can squeeze you in,' Lora replied cheerfully, 'the attic room is free if that would suit you?'

'Perfectly! And some hot food for supper?'

'Of course,' the landlady said with a smile.

She gestured to one of her stable boys, who began leading the horse around the back of the inn to where the stables were located, and the short bodyguard went with him. The merchant appeared in no rush to go inside the inn, and instead seemed happy to accept the mug of mead that was offered to him and watch the village festivities fondly.

'What brings you to Little Harrow?' Lora asked him conversationally.

'I'm just passing through I'm afraid, my dear,' the merchant replied. 'I'm on my way to Eaglestone.'

Merric had been doing his best to ignore the conversation, having no interest in the merchant's arrival now that he knew the man was no threat to him. However his ears pricked up at the mention of Eaglestone, and he inched closer to hear what they were saying.

'Oh? And what takes you there?' Lora said.

'I've got a dozen barrels of salted pork in my wagon,' the merchant said. 'I have to make good time, so I'll be setting off before dawn tomorrow. Would you mind sending someone to wake me? You will? You're too kind. Plenty of others will be heading that same way, and Lord Aric will only need to buy so much. It would be a shame to go all that way, only for my pork to be turned away. Say, you haven't had any other merchants come this way have you?' he asked as an afterthought.

'I haven't seen any,' Lora admitted. 'But we're a way off the main road here, so I don't suppose many would stop in our village. Is it a special occasion, for Lord Aric to require so much food?'

'Quite so, young lady, quite so! It's a wedding, and a wedding the likes of which we've never seen!'

Merric choked on his drink. A wedding? Fortunately Lora asked the question he was itching to ask himself.

'How lovely! I love a wedding. Who is getting married?'

'Ah now this is the wonder of it,' the merchant said. 'The marriage is that of his son, the new Duke of The Head himself. That's why I've come all this way from beyond the

Silver Peaks. Lord Aric will pay good coin for my pork; he'll want only the best for his son.'

'And who's the lucky lady?'

Merric held his breath in anticipation, all thoughts of Ana gone from his mind. The merchant took a long, slow drink of his ale, and Merric had to resist the temptation to run over and knock the mug from the merchant's jewel-encrusted fingers, so desperate was he to hear the answer.

Eventually the merchant lowered the mug again, and wiped the froth from his mouth with the back of his hand.

'Why, none other than the late Lord Roberd's only daughter. Lady Sophya Jacelyn.'

- CHAPTER FIFTEEN -

The truth is revealed

The Hall of Kings was impressive to look at, and a wonder to behold, but it was not welcoming. The vast, grey stone hall stretched on seemingly forever, larger than any other room in all the realm. The chequered floor was made from black and white marble, like a giant Kings and Castles gaming board. Overhead, the vaulted ceiling rose up and up, even grander than the most decorated priory. However, the vast open space was a cold and draughty place. It was especially chilly at this late hour, when the day was drawing to a close and the next would soon begin. Despite this, Henri stood loyally beside the throne, exhausted after a long day. He was the Royal Squire, and his place was beside the king at all times. King Cristoph of High Realm sat lazily in the throne, awaiting their visitor.

The huge double doors at the far end of the cavernous room opened with a distant crash, and a lone figure stepped through. He began the long walk towards the throne, along the narrow strip of red and blue patterned carpet that stretched the entire length of the hall. With each step the knight took his spurs made a metallic clang that echoed up and down the Hall of Kings. When the king of High Realm held his court, the hall would be filled with onlookers. But it was now the middle of the night, and the hall was empty apart from a few tired-looking royal guards. King Cristoph himself had needed to be awoken from his bed in order to greet their visitor, who had arrived unannounced and had requested an urgent audience.

The visitor was a knight by the look of him, clad in full armour as if for battle. His travel-stained surcoat was deep blue. He carried his helmet under his arm, and from its crest rose the carved likeness of a swan's head. Henri smirked, amused by how much knights liked to show off.

To be a knight was a mark of honour, and was a symbol of their valour and chivalry. After years of training with sword, lance and mace, all young noblemen who wanted to be a knight must stand vigil in a priory all night, praying to the Mother and swearing vows to uphold their honour and protect the helpless. Yet, once they were a knight, all ideas of honour and virtue seemed to disappear, to be replaced by a desire to show off and impress. Henri had seen many knights come and go from the Hall of Kings, eager to win the favour of the king.

The knight continued his journey up the hall, past the thirty-eight statues that lined the sides of the vast room. Each was near twice the height of a man, and depicted one of the thirty-eight kings of High Realm who had ruled before King Cristoph. They were carved from sea-granite, marble, ironrock, sandstone and many others. Every stone known to man was present in the statues, with each king wanting to outdo the others before them. Some had been bad kings, some had been good, and some had even been great.

At the far end of the hall from where Henri stood, nearest to the huge doors, stood King Eldred, the very first king who had left ancient Ouestoria and travelled with his companions across the Border Peaks to these lands. Halfway up the room was the statue of King Lycal the Lavish, who had a love for all things made of gold, and King Nyco the Young, who had been crowned when he was just seven years old and had died two years later. Nearest to the throne was the statue of King Rochus the Wise, the greatest king that had sat the throne of High Realm. He was King Cristoph's father, and the current king had never quite lived up to his father's legacy. One day King Cristoph would pass away too, and then he would have his own statue.

With a final chink of his spurs, the knight reached the throne and dropped to one knee. King Cristoph gestured for him to rise, with a lazy flick of the wrist.

'My apologies for the hour, your grace,' the knight said in a strong, deep voice. If he was nervous about addressing the king, it did not show.

'I fear being king leaves me with little time for sleep, Sir,' King Cristoph replied dramatically with a weary sigh.

Henri stopped himself from rolling his eyes. The king had been fast asleep when the Royal Squire had gone to his chambers to let him know that they had a visitor who had requested his audience. It had taken several minutes for Henri to rouse the king. It was unsurprising; that evening had been the summer celebrations, and the king had overindulged in both food and wine. If the folk of the realm could see the things that Henri saw then they would not look at their king in the same way.

He was known as King Cristoph the Victor, after the battle in which the armies of High Realm achieved victory against the Ouestorians, Henri's own people. However the king himself did not take part in the battle, although many of the common folk did not know this. His banner was there, fluttering high over their heads, as was his son in his golden armour. But the king himself was safely away from the fighting, many miles behind his army. Henri often wondered whether he should be renamed King Cristoph the Lazy. It had been his dukes that had saved the realm all those years ago, and since then the king had been happy to let the realm rule itself, ignorant to any dangers that threatened it. Fortunately the kingdoms of High Realm and Ouestoria were on friendly terms now, as Henri's appointment as King Cristoph's squire showed.

The king was old, and his hair was grey and his belly large. His rich blue and red clothes, the colours of the royal family of High Realm, were made of expensive silks and satins, but were ill fitting and stretched over his ever expanding body. His fingers were covered in rings and jewels, but were as fat as sausages. King Cristoph had never been impressive to look at, nor a wonder to behold. Unlike his son, Prince Iyan, who had led the army of The Kingsland to war for the past twenty years, the king had never shown desire to take part in warfare. It was tradition for the kings of High Realm to lead men into battle when war was unavoidable, setting a heroic example for their subjects to follow. King Cristoph, however, would struggle to even find armour to fit him. He much preferred to ride in a carriage than astride a warhorse, letting his son, and future king, represent him on the battlefield instead.

King Cristoph the Lazy – it was not just Henri who called him this behind closed doors.

'I have the honour of being Sir Horner Camoren, your grace,' the knight introduced himself. 'My father is Lord Warner Camoren, Baron of Pooltyn.'

'I've heard Lord Aric speak very highly of Lord Warner,' the king said, recalling.

The Lord Aric was a regular visitor to King's Keep, and it was rare for half a year to pass without him travelling to King Cristoph to offer his advice.

Sir Horner nodded.

'My father is Lord Aric's closest friend, and most loyal baron. He and I accompanied Lord Aric from The

Southstones as he journeyed east to Eagle Mount, along with his other most trusted knights and companions.'

'Ah yes,' King Cristoph said. 'I heard there was to be a tournament as part of his visit to The Head. Did you joust, Sir?'

'I did, your grace. I was unhorsed by the Blue Boar Knight; Sir Alton Hightop of Sprowstan, though it was a close bout.'

'A knight of my own dukedom!' the king chuckled. 'No shame in being beaten by a knight from one of the oldest and noblest families in The Kingsland. None at all!'

'Indeed not, your grace.' Sir Horner's face turn sombre. 'However I fear I haven't ridden all the way from Eagle Mount to the capital to discuss the tournament. I bring grave tidings.'

'Oh?' the smile faded from the king's face, and all signs of tiredness disappeared, to be replaced by a look of worry.

'Your grace, Lord Aric pains to inform you that Lord Roberd Jacelyn has been murdered.'

King Cristoph sat forward in his throne, stunned.

'Roberd Jacelyn? Murdered?'

Sir Horner bowed his head. 'His lady wife and son also.'

'This is grave news indeed,' the king murmured, flustered. 'Has the murderer been apprehended?'

'Yes and no,' Sir Horner confessed. 'They were slain by Lord Roberd's young ward, Merric Orrell. He's the orphaned child of the last Baron of Ryding, and has been the guest of Lord Roberd and his family for the many years. I fear he has escaped, though the Jacelyn soldiers who he persuaded to help him in his treason have been either killed or thrown into the dungeons.'

'Orrell…Orrell,' the king said, thinking. 'That family's name stirs a memory in me, though I cannot quite place it. You say he escaped? How is this possible?'

'We believe he may have had help, your grace. A poacher, who was in the dungeons of Eagle Mount at the time, also escaped, along with the traitor commander of Lord Roberd's personal guard. We think they may be aiding the Orrell boy.'

'Criminals helping criminals,' the king spat with disgust, 'they all deserve to lose their heads.'

Henri knelt and deftly cleaned up the spit from the marble floor with a silk cloth. Sir Horner either did not notice the Royal Squire, or else just ignored him. A good squire was neither seen nor heard.

'Whatever the Orrell boy's plan was, whatever he hoped to achieve, has been foiled by Lord Aric,' Sir Horner assured the king. 'He has named his son, Sir Rayden Monfort, the new Duke of The Head. He felt it important to maintain order during this chaos. No doubt the folk of The Head would be upset by the murder of their duke, and Sir Rayden offers them some comfort and stability.'

'A wise move, very wise,' King Cristoph murmured. 'Of course, only I can truly name a new duke in a situation like this, though I fully trust Aric's judgement. I therefore accept Sir Rayden's appointment to Duke of The Head. Aric knows what's best for my realm after all. He saved it once you know, at the Battle of King's Keep. It was right here, outside the walls of the capital.'

I wish I could have seen it, but I was no more than a child,' Sir Horner said, talking of the battle. 'I heard it was a great victory. The folk of The Southstones sing of it even now, from The Citadel to Weald.'

'Thank the Mother that Aric was in Eagle Mount when Roberd was murdered,' King Cristoph said. 'She only knows what would have happened if he wasn't. No doubt we'd have a rebel, and a murderer, ruling from Eagle Mount rather than a good man like Sir Rayden!'

Henri kept silent, as a good Royal Squire always did. It was not considered proper to talk when better folk were speaking. He had learnt that the hard way. His backside still ached when he remembered the beating he had once received from the king after making that mistake. His mind, however, never stopped working. His father used to tell him that he was too clever for his own good. The king was describing Lord Aric as a man who had heroically stopped a rebel from taking over The Head. What Henri himself was getting from the conversation was that Lord Aric and his family were now controlling half the realm. The Orrell boy's failed attempt to seize power had worked out very conveniently for Lord Aric.

King Cristoph was speaking again.

'Roberd had a daughter too, did he not? Saria, or Sara, or something like that.'

'He did, your grace, and she lives still, the Mother be praised. The Orrell boy was forced to flee once Sir Rayden led our forces against the rebels, before he could lay his hands on her too. She mourns the loss of her family, but she is safe. Lord Aric has seen fit to arrange a marriage between she and his son.'

'Such an honourable man,' the king said wistfully of Lord Aric. 'Marrying his own son to the poor Jacelyn girl will help her keep her family's memory alive.'

Or, Henri thought, having a Monfort ruling The Head would not go down well with the folk who lived there. Having him married to a Jacelyn would help make sure they all stay loyal.

'That is my duke's hope, your grace,' Sir Horner said.

'I thank you for taking the effort to ride all this way to tell me of this.'

The knight bowed again. 'It was my honour and duty, your grace. I only wish I had brought happier news.'

'There is no good news or bad news, just news,' the king replied, with an expression that he obviously thought made him look wise, but in fact just showed off his double chin. 'You have the hospitality of my castle, Sir. Rest here tonight, and then return to Lord Aric and Sir Rayden, though I suppose it's *Lord* Rayden now! I'm sure they'll appreciate your assistance in hunting down this Merric boy.

You may tell them that they have my full support, and I will aid them in any way I can.'

Sir Horner thanked the king, and with one last bow he turned and began making his way back down the long hall. The sound of his clinking spurs faded with him.

King Cristoph pressed his fingers together, and looked deep in thought.

'I say, what's happening in The Head? What would cause a boy to murder the man who had raised him?' he muttered.

Henri knew the king had not been asking him, but he chose to answer anyway.

'Only the Mother knows, your grace, and She's not telling.'

'She saw fit to gift me with a man as trustworthy and loyal to the crown as Aric Monfort,' King Cristoph replied, frowning at the Royal Squire for speaking to him in the Hall of Kings. This was a place for kings and lords, not common folk. 'We must be thankful for that.'

Henri raised his eyebrows, thinking that there may be more to Aric Monfort and his actions in The Head than Sir Horner had allowed himself to say. However, the Royal Squire had long since decided to keep out of the politics of the highborn folk of High Realm, so said no more.

King Cristoph the Lazy, Henri thought.

King Cristoph the Gullible, more like.

King Cristoph the Fool.

The merchant's words swam around Merric's head, and each time he heard them they made less and less sense. Sophya had been murdered, along with her brother and parents. The merchant must be mistaken. How could Rayden being marrying her? She was dead.

But was she?

Merric had not seen her killed, this was true, but he had been told she was dead. People had made him believe that none of the Jacelyns were left alive.

The merchant was still talking, unaware of the turmoil his words were creating in Merric's mind.

'…they're due to be married in three days, once the period of mourning has ended. The poor dear, losing her parents and brother in one night.'

Merric was hearing him speak, but the words were not registering in his head. Why would everyone tell him that Sophya had died, if she had not? Surely someone would have told him the truth. Merric thought of Sophya as a sister after all, so he deserved to know. It would be cruel to keep the truth from him. How could anyone allow him to believe that someone he loved had died? It was not the same kind of cruelty that had wielded the sword that had cut down Tristan, but a cruelty of another kind.

Surely Sir Gerard or Kasper would have told him. Perhaps they had also been lied to as well, and that was why they had not made Merric aware of the truth. However

Merric's thoughts went suddenly to the night before Sir Gerard had been killed. Mortin the minstrel had known, and had tried to tell Merric, but he had been stopped before he could say anything. And then the following morning, after the Monfort men had ambushed them, that yeoman had said that he had something he would tell him if Merric promised not to harm him. But he had died before he could say another word. At both times it has been Kasper who had stopped him from finding out the truth,

'Merric?'

He turned to see Kasper standing behind him, two empty ale cups in his hands. He had heard the conversation between the merchant and Lora on the way to refill the cups, and was watching Merric with a worried expression on his face.

'You knew,' Merric said, his voice shaking. He glared at Kasper, his eyes afire. 'You knew Sophya was still alive.'

With a slump of his shoulders and a sigh of defeat Kasper nodded.

Merric was speechless, and gaped at the man who he had grown to trust.

'How could you not tell me?'

When Kasper did not answer, Merric exploded in fury, drawing concerned glances from the villagers nearby.

'WHAT RIGHT DID YOU HAVE?'

Kasper seized him by his elbow and steered him away from where the folk would hear them. Merric shoved his hand off him.

313

'I know you're angry, and I'm sorry. I found out that Sophya Jacelyn had alone been spared when I was in the dungeons. Before we met up with you in the Greenwood, Gerard said that we weren't to tell you about Sophya, no matter what. When we found you, you were determined to return to Eagle Mount and you were set on throwing your life away in a foolhardy attempt at revenge. If you had known that Sophya was still alive then I knew we'd never have been able to stop you. I knew that Gerard had been right to decide to keep that knowledge from you.'

'So you chose to let me believe she was dead? She was like a sister to me!' Merric snarled.

'Yes. If there was a choice between you thinking all of the Jacelyns being dead, but you staying alive, or you knowing she was alive and then dying in some vain attempt to rescue her, then I knew which we must pick. Gerard made a choice, and a tough one at that. Sophya was beyond his help, but there was hope left for you.' Kasper's voice softened. 'It takes a great deal of courage, Merric, to draw your sword. I know, *I know*. But listen to me; it takes even more to know when to sheath it again. There are some things we cannot do anything about, and we have to learn to accept that. If we don't, then it will destroy us.'

'And you would abandon Sophya? What kind of man are you?' Merric accused.

'I take no pride in it,' Kasper said, looking at his feet.

The only reason Merric had agreed to leave Eagle Mount and his old life behind him was the thought that all

314

of the Jacelyns were gone. The idea that Sophya was alive, scared and alone, flooded him with determination. He had to return, to rescue her, to get revenge on the Monforts. But would that also bring about his own death? That was certainly what Kasper and Sir Gerard had been afraid would happen. However, Merric knew there was no valour in keeping himself safe when he knew that Sophya was in need of help. She was being kept prisoner by those who had murdered her family, and there could be no crueller fate than that. They may not be blood, but Merric was all the family that remained to her.

'Did you know that Sophya would be forced to marry Rayden?' Merric asked Kasper, accusingly.

'I didn't know,' Kasper replied, 'but I guessed. The Monforts have made themselves the rulers of The Head, but a Jacelyn has always lived in Eagle Mount, and the folk would never truly accept an outsider as their duke. By marrying his son to Sophya Jacelyn, Lord Aric could ensure that his grandson, Rayden's heir, would be half-Jacelyn, and his hold on The Head would be complete. The folk of The Head would be far more likely to follow their new ruler if they knew that Sophya was loyal to him.'

'Sophya won't ever be loyal to him,' Merric said.

She may have admired Rayden once, but she would now know that he was not the gallant knight she thought he was, but rather the cold-hearted murderer of her family.

'She will always be a prisoner; maybe not in chains or locked in a dungeon, but a prisoner nonetheless,' Merric continued.

Kasper nodded, but his expression was sad.

'There's nothing to be done, Merric.'

'There *is* something I can do,' Merric argued.

'You cannot succeed,' Kasper said warningly, his voice rising. 'You wouldn't get within a league of that castle. Half of Aric's men are out hunting you, and it's likely the king himself will be helping him as well by now. Even if you did reach the castle, you'd be captured before you could get close to her. Getting yourself killed won't save her, and nor will it keep the memory of the Jacelyns alive. You must survive, that was Gerard's last wish. There's nothing more valuable than the survival of innocence. The truth about the murder of Lord Roberd and his family will come out one day, but not with you dead.'

'You can't stop me from going!'

'Are you not listening to me?' Kasper asked. His temper was boiling over, and his face was turning red. 'I risked everything to bring you here. Gerard *died* protecting you, and Ana and Tomas gave up their old lives to accompany you, to keep you safe and allow you to start a new life here in my village. Is this how you would repay them, by throwing your life away? Aric knows you will have heard about the wedding, and will know that you'll want to try and stop it. Gods, maybe that is even his plan. All he wants is you captured or dead. He told the folk that you killed Lord Roberd and his family, and with your death he can appear the hero that avenged his memory. That will do nothing to help your cause, believe me. It'll just make the Monfort's grip over The Head even tighter.'

Merric was deaf to Kasper's words and warnings, despite part of him knowing the truth in what he said. He knew what he had to do. He had no choice. He could not live and know that Sophya lived in constant fear under the cruelty of the Monforts, and until she was safe he would never be able to rest, nor live with the feeling of guilt. He could do something about it, and even if he failed and was killed then at least he would die knowing he had done everything he could. Sophya would know that too, and know that not everyone had abandoned her.

Merric stepped away from Kasper, his mind made up. The archer grabbed him by the shoulder, knowing what he intended to do.

'No Merric,' he growled threateningly, 'I SAID NO!'

With all of the strength Merric could muster he punched out with his fist and struck Kasper clean across the face. Kasper grunted as he felt his nose break. Warm blood poured from his nose, and his grip on Merric's shoulder loosened slightly. Merric shrugged the man's hand away and ran into the darkness. Kasper's voice pursued him, loud in the night.

'You fool! Go! See if I care!'

Merric ran.

The darkness swallowed him up as he left Kasper behind. The night was moonless, and the village was pitch black. He stumbled onwards, knowing that he was going in the right direction, even in the darkness. He skidded to a halt outside Kasper's cottage, and could see that it was still dark inside; Maryl and Daysee must still be at the celebrations, which would continue long into the early hours of the morning.

He went round the corner of their cottage to where Nosy was tethered. Merric's jaw was set in determination, but he looked sadly at Tomas and Ana's horses. He wondered if he would ever see them again.

Nosy stopped chomping on the hay in front of him and looked at Merric with curious eyes as he began untying him from the hitching post. Merric threw his saddle onto the horse's back, and swung himself up. At that moment he heard a pair of footsteps approaching, and saw the light from a lantern bobbing as it came nearer.

'Where are you going?' Tomas said from behind the glare of the lantern.

He lowered the light and Merric saw that Ana stood beside him. She was not looking him in the eye.

'I heard Kasper's shout, and saw you running. What's wrong?' Tomas continued.

'I'm leaving.'

'What?' Tomas gasped.

'To go where?'

This time it was Ana that had spoken. She kept her eyes off Merric's, and looked instead at Nosy as he stood there shuffling his hooves.

Merric felt his heart lurch into his mouth as he looked at Ana, but pushed this from his mind.

'Back to Eagle Mount; Sophya is alive.'

Tomas's mouth dropped open in shock, and Ana finally looked at Merric properly.

'Truly?' she asked, shocked.

'Yes. She's to be married to Rayden,' Merric snarled in anger, causing his friends to take a step back in alarm.

'What are you going to do?' Tomas asked, his voice squeaking.

Merric looked hard at his friends, daring them to try and stop him as Kasper had.

'I'm going to stop it from happening. I'm going to save Sophya, and I'm going to get justice for Lord Roberd if I can.'

'We're coming with you,' Tomas said, trying to sound brave. 'Aren't we, Ana?'

Merric looked at Ana, who stared back at him with a pained expression. Their conversation earlier in the evening haunted her face..

'I promised to follow you, to help you where I could. I'm not leaving you now,' she said.

Relief flooded through Merric. The idea of leaving without them had filled him with dread. Ana went over to where their weapons were stored, and passed Merric his sword whilst she strapped her crossbow over her shoulder. It looked strange with the dress she was wearing.

Tomas looked confused all of a sudden. 'What about Kasper?'

'He's staying here.' Merric avoided their gazes.

'He's not coming with us?' Ana asked.

'There's no time to waste, we must leave now. Mount your horses, let's go.'

Merric feared that Kasper would turn up at any second, and try to persuade them to stop.

Once they were all mounted they spurred their horses and set off at a canter. They skirted the edge of the village so no one would see them leave. Once they reached the stream they turned onto the main road, and looking back they could see the fire in the village green surrounded by the happy folk singing and dancing.

The folk were at peace with the world, and leaving the village made Merric feel gloomy. He had just begun to feel at home there, but he knew now that Little Harrow had never truly been his home. He turned to his front again, and the three of them trotted over the small wooden bridge. Behind them they were leaving Kasper and his wife, and a life of safety and peace. In front of Merric was the open road, and nothing but danger and maybe even his own doom. The thought terrified him.

As they disappeared into the blackness of night Merric gave thanks that his friends were beside him.

- CHAPTER SIXTEEN -

On the road again

They rode for a couple of hours before stopping for the night, following the same track they had travelled along a few days earlier when they had first arrived in Little Harrow. Merric had wanted to continue, to cover as much ground as possible before coming to a halt, but Ana had insisted they stop. She pointed out that it was a moonless night, and it would not help them at all to have one of their horses trip on the heavily rutted farm track. Merric reluctantly agreed to stop, as long as they set off again at dawn the next morning. They had a long journey ahead of them.

They therefore found a small cluster of trees in a grassy meadow to the side of the road, which would provide a suitable place for them to camp for what was left of the night. They dismounted and led their horses to it, feeling weary after their long evening. Merric tethered their mounts to a tree where they were hidden from the road, while the others sleepily laid themselves down on the softest patch of mossy ground they could find. As they had not brought any of their things with them from Little Harrow, the three of them were forced to huddle together against the nightly chill, beneath the cloak Merric had been given by Kasper.

The past few hours were like a blur to Merric. Not long ago he had been enjoying the summer celebrations along with everyone else in the village, but so much had happened since then. The way he had ended things with Kasper left a sick feeling inside him, and as they had ridden through the darkness Merric had half expected the archer to come chasing after him. Lying awake beneath the trees, he strained his ears to try and pick out the sounds of a horse's hooves, but apart from the breeze in the leaves of the trees and the soft hooting of an owl the world was quiet. Merric wondered how Kasper's nose was after his punch had broken it. The clouds moved away overhead, and glittering stars appeared in the sky above them.

Ana lay just a few inches away from Merric, on the other side of Tomas, who was huddled fast asleep between them. Merric had been close to losing Ana as a friend today, and he wondered if their friendship would ever be the same again. She had agreed to join Merric on his journey back to Eagle Mount and whatever lay beyond, but there had been an awkwardness between them as they had ridden. Ana had kept her horse a few paces away from his, and spoken only when she needed to. Tomas had thought things seemed a bit strange, though he did not know why, and had looked back and forth between Ana and Merric for much of their ride.

The feelings Merric had felt towards Ana this evening were completely new to him. He kept on telling himself that she was just his friend, and that the feelings he had towards her were the kind that best friends have for each other. But he knew he was kidding himself. What was it she had said to him? *'I'm not going to wait around for you forever, Merric!'* She, too, must be experiencing feelings that were different from friendship towards him.

Merric was torn. He longed to speak to Ana, to find out how things stood between them. But he remembered the reason why they had fled Little Harrow in the middle of the night, and that far away in Eagle Mount Sophya was scared and alone. She was just a few days away from being forced to marry Rayden. Merric could not let himself be distracted by his feelings towards Ana, whether they were feelings of friendship or something more. There was something even more important at hand. He knew that Ana would understand that, or at least hoped she did.

Merric looked across at her in the darkness and could see the stars reflected in her eyes, and knew that he was not the only one lying awake.

* * *

Merric woke the others early and, with the sun still low in the sky, they heaved themselves wearily into their saddles. Their horses seemed eager to be on the move, and were happy to be on the road again after their brief stay at the village. The horses were raised by yeomen, and were trained to run great distances at speed, so were in their element. The same could not be said for Merric and the others. They had nothing with them that they could eat for breakfast, but as they set off they plucked some berries from the bushes that grew beside the road and ate these as they rode. There was dew on the grass to either side of the road, which made it look almost white in the morning's first light. Their clothes were damp from the dew, and the morning air chilled them. There were no clouds in the sky though, so the day promised to be a fair one.

Merric set a brisk pace, and they trotted their horses towards where the track would meet the Great East Road. If the merchant was right, the wedding was just three days away, so they had no time to lose. Their journey to Little Harrow had taken far longer than three days, but that was largely on foot, and they had taken the less direct route that had avoided the main road for fear of coming across the Monfort men who were searching for them. While the risks were still there, Merric knew they had to throw caution to the wind if they were to get to Eagle Mount in time.

They did not stop for several hours, until the dew had faded and they had reached the Great East Road and the churning waters of the Willowbank River beside it.

Before turning east, they rested beside the Willowbank in which, just days ago, Merric had almost drowned. His thoughts strayed briefly back to the mystery of his saviour on that day, but he quickly pushed it from his mind. Their horses drank gratefully from the cool water, while Ana, using the skills she had picked up from Kasper during their previous journey, managed to catch two small fish. Tomas lit a fire with a couple of flints, something he was becoming better and better at, and they dined quickly on one of the roasted fish.

Once finished they made to continue their journey, but Merric first wanted to speak to Ana. They were riding towards danger, and he did not like the strange atmosphere between them.

'Look, about last night,' Merric said, as Tomas was fetching their horses from the river.

'Merric, don't.'

'Don't?' Merric took a step back, afraid that she was going to get angry and shout at him again.

She saw his worried expression, and forced her face into a strained smile. 'I mean, don't worry about it.'

'Are you sure?'

'Of course, we'll talk about it another time. Once Sophya is safe,' Ana said.

Merric nodded and said no more. He wondered whether they would be alive to have that conversation in a few days' time.

The sun was high in the sky by now, and bright. After their short night's rest they would all have welcomed a longer break, but Merric knew they could not afford to. They remounted their horses and spurred onwards along the Great East Road. As they rode, Ana asked Merric why Kasper did not join them for their return journey. He had, after all, watched out for them as he led them all the way from the Greenwood to his village, and it seemed strange to them that he would not help them now. Merric did not want to lie to his friends, and so told them the truth. Tomas was shocked.

'You hit him?' he cried.

Ana did not say anything, and Merric could not tell what she was thinking. He hoped that Ana did not think that Kasper was right about it being silly trying to rescue Sophya. If she did, she kept such thoughts to herself.

They reached Oaktyn before long, and wary of their close call with the Monforts on their last visit they chose to skirt around the edge of the town, rather than follow the Great East Road through the centre. Merric looked back once they were on the main road again, and could see the oak tree and squat castle of the Oakheart family over the roofs of the town. He wondered how Lord Horin was faring. The poor elderly baron had not only had his lands taken away from him by the Monforts, but his sons had also been imprisoned as well. It was yet more misery brought on by Lord Aric and Rayden, and Merric swore that he would avenge them all.

With the town of Oaktyn behind them, Merric picked up the pace. He spurred Nosy into a canter, and Ana and Tomas did the same. The hooves of their horses kicked dust into the air from the road. Beyond Oaktyn, the Great East Road plunged into the northern lands of the Yielding, where the endless fields they passed were occasionally interrupted by small woods, farms, clusters of cottages, and the odd small castle where a knight lived. The road led down into a deep, wide valley, littered with neat orchards and meadows filled with cows and sheep grazing contentedly. There were few other travellers on the road, and those they did see were mainly just farmers herding their cattle from one field to another. None spoke to them, and Merric saw no reason to draw any unnecessary attention to themselves. As they reached the far side of the valley the ground levelled out again, and the Greenwood was in sight in the far distance, nothing more than a green smudge on the horizon, stretching as far as the eye could see both to the north and the south.

A few hours later the forest was looking closer, but still a long way off. Merric knew they would not reach it before nightfall, so he agreed to stop for the night and set off again in the morning. They set up their camp by a rocky outcrop off to the side of the road. The rocks would give them shelter from the wind that was picking up from the south, as well as hide them from any unwelcome eyes on the road.

They cooked and ate the other fish that Ana had caught, and were soon resting on the soft grassy ground. Ana and Tomas fell asleep quickly, exhausted from the day's journey. Merric stayed awake though, looking through the fading light at the trees of the forest far ahead of them.

Sir Gerard had died in the Greenwood, doing his best to protect Merric and his friends. He had sworn his life to Lord Roberd and his family, and gave his life for that oath. Merric now wondered if the knight had died for nothing. Sir Gerard had decided to not try and save Sophya himself, and Merric's own death may just be a day or two away. Beyond the forest stood Eagle Mount, and Merric did not know how he would feel when he saw the gleaming white towers of the castle again. Many sad memories laid there, memories of Lord Roberd who had treated Merric like a son, of Lady Cathreen who had loved him as one of her own, and Tristan who had thought of him as a brother.

But hope was there as well; hope in the form of Sophya, who Merric was determined to save from the grips of the Monfort family. Death and misery seemed to surround Merric, and he vowed he would make sure that Sophya did not share this fate. With this determination helping to bring peace to Merric, he slowly drifted off to sleep.

He woke at dawn to the songs of the birds gently sounding in his ears. He was stiff from sleeping on the ground and aching from the hours in the saddle. The land was beautiful in the early light, with the sun burning away the morning mists. He watched the birds circling overhead for a few minutes, and felt jealous of all those who woke this morning without worry or concern on their minds.

His friends slept on soundly, and Merric allowed them a few extra minutes. They had showed incredible loyalty by coming with him, so letting them have a little more rest was the least he could do. He could not afford them to have more than a few moments though. If the merchant was right, the wedding was due tomorrow afternoon, and they still had a lot of ground to cover. Leaving Ana and Tomas asleep, Merric led their horses down to a small stream and let them drink. After waiting as long as he could, and with nothing left to do to keep himself busy, Merric roused his friends with a gentle shake of their shoulders. Bleary-eyed and weary, they mounted their horses without a complaint, and got on their way again in the dawn light.

Before the sun had fully risen they had reached a small village that sat peacefully on the Great East Road. No folk were in sight, but smoke rose gently from the chimneys of the cottages. A notice had been nailed to a post in the centre of the town, and Ana went over to see what it said.

'You're getting famous,' she said to Merric, when she had re-joined them with the notice in her hand. 'There's a reward for information leading to your capture. One hundred gold pieces.'

Merric looked nervously round the village, but if any folk had seen him and recognised him then they cannot have been interested in claiming the reward, as there was no movement apart from a dog that barked at their passing.

They left the village behind them. Up ahead ran the Bluebottle River, which they had crossed further south a few days previously, and beyond that rose the trees of the Greenwood. They paused briefly to allow their horses to drink from the clear waters of the river. The dust from the road had made Merric's mouth dry, and he dipped his hands into the cool water and quenched his thirst. Once man and beast had drunk their fill, they rode over the bridge that spanned the lazily flowing water, and felt the forest close in around them.

The sunlight passed through the canopy of leaves above them, casting a dappling of light on the dirt road. They had many miles to cover, and they cantered along at a fair pace. The horses seemed to sense the urgency of their journey, and did not slow. Midday passed and the afternoon wore on. Their return journey through the Greenwood on horseback was much faster than their previous time in the forest, but to Merric the trees still felt never ending. They passed the small inn where, days ago, Merric had seen the Monfort yeomen relaxing.

Merric was thinking that they had not passed any other folk in a while when, as they galloped around a bend in the road, they found themselves face to face suddenly with a horseman who was travelling the opposite way.

The knight reined in his horse when he saw the three of them. Merric and his friends likewise pulled up abruptly, their horses skidding to a stop. The knight was clad in a red surcoat over his ring mail, with the image of a snake emblazoned across his chest. Merric drew in a breath sharply, panic rising in him. Was this knight a friend or foe? Did the knight know who they were? Merric did not recognise his snake symbol as being from a noble family from The Head. It was therefore likely that he was from The Southstones. Merric swallowed nervously.

The knight did not appear to be here to fight them though. His sword was in its scabbard at his side, and he made no move to unsheathe it. He was also not wearing his helmet. His head was covered only by the snug-fitting ring mail hood that was designed to be worn under a helmet. His eyes were studying the three travellers, but his expression was of boredom rather than of hostility.

'Clear the road, at once,' he ordered.

The command was blunt, his voice cold and drawling. Merric could barely control his relief. The knight did not know who they were, and had assumed them to be common folk who were hardly worth his attention.

'Make way there you urchins!' he barked when they did not move at once, his face turning stern.

Behind the knight Merric could hear the muffled thundering of the hooves of more horses. There seemed to be a large group of horsemen riding this way, westward along the road. Merric, Ana and Tomas therefore obediently dismounted and walked their horses to the verge beside the road in the shadow of the tall trees.

A moment later, in a flurry of hooves and jingling armour, around fifty more men rode into view. They were more knights, clad in all manner of colours which looked bright against the dull green and brown of the forest. Several were wearing white, bearing the symbol of the black marching knight of the Monforts.

Suddenly, Merric felt his stomach tighten, and Ana clutched hold of his wrist. At the centre of the group of horsemen rode Lord Aric himself astride his gleaming black horse. Merric, Ana and Tomas all bowed their heads, not out of respect, but to hide their faces.

Merric could barely breathe.

Lord Aric spotted the three young travellers and reined in his horse. His retinue of knights all did the same. He looked at their travel-worn clothes and laughed.

'Do you see, Sir Pollus,' Aric said in amusement, 'it is like I say; the folk here in The Head are inferior in every way. Look at these miserable creatures.'

'I see them, my lord,' a knight with a beard replied. 'You're absolutely right; pathetic excuses of peasants.'

'Let's see if they're as slow-witted as they look. You there,' Lord Aric said, speaking slowly and loudly, as though the three travellers were stupid. 'Who is your rightful duke?'

Merric, Ana and Tomas glanced at each other, their heads still bowed. If Merric looked up then Aric would no doubt recognise him.

'Come now, speak,' Lord Aric said, growing bored of mocking them. He drew his sword and pointed it threateningly at Merric. 'Are you too unintelligent to answer, or do you fear that your answer won't be to my liking?'

It was Ana who at last spoke. 'Rayden Monfort, milord. He's the true Duke of The Head.'

'There,' said Aric with the same booming laugh he had used so many times while at Eagle Mount as Lord Roberd's guest. 'Maybe they're not as brainless as they look.'

He spurred his horse into a trot and, followed by his company of knights, he rode away westwards. An elegant cart followed along behind, pulled by a teamster of strong horses and piled high with Lord Aric's possessions, before a collection of squires and servants brought up the rear.

Once the last of the horsemen had passed them and thundered away down the road, the knight with the snake embroidered on his surcoat touched his spurs to his horse's flanks and rode after them. When he was gone, Ana slowly looked round at Merric with wide eyes, her hand toying with the leaf-shaped silver amulet that she wore round her neck. Merric just let out a nervous laugh.

'I guess he's not staying around for the wedding then.'

His calm composure did not reveal his inner feelings. Anger had erupted in him when he had seen Lord Aric, and a part of him now wanted to charge after him and, even though he was one against many, try and cause as much pain to the man as he could. At the same time, Merric had felt fear. Had Lord Aric looked properly and see Merric's face then the game would have been up. Within seconds Merric would have been dead, or worse, captured. Seeing the Monfort duke surrounded by his heavily armed knights made Merric realise how foolhardy his task was.

'Well, at least there are fifty less Monfort men to face when we get to Eagle Mount,' Merric said, forcing a smile.

He indicated that they should get moving again, and neither Ana nor Tomas objected to this. They all wanted to put as much ground between them and Lord Aric and his men as they could. In a way, Merric was annoyed that Lord Aric appeared to be leaving The Head and returning to The Southstones. While it may make his task of rescuing Sophya a little easier, Merric had imagined taking out his revenge on both Rayden and his father. Lord Aric would just have to wait.

The trees began to thin as the evening loomed and, suddenly, the forest stopped altogether. They found themselves on the edge of the sweeping meadows and fields that led towards Eaglestone, and they reined in their horses. Merric could hardly believe that they had been able to cross the Greenwood in just a day, but even so they had reached the other side not a moment too soon. The sky above their heads was a deep blue, and the sun was beginning to set behind them to the west. They still needed to reach Eaglestone that night, as by the time the sun came up the next morning it would too late to rescue Sophya.

Merric, Ana and Tomas paused for a moment beside a little stream that trickled out of the Greenwood. Their horses dipped their muzzles in the water and drank, grateful after the dry and dusty road, while their riders stretched their aching muscles. Ana walked over to Merric, who stood as still as a statue. His hands clasped behind his back, with his eyes fixed to the east.

In the distance rose a gentle hill, and on that hill was a built a large town. Strong walls surrounded the town at the foot of the hill. As the hill rose, the buildings in the town grew steadily bigger, before it was topped by a beautiful castle built from white stone. Its walls dwarfed the town around it, and atop the castle keep were many towers, with the stone likeness of a great eagle, watching the land around it, at the top of the tallest.

Merric had not known how he would feel when he beheld Eagle Mount again, but now that he could see it all he could feel was affection. It was like seeing an old friend. He had grown up within those walls. There he had been tutored by Lord Roberd. He had played and fought with Tristan there, and had teased but loved Sophya. There he had first been introduced to Tomas, his honest servant who, for years since, had loyally served his master. Within the town outside the castle walls he had met Ana, his truest friend in the world. Even though their friendship had been tested, there was no one else he would rather have with him now.

Ana put her hand comfortingly on Merric's as he stood there, looking at the distant castle. Eagle Mount looked exactly as he remembered it. From this distance he could not even see the Monfort banners that fluttered from the walls. He was both excited to be returning to the castle, and at the same time dreading it. He did not know how he would feel stepping within its walls, knowing that Lord Roberd and the others were no longer there.

One thing at a time though. There was still a lot of things that could go wrong before he would get to the castle.

Merric, Ana and Tomas set off towards Eaglestone. The castle and town that surrounded it were still a few miles away, and night had fallen by the time they were close. The Great East Road passed right by Eaglestone's walls, and Merric reined in at a cluster of farm buildings half a mile from the town's gates. Here they dismounted and led their horses around the back of the buildings, where they found a small stable. The farmer was nearby and caught their eye. Ana went over to him, and after a quick discussion she came back and said that they would be able to leave their horses in his stable.

Merric patted Nosy on the neck.

'You wait here now, boy,' Merric said to him. 'When I get back, we might have to run like the wind, so get as much rest as you can, okay?'

There was some hay in the stable, and the horses tucked in greedily after their journey. Neither they nor their riders had eaten since the previous evening.

The town lay close, and from where they were they could clearly see the gatehouse built into the strong walls. Merric's eyes followed the well-travelled highway that veered off from the Great East Road and led up to Eaglestone's gatehouse. The highway was lined with well-tended trees; the home of the Jacelyn family had always been a welcoming place. This pleasant entrance to the town was ruined, though, by the cluster of heavily armed Monfort soldiers who milled around outside the gates.

'How do we get in?' Tomas said, looking at the soldiers, and asking the question that both Merric and Ana had been wondering.

They would never be able to sneak past the guards, and there was no other way into the town. Merric may have been able to climb the walls, but figures were patrolling the battlements, armed with longbows and crossbows; they would see and shoot Merric before he even got half way. They could not just walk up to the gate and hope not to be recognised either. The Monfort men at the gate would ask their business, and they would be sure to see through any story they made up.

Despite the day drawing to a close, the lands around the town were not deserted. A few travellers riding horses and driving wagons were on the road, heading to and from Eaglestone. Merric bit his lip, deep in thought, and then looked back up the road from the direction they had come.

Suddenly he smiled. 'I have an idea.'

* * *

Algon's large behind barely fitted on the seat atop the rickety wagon which rolled unsteadily towards the gates of Eaglestone. He pulled sharply on the reins to slow the two thin oxen that hauled the wagon along the road, coming to a stop in front of two of the Monfort soldiers who stood fully armed before the gates. Their padded coats bore the symbol of the black marching knight of the Monforts, as did their tall shields, and they looked at the fat farmer coldly. Algon regularly visited Eaglestone with his crops, and was usually greeted warmly by the Jacelyn soldiers. They were nowhere to be seen though, replaced instead by these unfriendly looking men who had been there ever since Rayden Monfort had taken over residence of Eagle Mount.

'Where are you going?' one of the Monfort soldiers asked gruffly.

'Up to the castle,' Algon replied, in as friendly a voice as he could summon.

He had his wife and seven children at home, and they depended on him selling his crops. He could not afford to be turned away from the town or, even worse, have his wagon and its contents confiscated. If he could sell this final crop of the year they would have enough money to see them through the winter. One of Algon's daughters was sick, and the healer in the village was not cheap.

'The castle?' the Monfort soldier asked. He nodded his head at the wagon 'What have you got in there?'

'Neeps, sir. For the wedding banquet tomorrow.'

'*Neeps?*' the first soldier said, looking at his mate with a frown. 'What in the name of the Mother are *neeps?*'

They were not familiar with the farmer's Yielding dialect.

'Neeps,' Algon said, panicking. He strained to think of another way of saying it, but could not think of any. 'They're neeps!'

Seeing the farmer's face turning red in concentration, the second soldier walked round to the back of the wagon and peered in. He turned back to his mate with a laugh.

'Turnips,' he said, sniggering at the farmer and his simple ways.

'What do they want with bloody turnips at the duke's wedding banquet?' the first soldier said curtly, not impressed.

Algon had a bead of sweat running down his forehead. Maybe they would not be able to afford little Sally's medicine this month after all. He was not about to give up though.

'You can do anything with neeps, sir! Neeps in pies, neep soup,' he said desperately, counting them off on his fingers, 'roasted neeps and tatties, mashed neeps, neeps fried with pease and onions.'

'Alright, alright,' the Monfort soldier said, waving him through the gate. 'Go through then, get out of here.'

'Thank you sirs, and have a fine evening.'

Algon breathed in relief, and cracked the reins. The wagon lurched into motion again, taking him through the gates and into the town. One of the Monfort soldiers grabbed a turnip off the wagon as it passed, and took a bite out of the vegetable.

'Eurgh!' Algon heard the man say, as he threw the turnip away. 'That's disgusting!'

The Lord's Way, the wide cobbled street beyond the gatehouse, twisted and turned between the buildings as it went up the hill and towards the high castle in the distance. Algon began making his way up the street, but once out of sight of the gatehouse he steered the wagon into a side road and came to a halt.

He banged twice on the seat of the wagon with his fist, and looking behind him he saw the three young strangers emerge from the pile of turnips and disappear into the shadows of an alley.

Algon wiped the sweat from his face, and rummaged in his patchwork cloak to extract the amulet that had been given to him as payment for smuggling the three of them into the town. It appeared to be made from silver, and took the form of a small leaf. He tucked it safely back into the folds of his cloak, and, with the memory of the two Monfort soldiers fresh in his mind, wondered whether the risk had been worth it.

CHAPTER SEVENTEEN

Eaglestone

Eaglestone's streets, normally so bustling and lively, were strangely quiet. That was the first thing Merric had noticed when he had climbed ungracefully from the pile of turnips on the back of the wagon, his already dirty clothes now covered in a layer of soil. At this hour the town was usually still fairly busy, with folk shutting up their workshops and heading home or to one of Eaglestone's dozens of taverns to relax after a hard day's work. However, this evening only a handful of folk could be seen, and they were hurrying past with their eyes down, not stopping to chat with anyone.

'It feels different, don't you think?' Ana said to Merric, watching the Monfort men who were patrolling the streets with the look of those who knew how to keep folk in line. 'Everything seems…tense. It's not the Eaglestone I remember.'

Merric just nodded, frowning. Many of the shops near to where they were stood were boarded up, as though the owners had left town or, more likely, had been imprisoned. On the wall of the nearest shop a notice had been nailed up. It was another poster offering a reward for information leading to Merric's capture.

Merric, Ana and Tomas had got inside the town walls with fairly little difficulty, but that had been the easy part. While the farmer had initially been hesitant to let them hide in his wagon, he had been quickly swayed when Ana had reluctantly presented him with her beloved silver amulets as payment. Now, they loitered in the dark entrance of an alleyway, and looked up the main street of Eaglestone that led up to the castle.

Merric had been relying on the town being busy, as this would allow them to blend in and make their way up towards Eagle Mount with little difficulty. With the streets being almost deserted this would be much harder. Without the protection offered by the crowds he knew they would be spotted quickly. But Merric would not give up. They had come this far, so had no choice but to keep going. All they needed to do for now was get to the castle, and Merric focused on that for the time being; just one step at a time. Once they reached the soaring walls of Eagle Mount he would then start worrying about the even harder task of finding their way to Sophya.

Merric gestured with his hand for his friends to follow him, before setting off down the alleyway at a fast walk. The buildings rose up on both sides of them, built from stone and wood and topped with the familiar blue roof tiles that made Eaglestone so unique. Merric kept himself half crouched, as though this might make his footsteps quieter. He soon realised though that sneaking along like this was likely to draw even more attention to them, so instead he straightened up and tried to look as calm and relaxed as he could.

In truth he felt far from calm, and half expected to hear the shouted challenge of a Monfort soldier at any time. Merric could hear the nervous breathing of Ana behind him, along with the shuffling footfalls of Tomas. He was about to turn round and tell them to quieten down, but he knew their hearts would be pounding and their nerves fraying, and him snapping at them would not help.

They were heading gradually upwards. It was not steep, and the back alley they were moving along gently twisted and turned as it made its way up the hill, parallel to The Lord's Way. It was best to stay off that main road, as it was sure to be heavily patrolled by the Monfort soldiers. The side roads would be much safer. However, the alley suddenly swerved sharply to the left, opening up unexpectedly into the Fountain Court. Merric had to admit that he did not know the back streets of Eaglestone as well as he ought to. They paused to take in their surroundings.

The Fountain Court was the name given to a section of The Lord's Way, around half way up to the castle, where the great cobbled street grew even wider to pass either side of a large round pool and fountain. Below the surface of the pool there glittered hundreds of copper coins that were flicked into it by the townsfolk, who believed that by doing so they would be blessed by luck and good fortune for the remainder of the day. The fountain was usually a glorious sight, with its cascading water rushing pleasantly into the pool, and in the hot days of the summer children happily splashed each other in the cool water. However in the darkness that had descended on the town since they had arrived, the fountain looked foreboding and lonely.

Like the rest of the town, the cobbled square surrounding the fountain was much quieter than usual. Normally a place where minstrels would stand and perform for the townsfolk throughout the evening, and peddlers would move around trying to sell toys and talismans, it was almost deserted this night. In the moonlight, a group of three Monfort soldiers could be seen stood huddled together not far from the fountain, passing a bottle between them. A burst of laughter came from them, and one of them hushed his friends as he looked nervously around. Suddenly a shout came from further up the street, and Merric edged backwards to make sure he and his friends were hidden in the shadows of the alley.

'What's so funny, you lot?'

The three soldiers snapped hurriedly to attention as their serjeant appeared in the square. One of them sneakily tucked the bottle into the back of his belt.

'Nothing, serjeant.'

'You heard his lordship earlier,' the serjeant said, his voice loud and commanding. 'He's expecting trouble, so be alert.'

'Yes, serjeant!' the soldiers said in unison.

When their serjeant had moved away again one of them turned to his mates.

'Do you really think the boy is coming back here?'

'Sir – sorry, *Lord* - Rayden seems to reckon so. He's made sure the wedding is no secret, and the boy is sure to come and try and stop it if he hears about it.'

'It would be certain death if he tries to get within a mile of this place. We'd skewer him where he stands.'

The soldier shook his spear to make the point.

'Yeah, well he's from The Head,' the youngest of the three said, 'folk from round here never was too bright.'

'Roberd Jacelyn was from The Head,' the eldest of the three countered, 'and he was as bright as anyone.'

'What?' scoffed the younger soldier. 'He spent his life daydreaming about flying eagles and the Mother know what else. He was a simpleton, that's what I've been told.'

'Not true.' The eldest soldier pointed at a scar on his brow. 'I got this at the Battle of King's Keep. I used to fight in King Cristoph's army of The Kingsland, before that Royal Land Charter was signed and the king gave some of his land to Lord Aric as thanks for the part he played in the battle. However, before the Lord Aric and the army of The Southstones arrived to help, we were already fighting hard. Roberd Jacelyn was a smart one. The prince was there, but he was all hot-headed and eager for a fight, and the duke from The Dale was too old. It was Roberd Jacelyn, I heard, who thought up our battle plan.'

The other two soldiers were too young to have taken part of the battle, but knew the story well.

'Yeah, but you weren't doing very good til us Monfort boys showed up.'

'We was doing just fine. I'm a Monfort man through and through now, but before the Land Charter was signed my home was over the border in The Kingsland, and I do have a small bit of pride for how well we was fighting before your papas arrived with the rest of Lord Aric's army.'

His mates just laughed. 'I told you your mind goes soft when you get old,' one of them said to the other.

The older soldier scowled at them.

Not wanting to get in trouble with their serjeant they chucked the empty bottle into the fountain with a small splash and hefted their spears, obediently watching the road as it led downhill back towards the gate. They were looking in the opposite direction to where Merric, Ana and Tomas lurked in the shadow of the alley though, and the serjeant had disappeared from sight.

Merric signalled to his friends, and cautiously they stepped out onto the wide cobbled street. The soldiers, who had their backs to them, did not hear their steps, so the three were able to edge quietly and quickly along without being challenged.

As they made their way through the Fountain Court, keeping to the shadows cast by the moonlight, they saw a new feature which had been added by the Monforts. At the far side of the Fountain Court, three sets of wooden stocks had been built. Two of the stocks were occupied by exhausted looking men, who had their heads and hands enclosed in the holes. They were not able to stand straight, nor were they able to sit down. Merric wondered who they were, and what they had done to deserve that punishment. Lord Roberd had never agreed with the idea of public punishment or execution, but clearly Rayden did not share this view.

Merric and his friends continued up The Lord's Way, but before The Fountain Court and the prisoners in the stocks had disappeared from view behind them, they heard a new noise.

'Merric, who's that?' Ana said, squinting up the street ahead of them.

Merric could not see anyone through the blackness, but straining his ears he could hear the sound of horses approaching. He could not tell who they belonged to, but knew that it was not likely to be someone they wanted to meet. Merric's head snapped from side to side, looking for a back alley or side road they could duck into, but could see none. There were only the rows of workshops and homes that lined the street. Directly to their right was a small, dark shop that seemed quiet, and Merric saw their only chance.

'In here,' he said, moving to the door and leaning against it with his shoulder.

The door did not budge, so he took a step back before slamming his body against it again. Once more the door did not open, but Merric felt it give way slightly. Tomas looked nervously back down the street to where the Monfort soldiers stood in the Fountain Court, worried that they could hear them. Merric gave the door one more shove, and was rewarded with the satisfying sound of the door snapping open. The three of them ducked inside, and Merric quickly closed the door again behind him. They gathered around the one cloudy glass window and peered silently out.

They only had seconds to wait before four horsemen trotted past where they were hiding. Three wore the uniform of the Monforts and had swords at their hips, but the other was dressed plainly in a tight fitting black robe. Merric's heart gave an angry flutter as he recognised Orderix, the Jacelyn's old Lord's Counsel.

Merric did not know what Lord Aric had promised Orderix in return for his help in betraying Lord Roberd, but he assumed it was gold or more power in The Head. Or both. Orderix was a selfish and greedy man, and it would not have taken much to convince him to betray his own duke. Merric recalled how Orderix had been eager for Kasper to suffer a humiliating death for having poached that deer, and Merric's hatred for the spider of a man grew.

'I don't care that he is from The Head,' Merric muttered as they watched Orderix pass their hiding place. 'That filth betrayed Lord Roberd and serves the Monforts now. I hope I can make him pay.'

He hated the smug look on Orderix's face as he rode along with the Monfort men in tow. He had sworn to serve the Jacelyn family, as his father had before him, and had worked for Lord Roberd for over ten years. He had been treated well, and was given no reason to betray his duke.

'Who-who's down there?' called a shaky voice from upstairs, causing Merric, Ana and Tomas to jump.

The shop was a cobblers, judging by the half-made shoes that littered the room and the strong smell of leather, and it seemed that the owner had heard them break open the door. Orderix and the Monfort men had passed them now, but Merric did not dare take Ana and Tomas back out into the main street. They had already had too many close calls. However, fearing that the cobbler upstairs would mistake them for common thieves and raise an alarm, they could not stay there either.

They hurried through to a back room. They darted through a second door and found themselves out in the open air again. The yard was cluttered with empty crates and a small well, and was surrounded by a fence. The fence was not high, and they quickly climbed it, with Tomas needing a hand from Ana. They were now in a neighbouring yard, which was filled with lines of dyed clothes that were drying in the still air. Without pausing they vaulted the next fence as well, keen to put as much distance between themselves and the nervous cobbler, not to mention Orderix and his Monfort soldier lackeys.

They arrived in a side street, and Merric and his friends took a moment to catch their breath. The town around them was silent again, and they could hear neither the sound of the cobbler pursuing them nor the footfalls of the Monfort men. Ana was the first to speak.

'We're not far from Forge Row here,' she said, squinting up the road through the darkness, 'we could go to my father's.'

'We can't,' Merric said. 'If the Monforts suspect I'm going to be coming back to Eaglestone, they're sure to be watching your place.'

Ana was clearly desperate to see her father again. After seeing how strictly the Monforts were ruling the town, she wanted to make sure he was safe and well. But this was not the only reason.

'We need somewhere safe to stop for a moment, to come up with a plan,' Ana said.

She could tell that Merric understood that she had a point, and so eagerly pressed on.

'Where this back road joins onto Forge Row you can see my house. We can wait there and see if it's safe before going in.'

Merric agreed, reluctantly.

'Okay, but we can only stay for a few minutes. We need to get into the castle and out again before it gets light.'

Ana led them at a jog down the road. It passed alleyways and back yards, twisting and turning, until it eventually opened up onto Forge Row, just as she had said it would. Merric felt the air turn warmer around them. The red-hot forges in the blacksmiths' workshops, which gave the road its name, were kept burning all night, and the very air seemed to shimmer in the warmth they were producing.

Merric, Ana and Tomas crouched at the corner where their small side road joined Forge Row, and peeked around the edge of a hand cart that had been left there. To the left, around fifty paces away, stood Ana's father's house. Like most other buildings nearby, it was a two-storey house. Downstairs was a blacksmith's workshop, which was open fronted showing a wide workbench, two heavy anvils and, at the back, its huge forge that was glowing orange and casting its light halfway across the road. Above the workshop was where Ana and her father lived. A light in an upstairs window showed that he was at home and awake.

All seemed peaceful and, apart from a skinny cat that slinked down the road, there was not living soul in sight.

'It seems quiet,' Ana said hopefully.

Merric agreed that it did, but he still felt the need to be cautious. The hairs on the back of his neck were prickling.

'Is there a back entrance?' he asked her.

'Of course. It opens up onto an alley behind.'

Ana pointed to the entrance of an alley directly across the road from where they crouched, and traced its route behind the row of blacksmiths' buildings with her finger.

'Okay, we'll go that way,' Merric said. 'You never know, someone could be watching from one of the other buildings.'

He was about to stand and dart across the road towards the alley when a familiar sound appeared. With a feeling of panic, he waved the other two back. He cursed their constant bad luck.

Orderix emerged out of the darkness at the far end of the road with his Monfort bodyguard, and to Merric's dismay he stopped his horse outside Ana's father's house. Orderix smartly dismounted from his horse, straightening his robes. Two of his bodyguards climbed down from their horses as well, loosening the swords in their scabbards, while the last man stayed in his saddle and peered up and down the road with a scowl on his face.

'What are they doing?' Ana whispered, and Merric could hear the worry in her voice.

He could only shake his head and shrug.

Orderix and his men had disappeared into the interior of the workshop, to where a door led upstairs. Merric heard a fist pounding on the door.

'Open up, in the name of Lord Rayden Monfort!'

Merric did not recognise the voice, so assumed it was one of the Monfort soldiers who was shouting. A creak let

Merric know that the door had opened, and another voice answered.

'What do you want?'

The voice was gruff, and completely without fear or intimidation.

'Danell the smithy?' the soldier asked.

'Aye,' Ana's father said impatiently, almost in boredom.

'I think you know why we're here.'

The sound of Orderix's oily voice made Merric tighten his fists into balls. Danell did not answer, so Orderix continued.

'We've received reports that you've been speaking ill of his lordship, and are showing public signs of resistance to his rightful rule of The Head.'

'And which lord is that?' Ana's father asked.

An angry curse came from one of the Monfort soldiers, but he was silenced by Orderix.

'That would be *your* lord,' the Jacelyn's previous Lord Council said.

'You're mistaken. I've never spoken ill of Lord Roberd.'

The soldier spluttered in anger again, but once more was hushed by Orderix.

'Roberd is dead,' Orderix said coldly. 'You now owe your loyalty to Lord Rayden Monfort, the true Duke of The Head.'

There was a pause before Danell responded.

'Loyalty is something you earn, not something you're owed. Naming yourself duke doesn't make you so, not in the eyes of us common folk. The Jacelyns have known that for a thousand years. I don't know how things are done in The Southstones, and frankly I don't care. But I do know how things are done in my own town.'

The silence that followed bristled with tension, and Merric and the others strained their ears to make sure they did not miss anything. Ana was itching to rush to her father's aid, but she knew she could not.

'One word from me, filth, and you could find yourself in the dungeons, never to see the cold light of day again.' Orderix's voice was threatening, but to Merric's surprise, Danell just laughed.

'Take your threats elsewhere, turncloak, I'm bored of your bleating. Go and rub your Monfort master's feet.'

Merric heard Danell close his door. Orderix and the soldiers came into view again as they left the workshop, looking furious. As they mounted their horses, Orderix looked back at Danell's house and shouted.

'You're behind on your quota for this week, smithy. If you don't meet the required number of horseshoes then I can assure you, we'll make things very unpleasant for your daughter when we find her. And we *will* find her.'

He turned his horse and spurred away, his bodyguards close behind.

Merric turned and looked at Ana. She looked shaken, but was proud of her father and the way that he was refusing to bow down to the Monforts and their bullying. Still, it was dangerous what he was doing. The Monforts would not take kindly to any folk who spoke out against them, and it was only Ana's father's position as a valuable blacksmith that was keeping him safe. That would not last though, if he continued to be seen as a threat to the Monforts. He could find himself in those stocks in the Fountain Court, or worse.

Still wary that spies might be watching Ana's house, waiting for her return, Merric and his friends ran across the road and ducked into the alley. Soon after, they found themselves at the back door to Danell's workshop. With her excitement hardly containing her, Ana pushed the door open and took one step into her home.

Suddenly a huge hand grabbed her by the scruff of her neck and thrust her against the wall.

'What are you doing back h…Ana?!'

'Yes, Da, it's me!'

The hand suddenly let go of her collar, and she and her father embraced. Merric and Tomas stepped into her home behind her, closing the door after them, and then stood awkwardly.

'Thank the Mother you're safe,' Danell said, still hugging his daughter.

Her father was a huge man with short hair and a thick beard. His arms were massive, built up over years of working with a hammer in hand, but the way he held his daughter was gentle and tender. Finally, he broke away from Ana, and turned to the others.

'You must be Merric.'

Despite Merric and Ana's friendship, her father had never met him before.

'Yes, sir,' Merric replied, but Danell waved the formality aside.

'No need to call me "sir",' he said.

'I'm so sorry I left, Da,' Ana said, 'I had to.'

'I know you did, my daughter. I hope the lad here knows how loyal a friend he has in you.'

Merric flushed at his words, but nodded and smiled at Ana, who grinned back at him.

'And who's this?' Danell said, looking at Tomas who stepped forward timidly and introduced himself. 'Never seen much use in servants myself,' the blacksmith said, not unkindly, 'but you must be doing well to keep up with these two.'

Tomas nodded shyly, and then spotted a sword lying on a workbench beside him. It was small, but delicately decorated with a pommel carved in the likeness of a rabbit. Danell noticed what the boy was looking at.

'That's a sword I'm making for a knight from near Elderwyne. His family symbol is a rabbit. Sometimes I think the noble folk are rather strange, no offence meant,' he bowed his head slightly to Merric. 'He wants it for his son, but I haven't heard from him since the Monforts seized The Head.'

Tomas looked fascinated by the sword and reached out to pick it up, but was stopped by Danell.

'Don't, my boy. My father always told me; never pick up a sword by the hilt unless you mean to swing it. You don't look like the type to wield a sword to me.'

Tomas reluctantly pulled his hand away from the sword, and looked at the others sheepishly. Ana grasped her father's hand warmly.

'I'm so glad to see you again, Da. Part of me thought I never would.'

'You're not the only one,' Danell replied, looking with joy at his daughter. 'Come, let's go upstairs where we'll be able to talk more freely.'

With a candle in hand to light the way, he led them up the stairs away from the workshop, and into the modest but comfortable living space above. Merric had never been in Ana's home before, and suddenly felt very aware that he was now.

'I'll be honest, Merric,' Danell said, 'I don't know if it's a good idea you being back in Eaglestone. The Monforts are after you, and they're almost fanatical about finding you. They're sure to guess that you'll be coming back here soon. What caused you to decide to come back?'

Merric explained to him how he had thought that all of the Jacelyns had been murdered, and that he had been prepared to start a new life away from the castle. Now that he had learned that Sophya was still alive, his only thought was to save her if he could.

'Don't get me wrong, I'm glad to see you all safe,' Danell said. 'Since you had to leave, things have gone from bad to worse here. The Monforts rule over us with an iron fist, and the smallest crime is punished severely. We're force-fed the lie that you murdered the Jacelyns, but we all know the truth. Most folk want to do something about it, but are too scared. Only yesterday two carpenters were arrested for suggesting that the Monfort soldiers ought to look inside the walls of Eagle Mount to find the Jacelyns' murderer, rather than look for you. If folk knew you were back they would rally beside you, to try and take back your family's home. But I confess that I don't believe it's a fight you could win.'

'I don't know what I can do to stop the Monforts, I'm only one person,' Merric admitted. 'That's not why I've come back.'

At Merric's words, Danell's face appeared to show a flash of disappointment, but it was gone in an instant.

'I have to try and help Sophya, to take her somewhere safe,' Merric continued. 'I can't allow her to suffer at the hands of Rayden Monfort. I owe her and her family that much at least.'

Danell nodded slowly. 'I understand. What can I do to help?'

'I need you to look after Tomas,' Merric said.

Tomas looked at his old master in alarm.

'That's fine,' Danell said, but Tomas's eyes were stuck on Merric.

'What do you mean?' he asked.

'I'm sorry, Tomas,' Merric said soothingly, 'but it's too dangerous. We're not looking to get into a fight, but we'd be fools not to prepare for one.'

'I'm coming with you!'

Merric just shook his head at him. 'I'm sorry.'

Tomas's eyes were brimming with tears, and Ana moved across to him and put her arm around his shoulders warmly.

'We'll be back before you know it,' she said, comforting him.

Tomas looked devastated. He had loyally followed his old master all this way, and the idea of not being with him at the end crushed him. Merric knew how much Tomas was hurting, but he knew he was doing the right thing. There was no one more loyal than Tomas, but they would have to move quickly. Merric was no expert with a sword, but if they got into a fight he knew he would be able to at least try and defend himself. He would not be able to defend the small boy as well.

'I'll keep an eye on him, until you get back,' Danell said, smiling reassuringly at Tomas and taking a seat at his table. 'So, do you have a plan?'

Merric had been half-forming a plan in his head for the past couple of days, but when he described it to the others he tried to make himself sound more confident than he felt.

'Eagle Mount's main gate will be shut, and even if it wasn't it would be too heavily guarded to approach. Fortunately, I know another way.'

'Another way into the castle?' Danell asked.

'Yes. There's a secret passage, which leads all the way from the town into the courtyard of Eagle Mount. I don't even think Lord Roberd knew about it, so the Monforts definitely won't.'

'But you know where it is?'

'I've been using it for years, whenever I wanted to come into town without anyone seeing me. Tomas and I used the tunnel to escape the castle when the Monforts took over.'

It had only been a few weeks since the night they had fled, but it seemed so much longer ago. So much had happened since then.

'Once in the courtyard we can make our way to the castle keep, using the stables as cover. That should keep us hidden from the guards on the castle walls. There's a trapdoor at the base of the keep which leads down into the kitchens. I've seen it being used by the servants to lower sacks of food to the kitchen. From the kitchen we can make our way up to Sophya's chamber, and once we have her we can leave in the same way.'

After a moment of thought, Danell spoke.

'It's a good enough plan. However, if the Monforts do know about the tunnel then they may block it up, or set up a trap there.'

Merric himself had been worrying about this same thing, but he tried to sound convincing.

'The Monforts don't know about the tunnel, I'm sure of it. And we passed Lord Aric in the Greenwood; he looked to be heading back to The Citadel, his castle in The Southstones. He took a good number of his knights with him, so hopefully we'll find the castle more lightly defended.'

'Okay,' Danell said, rising from his chair. 'You wouldn't stand a chance in the daylight, so you'll need to be back by morning. You had best go.'

They followed him back down to the workshop. As they prepared to leave, Tomas began to look sad again.

'We won't be long, I promise' Ana said to him.

Merric laid his hand on Tomas's shoulder.

'Thank you for everything you've done,' Merric said. 'You're not my servant anymore, you're my friend.'

Tomas bit back the tears and smiled at Merric. Danell squeezed Ana tightly in his arms again, and then shook Merric's hand.

'You two look out for each other, do you hear?' the blacksmith said.

He looked hesitant to let Ana out of his sight again, but he had long since given up trying to stop her from doing what she wanted. She was a determined young woman, and she reminded Danell of her mother. He smiled fondly.

Without another word, Merric and Ana stepped out of the back door and into the night once more. The walls of Eagle Mount rose up out of the night not far ahead. The journey over the past few weeks had been long and difficult, and had started and ended in the shadow of the castle that Merric knew so well.

How that journey would end though, he would have to find out.

- CHAPTER EIGHTEEN -

A strange homecoming

Now that they had a clear plan in their mind, Merric felt encouraged. Ana, too, appeared to be walking with more determination as they made their way along the back alley and further up the hill towards Eagle Mount, buoyant after being reunited with her father. However, the knowledge of what they were about to try and do still filled Merric with fear. He had spent the past weeks fleeing from the swords of the Monforts, but now he was willingly getting closer and closer to their sharp-edged blades.

Despite this though, for the first time in weeks, Merric felt like he was in control of something.

The walls of Eagle Mount towered above them as they got closer, looming over the town. In the moonlight the walls were closer to a ghostly purple in colour, rather than the familiar white stone that Merric had grown up surrounded by. He had never realised how intimidating and foreboding the castle could look to those outside it. To

Merric, Eagle Mount had been his home and the place in which he had grown up. It had meant safety, and security, but with the Jacelyns gone and the Monforts now ruling there, the castle was a fearsome and unfriendly place, into which Merric now had to venture.

High above them, at the top of the walls, the new rulers had planted large white flags bearing the black marching knight of the Monforts. It was a clear message to the folk of The Head; accept your new rulers. All along the top of the castle wall there were patrolling Monfort soldiers, the moonlight reflecting off their helmets and spear points as they paced up and down. They did not worry Merric though, as he and Ana were invisible to them in the shadows far below.

Merric led the way down the narrow streets. It did not matter that Ana knew the layout of the town better than he did, because he was aiming for a very specific tavern among many that stood in the town. The tavern, with the tunnel leading from its wine cellar, stood a stone's throw away from the castle walls, and they reached it within minutes. All was looking quiet, and no lights shone from the dark windows. It was the middle of the night, and most folk in the town would be asleep by now.

'The secret tunnel is here?' Ana asked, her voice showing her doubt. Her eyes had scanned the quiet tavern and the small yard beside it.

'We need to go down,' Merric replied, taking Ana round the back and squeezing through the gap in the fence.

He showed her the hole in the ground in the yard that led to the wine cellar. She nodded, and followed Merric over to the ladder before climbing quickly down. No one saw them or shouted a challenge, or asked them what they were doing. Merric took her over to where the hidden door was in the wine cellar, and pulled it open.

The passage beyond was pitch black, but Merric seized Ana's hand and held onto it as they went into the darkness. Ana followed Merric along the tunnel, her nose filled with the smell of damp earth.

She was suddenly very aware that she was still wearing the dress from the summer celebrations, and wished that she had more than just her crossbow and dagger for protection. Merric hoped that they would not need their weapons at all. The Monfort defenders of the castle would not expect Merric to get there without being seen, and would anticipate that the patrols in the streets of the town would find him first, if not the guards at the castle gates. An attacking army would never be able to sneak this close to the castle, but Merric and Ana had got this far without being seen, and that gave them a huge advantage.

The tunnel continued, the dirt floor uneven beneath their feet. Once or twice Ana winced as she felt cobwebs brush against her face. She was not afraid of enclosed spaces, but she certainly did not enjoy them either. She was relieved when she felt the floor of the tunnel beneath her feet turn to steps, and they began to climb. Eventually, Ana felt Merric slow, before coming to a complete stop. She reached up and felt the wooden boards of a trapdoor above her head.

'I think the coast is clear,' said Merric, who had been listening carefully with his ear pressed against the door.

He pushed the trapdoor upwards and silently climbed up into the dimly lit stable, with Ana close behind him. Merric put a finger to his lips and then signalled Ana to follow close behind him. The straw on the floor of the stable thankfully muffled their footsteps, so they did not wake or spook any of the sleeping horses as Merric and Ana edged towards the stable doors. If they had then their neighing might alert any Monfort soldiers who happened to be passing.

The doors of the stable were open, and they crept noiselessly through. To their left, only fifty paces away, was the gatehouse. It seemed a long time ago that Lord Aric and his men had marched through that gate, as the guests of Lord Roberd. The space behind the gate, which on that day had been filled with the neat rows of Jacelyn guards, standing smartly awaiting their visitors, was now empty. The vast keep faced the gatehouse across this open courtyard, and strangely the front doors of the keep were wide open, spilling yellow light down the handful of steps that led down to the courtyard before it. A couple of guards were beside the open doors, armed with spears and shields. They looked bored and tired, and slumped against the great stone blocks of the keep behind them. On the far side of the courtyard from where Merric stood were the barracks of the castle garrison. Once filled with the laughter and music of the Jacelyn soldiers who were relaxing off-duty, they were instead silent and dark.

Merric felt his eyes rise to a window on the third level of the castle keep. The shutters of his bedchamber window were open, but no light shone beyond. Merric wondered if the room had passed into the possession of someone new. It seemed a lifetime ago that he had last slept there. A small ledge ran beneath his chamber window, and Merric's eyes followed it to where the next darkened window stood. That had been where he had watched Tristan be murdered, and the memory brought a lump to his throat. The man who had delivered the killing blow to Tristan was right there in the castle keep somewhere, most likely asleep in Lord Roberd's old bed. He was now calling himself the Duke of The Head, but to Merric there would only ever be one man worthy of being called that, and he was dead. And tomorrow, Rayden would marry the sole surviving member of the Jacelyn family against her wishes, though not if Merric could do anything about it.

What Merric was looking for was located almost directly below his old bedchamber window, not far from the large roofed haystack that sat at the base of the keep's wall that had, on that fateful night, broken his fall and saved his life.

'That's it,' he whispered to Ana.

She followed his outstretched finger and looked to where he pointed. On the ground beside the keep there was a large double door built into the earth. When deliveries of flour or meat or other such things came in from the town or the land beyond, the trapdoors would be swung open to allow the supplies to be lowered directly down to the kitchens below. Tonight though, it was their way into the castle.

'Underground again,' Ana said, nodding her understanding.

She swallowed nervously as Merric set off at a run towards the trapdoor. She followed him, bent double to keep herself as small as she could in case any guards looked their way. With every step the keep grew larger, and towered ever higher over their heads. Within seconds, they had crossed the open space between the stables and the keep, and the eagle-topped tower was now too high above them to see.

As Ana caught her breath, Merric seized the heavy iron ring that was attached to the right-hand door and gave it an experimental tug. He grinned, full of nervous excitement.

'They should really keep this locked.'

With a glance around to make sure that none of the soldiers patrolling the outer wall were looking back into the castle, Merric pulled on the door, straining against its weight. Ana gave him a hand, and together they managed to swing it open to reveal a dark chute underneath. They carefully lowered the opened door onto the grass, not letting it make a sound, and then glanced down into the shaft. It could not drop more than fifteen feet, but the darkness stopped them from seeing the bottom. Merric was sure it would be safe. He took a deep breath.

'Here we go then,' he said, more to himself than to Ana.

'Here we go,' she echoed anyway.

Merric sat down next to the open trapdoor and lowered his legs over the edge. He waggled them there for a moment, plucking up his courage, before slowly inching himself down by his arms until he was hanging by his fingertips. He let go.

He dropped for only a couple of seconds before he felt his feet hit the hard stone floor at the bottom of the shaft. He stumbled as he landed, but managed to stay upright. Looking up he could see Ana in the moonlight, peering anxiously down into the hole just a few feet above his head. Merric called up to her in a whisper, saying it was fine to drop, and a moment later she landed next to him. He caught her as she landed, and in the dim light he saw her smile at him in thanks. Embarrassed, Merric hurriedly removed his hands from where he had caught her around the waist.

Merric looked around his surroundings as his eyes slowly adjusted to the darkness. Despite having spent most of his life in Eagle Mount, Merric had never before been in the kitchens of the castle. The basement level of the castle, which contained the kitchens and servants' quarters, was used solely by the servants, and was rarely visited by those they were there to serve. The chute had led down into a large store room, which, in the low light, appeared to be filled with barrels, crates and sacks of food. Most of it was likely for the wedding banquet the next day. There was a door at the other side of the room, and they moved silently over to it. The door took them through to the kitchen itself, a vast room which stretched across the full width of the castle keep above it. The kitchen was deserted, as expected in the middle of the night, so they were able to cross the large room without fear of being seen. Giant stone ovens lined one wall, and huge cauldrons sat over fire pits nearby. A large hearth was at the far end of the room with a spit mounted above it, where meats would be cooked over a roaring fire.

Long work benches stretched across Merric and Ana's path, and in the darkness Merric bumped into one, cracking his knee painfully against the hard wood. Rubbing his throbbing knee and cursing under his breath, Merric led Ana to the far corner of the kitchen, where a door led to a spiral staircase. The staircase was one of four which rose up within the towers that stood at each corner of the keep, and went all the way from the basement to the very top of the huge building. They were the quickest way to move around the castle.

'I think this is the southern staircase. All we need to do is climb all the way to the top level, which is where all the Jacelyns had their bedchambers,' Merric explained in a hushed voice. 'That is surely where Sophya will be.'

Ana nodded her understanding, and they began climbing the steep steps that rose up and up in a tight spiral. They passed a door to their left, which let them know that they had reached ground level, and they continued to climb. However, before they came to the door on the next floor up, they heard what they had been dreading.

The heavy tread of boots was echoing down from above, and getting louder, telling them that someone was marching down the staircase towards them.

Merric remembered the horrible feeling of being trapped on the staircase at Oaktyn Castle. He and Ana could not see further than a few steps ahead of them, but judging by how loud the footsteps were they knew that whoever was climbing down the stairs would come into view within seconds. Even with the darkness that filled the staircase, there was no chance of them not being spotted. With no other choice, Merric and Ana span round and hurried back down the way they had come, throwing themselves quickly through the door that they had just passed. They carefully shut the door behind them again, and pressed their ears to the wood. The footsteps got louder, before finally faded away again as their owner continued down towards the kitchens a floor below. Merric breathed a sigh of relief, and rested his forehead against the door. *That was just a minor obstacle*, he told himself. *We're still doing well.*

They had emerged into a dark passageway on the ground level of the keep, which led towards the main entrance. With the owner of the footsteps now down in the kitchens, Merric made to open the door which led back into the spiral staircase again. Ana reached out and stopped him.

'What?' he asked her.

'Shh!'

She had put a finger to her ear, and so Merric strained to listen. Above them were the faint sounds of voices, and more footsteps in the stairwell.

'Is there another way we can go?' Ana whispered.

This staircase was the quickest route, and Merric was frustrated that they could no longer go this way. He thought for a moment, and then nodded. Grateful to not have to fight her way up the stairs, Ana began making her way down the passageway. An urgent whisper from Merric stopped her.

'What is it?' Ana hissed.

Merric did not reply, but hurried her back with a frantic gesture with his hand.

'Those doors,' he said, when she was back at his side, 'are the quarters of the Eagle Guard. Or, they used to be. Now I bet they're filled with Monfort men. It's too risky to go that way, if one of them came out...'

Ana looked warily at the closed doors which lined the passageway.

'So which way do we go?'

'Through there.' Merric indicated a door next to them, which sat opposite the one which led into the staircase. It was a small door, and Ana had not noticed it before.

'Okay,' she said, as Merric gently pushed the door open.

It creaked, and the sound echoed loudly, causing Ana to flinch. However it was the sight beyond the door that made her truly stop in her tracks.

'Really, Merric?' Ana said, 'I thought we were trying to keep a low profile.'

The door had led them into the huge and cavernous Grand Hall. Ana had never seen a room so big, and the sight of it took her breath away. Stepping through the door they emerged at the top of the Grand Hall, on the raised platform where Lord Roberd's chair had sat. To their left, the room stretched back towards the large double doors which led into the entrance hall beyond. Above the doors was the minstrel's gallery, which was ominously dark and silent. For a moment Merric thought he saw something move up there in the shadows of the balcony, but he knew it was just his mind playing tricks on him. His attention was drawn to the floor of the hall. The long tables which could seat hundreds had been cleared away, to make room for the rows and rows of guests that would stand and watch the wedding that was due to take place the next day. The tall walls of the room were bare, the decorative shields of the barons gone, but the high vaulted ceiling was covered in the banners of the Monfort family. Clearly the Monforts had not taken long to take over this ancient and noble room of the Jacelyns.

Ana's gaze was on the enormous stained glass window that filled most of the back wall of the Grand Hall. The scene of Jace atop his giant eagle was still there, though in the moonlight all the colourful pieces of glass glowed in shades of deep blue and purple. Ana had never seen anything like it, and Merric had to put his hand on her arm to draw her attention away from it. They did not have time for sightseeing.

'We're going through there,' Merric said to her, indicating an identical door across the room opposite the one they had entered through. These two doors were used by servants when they brought food up to the Grand Hall from the kitchens below.

They hurried across to it, Merric not allowing his eyes to be drawn to the empty chair that Lord Roberd had ruled The Head from for many years. Ana opened the door when they reached it, and they emerged into a passageway just like the one they had been in moments ago, but on the opposite side of the keep. The passageway led off into the darkness, passing more rooms that had once housed more men of the Eagle Guard, but Merric and Ana instead crossed the passageway and went through another door that led into another spiral staircase. This one was located in the northern tower of the keep, and also led all the way up to the top level. It would bring them out further away from

Sophya's bedchamber than the southern staircase would have, and it was a delay they could not afford, not with dawn so close.

There was silence above them, so they hurried up the spiralling stairs, not noticing the protesting muscles in their legs from the tiring climb. They passed two more doors which led out onto the next two floors, before arriving at a third. They were now at the highest floor of the castle keep. The stairs continued upwards from this spot, but they only led to the roof of the keep and the top of the tower. After their last adventure on the roof of a castle, Merric had no desire to go up there.

After listening for a moment at the door, Merric gently pushed it open, and Ana instantly knew that they were close to where the Jacelyn family's bedchambers had been. Underfoot there was soft carpet laid on top of the hard wooden floorboards, and the bare walls were decorated with rich paintings and tapestries that were illuminated by burning torches attached to silver brackets on the walls. It was far more luxurious than anything she had ever seen before.

Merric and Ana began creeping along the passageway, their footsteps muffled by the carpet, but they were unnerved by the bright light from the torches. There were no shadows to hide in here, and they were grateful that most of the castle was asleep at this hour. They came to a point where the passageway turned to the left, and Merric poked his head around the corner.

Doors were evenly spaced along the passageway. The nearest door on the left led to the chamber where Tristan used to sleep, and beyond that was the door of Sophya's bedchamber. Opposite these doors, on the other side of the passageway, with windows that gave magnificent views of Eaglestone and the lands south of the town, was the master bedchamber that used to belong to Lord Roberd and Lady Cathreen. All of this was what Merric had expected to see. What he had not counted on seeing was the spotlessly dressed Monfort soldier who stood smartly outside the master bedchamber's richly decorated door.

Merric whipped his head out of sight, fearing that the guard might have seen it out of the corner of his eye.

'What is it?' Ana asked him, so quietly that Merric could barely hear her.

Her eyes were wide with alarm.

'There's a guard down there,' he mouthed.

'What do we do?' she mouthed back, her heart dropping.

Merric was thinking. The guard was in their way, and there was no way they could get past him. If they had been able to go up the other spiral staircase, and so had approached the passageway from the other direction, then there was a chance that they may have been able to make it to Sophya's door without the Monfort soldier seeing them. There was no time to go back and try that staircase again though.

Merric fingered the sword at his waist, worried about what he knew he would have to do. It would take him several seconds to get to the soldier, even at a sprint, and in that time the Monfort man was sure to see him coming and ready his weapons to fight or, even worse, call out and raise the alarm. If anyone knew that Merric and Ana were in the castle then they would be done for. There was no way they would be able to fight their way through everyone. Ana offered up a quick prayer to the Mother, asking for Her help just one more time.

The sudden sound of muffled footsteps drew Merric's attention, and he peered carefully around the corner again to see Orderix approaching Lord Roberd's old bedchamber from the far end of the passageway.

'State your business,' the Monfort soldier challenged him.

'Get out of my way!'

Clearly Orderix had some authority over the Monfort men, as the soldier obediently stepped aside and Orderix went through the door. The soldier closed it behind him, and resumed his position in front of the door.

Voices could be heard from behind the door; the low murmuring of Orderix and the louder sound of Rayden shouting at him. Words like "useless" and "pathetic" could be heard. It sounded like Rayden had been less than impressed with the performance of his new ally.

The Monfort soldier outside the door grinned. While Orderix may have authority, he was clearly not liked. The soldier was enjoying hearing the Lord's Counsel being told off, and was no doubt already looking forward to telling his mates about it when he came off duty.

Merric was biting his lip, still thinking about how to get past the soldier, when the solution presented itself from the most unlikely place imaginable.

'Guard!' called the drawling voice of Rayden Monfort from inside the master bedchamber. 'Get in here. I need you to deliver a message for me.'

The hatred that surged within Merric at the sound of Rayden's voice quickly disappeared as he watched the Monfort soldier go through the door behind him, leaving the passageway deserted. Ana's prayer had been answered, and Merric knew they could not waste a moment.

'Quickly,' he said, his voice filled with eagerness.

He could not believe his luck. Ana hurried after him as Merric ran along the passageway, trying to keep his footsteps as quiet as possible on the carpeted floor. He half expected the door of the master bedchamber to open again, and the soldier to come out and see the two young intruders, but their fortune held out. Within seconds they were in front of Sophya's door. Without pausing, and with a burst of excitement, Merric twisted the handle and pushed the door open.

He had expected to find Sophya asleep in her four-poster bed, but she was awake. She was stood with her back to her door, gazing out of the window that looked north towards the distant mountains. Unlike Merric's old bedchamber downstairs, the windows on this floor had glass in them. Sophya's eyes saw Merric's reflection in the glass, and she spun around in alarm at his sudden appearance.

Merric closed the door behind Ana and himself, and took a step towards Sophya, a smile spreading across his face. Sophya's eyes were wide with shock, and she appeared lost for words.

'Merric?' she said simply, disbelieving.

'Sophya,' Merric replied, overwhelmed with joy at seeing her, 'I never thought I would see you again, I thought you were dead, I-'

To Merric's surprise, Sophya shuffled backwards until her back was up against the window. She, too, seemed overwhelmed at their reunion, but her face did not seem to be showing happiness.

'I'm here to get you,' Merric said, trying to reassure her.

He wondered whether Sophya had given up hope of someone coming to help her, to stop her forced marriage to Rayden.

She just stared at him, with her wide, shocked eyes. Merric opened his mouth to say that she was safe, and that he was going to take her far from the Monfort family's reach, but before he could do so he was stopped by Sophya's voice.

There were lots of things Merric imagined Sophya would say when she saw him again, and they had gone round and round his head throughout his journey from

Little Harrow to this very chamber; words of relief, of happiness, of gratitude. But only one word came out of Sophya's mouth, and it was said at a shout so loud that Merric almost fell backwards in surprise. It was the last thing he could ever have imagined her saying, and the word made his heart drop lower than it had ever gone before.

'GUARDS!'

- CHAPTER NINETEEN -

A taste of defeat

Merric did not move. He was too stunned to speak, too shocked even to think. It was over, the Monforts had won. Merric just stared at Sophya, who looked back at him in terror. He did not notice when Ana grabbed his shoulder and frantically tried to pull him back towards the door, or when she shouted 'we've got to go!' at him. His feet were glued to the floor, and he would not have been able to move even if he had wanted to.

'GUARDS!' Sophya screamed again, her eyes wide with fear as she tried to put her bed between herself and Merric, as though she feared he was about to lunge at her.

There was a heavy pounding of feet approaching beyond the chamber door. Ana gave up trying to get Merric to move as she heard the sound, and span round to face the approaching danger.

The door to Sophya's bedchamber burst open with a crash, and Rayden Monfort, handsomely dressed in a crimson velvet doublet, charged into the room, closely followed by two Monfort soldiers. Orderix was there too, peering over their shoulders.

Rayden stopped in his tracks when he saw the intruders. Ana shot her crossbow at directly at him, who saw it coming and jerked his head out of the way. The crossbow bolt flew harmlessly past him and struck the door with a thud.

'Grab them!' Rayden shouted at his men.

Ana dropped her crossbow and whipped her small daggers from her belt. She swiped it viciously at the first of the men to reach for Merric, yelling at her friend to draw his sword and help. The soldier dived to one side to avoid Ana's blade, but the second man pushed her aside and seized Merric.

'No!' Ana screamed, as she rushed at the man who had grabbed hold of Merric.

He was a large man with a bushy red beard, and he effortlessly pushed Ana away again with one meaty hand, while keeping a firm grip on his Merric.

Merric was still in shock, and did not resist his captor. The Sophya who Merric had known, who had been like a sister to him, could not be the same person who now cowered in fear of him. It did not make any sense, and Merric could not understand why should would raise the alarm. She still looked terrified of Merric, as though he wanted to hurt her.

Sophya moved over to the safety of Rayden, who put a protective arm around her and looked down at Merric with a look of triumph on his face. The bearded man who held onto Merric reached round and pulled the sword from his captive's belt, in case Merric came to his senses and made a move to try and use it.

Ana made one last ditch attempt to rescue Merric from the clutches of the Monfort soldier. She was unwilling to give in and let them take him, not if she could do anything about it. The other soldier had got back to his feet, and swung the wooden shaft of his spear at her. The blow struck her across the head with a loud crack. She fell heavily to the floor, knocked out cold.

'I knew you'd come back,' Rayden said, victory in his eyes.

Merric was still staring at Sophya, oblivious to everything else that was happening.

'Sophya…' he said weakly, 'why?'

Rayden turned angry, and he pushed his future wife safely behind him.

'How dare you speak to her!' he roared. 'You murdered her mother and father! You killed her brother when he tried to stop you, and now you've come here to finish the job and kill her too!'

'That's not true,' Merric said, a tear rolling down his cheek, willing Sophya to believe him.

Rayden's cold lie had brought Merric to his senses, and he suddenly noticed for the first time the strong arms that were restraining him. He struggled and strained, and tried to fight free. He wanted to reach Rayden, to hurt him, to kill him, but the Monfort soldier who held onto him was too strong. His grip was like iron.

'It's not true Sophya, you have to believe me!' Merric begged.

It was then that Merric saw Ana lying on the floor next to him. She was breathing, but not moving. The sight of his best friend hurt and at the mercy of the Monfort men took all fight out of Merric, and he knew there was nothing he could do.

He had lost.

The taste of defeat filled his mouth, and he could not swallow it away. He slumped weakly against the bearded soldier who kept a tight hold of him.

Sophya's face appeared behind Rayden's strong arms and looked at Merric. He returned her gaze, his eyes misted with tears. He looked pleadingly at her, begging her to believe the truth. But he knew she did not.

'Please, Sophya.'

'You murdered them,' Sophya said simply, her voice small.

'Get them out of my sight,' Rayden ordered, and the soldier dragged half carried and half dragged Merric towards the door.

The other man picked up Ana's motionless body and followed.

'Take them to the dungeons,' Rayden snarled, 'Let them rot in the cells until my lady and I have decided their fate.'

* * *

The dungeons would have been pitch-black, had it not been for the small, greasy torch that burned outside their cell. The light from the flickering flames shone feebly through the bars in the cell door, giving just enough light for Merric to see by.

Ana, going in and out of consciousness from the heavy blow to her head, lay in a corner of the cell. Merric had made her a pillow out of his cloak and slid it gently under her head, but there was little more he could do to make her comfortable. There was a chipped jug of water beside the cell door, and Merric used this to clean the small cut on the back of Ana's head, and wash the matted blood from her hair. When he had done all he could for his friend, Merric paced up and down the small cell, trying to understand what had happened. The initial shock had begun to fade, to be replaced by deep confusion.

It was this confusion that bothered Merric the most. Far from being relieved to see Merric, and overjoyed to have the opportunity to be freed from the clutches of the Monforts, Sophya had been convinced that Merric was there to hurt her, even kill her. How could she ever think that? She had known him for years, and would know that he would never try and hurt her. The memory of her face, so fearful at the sight of him, haunted Merric. It brought a sick feeling to his stomach every time he remembered it.

The Monforts had done something to her, Merric decided. He had always imagined that Sophya was being forced to marry Rayden against her will, in fear of the consequences if she did not. But it seemed that she was actually marrying him willingly, and gladly. Despite the rest of the folk living in The Head believing the truth, Rayden and his father had somehow convinced Sophya that Merric had murdered her family, and that they were there to protect her. Merric could not understand how she could ever believe that he would do something like that to the Jacelyns.

The more Merric paced, and the longer he spent dwelling on it, the more he began to understand.

Sophya had lost her entire family in one fateful night, and the grief Merric had experienced would have been nothing compared to what she must have been feeling. If Rayden had been gentle and kind to Sophya, and had helped comfort her at that terrible time, then it was likely that he could have gotten her to believe anything he wanted. She had also been infatuated with the handsome, young Monfort knight from the moment she first saw him, so she would probably have welcomed Rayden's marriage proposal with open arms. Sophya would have had no idea that she was being used by Lord Aric and Rayden. Even now, she was theirs to control. They may even be able to use her to eventually persuade all the folk of The Head to become loyal to the Monforts.

Merric was not angry at Sophya. Far from it. She was not to blame. The Monforts were using her, and she was as much a victim as Merric was. He just wished there was something he could do to help her. However, the thick stone walls of the cell that imprisoned Merric told him that his wish would not be answered.

He did not know how much time had passed since they had been taken down to the dungeons. With no windows to see the sky outside, it could have been hours or days since they had been thrown roughly into the cell by the two Monfort soldiers. Merric looked over at Ana, who was lying awkwardly on the hard stone floor. She had followed him all this way. Without question she had gone with him into the one place they should have avoided, trusting that Merric would protect her. Now, because of him, they would both likely to be dead before long. She had never questioned her loyalty to him, despite her having many reasons to do so, and Merric was repaying her now with failure. Merric thought guiltily of Tomas and Danell, who even now would be waiting for their return.

The jangling of keys sounded outside the cell, and with a loud metallic screech the door was swung open. The toothless jailer stepped to one side, allowing Rayden Monfort himself to walk into the small cell. He carried a burning torch, and held it up so that he could observe his captives better. He studied Merric for a few moments, before speaking.

'You're smaller than I remember. Then again, I barely took any notice of you; you're nothing more than the orphan boy of some minor baron,' Rayden said with a smirk.

Merric did not reply, not wanting to give Rayden the satisfaction of knowing that his words were making his angry.

'You shouldn't have come back, you stupid boy,' Rayden went on. 'What did you think you'd do, come back here and whisk the girl away? What hope did you even have?'

Merric remained silent.

Rayden's long, black hair fell down each side of his handsome face, and he smiled menacingly as he looked down at his captive.

'The Jacelyns are finished, and none now dare oppose the might of the Monforts,' Rayden said with passion, marching up and down the small room. 'The Head is ours, this horrible little castle is ours, and you have nothing. You *are* nothing.' He stopped his walking and hissed these last words at his captive. 'The girl will marry me this afternoon, and then my hold over The Head will be complete. With her by my side, no one would dare oppose me, or question my right to rule. My son will be half a Jacelyn, but I'll soon stamp that softness out of him, leaving nothing but

Monfort strength. You've lost, boy, and there's nothing you can do to stop me.'

'Sophya will realise the truth,' Merric said, ending his silence. 'One day she'll know that I'm innocent and that you and your father murdered her family, not me.'

'What do I care if she does?' Rayden asked, unconcerned. 'It'll be too late. She'll be my wife by law, and she will bear me a son, regardless of whether I fill her heart with love or hate. In fact, I might tell her how I killed her pathetic parents and brother tonight as a wedding gift, how about that? Why should I care about her feelings? Once she is my wife, there's nothing she can do about it.'

'I don't know why you're doing this. I don't know what Aric wants, but he'll never get it,' Merric said, struggling to keep his voice steady. 'You're pure evil. Your whole family is.'

Rayden just laughed.

'What is "evil"? There are just those who are winners, and those who are losers; there's no good or bad. I am a winner, and history will remember what my father and I will soon achieve. You,' he pointed the burning torch at Merric, causing him to flinch away from the flame, 'and your beloved Jacelyns, are losers.'

'You'll never win over the folk of The Head,' Merric said, defiantly. 'They know the truth, and they'll never respect you as their duke. They'll rise up against you, I guarantee it. You won't live to see the coming winter, let alone whatever it is you and your father are planning on achieving.'

'I think not,' Rayden said dismissively, moving back towards the door to the cell. 'And I care not what the commoners think anyway. Once we've accomplished what we've set out to do, this land can swallow itself up for all I care. The Head isn't the real prize, we're thinking bigger. Still, a few executions will sort the folk out, and send a clear message to those who choose to object to my rule. I think we'll start with you and your little friend there. After that, we'll execute her precious father, and all of the Jacelyn soldiers that we have locked up down here with you. But first, I have a wedding to get to.'

Merric, his hatred overcoming him, lunged towards Rayden. The cell door swung shut with a clang before he could reach him, and Merric smashed painfully into it. He slumped down onto the floor with his back to the cell wall, gathered his knees against his chest, and buried his head in his arms.

A short while later the dungeon door was unlocked and opened again. This time it was Orderix who entered.

'You!' Merric snarled.

Orderix looked tired and stressed. He skin was pale, and there were bags under his eyes.

'How did you get into the castle?' he asked by way of welcome.

Merric ignored the question.

'You look unwell, Lord's Counsel,' he said, without any sympathy. 'Are things not going as well as you had hoped with your new masters?'

'SILENCE!' Orderix screeched, and struck Merric across the cheek with the back of his hand. 'You will answer me!'

'I won't. If Rayden sent you here to find out how I snuck in to Eagle Mount then you're going to have to run back to him and explain that you've failed at yet another task. He's not going to be very happy with you is he.'

'I can make things very uncomfortable for you, you loathsome creature, so I suggest you start co-operating.' Orderix said, but the panic in his eyes told Merric that he knew his words were true.

'Why should I? I'm dead already, there's no way the Monforts will let me live. And I expect they'll have a similar plan for you if you continue to disappoint them. What did you think you could hope to achieve?' Merric felt a grim satisfaction in seeing the anxiety on Orderix's face. 'I bet the Monforts thought you'd be a useful ally to have, but really you're just all talk.'

Orderix's face turn green.

'I won't be spoken to like this,' he squawked. 'You will obey me!'

Despite the hopeless situation he was in, Merric smirked.

'How does it feel, knowing you've betrayed your duke? And for what, gold? Gold won't protect you.

Orderix tried to slap him again, but Merric dodged out of the way. Without another word Orderix left, slamming the cell door shut behind him, fleeing like a dog with its tail between its legs.

* * *

'Merric.'

Ana was roughly shaking him awake. How he had managed to fall asleep, with everything that was going on, was a mystery to him.

'Ana,' Merric mumbled, rubbing his eyes. Seeing her awake swept the tiredness from him and he sat up suddenly. 'Thank goodness you're okay! How are you feeling?'

She looked terribly pale. The blow to her head must have been aching terribly.

'Dreadful,' Ana said, smiling grimly at him.

Merric took hold of her hand and squeezed it tightly.

'I'm so sorry,' he said to her, 'you don't deserve this.'

'Neither of us does. But we had to come here and try, didn't we?' Ana spoke slowly, and her words were slightly slurred. 'What do you think happened to Sophya, why did she raise the alarm?'

Merric explained his theory about how the Monforts had managed to convince her of their side of the story, and filled her in on his conversation with Rayden.

'That makes sense I suppose,' Ana said, when he had finished. 'The real question though, is what are we going to do about it?'

'What do you mean?' Merric said.

In the dim light from the torch outside the door, Merric saw his friend slump herself down on the floor next to him.

'How are we going to help her realise the truth?' she said.

Merric looked at Ana sadly.

'There's nothing we can do for her now, it's all over. She'll be married to Rayden any moment now, and we're to be executed.'

He watched Ana's expression in the dull light to see how she reacted to this. He thought it best not to tell her that her father was going to be arrested too, as he knew that would not help. If they were going to die, it was better that she died thinking her father would be safe.

If Ana was scared to die, then she did not show it.

'What do you think it is that Rayden and his father want?' she said instead.

Merric could only shrug and shake his head. He recalled Rayden's earlier words.

Once we've accomplished what we've set out to do, this land can swallow itself up for all I care. The Head isn't the real prize, we're thinking bigger.

What did he mean by that? Merric had assumed that the Monforts had wanted to seize The Head to make themselves more powerful. The more land you controlled, the more power you had; more men to fight in the Monfort army, and more folk to tax. With the coastal town of Lynport in their grip they would also have full control over all trade coming into High Realm by ship from kingdoms across the sea. But what Rayden had said suggested to Merric that this was not what he and his father wanted. If it was not the land, was there something in particular that they wanted from The Head? It was a mystery to Merric, and one that he feared he would never see solved.

Ana's voice brought his attention back to the present.

'Well, whatever it is they want, it's up to us to stop them,' she said.

'But what can we do? We're locked in here, and I can't see Rayden letting us out willingly.'

'Then we'll just have to get ourselves out, won't we. There must be a way, we just have to find it,' Ana said, standing with a wince. She began walking around the small cell, inspecting every corner.

Merric had not wanted to give up hope, but he was just being realistic.

'Ana, we're underground, in the middle of the castle which is crawling with Rayden's men, and this door is five inches thi…'

The rest of Merric's sentence was suddenly interrupted by the sounds of a commotion outside the cell.

'Who in the name of the Mother are you?' came the curt voice of the jailer. He sounded as though he had just been awoken from a slumber, and was incredibly unhappy about it.

'Where are they being held?'

The second voice was faint and muffled through the thick stone wall of their cell. The owner of the voice sounded fierce though.

'I demand to know who you are! Did Lord Rayden send you? I'm under orders from the duke himself; no one is to see or speak to the prisoners without his permission.'

There was a sudden sharp sound and the jailer whimpered in fright.

'Tell me which cell they're in,' the second voice commanded.

'Over there!' the jailer sounded scared, and it seemed that the intruder was holding a knife to his throat. 'That last cell down the passageway.'

'Thank you.'

There a loud thud, followed by the sound of an unconscious body falling heavily to the floor. Then came a rattle of keys, as the intruder pulled them from the hook on the belt of the knocked out jailer.

Footsteps sounded, and got louder as they neared. Merric and Ana edged away from the cell door as they heard the loud click of a key being turned in the lock. The door slowly opened, but the flaming torch on the wall outside silhouetted the intruder so Merric could not see who it was. He was tall and hooded, and held a knife out in front of him. After a moment of glancing around the dark cell, the intruder stepped into the room and lowered his hood, revealing, in the dim light, a shock of long dirty blond hair.

'Kasper!' Ana cried, and despite the pain in her head she went to him, hugging him tightly.

Kasper was surprised by her affection, and seemed embarrassed by it. He then looked nervously at Merric.

'I'm sorry, Merric,' Kasper said, 'I should never have abandoned you.'

Merric shuffled his feet. He knew that he was the one who had been in the wrong that night in Little Harrow. Kasper had simply been looking out for him.

'It's me that's sorry, honestly. I should never have hit you,' Merric said.

'No,' Kasper said, taking a step towards him, 'you should have. I deserved it. I knew that you were going to come back here, with or without my help. I swore to protect you, but still I let you go. I should have come with you. If something had happened to you, to any of you I…I'd have never forgiven myself.'

Kasper reached out with his strong hand, and Merric shook it.

'I can't believe you're here,' Ana said. 'How did you get in?'

Kasper just laughed softly.

'I have my ways, as you have yours. I broke out of these dungeons once, remember? When you have friends to help, you don't let anything get in your way. I also have unfinished business with that piece of filth, Orderix. But we need to go now, quickly.'

'Wait a moment,' Ana said, looking to Merric, 'go where though? Away from here, or to help Sophya?'

Merric knew his answer straight away.

'I've got to finish what I started. The Monforts have Sophya trapped. I can help her to see the truth, I know I can. I can save her from a life of misery under Rayden.'

Ana knew Merric would say that, but also knew it would not be that easy.

'How though?' she asked him. 'Sophya will be surrounded by the Monforts. We won't be able to get near her, let alone rescue her. And don't forget that right now she doesn't want to be saved.'

Merric paused before speaking, choosing his words carefully.

'I'm going to save her the only way I can. I'm going to kill Rayden Monfort.'

There was silence in the cell, broken only by the sound of Kasper's footsteps as he moved to the cell door and glanced nervously out in case guards were approaching. They needed to move, and this was taking too long.

'You're going to do what?' Ana said, stunned.

'Rayden rules Eagle Mount now. If I can kill him, then not only will Sophya be free, but The Head will be free as well.'

'But how could you defeat him?' Ana pleaded. 'He's a knight, one of the best in the realm.'

'The best, apparently,' Kasper added from the doorway, 'if you believe everything he says.'

'Exactly,' Ana said, 'and you're, well, you're not a fighter, Merric. How can you beat him?'

'I don't know,' Merric confessed, but I'll think of something. I have to. Kasper, will you help me?'

'I'm not going to abandon you again.'

'Okay,' Ana sighed, making to follow them, 'it might be a foolhardy idea, but I'm not leaving you either.'

'No,' Merric said abruptly, stopping her in her tracks.

'What do you mean? Of course I'm coming.'

'I can't let anything happen to you, not after everything you've done.'

Ana opened her mouth to object, but Merric stopped her.

'I wish you could be with me, Ana, to finish this. But you're hurt, you can barely stand.'

The idea of not being with him was almost more than Ana could bear. She now knew how Tomas had felt back in her home, when Merric had told him to stay with her father. She knew he was right though. She still felt lightheaded and groggy. And knew she would do more harm than good.

'There's something you can do for me though,' Merric said.

Ana would do anything he asked, to help him.

'What is it?' she said, struggling to fight back her tears.

'In these other cells there are the Jacelyn soldiers who were captured that night. Free them. Kasper, give her the keys. I could really use their help.'

'I'll do it,' Ana said, 'but promise me you won't die.'

She looked deeply into Merric's eyes, and he noticed for the first time just how pretty hers were.

'Ana-'

'Promise me!'

Without thinking, Merric put his arms around Ana and pulled her in close. He kissed her full on the lips. She recoiled in surprise for a moment, but then Merric felt her kiss him back. To Merric, the cell had disappeared, and Kasper, and all thoughts of Sophya, and of Rayden Monfort and his evil father. Nothing existed except he and Ana, and he was aware of nothing but her. It was as though the worries and feelings of the past weeks had all been building up to this moment where they would simply disappear, and Merric did not want it to end. Selfishly he wanted to forget about all about Sophya, and stay here with Ana. But he knew he could not.

The moment seemed to last forever, until Kasper cleared his throat and the two separated at last. Ana smiled at him. Despite the danger, and what Merric was about to do, she had never been happier.

'I promise,' Merric said clumsily, wishing he could have said more.

Kasper tossed the keys to Ana, and Merric followed him out of the cell door. As he glanced back for one last look at Ana, Merric could see tears rolling her still smiling face.

Kasper led Merric past the unconscious form of the jailer on the dirty floor in the passage outside the cell, and they made their way to a staircase that led up and into the heart of the castle. As he climbed the stairs, rising from the depths of the dungeons, Merric felt the fate of all The Head rise with him. He had this chance to save these lands, and he swore that he would succeed or die trying.

Merric noticed the air getting fresher as they left the dungeons behind them, and his mind wanted to wander to thoughts of Ana. Reluctantly he shook all thoughts of her from his mind, knowing that he could not let himself be distracted. But thinking of her was easier, and more pleasant, than thinking of what lay ahead of him.

As they climbed the stairs, twisting round and round, they passed a door which led to the kitchens in the castle basement. They were almost back on ground level. Merric hated the feeling of being underground, and was glad to almost be away from it.

'What made you follow us?' Merric asked Kasper, who was walking ahead of him. 'I never thought I'd see you again.'

Kasper sighed. 'In truth, Merric, I wanted to come and find you the moment you ran away from me that night.'

Merric once more recalled hitting the archer, and turned deep red.

'I was too cowardly though, I admit. I was too ashamed of the things I'd said, so I didn't come after you. Not even after old Hamm the farmer told me that he'd seen you leaving the village. I barely slept that night, and by morning I'd made up my mind. I saddled my horse and came after you. I thought I'd catch you up, but you must have been even more determined to get back here than I thought. You were too far ahead of me. By the time I arrived in Eaglestone this morning, there were rumours among the townsfolk saying that you'd been spotted in the town, and I prayed that I wouldn't be too late. I then heard some Monfort men speak of your capture, and feared the worst. I had to try and help you if I could.'

'Your timing couldn't have been any better.'

'I like to make an entrance,' Kasper smiled, before turning and looking at Merric seriously. 'I'm going to help you, like I promised. But then after that, I have a personal score to settle with Orderix, wherever he is now. That piece of filth has terrorised us common folk for long enough.'

'He's here still, in the castle,' Merric said. 'He's working for the Monforts now. Getting friendly with the Monforts must have been his side of the bargain when he agreed to help betray the Jacelyns.'

'He's here? That'll make things easier.'

Merric went quiet for a moment.

'He's a horrible piece of work. I always knew he was an unpleasant and cold man, but he may even be worse than the Monforts. I don't know what Aric and Rayden's

402

aim is, but I do know what Orderix's is; greed and power, that's all he wants.'

'There's nothing worse than a man whose loyalty can be bought with gold,' Kasper agreed.

As they climbed up to the next floor they reached a door that led out into the main entrance hall of the keep. Beyond, they could hear the loud murmuring of dozens of voices. Merric listened.

'That sounds like the wedding guests arriving. Thank goodness we're not already too late.'

'Hold up a moment though,' Kasper said, putting his arm in front of Merric, as though he feared the boy would charge through the door without thinking. 'You need a weapon; we can't go trying to save Sophya without a blade in your hand. Where is the armoury?'

The archer had his longbow slung across his back, and he wore a short sword at his belt as well. He was prepared for a fight, but Merric clearly was not.

Merric's heart sank, knowing that Kasper was right. He had been so determined to finish things that he had not even thought about a sword.

'The armoury is by the barracks of the Eagle Guard, but that's through the entrance hall. We'd never make. Hang on,' Merric said suddenly, his face brightening as a thought occurred to him. 'We don't need an armoury! I've got a better idea.'

He gestured for Kasper to continue climbing the stairs, and they hurried upwards. When they reached a door two floors above the entrance hall, Merric carefully pushed it open. Seeing the passageway beyond empty, they snuck out and began making their way past the closed doors that lined each side. After the noise downstairs, this part of the castle keep seemed eerily quiet.

'Where are we going?' Kasper asked.

Merric did not reply, but just hurried on before finally stopping at a familiar plain door. He pushed it open. As he did so, he saw that the lock and the edge of the door were still broken and splintered. Kasper glanced at the damaged door which looked like it had been opened with force, and remembered Merric's story of that fateful night when the Jacelyns were murdered.

'This was your bedchamber?'

'Yes,' Merric said, looking around the room.

It looked just the way he remembered it. The sheets were still hanging off the bed from when he had hurriedly got up, and the shutters on the window were open and swinging in the breeze from where he had climbed out onto the ledge beyond in order to escape. Daylight streamed through the open window. Clearly the Monforts had no use for this chamber, so had not bothered to tidy it.

Merric's eyes moved to the wardrobe that stood in one corner of the bedchamber. He slowly walked over to it and pulled open the doors, and was greeted by the usual sight of messily folded clothes. He reached up into the pile of clothes and panicked slightly for a moment, worrying that it was gone. He then found what he was looking for as his hand closed around the hilt of a sword. He pulled it from its hiding place.

'This belonged to my father,' Merric said.

He had rarely looked at the old sword, thinking of it as just another sad reminder of the fact that he was part of a family he could not remember. He knew that he ought to be proud to own his father's sword, but he never had felt that way about it.

For the first time in his life, Merric looked at the sword properly. While not as decorative or elegant as the blade carried by many knights, it was skilfully made by a blacksmith who knew his craft well. The sword was encased in a scabbard made from deep red leather. The cross bar of the sword, which protected the wielder's hand, was forged from spotless silver, and below that the hand grip was carved from rich mahogany and bound in supple leather. The pommel was silver like the cross bar, but now that he looked closely, Merric could see that the likeness of a stag's head had been carved into it; the symbol of the Orrell family.

Kasper was taken aback by the sight of the sword. Despite the danger and the urgency of the moment, he moved away from where he kept watch at the bedchamber door, and stood behind Merric. He admired the blade over Merric's shoulder.

'A magnificent sword,' he said approvingly.

'This is *Hopebearer*,' Merric said, cradling the sword in both hands, 'the sword of the Orrell family.'

'It belonged to your father?'

'Yes, and my grandfather before him. It's belonged to the Barons of Ryding for hundreds of years.'

When he was old enough to understand, Lord Roberd had told Merric about his family's history. He would tell Merric how important it was to know where he had come from, especially as his parents were not there to tell him themselves. This sword was part of the history of the Orrells. Five hundred years ago, the lands surrounding Ryding had suffered from a sickness that gripped much of High Realm. The sickness struck down lords and common folk alike. After the death of his father from the illness, an Orrell boy aged just seven years old was named the new baron. The sickness passed, but none knew how the folk of Ryding would ever recover from their losses, especially with just a young boy as their baron.

They foresaw dark times ahead. A blacksmith saw promise in the boy though, and knew he would lead them all to greatness once more. He therefore forged his young baron this sword, naming it *Hopebearer*. He had so much faith in the boy that he even sold everything he owned in order to afford the expensive silver he needed to complete the work on the sword. His trust was well placed, as the young boy went on to be one of the most loved and greatest barons Ryding had seen. Ever since then, the sword had been passed on to the new baron of Ryding, as a memory of what they had overcome. The last baron to carry

Hopebearer had been Lord Willarm Orrell, and now it belonged to Merric.

Kasper looked at the blade with wide eyes. 'You must be proud to own it. Your father carried this sword into battle, and your ancestors before him. It's a sword of lords, not of common men.'

'I'm not the Baron of Ryding though,' Merric shrugged, 'I am nothing more than a common man.'

He drew the sword from the scabbard, to see if the blade was still sharp. In doing so, he spotted something he had never seen before, nor had ever known was there. There were words engraved into the length of the steel blade. Merric moved over to the window, to read the words in the light.

Unity gives strength to hope

Kasper read the words. 'What does it mean?'

Merric did not know, but the words were filling him with courage, and for the first time in his life he felt proud to be an Orrell, to be his father's son.

'On my own I would have no chance of stopping Rayden, but with you and Ana and Tomas there is hope... even if it's only a glimmer of hope.'

Kasper put his hand on Merric's shoulder.

'You haven't just got us with you, Merric; you've got the whole of The Head with you too.'

- CHAPTER TWENTY -

The wedding

With the words inscribed on the blade giving him encouragement, Merric buckled *Hopebearer* around his waist. He looked at Kasper.

'I'm ready. The wedding will be in the Grand Hall, so that's where we need to go. All doors into the hall will be heavily guarded though. The entrance hall will be out of the question.'

'I'm all ears then,' Kasper said, trusting in Merric's knowledge of the castle to think of a plan.

Merric thought for a moment, before deciding on a plan.

'The minstrel's gallery; it's a balcony that overlooks the Grand Hall. It will get us right above the wedding, and I bet you it won't be guarded, not strongly anyway.'

'That sounds as good a plan as we're likely to have. How do we get there?'

Merric led the way out of his chamber again, feeling more confident with the Orrell sword at his hip and a plan in his mind. Kasper paced beside him, and for the first time Merric noticed that the archer was wearing a shirt of ring mail beneath his well-worn travel cloak. He had left Little Harrow knowing he was going towards danger. Merric wondered whether Kasper expected to see his wife or daughter again. He was a proud man, and did not shy from danger in order to do what he felt was right. Merric was incredibly grateful to him for rescuing them, and for staying at his side even now.

They went down a floor and emerged onto a landing that gave a view of the entrance hall below. A large staircase swept down towards the main doors into the keep. The entrance hall below was filled with Monfort soldiers milling around, having ushered the guests into the Grand Hall ready for the ceremony.

'The Grand Hall is through those doors.' Merric pointed to a set of double doors at the end of the entrance hall directly opposite the main doors of the keep.

'I'm glad we're not going that way,' Kasper commented.

He was looking at the soldiers that filled the space below them. They seemed relaxed, but all were fully armoured and dangerous.

Merric and Kasper hurried away from the landing until they came face to face with the door to Lord Roberd's study. Merric did not look at it, worried about the sad memories that would flood back to him if he did. He instead turned left, stopping when they reached a small door that led to the gallery. Kasper opened the door a crack and peeked through, before silently edging out onto the balcony.

On the gallery there was a single Monfort soldier, but his spear was propped up against the wall behind him. He was leant casually against the handrail, watching the goings on down in the Grand Hall below. Before he had even noticed that the door he was meant to be guarding had been opened, Kasper had clapped a hand over the man's mouth to prevent him from shouting out in alarm. He put the struggling soldier into a headlock until he felt him go limp. Kasper silently laid the unconscious man down. With the coast clear, Merric walked out onto the balcony, unable to believe that the end of his quest was in sight.

If the Grand Hall had looked impressive to Ana the previous night, she would have been even more impressed by the view from the gallery today. The huge white Monfort banners that hung from the ceiling came down almost to Merric and Kasper's eye level as they crouched in their hiding place. Below, the previously empty space of the Grand Hall was now filled with rows and rows of guests who all stood facing the raised stage at the far end of the hall. They were all looking at Rayden and Sophya, who stood beneath the huge stained-glass window that bathed them in a colourful light. In honour of her family, Sophya was wearing a long flowing gown of Jacelyn sky blue, with golden coloured flowers in her curled hair. Rayden was clad in an immaculate white doublet with a matching snow-white cloak at his shoulders. Being a knight he wore his sword at his side, and Merric felt a surge of anger when he spotted the smaller blade on his other hip. It was Tristan's eagle dagger, which had been given to him by Lord Roberd when he was first knighted; Rayden must have stolen it from Tristan after he had murdered him.

Arch Prior Simeon stood facing the couple, in his finest ceremonial robes. His hands were clutched together nervously. It did not look as though the Arch Prior had been mistreated at the hands of the Monforts, but he clearly was not happy about serving those who had murdered Lord Roberd and his family. Merric wondered what threats had driven him to agree to conduct the wedding ceremony. To either side of the Grand Hall stood just three Monfort soldiers, looking spotless in highly-polished ring mail and brand new white surcoats, rather than their usual uniforms. Aside from them there were no further guards in the hall. Clearly Rayden did not consider himself to be in danger.

The wedding guests, from what Merric could see, were mainly rich townsfolk and wealthy merchants from Eaglestone and the surrounding villages. None appeared to be overly fond of attending the wedding, and Merric expected that the Monforts had told them that their attendance was not optional. For appearance's sake, Rayden had to give the impression of the wedding being completely normal, and that meant having guests. Most seemed to be looking at Sophya in sympathy, or else giving Rayden and his soldiers looks of dislike.

Kasper glanced around the huge room several times, before clicking his tongue and scowling. Merric knew what he was thinking. He was looking for Orderix, but the Lord's Counsel was not present. Merric had already searched for the man himself. Orderix may have been useful to the Monforts in helping them to overthrow the Jacelyns and take control of The Head, but it seemed that they hardly thought him to be important enough to be a guest at Rayden's wedding. It's likely they disliked the greedy man as much as everyone else did, and that gave Merric a grim satisfaction.

The wedding ceremony was already nearing its end. Arch Prior Simeon had finished speaking and, in High Realm's noble tradition, Sophya was presenting Rayden with a shield as a gift. It was made from rare snow oak wood, bright white in colour. The marching knight of the Monforts displayed on it, formed from hundreds of rare black jewels from the icy wastes beyond The Southstones.

'I give you this shield, as your wife, to keep you safe from harm in battle, so that you will always return to me.'

Sophya's high voice drifted across the Grand Hall, all the way to where Merric crouched. Like all young girls in High Realm who dreamed of marriage, she had memorised the ceremonial words years ago. Rayden took the shield with a bow, before giving it back to her.

'And as your husband, I ask that you keep this shield, as a reminder that I will always protect you.'

As Rayden finished saying the words, the assembled guests politely applauded, as was expected of them. A servant stepped forward and took the shield from Sophya, moving it out of the way. Arch Prior Simeon then asked Rayden to take Sophya's hand, ready to make his vows. Once this was done, and Sophya had done the same, they would be married. Now was the time for Merric to act.

From their high vantage point on the gallery they had a clear line of sight towards Rayden, and so Kasper unslung his longbow and looked at Merric with raised eyebrows. Merric knew he was asking if he should put an arrow into Rayden, so he shook his head quickly. There was no honour in that. He wanted Rayden to know who he was fighting, and who was going to beat him. He wanted to see the fear in Rayden's eyes. And if Merric was to fail, then he wanted to have lost with a sword in his hand and courage in his heart. Kasper and his longbow had their uses though.

'Will you keep those men occupied?' Merric asked him, pointing at the Monfort soldiers who stood at either side of the Grand Hall. There was no way Merric would be able to challenge Rayden to a one-on-one fight if they were there to step in and protect him.

'With pleasure,' Kasper said, stringing the longbow. It was made from powerful ironwood, and it took a strong man to be able to pull the bowstring back. Kasper made it

413

look easy when he flexed the wood and slipped the bowstring into place.

Merric made to move, but hesitated for a moment.

'If anything should happen to me…' he whispered.

Kasper just shook his head, silencing Merric.

'I'll keep an eye out for you.' He touched the sword at Merric's hip. 'Remember the words on your father's sword; *your* sword. You have all of our strength behind you. I'll talk to you again soon.'

Kasper stretched out a hand, and after a brief pause, Merric shook it.

Several great pillars stood along the sides of the Grand Hall, stretching from the floor all the way to the vaulted ceiling high above. One of these was immediately next to the minstrel's gallery, and Merric knew that was his way down to the floor. The pillars were highly decorated, with scenes from the history of High Realm carved into the stone. This would give Merric firm handholds which could be used to help him climb down from the gallery to the floor below.

Merric moved over to the wall, and peeked over the edge of the gallery. It seemed like a long drop. He climbed over the handrail of the gallery, reaching over and grabbing hold of the rough carvings on the pillar. Feeling suddenly exposed, he glanced around quickly, but could see that no one was looking his way; all attention was on Rayden and Sophya at the front of the hall. Rayden had started to say his vows. Merric slowly began shuffling down the pillar, his hands and feet looking for safe holds. He felt his foot touch an iron torch bracket that was bolted into the pillar. The daylight streaming into the Grand Hall meant that the torch did not need to be lit, and so Merric used it to help with his climb down.

He finally reached the floor, and was glad for the feeling of solid ground beneath his feet again. The descent had done nothing to calm his nerves. He glanced up at the gallery and saw Kasper peeping down at him. The hunter nodded down at him and readied his longbow. Kasper's hands looked steady and calm, and Merric wished he felt the same. His hands were sweaty and were shaking slightly, though whether from fear or something else Merric could not tell. He could not turn back now though, and had no choice but to go on. Steeling himself, he began to move towards the front of the hall, wondering with each step whether he was walking towards his own death.

Down the centre of the hall, between the rows of standing guests, an aisle ran all the way from the main doors below the gallery behind Merric to the raised stage at the far end of the Grand Hall. When Merric reached the rearmost line of guests he took a deep breath, and began walking down the aisle towards his enemy. Rayden and Sophya were unaware of Merric's arrival in the Grand Hall, and were stood facing Arch Prior Simeon, dwarfed by the colourful glass likeness of Jace and his eagle. It was now Sophya's turn to speak her vows to Rayden.

415

The first guests to notice Merric, as he walked past the rearmost rows, looked at him in mild interest. They did not recognise him, and assumed that he was a part of the wedding ceremony. They eyed his worn and dirty clothes and unwashed hair with curiosity. The next few rows of guests, as he passed them, looked at the sword at his hip in confusion. With the exception of Rayden Monfort and his soldiers, no one had been allowed to carry a weapon of any kind into the Grand Hall, and one older lady had even had her knitting needles taken from her. Yet this boy, who was striding stiffly up towards the stage, was making no effort to hide the sword he was carrying at his waist.

As Merric neared the front of the hall, his heart was thumping so loudly that he was certain that even his footsteps on the stone floor must be drowned out by the sound of it. Still neither Rayden or Sophya, nor the elderly Arch Prior, had noticed Merric's approach. By now though some of the guests had recognised Merric's face. Nearly all were still mourning the loss of their beloved Lord Roberd, as well as his wife and son, and seeing Merric brought a sudden hope to them. Clearly they, too, did not believe the lies being spread by the Monforts, and excited murmuring broke out among them. The Monfort soldiers at each side of the room were not able to see Merric, who was shorter than most grown men and so was blocked from view by the rows of standing guests. They shuffled nervously, fingering their spears and craning their necks as they tried to see what had caused the unexpected stir of excitement in the room.

Frowning in irritation at the noises coming from the guests, Rayden at last tore his attention away from Arch Prior Simeon, and turned around.

Rayden's eyes locked onto Merric's, and his mouth opened slightly in surprise. This soon vanished, as his mouth curled up into a wicked smile that nearly sent Merric running in fear. Sophya gave a small gasp as she saw Merric, and edged away from him. Arch Prior Simeon just blinked in disbelief at the sight of him.

The excited murmuring from the guests had ceased, and the Grand Hall was now deathly silent in anticipation. No one moved, not even the soldiers who finally had sight of the new arrival. They were looking at Rayden, waiting for his orders.

It was Rayden who finally broke the silence, but his words were directed at Merric and not his men.

'You don't know when to give up, do you?'

He smiled as he spoke, and abandoned Sophya to take a few slow steps towards Merric. He appeared unconcerned, and kept his hands away from the hilt of his sword. The arrival of Merric did not seem to worry him in the slightest.

Merric's heart was in his mouth, and he could barely walk from the fear he was feeling. He stopped when he was a few paces away from the stage on which Rayden and Sophya stood, and those guests nearest to them began to edge away. Rayden towered over Merric, and he looked strangely pleased to see him. He did not know how Merric

417

had escaped the dungeons far below them, but seemed to relish the opportunity to end things here and now, rather than go through the formality of a trial and execution. Rayden's grey eyes bore into Merric as he stood there, and what little courage Merric had left slowly drained away from him. Rayden Monfort was a knight, one of the greatest knights in the realm, if not *the* greatest. Who was Merric to try and stand against him?

Merric did not know what to say in response to Rayden's taunt, so instead looked over to where Sophya stood beside Arch Prior Simeon.

She was staring at Merric, but her eyes showed him that her fear of him was matched by her curiosity at his sudden appearance. If he had been able to escape the dungeons somehow, then why come closer to danger rather than flee the castle and get as far away as he could? Surely he could not be that determined to murder her, so was there more to Merric's story than Rayden had told her?

Merric could see this confusion and doubt on her face, and knew that he had to act now; he had to help her realise the truth. Swallowing his fear, he grasped the hilt of *Hopebearer*, and looked back up at Rayden.

'I know when to give up,' he said loudly, so that the whole room could hear. 'But it's not now, not while you're still breathing.'

The smile on Rayden's face just got wider, so Merric pressed on.

'I'll give up once you and your father have paid for the murder of Lord Roberd Jacelyn, his wife, Lady Cathreen Jacelyn, and his son, Sir Tristan Jacelyn; once you've answered for the loyal men who served the Jacelyn family that you've killed; once justice has been done for those that you have kept locked up for not believing your lies; and once the folk of The Head have revenge for the reign of terror that you have forced them to live under. Only then will I give up.'

Silence filled the Grand Hall. Nearly all the guests knew that the Monforts were the real enemy, but none had ever heard anyone be brave enough to say it openly to Rayden's face. The Monfort soldiers knew what had truly happened that night, and Arch Prior Simeon would never have believed that Merric had committed the murders. Rayden of course knew that the words were true, but the only person Merric wanted to believe him right now was Sophya. She was the only one who had believed the Monfort's lies, through no fault of her own. Merric wanted to look at her, to beg her to understand that what he was saying was true. But he dared not take his eyes off Rayden.

And Rayden just laughed.

It was a slow, cruel laugh. The sound echoed throughout the Grand Hall, right up to where Kasper crouched anxiously in the gallery. Sophya looked at Rayden, as though desperate to hear her future husband say that Merric's words were lies; to hear him deny it.

Rayden stopped laughing at last, and he saw Merric's hand clutching his sheathed sword. Rayden moved his hand down to the hilt of his own blade. A large ruby was laid into the pommel of the sword, and it caught the light as Rayden shifted his position. He drew the sword slightly, baring a few inches of cold steel threateningly, before dropping it back into place again. He was toying with Merric, knowing that his skills with a sword far outweighed his opponent's.

'I'm afraid you'll be waiting a long time to give up if you're wanting all that to happen,' Rayden said, mocking Merric. 'Guards, grab him!'

The six Monfort soldiers immediately darted forward, their spears pointed at Merric, who took a step back. A sudden whooshing sound filled the air, and an arrow struck the first man in the chest. He looked at it in surprise, before stumbling and falling to the floor. The others looked up in alarm, to see where the shot had come from. High up in the gallery Kasper was stood, one leg up on the handrail, with another arrow already notched onto his bowstring. The guests, suddenly realising they were caught in the middle, turned and fled back towards the doors beneath the gallery which led to the entrance hall beyond. As they ran, Kasper's second arrow flew over their heads, striking another of the Monfort men behind them. The remaining four soldiers, fearful of the archer who had already taken out two of their number, turned their attention away from Merric. They lifted their large shields to try and protect themselves from

Kasper's arrows, and began shuffling cautiously towards him at the far end of the hall. One tried to shout to the other soldiers who crowded the entrance hall beyond the far doors, wanting them to rush upstairs and attack the archer from behind. His voice was drowned out by the alarmed cries of the guests as they hammered on the doors, trying to get out, and so his shout went unheard.

Seeing his men distracted, Rayden scowled and began advancing towards Merric himself. As he slowly descended the few steps that led down from the stage to the floor, Rayden drew his sword. The steel rang with a musical menace around the stone walls, and the sound chilled Merric to the bone. His palms were slick with sweat, but he forced his hand to pull *Hopebearer* from its red leather scabbard. Rayden's eyes moved up and down the Orrell family sword, reluctantly acknowledging the quality of the blade. His appreciation of the sword soon disappeared when he turned his attention back to the boy who was holding it.

Merric did not feel confident at all as he stood there, alone, just a few feet away from Rayden. His eyes were drawn again to the words engraved on the blade.

Unity gives strength to hope

He was not truly alone, he knew. His mind wandered to Kasper, and to Ana and Tomas, and all the others that had helped him; brave Sir Gerard, cut down whilst he protected Merric; Hary the farmer, who had not known who Merric was but had helped him all the same; the folk of Little Harrow who had taken him and his friends in; Ana's father who, even whilst being terrorised by the Monforts, had never lost support for Merric, nor believed the lies being spread about him. Merric did not know how he could hope to beat Rayden, and wondered if he was simply doing exactly what Rayden had wanted him to. However, with all of The Head behind him, Merric knew he had to try.

The Grand Hall, so busy a few moments ago, was now almost deserted. The wedding guests had managed to force the doors at the far end of the hall open, and were trying to flee into the entrance hall beyond. The door was large, but not large enough to let them all pass at the same time, and a bottleneck was being formed from the panicked folk. The Monfort soldiers beyond the doors were trying to get through into the Grand Hall, to see what had caused this disturbance, and this was making the jam ever worse. The four remaining soldiers had made it almost level with the minstrel gallery, and had made a solid barrier over their heads with their shields. Kasper was happy to shoot arrow after arrow at the wooden shields though, keeping them distracted and away from Merric. Sophya had shrunk against the wall beneath the great stained glass window, her eyes flicking between Rayden and Merric. Arch Prior Simeon had not fled from the Grand Hall with everyone else, and stood protectively in front of her. His hands were raised as though to request that they both put down their swords, but his face did not look like he dared to interfere.

All of this was happening, but Merric was noticing none of it.

'What's the matter? Lost your nerve?'

Rayden's taunt angered Merric, and he wondered if that was because there was some truth in his words. He was terrified. Merric tightened his grip on *Hopebearer*, and tried to steady his breathing. He had only wielded a sword in battle once, and the heavy blade felt unnatural in his hands.

'I'm going to cut you down,' Rayden continued confidently, 'just as I cut down Tristan. Like you, he was just a stupid boy, playing at being a knight; he was a disgrace to knights across the entire realm.'

He began slowly circling around Merric, who was forced to do the same to stop Rayden from getting behind him.

There was a small whimper from behind Arch Prior Simeon, and Sophya's eyes appeared over his shoulder, wide with shock. She had heard Rayden's words. This was not how Rayden had acted around her before, always being comforting and saying sweet things. This could not be the same man who had been a perfect, chivalrous knight towards her over the past few weeks.

Merric could see Sophya out of the corner of his eye. There was a devastated expression on her face, from hearing a man who she thought loved her gloating about murdering her brother. Merric was encouraged though, knowing that she was beginning to understand the truth.

'We disagree about what is a disgrace to knighthood,' Merric said to Rayden. 'Murdering a helpless mother and father as they slept, that's not the actions of a gallant knight of the realm. Killing your opponent who was defeated and defenceless and at your knees, where is the honour in that?'

Rayden was infuriated by Merric's words. He would not be spoken to like that by a simple boy. Suddenly, and with a snarl, he lunged forward with his long sword, taking Merric by surprise. Merric had to wildly sweep *Hopebearer* across to parry Rayden's sword aside, but the quick attack had knocked him off his balance. He recovered quickly to clumsily block two more strikes, and was shocked by how fast Rayden moved. One minute his sword was coming at him high from the right, before suddenly sweeping at him from low to the left. Merric had seen Rayden fight twice, once during the jousting tournament and again when he had fought Tristan that night, but he could not have been prepared for his speed and skill with a sword. He was strong too, and his blows were making Merric's arms numb.

Rayden paused for a moment, clearly enjoying toying with his young opponent. Merric took the opportunity to recover his breath. Rayden did not even look like he had broken a sweat, and was relaxed, smirking down at Merric.

'Tell me it's not true,' Sophya said to Rayden, her voice shaking. 'Say you didn't do it. Merric is lying.'

Rayden just ignored her, and Sophya burst into tears.

424

'I'm so sorry, Merric,' she sobbed. 'I shouldn't have believed the lies he told me. What…what have I done?'

She looked in anguish at her wedding gown, and began ripping the decorative flowers from her hair

Merric looked across at her and their eyes met. For the first time since he arrived back at Eagle Mount the previous night, Merric felt like he was looking at the girl he had grown up with. The girl from last night was a stranger, a creation of Rayden and his father, but now she was gone. Merric tried to give her a smile of encouragement.

'Shut up,' Rayden spat at Sophya, tired of her talking.

She looked back at him in fear, and tears were streaming freely down her face.

'Why are you doing this?' she begged, as Arch Prior Simeon tried to comfort her.

Rayden just shook his head in frustration and turned back to Merric, raising his sword once more.

'I'm going to save you,' Merric promised Sophya, looking past Rayden at her, 'and I'm going to save Eagle Mount.'

Rayden laughed humourlessly at Merric's words, and the smile did not leave his face when Merric suddenly went on the attack himself. He lazily blocked and parried Merric's first blows, not even bothering to move his feet. The attacks were weak and predictable, and Rayden acted as though they were more of an annoyance than anything else, like he was merely swatting away an irritating fly. Despite what he had said to Sophya, Merric knew he could not hope to win, but he wanted to inflict as much pain on Rayden as he could. He wanted revenge, for Sophya, and for her murdered family. This desire drove his blade again and again. Whenever Rayden expected Merric to tire, the sword strikes became harder and faster, and Rayden found himself suddenly having to work a bit harder to block the blows. To his own surprise, the smirk on his face slowly turned to a grimace.

Merric had never known pain like it before, but his arms burned like fire from the effort. His muscles were screaming at him, begging him to stop, but he kept swinging *Hopebearer* viciously at Rayden. He tried to remember everything Sir Gerard had told him. After every blow he lifted his sword high above his head, ready to bring it swinging down again. He had no energy left, but he could see the sudden worry on his opponent's face, and he knew that Rayden had not been expecting such fierceness in him. Seeing the realisation of the truth on Sophya's face had filled Merric with a determination, and he would stop at nothing to try and defeat the man who had caused so much pain and grief to her family. His sword blows kept on coming. For the first time, he felt like he could beat Rayden.

He could win.

'Enough!' roared Rayden eventually, and after deflecting a final blow from Merric he kicked out hard.

Rayden's booted foot struck Merric's chest, and Merric felt the wind get knocked out of his lungs. Surprised by the attack, he fell heavily back onto the stone floor. *Hopebearer* slipped out of his hand, and clattered loudly on the stone beside him.

'Enough,' Rayden repeated, stepping up to the prone Merric.

He aimed his sword at Merric's throat. He looked furious, and had put up with enough of his young opponent's attempt at beating him.

Behind Merric, Kasper had run out of arrows and so had followed Merric down the pillar from the gallery to the floor of the Grand Hall. He had tried to fight all four Monfort soldiers at once with his short sword, but had been overcome by them. He was not lacking for bravery, but his ability with a sword was not the same as his skill with his longbow. The Monfort soldiers now had him pinned up against the wall, defenceless and at their mercy. As Merric laid there on the floor, breathing heavily, he watched them threatening the archer with their spears. Merric felt a surge of guilt; Kasper was trying to protect him, and because of that his wife and daughter were never going to see him again. Kasper was not giving up though, and was defiantly swatting the spear tips away with his sword.

The crowd of guests had finally all got through the door at the far end of the hall beyond Kasper and his attackers, and now dozens more Monfort soldiers were filing into the Grand Hall. Their swords were drawn, but when they saw that both of the intruders were defeated, they relaxed. Rayden looked triumphantly down at Merric, his anger and frustration passing.

'You've had your fun, boy, but now you've lost. *I'm* Duke of The Head, and there's nothing more you can do about it. Every second you fight extends your miserable little life by another breath, but you cannot win. I'm going to kill you, but before I do, know this; I'm going to marry your precious Sophya, whether she wishes to be my wife or not. Then these lands will be mine by right, and there's nothing anyone can do to stop me, not even the Mother herself. Don't worry though, my lord father and I have big plans for the realm. It's just a shame that you won't live to see them come to fruition.'

Sophya had collapsed to her knees, still unable to believe that everything she had been told was a lie. She thought of the night before, when Merric had tried to sneak her out of the castle. It was because of her that Merric was captured. If she had gone with him then they could have been leagues way from the castle by now. Arch Prior Simeon put a comforting arm around her, trying to pull her back to her feet, but his own face was filled with despair. He watched Rayden standing over Merric, with sorrow in his old eyes. He wished he could have done something himself to help, but he was duty bound to serve the priory and take no part in the quarrels of the realm.

Merric refused to give Rayden the satisfaction of going quietly, but nor would he beg for his life.

'Eagle Mount was built by Jace a thousand years ago, and a Jacelyn has ruled here ever since.' Merric said, grasping the hilt of his sword again and slowly climbing back to his feet.

His breathing was heavy and laboured from the pain in his chest. Rayden let him stand, thinking that he would gladly knock the boy back down again if that's what he really wanted.

'You are not the Duke of The Head,' Merric said. 'The Duke of The Head is dead, because you murdered him. His son and heir is gone as well, because of you. Sophya is the last member of the Jacelyn family. One day she *will* marry, and her husband will take the Jacelyn name and be the next duke, and their son after him. But that man won't be you.'

Merric looked up at the stained glass window that towered behind Rayden. Jace the Eagle Rider, mounted on his giant eagle, looked down with pride at Merric standing up to the evil of the Monforts. It felt to Merric that he was in the presence of an old friend.

Rayden snarled and lifted his sword above his head with both hands. He had listened enough to the boy who continued to defy him, and wanted to end it. With incredible strength he chopped his sword down at Merric in a powerful two-handed swing. Merric had to use all of his remaining energy to block the strike with *Hopebearer*, and the Rayden's powerful blow made Merric's arms ache and hurt even more. Rayden continued his attack, repeatedly bringing his sword down towards his opponent, but each time Merric parried the blows.

Rayden's eyes were filled with frenzied hatred towards Merric, while Merric himself felt calmer than he expected to be in the face of his death. He watched Rayden tighten his grip on the hilt of his sword, and begin the motion of swinging the blade down towards Merric's unprotected head one last time. Merric did not try and block the strike. Instead, with all the energy he had left, he launched his own attack and swung *Hopebearer* upwards to meet Rayden's own swinging sword. The two blades met with an echoing ring, and a shower of sparks sprayed into the air.

The blade of Rayden's sword shattered.

The top two-thirds of the blade snapped clean off and fell to the stone floor, where it broke into countless pieces. Rayden looked in shock at the remaining shard of metal that he held in his hands.

Merric took a step back, stunned, breathing heavily. Rayden continued to stare in astonishment at his broken sword. The sword had been forged by the finest blacksmith in The Southstones, and with it he had been unbeaten. He had carried it since he had been old enough to lift it, and it was as much a part of his arm as his own hand. And yet, here in this quiet hall of Eagle Mount, it had been broken by this boy; a small boy, ordinary, and not even a knight. How could he possibly have had the strength needed to break the sword?

Merric looked at *Hopebearer*, which showed no signs of damage at all from the battle. There were no dents or scratches in the flawless blade, and it continued to shine in the light pouring in through the stained glass window. The words along the blade shone brighter than anything else.

Unity gives strength to hope

'This is *Hopebearer*,' Merric said proudly, raising his sword so that Rayden could see it clearly. 'You're right, the Jacelyn's may nearly all be gone. You've seen to that yourself. However you didn't reckon on one thing.'

Rayden turned his head to look at Merric, his face contorted in rage.

'Yes? And what's that?' he spat.

Merric looked directly into the eyes of his enemy, feeling far taller than his five feet.

'You didn't count on the Orrells. We might be a small family, but we've always been close to the Jacelyns...'

Rayden almost seemed to recoil from Merric, seeing the determination in the younger boy's eyes for the first time.

Merric felt a thousand years' worth of Orrells standing with him, and had never been prouder of his heritage.

'...And there's still one of us left.'

The remains of Rayden's sword dropped to the floor as he fell to his knees.

431

'Mercy!' he said, keeping his head lowered so that Merric could not see his face. 'I beg you. It was my father; he made me do it all. It's his plans, I just do what he asks of me.'

Merric was disgusted.

'Did you offer mercy to those that you murdered?'

The Monfort soldiers were edging towards him, seeing Rayden in danger. Sensing the threat, Merric shouted over his shoulder at them.

'Stay back! Don't come any closer!' He turned back to Rayden. 'I'm not a murderer; I'm not like you. If you swear, on whatever shred of honour you have left as a knight, that you won't try to escape, I'll spare your life.'

'I swear it, I promise,' Rayden said, still on his knees, and still avoiding Merric's eyes.

'Order your men to lay down their weapons. They will be free to return to The Southstones, but you and your father will be taken to the king. You will confess your crimes to him, and he will decide your fate.'

Rayden just nodded his head, looking defeated. Merric pointed at Sophya, whose eyes were wet with tears.

'You murdered her family, and you were going to give her a life of misery. This is better than you deserve.'

While Merric was speaking, he did not notice Rayden's hand move down to his hip.

'Merric, watch out!' Sophya cried, spotting the danger.

Rayden leapt to his feet, Tristan's eagle dagger in his hand.

'Kill the archer!' Rayden screamed at his soldiers who were restraining Kasper, who looked up at him in surprise. 'Kill the men down in the dungeons, kill everyone in the town. Kill them all!'

Rayden lunged forward with Tristan's dagger, the blade aimed straight for Merric's heart. The move took Merric by surprise, who had believed Rayden's cries for mercy to be genuine. He should have known that Rayden was a good liar.

Acting on instinct, Merric brought *Hopebearer* up as quickly as he could and pointed the blade at Rayden, who saw the danger too late. With a cry, his own leap forward took him straight onto Merric's outstretched sword. The fury and determination in Rayden's eyes turned to disbelief when he felt the pain.

Impaled on *Hopebearer*, he tried to swipe the dagger at Merric, but could not reach. As he felt his strength leave him, Rayden looked at Merric with loathing in his eyes. Merric was pale, stunned by what he had done. His arms were shaking, but he kept the sword up, seeing the blood appearing on Rayden's pure white doublet where *Hopebearer* had pierced him.

'You can't beat me!' Rayden snarled, his voice growing weaker. 'You can't....'

He tried to strike Merric one more time with the dagger, the blade cutting through nothing but air. With one last look of hatred, Rayden's eyes slowly closed and he fell to the floor. Merric, unable to hold on, let go of the sword as it fell with him.

There was silence absolute silence in the Grand Hall, and Rayden Monfort moved no more.

- CHAPTER TWENTY ONE -

The battle for Eagle Mount

Angry shouts came from behind Merric, as the Monfort soldiers recovered from the shock of seeing Rayden killed. As one they charged towards Merric. Even the men who had been holding onto Kasper let go of their captive, and joined the rush. Merric just stood there, watching the men as they charged towards him.

'Run, Merric!' shouted Arch Prior Simeon.

The elderly man grabbed hold of Sophya, and began dragging her to the relative safety of a side door. Sophya was kicking and screaming, pleading with Merric to come with them. She was desperate to not lose Merric, after realising the truth of the events over the past weeks. It was too late though, Merric would never be able to reach the door before the Monfort soldiers caught him.

Merric looked at the faces of the men who were charging at him. They had no leader, but were determined to take revenge on the boy who had taken Rayden from them. Merric was exhausted from the fight and *Hopebearer* was lying beneath Rayden's body. He knew he could not hope to defend himself against the Monfort soldiers.

It seemed unfair. He had achieved the impossible in defeating Rayden, and he had vengeance for the murder of the Jacelyns, but he would only be able to briefly enjoy that success before he would himself be killed. He would never get to see Sophya's happiness at being free from the Monforts, and he hoped that Arch Prior Simeon would be able to get her to safety before the Monfort men sought to take their anger out on her too.

Merric thought of Lord Aric, by now likely back in The Southstones. The reason why he had wanted to claim The Head for the Monforts was still a mystery to Merric, and he was disappointed that he would never find out.

His mind then wandered to Tomas, and he hoped that his servant knew how much he meant to Merric. They had become friends, and Tomas's loyalty to Merric had never wavered.

Merric watched Kasper charging after the Monfort soldiers, but he must have known that by trying to save Merric he was only running towards his own death as well.

Finally, Merric's mind settled on Ana. The two had finally opened their hearts to each other, and admitted their true feelings. It had only been for a moment, and Merric wished it could have lasted forever.

The nearest Monfort soldier was racing towards him, and Merric recognised his thick red beard. He was one of the soldiers from the night before, in Sophya's bedchamber, and judging by the white cloak hanging from his shoulders he had been made into a serjeant for his part in Merric's capture. Of all the soldiers in the Grand Hall, he looked to be the one most determined to get vengeance for the loss of Rayden. As he got nearer to Merric he lifted his axe, ready to swing it down towards the boy who stood beside the body of the Monfort knight.

And Merric did not even try to stop him.

A sudden shocked shout sounded from behind the red-bearded serjeant, and he turned his head in surprise, checking the swing of his axe. He echoed the cry of surprise, and then sounded a warning to his men. The charge of the Monfort soldiers stopped suddenly, as all men skidded to a stop and turned their backs on Merric. Panic seemed to spread through their ranks, as they hurriedly organised themselves into ordered rows.

Merric peered past them, curious as to what had distracted them from killing him.

Through the doorway at the far end of the Grand Hall came two men, both large and muscled. One had short cropped hair and a beard, whilst the other had longer hair that was matted with dirt. Both were dressed in ragged clothes, but they were unmistakable. Behind Sir Orsten and Sir Oskar Oakheart were dozens of men wearing the uniform of Jacelyn soldiers, though after weeks in the dungeons their clothes were filthy and their faces were unshaven and covered in grime. They had hurriedly armed themselves from the armoury, and clutched an odd assortment of swords and spears, axes and maces. They may have looked like a rabble, but they were united in their desire to come to the aid of Merric.

A further shout of warning came from the Monfort soldiers, and one pointed up at the gallery. More Jacelyn soldiers, freshly escaped from the dungeons, were massing up there. They were armed with longbows and crossbows, and at their centre was a girl with dirty blonde hair wielding a crossbow of her own, and still wearing her dress from the summer celebrations. She had a look of determination on her face as she shouted out orders to the Jacelyn soldiers with her. Merric looked in wonder up at Ana, as she aimed her crossbow down at the Monfort men, and shot the bolt at them. The Jacelyn men around her aimed and loosed their arrows and crossbow bolts as well, while below them the Oakheart brothers led the charge forwards with a bellowing cry.

Merric had forgotten that Sir Orsten and Sir Oskar had been taken from their father, and were in the dungeons here in Eagle Mount, but at this moment he was so happy that they had been. They were fearsome warriors, and their presence encouraged the Jacelyn soldiers, and put fear into the hearts of the Monfort men.

'On!' Sir Orsten roared at the men around him, and they echoed his war cry.

'Charge!' bellowed the red-bearded Monfort serjeant, recovering from the surprise of the sudden appearance of the Jacelyn prisoners.

His men charged towards the Jacelyn force, and the two sides crashed together with the echoing noise of steel striking steel. Men shouted while others cried out, and blades rose and fell.

Kasper skirted around the battle, and ran over to Merric.

'Are you okay?' he asked, breathing heavily.

'Yes,' Merric said, feeling the adrenaline pumping through him. 'We've got to help them.'

He stooped and recovered *Hopebearer* from where it lay on the ground. Kasper hefted his own sword and nodded, and side by side they ran into the battle between the Monfort and Jacelyn men. Merric chopped left and right with *Hopebearer*. The arrival of the Jacelyn prisoners had lifted his heart and he was proud to fight alongside them.

Silently, men closed in around Merric, but they were not Monfort soldiers. They were missing their armour and spotless surcoats, but from their fearless expressions and the way they fought off any Monfort man who tried to harm Merric, he knew that they were the members of the Eagle Guard. They were sworn to defend the Duke of The Head and his family. Lord Roberd may have been killed, but clearly they still thought of Merric as being part of his family. They followed orders without question, and would not hesitate to give up their own lives to protect him. They had been powerless to protect Lord Roberd from the murdering blades of Rayden, and they were determined to make up for that now.

The Monfort soldiers, outnumbered by the escaped Jacelyn prisoners and terrified of the Oakheart brothers who led them, were slowly heading back towards the door that led to the entrance hall. To make matters worse for them, they were harried the whole time by the arrows and bolts raining down on them from the minstrel's gallery above. As they retreated towards the entrance hall they left many of their number lying dead on the floor of the Grand Hall.

As the fight spilled out into the entrance hall, Sir Orsten and Sir Oskar led the pursuit. Merric looked up as he passed through the doors from the Grand Hall and saw Orderix standing at the top of the wide staircase that led up to the floor above. Orderix was looking at the battle in horror, all the colour drained from his face. He had picked a side, and now that side was losing.

'Kasper!' Merric shouted.

'I've seen him,' the archer said quietly, looking up at the thin man.

Kasper's expression was determined, and his eyes locked on to Orderix's. Seeing that the situation was desperate, Orderix darted down the stairs, taking them three at a time, and made to flee out of the huge oak doors that led outside.

'Forward!' Kasper shouted at the Jacelyn soldiers around him, eager to get to Orderix, 'push them back!'

The Jacelyn soldiers answered him with a cheer, and with a renewed energy they forced the Monforts men back, step by step, towards the open doors of the keep's main entrance. Ana and the archers appeared at the top of the staircase, having hurried round from the gallery, and continued shooting down at the retreating Monfort soldiers. This sped up their retreat, and even with the desperate shouts of encouragement from the red-bearded serjeant, the Monfort men continued to edge backwards.

Before he knew it, Merric felt the sunlight and air on his face. The Monfort men had been forced through the front doors and down the short flight of steps that led into the courtyard. Both sides took a moment to catch their breath.

The remaining Monfort soldiers were gathered in the centre of the courtyard, in the shadow of the castle keep. They were looking hurt and beaten, but refused to give up. The bearded serjeant was walking up and down the front of the band of survivors, shouting at them to avenge Rayden, and fight for the honour of Lord Aric and the Monforts.

The Jacelyn soldiers ordered themselves, ready for one last attack. The men armed with swords and axes put themselves at the front, and those with spears stood behind them. All were eager to get back into the fray, though none more so than Sir Orsten and Sir Oskar. The Oakheart brothers saw their imprisonment as an insult to their honour as knights, and were determined to get their own back on the men who had harmed their father. Merric pushed his way forward, the Eagle Guard following him every step, until he was stood beside the Oakheart brothers in the front rank of the Jacelyn force. Merric had seen the Oakheart brothers during their capture outside Oaktyn castle, but they had never met him before.

'You're Merric?' Sir Oskar asked him.

'I am,' Merric replied. 'Thank you, your timing couldn't have been better.'

'You don't need to thank us. I don't need an excuse to fight Monforts,' Sir Orsten said, grinning as he lifted the big two-handed mace he carried.

Sir Oskar winced.

'You'll forgive my brother. What he meant to say was that we're honoured to fight in the name of Lord Roberd.'

'My twin has always been shy of the sight of blood. He'd rather talk than fight,' Sir Orsten laughed.

Sir Oskar, whose sword was nonetheless red with blood, ignored him.

'We should finish this,' Kasper said.

He seened frustrated at having lost sight of Orderix,

'It seems too easy,' Sir Oskar mused aloud. 'There are too few of them.'

As if in response to his words, a mass of fresh Monfort soldiers came flooding out of the barracks, and from the gate that led back into Eaglestone, eager to reinforce their companions. In their midst were men clad in full armour and colourful surcoats; knights from The Southstones who had stayed to help keep control in The Head after Lord Aric had gone back to his own dukedom. More and more Monfort men were arriving, and the mass of men in the middle of the courtyard was growing bigger.

'Oh, that's more like it.' Sir Orsten said, but even he did not like their chances now.

Merric watched as the flood of Monfort soldiers formed a large semi-circle around the band of Jacelyn men, who stood with the steps and front door of the castle keep behind them. A group of Monfort men closed the huge gates that led into the town, and dropped a heavy locking bar into place.

The Jacelyn soldiers were now trapped, and outnumbered by the Monforts at least three to one. After their gallant effort, it was looking like a battle Merric and the Jacelyn soldiers could not win. No one would think that from the look of the faces of the men who stood around Merric though. Despite the state of them from weeks locked in the dungeons deep below where they now stood, the Jacelyn soldiers looked proud and determined. When faced with the choice of going back into the darkness of the dungeons or being killed with a sword in hand, none had to even think about which they would chose. Most had cuts and injuries from the fight in the keep, but all seemed blind to any pain.

Merric sensed the Eagle Guard staying close to him, protecting him from any sudden attack from the Monforts, but he knew it was futile. They would be beaten, and if they were not all killed then they would be locked up in the dungeons again. Lord Aric, hearing of the death of his son, would appoint another to become Duke of The Head, and poor Sophya would be forced to marry whoever that might be instead. Was there anything at all that they could do to stop that from happening? Merric had to think of something that would stop everything they had achieved from being done in vain.

'My lord?'

Merric looked up to see a Jacelyn soldier, a cut on his cheek, looking down at him. It felt strange to see this man, three times his age and twice his size, address him in this way.

'Yes?'

'What are your orders?'

Kasper looked across at Merric.

'I don't know about you, but I have no intention of going down without fighting.'

'The Oakhearts never give in,' Sir Orsten agreed.

'Nor are we known for our common sense,' Sir Oskar added with a sigh. His brother clapped him on the shoulder with a grin.

Merric turned to one of the Eagle Guards that stood beside him

'Take two of your best fighters and find Sophya,' he told him. 'Protect her. Do whatever you can for her, and help her to escape if you can. Stay with her, and see that she comes to no harm.'

The man nodded and barked to two of the other Eagle Guards.

'Brant! Bromwell! Come with me.'

The three of them disappeared back into the castle keep, passing Ana and her archers as they joined the Jacelyn soldiers gathered outside. Ana looked at the mass of Monfort men that surrounded their small force, and then turned to Merric with a grim expression on her face. Merric smiled reassuringly at her.

He felt reassured that he had done all he could to protect Sophya, but wished he could send Ana away as well. He knew she would not leave even if he asked her to though, and part of him would not be able to bear saying goodbye to her again. Swallowing, he addressed the men around him. He felt self-conscious raising his voice, but knew that he had to say something.

'You may know me, or you might not. You will all know Lord Roberd though; a man we all loved and cherished, the same as he loved and cherished every one of us. Years ago, he saved me. He raised me as one of his own. These men before us took Lord Roberd away from us. They took Lady Cathreen away from us, and they took Sir Tristan from us too.'

At the sound of Tristan's name, several of the Jacelyn soldiers roared angrily at the Monforts before them. Lord Roberd was loved, and his lady wife respected. Tristan, though, was the pride of The Head. He was the greatest knight The Head had ever seen. If he had died in battle then that would have been one thing, but their beloved knight had been murdered, when he was unarmed and defenceless. Merric used the men's anger and desire for revenge to inspire them.

'They took Eagle Mount from us, they took all The Head from us. You men were all locked away because you defied them, because you did not listen to their lies. Any duke, whether he be Jacelyn or Monfort, needs good men. Aric and Rayden would have taken you in and clad you in white. They would have let you keep your lives and serve under the banner of the black marching knight. But you're proud men, and loyal men. You've stayed true to the Jacelyns, even when they locked you in the dungeons and threatened you with death.'

'This is Merric, the ward of Lord Roberd,' Kasper said to them, when Merric's voice trailed off.

The Jacelyn soldiers around him did not know who Kasper was, but in this moment they listened to him eagerly.

'The Monforts blamed the murders of the Jacelyn family on him, and accused you all of being his accomplices. They said you all fight for him, and they weren't wrong; you fight for him now, for the honour of the Jacelyns and the memory of Lord Roberd.'

In front of them, a fifty Monfort archers loaded their crossbows.

446

'Now is your chance for revenge,' Merric continued, emboldened by Kasper's words. 'Vengeance for Lord Roberd, and justice for The Head!'

The Jacelyn soldiers cheered, raising their weapons into the air. The Eagle Guard around Merric, chosen because of their courage and discipline, remained silent, but their faces showed the pride they felt at being able to fight for the golden eagle symbol of the Jacelyn family one last time. Some of the Jacelyn men carried shields, and they crashed their spears and swords against them loudly.

'Take aim!' came a shout from the Monfort ranks, and Merric saw several of the crossbows point directly at him. He knew that at any moment they would shoot their bolts right at him, and he wondered whether it would hurt to die. Like the men around him though, he would not go down without a fight. Before he could lose his courage, he raised *Hopebearer* high above his head.

'For Lord Roberd!' Merric shouted, as loud as he could.

At his cry the Jacelyn soldiers began sprinting across the courtyard towards the Monfort men. Merric ran with them, with Kasper at his side and the Eagle Guard around him. Ana remained on the steps along with the archers, and they shot their longbows and crossbows at the mass of Monfort men. Merric felt his courage soar at the sight of the Jacelyn men charging alongside him, and even though he knew he was running towards his own death, he did not feel any fear. Somewhere above him he knew Lord Roberd was looking down on him, a proud smile on his face.

Looking directly at a Monfort crossbowman, Merric charged with all the might he could muster, waiting for the bolts to strike him. A Monfort serjeant, who commanded the archers, gave the order to shoot. Bolts flew through the air towards them, but somehow none hit Merric. Some hit Jacelyn soldiers, who fell to the ground with cries, whilst others went over their heads to harmlessly strike the stone of the castle keep behind them.

Before the crossbowmen had a chance to reload, the Jacelyns were upon them. Monfort soldiers wielding swords and spears pushed past the crossbowmen, and launched themselves on their enemies. Sir Orsten swung his huge mace in a wide arc, and any Monfort men who did not get out of the way of his vicious attacks were beaten down. While his brother bellowed his war cries, Sir Oskar stayed silent, a grim look on his face as he used his sword against the men in front of him. Merric found himself face to face with a knight wearing a purple surcoat bearing the symbol of a silver fish on its breast. The knight lunged and slashed at Merric with no regard for his own safety. Merric hurriedly blocked and parried the attacks, before the Eagle Guard pushed past him and barrelled into the knight. Merric did not see what happened next, but as the Eagle Guard moved forward a moment later he saw a knight wearing a purple surcoat lying face down on the ground.

The Monforts had been taken aback by the ferociousness and determination of the Jacelyn charge, but now their sheer weight of numbers was starting to take effect. The Jacelyn soldiers were tiring, and even the huge Sir Orsten seemed to be swinging his mace with less ferocity. While the Jacelyn charge had forced the Monfort soldiers back, they were now starting to lose the ground they had won and were being beaten back again.

Merric fended off attack after attack by the Monfort men near him, and when he managed to get past the defences of one of them with *Hopebearer* and sent the soldier tumbling to the ground, he was just replaced by three more. Merric knew it was hopeless, and that the end was near.

Kasper was fighting off two Monfort men at once. He slew one of them, but the second got behind him and would have killed him had it not been for Ana's crossbow bolt that she shot from her position on the steps of the keep.

An angry shout came from behind Merric, and he turned to see that Sir Orsten had been knocked off his feet by four Monfort soldiers, and the knight was unable to stand up and fight them all off at the same time. His brother was unable to come to his aid, being surrounded by enemies himself. Merric rushed over to Sir Orsten, pushing past a pair of Jacelyn and Monfort soldiers who were duelling with spears. Merric slashed his sword at one of the men who was attacking Sir Orsten, before shoving another one away from the Oakheart knight. A third Monfort soldier turned towards Merric with a snarl on his face, but his sword swipe was rushed and clumsy. Sir Orsten had got back to his feet, and one tired swing of his mace was enough to take the man down. The fourth soldier turned to look for an easier target than the Oakheart knight.

'You have my thanks,' Sir Orsten said to Merric.

A surge of Monfort men running towards them was halted only by the timely arrival of the Eagle Guard, who stood between Merric and Sir Orsten and the Monfort soldiers. They were being forced backwards slowly though, and more than one of the Eagle Guard was struck down.

'For all the good it does,' Merric said, shaking his head sadly.

The ground was littered with bodies. Despite more of the dead wearing the uniform of Monforts, the Jacelyn soldiers were still vastly outnumbered.

'We knew this was a fight that we may not win,' Sir Oskar said, arriving beside them with a cut on his cheek.

He had lost his sword somewhere in the battle, and was now armed with a battered spear that he had picked up. Kasper joined them, somehow free of injuries himself, though his short sword was red with blood.

'I'll stay beside you,' Kasper said to Merric, 'until the end.'

'And us,' Sir Orsten said, and his brother nodded.

'Merric-' Ana had come alongside him, her quiver empty of crossbow bolts.

She threw her arms around his neck.

'You shouldn't be here,' Merric said to her.

'But I'm glad I am.'

She said no more, and neither did Merric. It was not necessary.

The Eagle Guard were breaking, overwhelmed by the sheer number of enemies, and to their left and right the number of Jacelyn soldiers still fighting was far fewer than who had charged across the courtyard.

'So, this is where it ends,' Merric muttered, and Ana squeezed his hand tightly.

He did not want her to die too, but at the same time he was also glad that she was there with him, at the end of their adventure. He glanced back up at the keep of Eagle Mount, his eyes following the towers as they rose into the sky, before settling on the giant eagle that sat at the highest point. What better place would there be to die than here?

'We fought valiantly. They'll write songs about this,' Sir Oskar said, before frowning in confusion. 'In fact, I can already hear the drumming. Am I going mad?'

'You may well be mad, brother,' Sir Orsten said, 'but you're not imagining the drumming; I can hear it too.'

It was coming from the gates which led out of the castle. The loud hammering sound was echoing around the courtyard, and as Merric watched, the great oak gates began to bow inwards. As the hammering grew louder and louder, Jacelyn soldiers and Monfort men alike stopped fighting, and looked in confusion at the gates which were bending and flexing even as they watched. It looked as though a giant was trying to force the gates open, but no such creature existing outside the bedtime stories of children.

Two cloaked Monfort men came running from the castle stables and sprinted towards the gate. One was huge and muscly with a giant hammer slung over his shoulder, the other short and round. There was something familiar about the way the short one ran, struggling to keep up with his companion. Merric watched as they reached the gate, and with grunts of effort up they lifted the locking bar from its brackets, and threw it down.

With a huge crash, the now unlocked gates burst open. It had not been a giant that had been pushing on the gate, but hundreds of folk. Thousands of folk. They surged through the destroyed gate, screaming and yelling at the tops of their voices. The flood seemed never ending, like a tidal wave of folk charging through the gateway from the town beyond.

The folk of Eaglestone had arrived.

Farmers, bakers, blacksmiths, merchants, cobblers, innkeepers, and all their wives, were pouring through the gate. They were armed with anything they had to hand, from butchers' cleavers and blacksmiths' hammers, to farmers' rakes and bakers' rolling pins. Some were even armed with swords and axes that they had been storing for such a day as this. Children and dogs ran behind their parents, wielding toy swords made from wood. Men shouted, and women yelled and dogs barked. The folk of

Eaglestone, eager to help wipe all trace of the Monforts from their home, were charging at the very men who had been terrorising them for these past weeks. Merric was overwhelmed by the sight of all folk, men and women, old and young, all coming together for what they knew was right.

And leading the charge was Tomas, his small legs pumping as hard as they good and fierce pride on his face.

Danell was close behind him, swinging his huge hammer, while Tomas brandished the short sword he had seen at Ana's house. He yelled wordlessly as he ran. Even though he was smaller than most, he ran faster than all and shouted even louder. He was fighting for Merric, and for Ana, and his love for them was giving him a courage he had never known was within him.

They had thrown off their disguises, and revealed themselves as the two who had unlocked the gate. They must have entered the castle through the tunnel that Merric and Ana had used.

'Yes!' Merric cried, 'yes Tomas! Onwards, men!'

The surviving Jacelyn men, with a final burst of effort, pushed forwards, and the Monfort soldiers broke. Their spirit was gone. In the face of such outnumbering forces, the Monfort soldiers threw down their weapons in defeat. With the townsfolk on one side of them, and the remaining Jacelyn soldiers on the other, they stood no chance. They could not fight the whole town.

As the Monfort soldiers raised their hands in surrender, they called for mercy, just as Rayden had done. However unlike with Rayden, Merric knew they meant it. The townsfolk swarmed over the Monfort soldiers, picking up their discarded weapons and forcing the men down onto the ground. Dogs jumped up and down beside them, their tails wagging and their tongues lolling in their mouths in excitement. Children happily kicked the Monfort men in the shins, thinking it was all a good game.

The surviving Jacelyn soldiers dropped to their knees and gave thanks to the Mother, before going to the townsfolk and helping them to secure the Monfort prisoners. Merric watched as one Jacelyn soldier tried to thank a carpenter who was armed with nothing more than a heavy mallet. The carpenter waved off his thanks.

'Lord Roberd was my duke as well, I'm just doing my bit,' he said.

There was a sudden shout and Merric saw a horse gallop out of the stables at the edge of the courtyard. On its back sat Orderix, his black robes billowing out behind him. He charged the horse towards the gate, scattering townsfolk as they dived out of his way. Angry shouts followed him as he rode off, hunched in the saddle as though determined to get every bit of speed out of his horse that he could.

'Move! Move it!' yelled Kasper, as he sprinted after Orderix.

Merric hurried along behind him. Kasper was unslinging his longbow as he ran, and scooped a stray arrow from the discarded weapons on the ground. By the time he had cleared the crowd and ran through the castle gate, Orderix was already at the far side of The Square. He was galloping down the Lord's Way, which twisted and turned towards the distant gate that led out of Eaglestone and into the countryside. No doubt he hoped to reach The Southstones, though whether Lord Aric would welcome him or not was a different matter.

'I'm sorry,' Merric said to Kasper, catching his breath.

They watched the distant figure ride further and further away. Kasper had been determined to get his revenge on Orderix, after the way the Lord's Counsel had treated the common folk. From his time in the dungeons, Kasper had learned that he was not alone. Orderix had a hatred of all folk he believed to be lesser than himself.

Kasper did not say anything in reply to Merric, but slowly reached into the quiver on his back and drew out the single arrow he had picked up. He carefully notched it onto the bow string, putting two fingers either side of it to keep it in place. He aimed his longbow at the distant figure, and began pulling the string back. He kept pulling the string back until it passed his chin and reached his ear, but Merric knew that Orderix was too far away to hit.

Kasper slowly raised the bow until he was aiming almost directly at the sun high above him, but his eye was still fixed on the tiny shape that was Orderix galloping away in the distance. Kasper paused for a long moment, before finally letting go of the bowstring.

The string flew forward with a twang, and the arrow shot up towards the sun. Everything else was silent, and Merric was only aware of the soft rushing sound of the arrow soaring through the sky. It climbed up and up, turning to a speck in the blue sky, before it reached the top of its arc and then started to fall. It seemed to pick up speed as it fell, its aim perfectly in line with the fleeing mounted figure. Merric lost sight of the arrow as it dropped down into the street far ahead, and he assumed that the shot had missed. It would have been an impossible shot.

After a moment though, the distant horse appeared to slow, before coming to a complete stop. The black-robed figure atop it slid, almost gracefully, from the saddle, to fall into a crumpled heap in the street.

Merric looked in amazement across at Kasper, who still had his bow raised towards the sun. The expression on his face was blank, but with a huge amount of satisfaction he lowered his bow and unstrung it casually.

Merric was stunned.

'You did it!'

Kasper turned to Merric, and put a strong hand on his shoulder. He smiled at him, before nodding back at the castle. High above them, from one of the towers that crowned the keep, someone raised the sky blue banner of the Jacelyns. The golden eagle flapped nobly in the wind over Eagle Mount once more.

'No,' Kasper said, 'you did it.'

***

The knight with the scarred face looked down at the body of Orderix lying in the street.

'Good riddance,' he muttered, knowing that putting any faith in the Jacelyn's old Lord's Council had been a mistake by Rayden Monfort.

It was not a mistake that Lord Aric would have made. The scarred knight looked up at Eagle Mount, and could just make out the boy and the archer as they stepped back through the gate and into the castle.

Rubbing his bald head, the knight knew that the castle was lost, and that Rayden was most likely killed. He could not pretend to be saddened by this news, but he knew that Lord Aric would be furious about the setback. Knowing that he could be of no more service to the Monforts here, the scarred knight snatched a rough brown cloak off the body of the Eaglestone shop owner who lay dead in the alleyway behind him, and pulled it on, tugging the hood over his distinctive features. Taking hold of the bridle of Orderix's horse, he mounted and spurred it towards the gate that led out of the town. He had a lot of work to do.

And unlike Rayden, *he* would not disappoint Lord Aric.

CHAPTER TWENTY TWO

The final secret

The chamber that had been chosen as the room of mourning for the bodies of Lord Roberd, Lady Cathreen and Tristan was warm and comforting, made so by the hundreds of scented candles that filled the room. In the centre of the chamber stood the three elegantly carved stone caskets, which was where the Jacelyns had been laid to rest. A stonemason must have been busy in the weeks since they had died, as each was topped by a carved likeness of their occupant, made from the same rich white marble used for the caskets themselves. Merric was glad to see that Lord Roberd and his family had been given the respect they deserved.

Thin white curtains hung in front of the windows, giving a pleasant muted light to the chamber, and Merric felt at peace as he stood before the caskets that contained those who he had loved as a family. He was grateful that the Monforts had followed the traditions of The Head, and had decreed that the caskets would remain on display, to allow mourners to travel from across The Head to pay their final respects. Merric had feared he was going to be too late, as this would be his only chance to say goodbye. Afterwards, the three caskets would be taken to the Grand Priory outside the castle walls, and down into the Jacelyn family crypt below, to be laid to rest beside their ancestors.

Merric was alone in the chamber, and glad it was that way. He did not want anyone else to see his grief. Since the day they had been killed, Merric had not had a moment to mourn Lord Roberd and his family, and had been forced to try and move on without a chance to properly say farewell. Despite it being a month since they had died, standing there beside their caskets, he felt sadness wash over him. It was almost more than he could bear. Blinking away his tears, Merric looked down at the dagger that he held in his hands. It was Tristan's; decorated with the head and wings of a golden eagle. The dagger had been taken from Tristan by Rayden Monfort after he murdered him, but now Merric was able to return it to its rightful owner.

He moved over to Tristan's casket, and looked down at the stone likeness of the young Jacelyn knight. The stonemason must have known him well, and chiselled his features with love and care. He had been carved as though he was sleeping. His eyes were closed, and his hands clasped together over his armoured chest. Merric was pleased that the stonemason had carved him to be wearing his armour; he was a knight after all, and that was how he should have been remembered; always standing up for what was right, and putting the safety of others before his own.

Merric placed the dagger in Tristan's stone hands, and then took a step back. He looked across at the caskets of Lord Roberd and Lady Cathreen. Each had been carved like Tristan, with their eyes closed as though sleeping, but Lord Roberd's left hand was outstretched and his lady wife's right hand was reaching towards his. In the Jacelyn crypt, the two caskets would be placed close together, so that they could be with each other for eternity.

A day had passed since the Battle of Eagle Mount, as the folk of The Head were already calling it. The day had gone by like a blur to Merric. He remembered walking with Kasper back through the gates of the castle and seeing the crowds that filled the courtyard. Jacelyn soldiers were leading their Monfort prisoners into the nearby barrack building, which would serve as a temporary prison for the dozens of captives. The townsfolk had already begun lifting the bodies of those who had fallen, Jacelyn and Monfort alike, and were laying them neatly to one side. A couple of farmers had hurried off to bring back their carts, and these would be used to take the bodies down to the grassy fields outside the town walls where they could be buried. The folk of The Head would give their fallen enemies the decency of a respectful burial, something Merric did not expect the Monforts would have done for them.

As they had seen Merric enter the courtyard, the Jacelyn soldiers took up a chant.

'Merric! Merric! Merric!' they had shouted.

Soon, the townsfolk were joining in too, and all around him Merric could hear his name being called. Fists were punched into the air, and hands clapped him on the back. Embarrassed by the attention, Merric had hurried up the steps and into the entrance hall of the keep. There were more bodies here, and he was reminded of the blood that had been spilled so that Eagle Mount could be freed of the grip of the Monforts.

It was here that he had found Ana and Tomas, arms around each other in relief.

'Merric!' Tomas had cried, and hurried over to him.

Merric had then realised how exhausted he was, and almost collapsed onto Tomas. Ana had come to his rescue, along with Kasper, and together the three of them managed to somehow get Merric upstairs to his old bedchamber. They took *Hopebearer* from his hand, where he had clutched it still, and laid him gently down onto his bed.

He could not have said how long he had slept for, but when he awoke again a new day had dawned and the sun was pouring in through his window. At first he felt the same uncertainty and sense of danger that he had felt almost every morning since the Jacelyns had been murdered, before he remembered the previous day's events. He could not come to terms with the fact that it was over. Eagle Mount was his home again, and Rayden and the Monforts were gone.

'Have you slept?' Merric had asked Ana when he awoke.

She was sat beside his bed. There were red rings around her eyes, but she smiled at him.

'Some,' she said, and Merric tutted wearily at her.

'I can't believe it,' he said, rubbing both hands over his face. 'I can't believe we did it.'

'You did it,' Ana pointed out, but Merric would have none of it.

'I couldn't have done it without you.'

Ana did not reply, and just squeezed his hand warmly.

Once he was washed and had changed into clean clothes, Merric had then gone to find Sophya. He found her in her own bedchamber. She was overjoyed to see him, but was still ashamed of how she had acted over the past few weeks. She had led Merric to the chamber where her father, mother and brother had been laid to rest for the mourning period. She left him there, having spent the past few weeks grieving for them herself. It was now Merric's turn.

As he stood there now, looking at the caskets, Merric heard someone else quietly enter the chamber. He turned to see Arch Prior Simeon walk up beside him and look sombrely at the stone carving of Lord Roberd on top of his casket.

'He would have been very proud of you,' the Arch Prior wheezed. 'What you did took a manner of courage that most of us could only dream of possessing.'

Merric was grateful for Simeon's words, but still found the praise he was receiving to be misplaced. He did not deserve to be hailed as a hero. He never knew what to say to it.

'What will happen now?' he said.

'A new duke will rule Eagle Mount,' Arch Prior Simeon said simply. 'The Head has endured for a thousand years, and will continue to do so now, I'm certain.'

'But who?' Merric asked, 'Sophya? I thought the Duke of The Head was always a Jacelyn of the male line? Or will she rule as regent, until she has a son who is old enough?'

'No, you're quite right,' Simeon said, squinting up at Merric.

The Arch Prior was getting very old now, and his eyesight was not what it used to be. He was stooped, and the thin white hair on top of his head only came up to Merric's chest.

'The laws state that only a male may be duke,' Simeon continued, 'although that's starting to sound very outdated to me, don't you think?'

'So Sophya will rule as regent?'

The Arch Prior sighed.

'She will not, and nor would she want to. I spoke to her this morning, and she's very ashamed that she believed

Rayden's lies. I told her that no one blames her, but she feels terribly about how she believed that you were responsible for all the dreadful things that have happened here. The title of duke will therefore pass onto the one remaining Jacelyn of the male line.'

'But there are no other Jacelyns,' Merric said, confused.

Simeon just looked at Merric for a moment before replying. His expression was hard to read.

'There's something I must tell you,' he said, turning to look at the three caskets. 'Lord Roberd wanted to tell you. Oh, how he wanted to tell you! But the right time never came. You deserved to have heard it from him, but since we are robbed of that great man, then I must speak on his behalf.'

'What must you tell me?' Merric said, slowly

'I must tell you about a conversation that Lord Roberd had with me, many years ago, soon after you were first brought to this castle. I'm an old man, forgive me, but let me take you back on a journey into my memory.'

The elderly Arch Prior spoke, and Merric listened.

* * *

The Square was thick with snow as Simeon hurried across the wide open space, his thick robes helping to keep the cold away. He gave a friendly wave to the soldiers who gathered around a burning brazier beside the gate of Eagle

Mount, warming their hands on the bright flames. They returned his greeting, and then directed their attention back to the fire. The Arch Prior crossed the castle courtyard, and then climbed the short flight of steps that led into the castle keep. Once in the entrance hall and out of the chill he shook the snowflakes from his robes, and looked up when he heard footsteps heading towards him.

'My apologies, Arch Prior, for bringing you away from the priory on such a cold day,' Lord Roberd said, walking up to him.

'Not at all, not at all,' Simeon said merrily, 'the cold is good for my joints. I find it most invigorating.'

Lord Roberd let himself smile.

'Would you accompany me to my study? What I need to talk to you about is not for others to hear.'

'Of course,' the Simeon said.

His Lordship had rarely looked this serious, so the Arch Prior walked with him towards the staircase that led upstairs. Lord Roberd did not speak as they walked, but his face looked troubled. Simeon was glad that he had been summoned, as it could not be good for the Duke of The Head to have such worries on his mind. A worry shared is a worry halved, is what the Arch Prior liked to say. When they reached the study, Lord Roberd seated himself down and politely gestured for Simeon to do the same. The room was cosy and warm, heated by a roaring fire in the hearth. Had it not been for the look of worry on Lord Roberd's face, Simeon thought he could have fallen into a comfortable doze. The duke kept silent, as though wondering how to begin. To help, Simeon therefore chose to break the silence himself.

'How's the boy?' he asked.

Lord Roberd smiled fondly, but his eyes still showed worry.

'He is well. Naturally the castle feels strange to him, but he will settle I am sure. He's already taken to tormenting Sophya.'

The Arch Prior chuckled, and looked at Lord Roberd with raised eyebrows, as though inviting him to start the conversation that he had summoned him here for.

'It is strange that you should ask about Merric, as it is for him that I have suffered sleepless nights. Arch Prior, I have asked you to come here today so that I could confess. I have a troubled mind, and I need to speak to someone about it.'

Lord Roberd, a proud man, looked at his hands as he said it.

Simeon had not been expecting this, and his face showed the surprise. He changed his expression quickly before Lord Roberd could notice.

'I see. I'll hear your confession, of course, and advise you on it if that's what you desire?'

'Thank you.' Lord Roberd seemed relieved. He thought for a moment before continuing. 'I am feeling guilt.'

'And pray tell me what is it you're feeling guilty about, my lord.'

'I had received a warning that a band of raiders was scouring the south-west lands of The Head, but I had ignored the report, not believing it. It was not until I received two further reports of these attacks that I finally acted. To make up for my earlier lack of judgement, I myself led my soldiers and knights south to counter the threat, but as I arrived at the village of Ryding I realised I was too late.'

Lord Roberd paused, but Simeon did not interrupt him. After a brief hesitation, the duke continued.

'I could see a cloud of smoke coming from the valley ahead of me, and by the time we reached it the whole village was ablaze. The villagers had all been put to the sword. The remaining raiders who were still there, plundering and pillaging, fled at the sight of us, so we were not even able to hold the perpetrators to justice.'

'You hold yourself to blame for the destruction of Ryding,' Simeon said with a nod, understanding.

'Of course I do,' Lord Roberd's voice, usually so proud, was quiet and hollow. 'Had I acted sooner we could have stopped the attack from taking place. Lord Willarm and Lady Chanelyse were good and honest, and did not deserve this fate; to be abandoned by their duke at their time of greatest need.'

'You did not abandon them my lord; you did all you could to help. And you found their son, you saved him.'

'He was the only living soul we found following the destruction of the village. He was stood, alone and afraid, in the centre of the burning cottages. I had failed the folk of Ryding, who I was sworn to defend, and I abandoned Lord Willarm, who should have been able to trust me to fulfil my duty as duke. I took in Merric, and have sworn to raise him as my own, but that cannot possibly right the wrongs I have done.'

'You didn't abandon Lord Willarm, or the folk of Ryding,' Arch Prior Simeon soothed. 'You did everything in your power to defend them, and the only person blaming you for their destruction is yourself, my lord. Lord Willarm was a loyal baron of yours, and knew that you returned the devotion he showed you.'

Lord Roberd laughed, a dry, humourless laugh.

'Willarm had no love towards me, and I deserved none. He died before I could make amends, and he went to the grave not knowing how sorry I am for causing us to grow apart.'

'My lord?'

Simeon was confused now, no longer understanding.

Lord Roberd knew that the Prior would be unaware of what he was speaking about, and so explained his words.

'Willarm and I were born from our lady mother within minutes of each other, and our father loved us equally. He said that it was purely by chance that Willarm was born slightly before me, and that it should not necessarily make him next in line to be Duke of The Head.

He therefore told us that on our tenth birthday he would bring us together, and choose who he would name as his true heir. Our tenth birthday arrived, and we both stood before our lord father. He named me his heir, destined to rule The Head when he died. Willarm was angered by this decision, of course. Not only was he the older of the two of us, but he was also the more skilled with sword and lance. And yet our father chose me. Willarm was furious, and while he tried to learn to live with his disappointment, he ended up leaving Eagle Mount a few years later. After a fruitless time of wandering, selling his sword-arm to the highest bidder, he went to Ryding. There the current baron took him in, and he eventually married my brother to his daughter, Chanelyse. With no son, the baron's heir was therefore Willarm. I do not believe he married Chanelyse as a way of getting power; I think he genuinely loved her. Willarm became the new baron of Ryding around the same time that our father died and I was named Duke of The Head.'

Lord Roberd rose from behind his large desk and paced over to the fire, looking deep into the flames.

'He was the perfect baron that a duke could ever ask for; answering my summons when I required his services, and sending his soldiers and raising his levies when war was upon us. However, as a brother, he did not exist. And I, I am ashamed to say, never tried to make amends with him. I was the cause of his anger, purely by being named our father's heir, and only I could resolve it. However, I was too proud to go to him and beg for his forgiveness, so we continued acting as though neither of us had a brother. I never spoke of him, and apart from his wife and father-in-law, Willarm told no one that he was born a Jacelyn. And now he is gone. I failed to save him, and he died knowing that.'

Simeon stayed silent. He had known none of this. He had not arrived in The Head to serve as Arch Prior until a year after Lord Roberd had become duke.

'And now I care for his son,' Lord Roberd continued. 'Merric is not only the son of one of my barons, but he is also my nephew. He is half Orrell of Ryding, and half Jacelyn of Eagle Mount. Tristan is my heir, but after him Merric would be next in line. But how can I tell him this? I am too ashamed of what I have done, and what I failed to do. What would he think of me? Would he forgive me for how I let down his father?'

'There would be nothing to forgive,' Simeon said, joining Lord Roberd by the fire. 'There is nothing you've done wrong, other than having once been a young boy who had a brother. Would you believe that before I joined the priory and devoted my life to the Mother I, too, had a brother? We fought and fought, and on more than one occasion I told him that I hated him. I always regretted saying such things afterwards of course, but I was also too stubborn to apologise to him. He knew that I never meant what I said. We do and say things in the moment that we don't mean, and Lord Willarm will have been the same. He

470

didn't hate you my lord, and he knew that you had only love towards him. You were both proud men, so naturally found it hard to admit when you were wrong, and found it even harder to admit it to each other.'

Lord Roberd smiled weakly at him.

'Thank you, Arch Prior.'

The trouble in his eyes was fading, as though speaking to him about it was enough. To keep such a worry to himself had been an enormous strain.

'I will raise Merric as my own, and I will never leave him wanting, this I vow. And when the time is right, when he is old enough, I will tell him the truth. He may hate me, or he may love me still, but he will be a man and I will respect his feelings either way. I see great things in him, like his father, and I cannot wait to see the man he becomes.'

* * *

Arch Prior Simeon had stopped talking, and was peering at Merric, trying to judge his expression. He was worried that it would be a lot to take in. It took Merric a few moments to notice that the elderly man's story was finished, but even then he did not know what to say. There was too much going around his head for any of it to make sense.

One thing came to Merric's mind suddenly. Though it was not important, he said it anyway, just to break the silence.

'That's what you almost told me,' he said. 'At the banquet to mark the end of Aric's visit, you told me that my father and Lord Roberd weren't on speaking terms.'

'Oh, yes, and my apologies again for that. The wine, it…well, it doesn't matter,' Simeon said uncomfortably. 'I know this must be a shock to you, but do you understand what this means?'

'Yes,' Merric said simply. 'Lord Roberd was my uncle, and Lady Cathreen my aunt. Tristan….he was my cousin. And Sophya too, she's my cousin.'

He realised with a jolt that this meant that he still had some family left. Real family. He and Sophya were cousins, and they shared the same blood. To have a living family member meant more to him then he could have imagined.

'But, you know what it truly means?' Simeon asked slowly, wanting to make sure that Merric properly realised.

'I'm half Jacelyn,' Merric said in wonder, still not believing it. 'And it means that…'

His eyes went wide.

'After Tristan died, *I* became Lord Roberd's heir.'

The Arch Prior nodded. 'It means that you're now Duke of The Head.'

The shock of this hit Merric. '…I'm the *duke?*'

'With Lord Roberd and Tristan gone, it's now up to you to lead the folk of The Head. They need leadership now more than ever; a good leader, not like Rayden Monfort had been.'

Merric did not know what to say.

'But I don't know how to lead,' he stammered. 'How can I expect folk to follow me? Sophya should be regent, until she has a son. Or the laws should be changed, to allow her to rule The Head.'

Arch Prior Simeon offered Merric a reassuring smile. The elderly man felt a confidence in him that Merric did not see in himself.

'The greatest leaders are not those who want it most, but rather those who bear the burden of leadership when they know they have to put personal choices aside. The folk are already hailing you as a hero. They look up to you, and admire you. You're someone they're ready to follow, unlike Rayden Monfort, who demanded loyalty, rather than earned it. I spoke to young Ana earlier and she told me about your victory over the bullying miller in Little Harrow. You led the village folk then, and you led the people of The Head yesterday.'

Merric could think of nothing to say. He was still trying to come to terms with the fact that he had been half a Jacelyn all along. All this time that Lord Roberd had been treating him as though he was part of his family, he had been family after all. He felt even more love and respect for Lord Roberd now, knowing the guilt he had felt when Merric's parents had been killed. Like Simeon, Merric knew that Lord Roberd had nothing he should feel guilty about. He had done nothing wrong, other than have a brother who was just as proud and perhaps just as stubborn as he had been.

Merric looked down at the carved stone face of Lord Roberd, and felt a deep sadness in his heart. He had been his uncle, and Merric wished he had known that whilst he was still alive. He knew that Lord Roberd had had his reasons for not telling him, and was going explain the truth to him when he knew Merric was ready to hear it. Only, that time had never come.

And now Merric was duke. He knew the laws of the land; if he was truly the nephew of Lord Roberd then, after Tristan, he was indeed Lord Roberd's heir. It was up to Merric to lead The Head. He was not the youngest to ever be named one of the three dukes of High Realm, but all others before him had known that their time was coming. They had years to learn the ways of their fathers, and step up to the role when their time came. Up until now, Merric had not even his wildest of dreams entertained the idea that he would be duke one day. He did not even know where to begin.

Arch Prior Simeon was speaking again.

'Rayden Monfort has been defeated, and all trace of his rule here in Eagle Mount has been erased. There are still Monfort men scattered throughout The Head, though I expect that with Rayden gone the barons will have the strength to see to them. Lord Aric will not likely give in though, and in The Citadel he will rebuild the strength needed to assault our lands. I offer you my counsel, my lord, and that is to prepare for Lord Aric to make moves against The Head. He has tried to take the Jacelyn lands through intrigue and plots, and failed. Now he will try again through force. I've heard that he has the support of the king as well, which will make the time before us particularly difficult.'

'So, all I've done is bring war to The Head?' Merric asked.

Simeon shook his head. 'The Monforts brought the war themselves, when they took the lives of Lord Roberd and his family. You though, Merric, have brought our folk *hope*. I'm sworn to serve the Mother, and they say She take no sides in the wars of men. But this will be a war between good and evil, and in this you know which side the Mother will always be on. But it's not just the Mother who will lend you strength to combat this evil, Merric, you have friends around you, and all the swords of The Head.'

A while later Merric left the chamber, his mind filled with the responsibility that had just been put onto his young shoulders. He was a boy of fourteen, skinny in body and more confident with a book in his hand than a sword. And now he was to rule a whole dukedom, and lead it into an inevitable war. That, he decided though, could wait until tomorrow.

He stopped short when he saw who was waiting in the passageway outside. Twenty of the Eagle Guard, splendidly dressed once more in their shining armour and spotless sky blue surcoats, stood to attention facing him.

Their faces were covered by their helmets, and they were stood as still as stone. They had yet to elect their new captain, following the death of Sir Gerard in the Greenwood, so one of their number stepped forward and dropped to one knee.

'My duke,' he said, his voice slightly muffled by his helmet, 'we live to serve you, and if required, give our lives to your protection.'

Merric nodded awkwardly at him. He had heard the words spoken by new members of the Eagle Guard when they joined its honoured ranks, but these were always uttered to Lord Roberd, not him. It felt strange to hear a man say it to him. The man returned to his place in the line.

Beside the Eagle Guard, Merric spotted four people who managed to bring a smile, and then a grin, to his face. Sophya beamed at him. Arch Prior Simeon had likely already told her what he had been about to tell Merric. She had lost her family, but regained a part of it in a way she had never imagined.

'Cousins, are we?' she said to him, 'That sounds wonderful to me.'

Tomas was stood next to her, looking at Merric in shock and amazement. His mouth opened and closed like a fish, but no words came out. Kasper laughed at the small boy, and looked at Merric.

'To think I almost didn't follow you; what a fool I was. If you'll forgive me for that, then I'm here to continue serving you, my duke. I offer you my bow arm, for as long as you find a use for it.'

Merric smiled at him, before looking at the last person in the passageway. Ana seemed to be having more trouble understanding all of this than Merric did. She looked confused, and worried. Like her, Merric wondered what this all meant for him and Ana. If he was a duke, then he would be expected to one day marry a noble lady, and he did not know where that would leave her.

But for now, he just kissed her. Ana grinned and kissed him back. It was even better than the last time in the dungeons, and Merric was not even embarrassed that everyone was watching them. No words were spoken between them, as no words were needed.

Merric did not know what trials and difficulties the coming months would bring, and where this new road would take him, but he knew that his friends would be beside him every step of the way.

Epilogue

The boy sobbed uncontrollably as he wandered between the burning cottages, trying to find his parents. He felt lost without them. Through the darkness and the smoke all he could see was folk running and screaming, and men with burning torches and great axes in their hands. Everywhere he looked there was flames, and fear.

As he stumbled along the road that led between the buildings, barefooted and terrified, no one seemed to notice him, or even care. The boy coughed and choked as the smoke found its way into his throat, and he urged himself onwards, to try and find whatever family he had left.

Before he knew it, the village was quiet again. The screaming seemed to have stopped, and there was no sound other than the crackling of the fires that were burning around him. A lone voice was cried out, but the boy could not tell if it was his own or not.

As a gust of wind cleared some of the smoke from the road before him, the boy saw the terrifying, huge man standing in front of the flames. His sword was in his hand,

and he stared back at the small boy with cold eyes behind a scarred face. The boy wanted to run, but knew he could not. He knew he could not escape.

At that moment the boy felt a hand clap him on the shoulder. He tried to cry out in terror, but no sound would come. He turned to see that the hand belonged to a tall man, dressed in a suit of fine armour topped with a surcoat of sky blue, with a golden eagle sewn onto the chest. The knight dropped down onto one knee in front of the boy, while dozens of soldiers dressed just like him rushed into the village, sending the scarred man fleeing into the night.

The knight removed his helmet and looked at the boy with piercing blue eyes. He had a head framed with brown hair flecked with the first signs of grey, but eyes showed warmth and comfort. He gathered the boy up in his arms, and his bushy beard tickled the boy's face. In spite of the horrors surrounding them, the boy giggled, and the knight smiled down at him. The boy wrapped his arms tightly around him, and for the first time, felt truly safe.

Acknowledgements

This book has been four years in the making. I have loved every moment of it, but it has not always been easy. I could not have done it without the help, support and encouragement of others.

I want to thank all those who have given their time to read the manuscript of this book and give me their feedback. In particular, I would like to thank Bradley Powell, Neil Adkin, Claire Long, Mark Farrell, Paul Jenkins, Chanel Clarke, Rob Simms, Leo Helps, Jo Boyer and Joe Roberts, as well as many others. How much I appreciate your time and effort in helping me with this book cannot be overstated.

I would also like to thank my mother and father, Juliet and Bob Wright, for fuelling my passion for reading, and for being my biggest fans throughout this journey.

I want to thank the incredible Dorothy Kimmings, who I am proud to call my great aunt. To say you were an inspiration for me writing my own book would be an understatement.

Christopher Badcock, I could never have completed this book without your enthusiasm and passion. This journey would not have been the same had I not shared it with you.

Last, but always first in my heart, I want to thank Laura May. Thank you for your patience, encouragement and unwavering belief in me. This book is dedicated to you.

Printed in Great Britain
by Amazon